*Edwin Mullhouse: The Life and Death
of an American Writer*

Portrait of a Romantic

PORTRAIT
OF A ROMANTIC

PORTRAIT
OF A
ROMANTIC

STEVEN
MILLHAUSER

ALFRED A. KNOPF   NEW YORK   1977

THIS IS A BORZOI BOOK
PUBLISHED BY ALFRED A. KNOPF, INC.

Copyright © 1977 by Steven Millhauser

Library of Congress Cataloging in Publication Data

Millhauser, Steven.   Portrait of a romantic.

I. Title.
PZ4.M6515P03 [PS3563.I422] 813'.5'4   77-4133
ISBN 0-394-41165-X

Manufactured in the United States of America

FIRST EDITION

PORTRAIT
OF A ROMANTIC

1

MOTHER OF MYSELF, myself I sing: lord of loners, duke of dreams, king of the clowns. Youth and death I sing, sunbeams and moonbeams, laws and breakers of laws. I, Arthur Grumm, lover and killer.

And you, dark angels of my adolescence: you too I sing, O restless ones. Setting forth this day in my twenty-ninth year, on the voyage of my dreaming youth. I, Arthur Grumm . . .

I was born in the shady corner of a sunny Connecticut town. My father was a bookkeeper in a firm that manufactured brakelining and my mother was a first-grade teacher. We lived on the bottom floor of an old two-family house, on a street of old two-family houses. The top floor was occupied by Mrs. Schneider and her three white cats: Wynken, Blinken, and Nod. My favorite image of those days is the dirt-patched back yard with its thick-trunked maple and its high border of dark green hedge. I was fond of the shiny sharp leaves, the white hedge-blossoms, the furry, drowsy bumblebees . . . those furry, drowsy bumblebees . . . Through the sudden spaces I would catch bright glimpses of a universe forbidden to my earliest years, for just beyond the hedge the world sloped down to a bushy field crossed in the distance by the concrete banks of a sunken and invisible stream, beyond which a brown slope rose to the dazzling white side of a body shop. On furry, drowsy summer afternoons I liked to lie on my stomach in a shady corner of lawn and gaze for hours through one of the brown hedge-arches at that forbidden wonderland, where older boys fought with rocks or hunted for snakes with sticks and sun-flashing jars; or I would swing higher and higher on the wooden rope-swing that hung from the maple until, over the top of the white-flowering hedgerow, I caught a sudden glimpse of the far concrete stream, crossed diagonally, as in an artful advertisement, by the precise green leaves of a single hedge-stem.

A clothesline on a pulley ran from the tree to one of the square gray posts of the long back porch. It is on the back porch beside that post, with a wicker basket at her feet and a red bag of clothespins hanging from the rail, that I best recall my mother, frowning at the sun and reaching up her immense arms to push out the line. For me she will always be the massive Mommy of my earliest years, with her bouncy cheeks and her braided pile of lustrous red-brown hair. As she bent down to the basket I would search among the braided coils for the gleams of her tortoise-shell combs. I was allowed—and suddenly it is all so boring that I really cannot continue. My Mommy, my Daddy, my boring childhood, did they exist at all? And if so, what of it? Let them rest in peace, let them rot in peace, let us stop this nonsense at once. And how I long to mock you, how I long to insult you!—you, Reader, you dull, smug reader; frowning at the page at this very moment. Oh, it is all so boring, so boring... if that's the word I want... Gleams of her tortoise-shell combs. I was allowed to hand her the clothespins, which were of two kinds. "It doesn't matter," she would say, "any old one will do," even though one had a spring and could be opened and shut, while the other was stiff and had a little head like a man. "I said it doesn't matter, they're both the same. Lord! what questions. If there's one thing you can be sure of it's this, Arthur: when you've seen one clothespin you've seen them all, believe you me." And so, while she fastened clothes to the line, I clipped the spring-clothespins secretly to her hem. Suddenly she would feel the row against her leg and look down. Placing a hand on her chest, and rolling up her great brown eyes, she would say: "Oh, sigh. Pooooooor me. Here I thought I was Martha Grumm, but I'm only a poor clothesline hangin' from a tree." And sniffing deeply, and wrinkling her forehead at me, she would pretend to wipe away tears.

My father exists in the memory of those days as two distinct creatures: a sad dignified gentleman in a gray pressed suit, sighing wearily as he left for work, and a boisterous companion in baggy pants, dancing a comic hornpipe under his own finger. When he came home from work he would smile sadly at mother and me, and falling wearily into the brown softness of his chair, from which I would see, on sunny afternoons, swirls of silent dustmotes rise, he would sit motionless and frowning with his feet up on the red leather hassock, his plump white cheek on the back of a hand, and the knot of his necktie pulled down below his open top button. After a while he would push himself heavily to his feet. I would watch his large gray back fading slowly from the room. Then from far away I would hear a faint scrape of hangers and a soft clash of brass from the loops of drawers—and suddenly he would burst forth in slippers and rumpled pants, with his hair sticking up in odd places and the sleeves of his red-and-black lumberjack shirt rolled up to the elbows. How he loved to play! With a whoop! and hey! Oh, he threw himself into games and hobbies and trips and plans with an eagerness that far surpassed my own. Seated beside me at the kitchen table, before the outspread treasures of an unassembled model ship, he would pore over the black-and-white page of diagrammed instructions, more fascinating to him than the colored map of the world, while I stared dreamily at the tube of glue, the razor blade, the large pale balsawood hulk of the ship, the metal lifeboats, the brass chains, the little bottles of black and gold paint, and the shiny boxcover showing a three-master in all the splendor of its paint and rigging. After a while he would look up, and smacking his fist into his palm would cry: "Hooo! what a doozy. Pass me the sander, Artie. What a peach of a boat." Even as a child I could sense that my father disliked his work, preferring to play at home among his family and hobbies, and I have no doubt that this division in my father's soul played its little part in my own darker blossoming. It was my father who taught me how to hold a bat and throw a baseball, how to distinguish quartz from feldspar, and how to identify the poison ivy and poison sumac that grew here and there on the slope beyond our hedge, down which he finally led me, along a narrow dirt path, one sunny summer day.

2

MY OLD BROWN SHOES had just been resoled and I kept slipping on the steep path as I clung to my father's hand. Leafy weeds brushed my bare legs. A black-spotted red ladybug, watching me from a dark green frond, seemed to crack in half as she rose in flight. In the hot hazy-blue sky a pale moon trembled, translucent. And if I remember these details, and all the others, it is only because I deliberately impressed them on my mind, in an effort to distract myself from the terrible joy that I felt as an oppressive force in my temples, at the place where the veins beat. For already, already I showed signs of the excitable temperament that is the dangerous other side of my dreamy, drowsy nature. You must understand that month after month I had dreamed of the blue stream hidden by the banks of concrete; I longed to possess it with my eyes as a hungry person longs to possess a piece of fruit with his teeth and tongue. As we marched across the field we kept to a dim path winding among pricker bushes and weeds. Here and there bent bottle-caps glittered. A stiff popsicle wrapper, stained dark orange and still clinging to its stick, lay beside two pieces of chalk-white excrement. On the broken-off neck of a soda-bottle, colorless and sparkling in the sunlight, a small brown grasshopper sat motionless. At one point my father stopped to pick up a flat purple stone with a white line in it, which he examined with a frown and tossed away. As we approached the near concrete ledge I could see the opposite wall dropping lower and lower and at any moment I expected to see the blue rushing river of my dreams. Seedy green stem-tops appeared. Father refused to let me set foot on the dangerous ledge and I had to strain forward, gripping his hand, in order to see the hidden stream.

Tall spears of grass, low dark ferns, shiny green stems with caterpillar tops, spinach-green and lettuce-green lacy and leafy weeds grew in ripe confusion on both banks down to the wavy outline of a sunny stream-bed. The hard dry stream-path, littered with plump little rocks and glittering bits of broken glass, darkened here and there to wet brown patches of gleaming mud. A dark green soda-bottle with a bit of tilted liquid and a bent white straw leaned against the inner rim of a sun-faded rubber tire that lay half in weeds and half in the dusty stream. Not too far away a gray upside-down ankle-sneaker, without a lace, revealed like a vast thumbprint the worn pattern of its sole. The thumbprint rippled, the weeds blurred and melted, the rocks began to flow, and I burst into tears so copious that my father's face, which had shown first alarm, and then tenderness, changed finally to disapproval, as squatting before me and gripping me by the shoulders he said: "What's the matter with you! Hey? What's the matter with you!"

3

"THE BOY'S A DREAMER," sighed my father at about this time, and if by that he meant I preferred lying in my room on the cool side of the house with a colorful picturebook open before me to running about on the hot black street in the fierce yellow glare of the malignant sun, I suppose he was right. On languorous summer evenings, lying on my stomach before the hedge, I would watch the big round sun, glowing like a large caution light, slip down behind the roof of the darkening white body shop. When I turned away I would see spots of orange light dancing on the lawn... Oh, I was an ardent, an agile dreamer! Those somnolent summer afternoons... And don't you love those dreaming dots, which cause a sentence not so much to end as to dissolve... As when, on a blazing summer day, a hard highway dissolves into a distant shimmer... In general I was a quiet, solitary, slightly blurred little boy. The only photograph surviving from those years, which my father carried in one of the scratched windows of his wallet, shows me seated in my mother's lap on a wooden park bench. Something must have caught my attention, for my face is blurred above the sharp details of my wintercoat, with its large four-holed buttons and its gleaming belt-buckle, shaped like a capital D.

My father failed to realize that if I was a dreamer he himself was at least partly to blame. Even then I must have understood dimly that his hobbies were nothing but his dreams—bright gashes of color amid the browns and grays of his everyday life. In the center of his stately mahogany bureau, beneath the dignified underwear drawer with its dark rows of balled socks and its neat piles of folded underpants, lay a bright treasury of cream-colored approval cards with orange and purple stamps tucked into all three rows, pale blue envelopes from foreign countries, spilled packages of greenish hinges, little cellophane packets with mint sets inside... Once my father took me with him to the brown-and-ochre post office, where he went to purchase a plate-block of every new American stamp. Gripping me under the armpits, he held me up so that I could see the man behind the window tear carefully from a crimson-and-blue sheet the block of four precious stamps with the number in the margin.

Deep in the cluttered cellar, beyond the washing machine and the deep square sink, beyond Mrs. Schneider's old black trunks and broken chairs, the cartons of rocks began. They extended to the workbench with its black vise, a workbench entirely covered with small chipped rocks, among which lay an all-metal hammer with a long narrow head. Past the workbench, around the corner, stood a large brown bookcase topped by a dusty whaling ship and housing a display of Connecticut minerals that father had found himself. Each specimen sat behind a neatly printed label. There were creamy barite crystals and green malachite from Cheshire, dark garnets from Roxbury, black tourmaline and golden beryl and lilac lepidolite from Portland, large silvery sheets of mica from Branchville; and the names of those towns were as colorful to me as names like Greenland and the Gold Coast in father's maroon album. This bookcase was father's pride and joy, but I was attracted to the more glamorous collection in a smaller bookcase, where he displayed the crystals and minerals he had not found himself: transparent pale-purple fluorite crystals shaped like pyramids placed bottom to bottom, silky white strands of asbestos, yellow wulfenite crystals like little squares of butterscotch, a glass-clear quartz crystal four inches high, and my own favorite, a yawning geode toothed with tiny crystals of dark-sparkling amethyst. The bottom shelf of this bookcase was taken up by a plain set of minerals much less interesting than the shining crystals, and I remember being puzzled until one evening, promising me a surprise, father led me down to his minerals and removed from a cardboard box an object that looked like a black flashlight with a black cord attached. He plugged it in and turned out the light; in the darkness the strange flashlight gave off a dull purplish glow. And as he turned the purple light upon the plain minerals at the bottom of his crystal collection, there arose from the darkness, as from the luminous dial of some fantastic watch, glowing gashes and splashes of yellow-green, green-blue, lemon, rose, and orange-vermilion.

If my love of dreaming derives from my father, it is to my mother that I owe my high sense of order in the scheme of things: of the folded napkin and the closed drawer, the pressed pantsleg and the polished toe, the ironed hour and the tucked-in afternoon. And perhaps it is to her as well that I owe my fatal attraction to all their wild opposites. Mother's mission was nothing less than the maintenance of order in the universe, as I sensed most violently on drowsy summer mornings. Dressed in her flowing smock, armed with rags and bottles and ominous machines, she marched through the house doing battle with the forces of disarray. She was nothing less than an artist, my mother, and her masterpiece was the living room. She polished the brass candlesticks until they glowed like spoons, she waxed the mahogany lamp-table until it became a brown mirror reflecting the green-shaded porcelain lamp, and with the sucking snorting pink-nosed silver snout of her formidable vacuum cleaner she gobbled up the rug, poked under cushions, swept across the blinds, swept across the very joints of wall and ceiling, her great head thrown back, her eyes blazing, her nostrils flared, as if she were scenting an enemy.

On other occasions, in other uniforms, she would descend upon the helpless back yard, where seated on tasseled cushions by borders of grass, or standing on stepladders beside hedges and trees, armed with other weapons she would do her best to dust and polish and vacuum-clean great Nature Herself, while I, by her side, dreamed among dandelions in all the freedom of my silent and tumultuous youth.

4

ACTUALLY IT WAS ALL RATHER BORING. With my chin in my hand I would gaze for hours at father chipping rocks on the cellar workbench, until he could stand it no longer and would tell me to run along and play with my "friends." I liked to watch mother sprawled asleep on the couch with her mouth open and her legs stuck under the slanting pillow. Sometimes, when she sat on the edge of her bed and drew from a little glass bottle a cap with a slender black brush, she would let me blow on her glistening fingernails. I enjoyed walking back and forth through dusty beams of sunlight, catching pieces of fluff that floated in the air, and pressing down the slats of venetian blinds, which sprang up with a clatter. My favorite toy was a dome that snowed when you shook it, but what I liked was not the snow but the mysterious water that forever submerged the blue boy, the brown house, and the three green trees. Alone, in the dark, I would build a brick wall. I would place the heavy red bricks carefully end to end, ten to a row, always moving from left to right. Slowly my wall would rise to my knees, my waist, my neck, until I would have to stand on a little bench for the last row of all. The whole process must have taken well over an hour. When everything was done I would stand back and admire my work. Then I would walk up to it, and spreading out my arms, and closing my eyes, I would stand motionless for a moment before swooning forward, a voluptuous destroyer; that silent crash . . .

By some accident the children in my neighborhood were several years older than I and so excluded me from their dusty games. Mother was at first my sole daytime companion but soon began to disappear, returning at lunchtime and a quarter to four, and leaving me in the meantime in the drowsy company of Mrs. Schneider and her yawning cats, among the faded green parrots of a maroon rug. Such isolation can only have increased my tendency to dream. But I must not exaggerate my solitude. In the evenings I romped and frisked with father, at night mother read to me, and spring and summer weekends were a green-and-blue festival of blackberrying, swimming, and searching for minerals in the white stone-heaps of abandoned quarries in green hills. And if it is true that I was a solitary sort of child, seeking out the dark places of summer and growing contentedly pale beside the winter reading-light, it is also true that from the very beginning I have tended to form passionate, secretive, and disastrous attachments.

Now it was father's custom, in those days, to exchange weekend visits with his smiling brother, who lived in a white house on a shady street in a green town some distance away. I was fond of Uncle Manny, who called me Arthur Parthur, always asked me to pick a card, and blew fat, white, slowly swirling smoke-rings which I enjoyed smashing. He wore a drooping watch-chain on his shiny brown vest, and I liked to lift the chain and watch the heavy circle rise from the pocket like a sun. I was even fonder of Auntie Lou, who had pink toenails and green eyelids, wore bright red pedalpushers and flowery halters, and screamed with laughter on two distinct notes: "*Ah* he-he-he. *Ah* he-he-he." She gave me fat chocolate lollipops wrapped in waxy polka-dot paper and she liked to rub her plump hand up and down on the back of my neck. The grownups sat in the living room, or on lawnchairs outside, while Marjorie and I went off to play by ourselves.

We were six years old. It was a sunny day, but the afternoon was dying. We were in Marjorie's webbed cellar, odorous of moist newspapers. I counted to twenty-five, shouting so as not to hear the direction of her footsteps, and then set off in search of her. I stamped around the first corner, hurrying softly back in hope of catching her by surprise, but this time she remained well hidden and I could not find her for a while. She was standing on a black pipe behind the dangerous hot-water tank. I knew I could beat her back and so did not immediately rush for home but stood grinning at her, my little captive. And suddenly she bent over, as if to scratch her knee, and rising abruptly she lifted her blue-and-white-checked dress. She thrust it down instantly, with a shrill little laugh, but what had struck me was her shining-dark eyes, gazing solemnly at me over her upheld hem. As I ran for home my cheeks were aflame as if I had done something bad. Again I counted to twenty-five, and as I pressed my eyes into my arm I saw her standing on the black pipe behind the dangerous hot-water tank, gazing at me with shining-dark eyes. Again I set off in search of her. Swiftly and softly I made my way to the hot-water tank, fearfully I peered into the forbidden shadows ... Marjorie sprang out from under the stairs and ran triumphantly home. When it was my turn to hide I hesitated for a moment and then climbed into a cobwebbed barrel. But looking up I felt oddly exposed, and climbing out, and wiping the sticky web-threads from my lips and eyes, I made my way to the dangerous hot-water tank. Standing on the slippery black pipe, pressing my back against the scratchy wall, breathing heavily in the dusty dankness, I listened to the leathery and gently crunchy patter of approaching footsteps, and as I listened my cheeks felt flushed, my heart beat faster, I felt a drowsy, swooning sensation, if I suddenly cried out she would scream with confusion and excitement, she would freeze in her tracks, I would leap out and rush for home, she would burst into tears of rage, suddenly in the dim space between the tank and wall she appeared, looking at me with luminous and expectant eyes, ripples passed across my stomach and I knew what I was supposed to do, what I longed to do, what I could never do, what I was about to do when all at once the kitchen door slammed shut above us and I heard mother saying "in August whether he" and I could not, and I did not.

We were blackberrying in a prickly field full of high bushes and a few crippled leafless trees. Each of us had a pot from the kitchen. I recall the heavy thump of the first berries dropped in the pot; the small dark leaves so troublesome to detach; purple-red fingertips. I had to go to the bathroom. "Hooha," father was saying, "now that's what I call a beaut of a berry, Lou, a beaut of a berry," and Uncle Manny was saying "Mmmmm nyum nyum nyum deelooshus. Deelectabubble." I placed my pot on a flat rock and crept away along a grass-grown dirt path toward a bushy hillock nearby. I climbed the hillock, looking down at Auntie Lou's bright red kerchief beside father's blond head, and scampered down the other side. Beside a tall bush I let down my shorts, but not my undershorts, and with an ache of pleasure began to splash onto the dark leaves, which gleamed in the sunlight. As the stream began to weaken I splashed onto my right shoe, which shone suddenly as if polished, and felt a hot trickle on my leg. A sudden noise made me whirl to one side, where I saw my cousin Marjorie standing some ten feet away. She was wearing her gray pot like a hat. She was watching me with a frown of earnestness, her lips parted slightly and one hand suspended in the act of raising a blackberry to her purple mouth.

Trips to Lake Sassacus were not mere swimming trips but day-long expeditions, centering around the picnic table and the charcoal fire in a setting of pine trees, distant red canoes, and reflections of hills in lakewater. Swimming was allowed in only a small section of the lake, bounded by white barrels whose lucid reflections rippled when a motorboat sped past on the other side. Marjorie and I liked to watch father make a fire, and sometimes I was allowed to shake out the little pillow-shaped pieces of charcoal into the circle of blackened stones. When father sprinkled the charcoal with lighter fluid and struck a match, I stepped away, waiting tensely for the sudden whoosh of flame. Usually we stayed until dusk, and as we drove home in the early darkness of woods and hills, along a narrow winding road bordered by short brown posts with shimmering silver strips, Marjorie and I sang songs with father, who drove with one hand and conducted with the other while mother watched the road anxiously.

One unusual feature of Lake Sassacus was the bathhouse, a long unpainted wooden structure divided into dank closets. The men changed on one side, the women on the other. It was our custom to change immediately after parking and then to carry the thermos jugs, aluminum folding chairs, picnic baskets, and patched inner tube to a damp table overlooking the lake. I changed with father and Marjorie changed with Auntie Lou, but she was released early to wait outside with father and Uncle Manny and me while the women, in Uncle Manny's words, took their own sweet time about it. One day as we waited on the men's side, Marjorie and I grew bored. We began to walk down the length of the building, glancing at the white hairy feet that sometimes showed beneath the raised doors. Father and Uncle Manny were talking and did not see us turn the corner. We began to walk along the other side, where I noticed an occa-

sional red toenail, an occasional hand reaching down to retrieve
a silky garment. All at once a door opened inward and a black-
haired witch in a black bathing suit stepped out, holding over
her arm a pile of red and white clothes. For a moment she
frowned at us. Then thrusting on a pair of green sunglasses she
walked briskly away, glaring at the ground and uttering little
hisses as she stepped on pebbles.

With a shrill little laugh Marjorie climbed up inside. I climbed
in after her. She closed the door, and standing on my toes and
pressing one cheek painfully against the wood I strained up, up,
up, up, to move the small dark block of wood into place. I
turned around, and in the brown dusk of that forbidden room,
with its pattern of dark dampness on the walls, I stood with my
heels in sunlight and my toes in darkness, waiting with a pounding heart. Slowly Marjorie began to count. And as I stood there
with my heels in sunlight and my toes in darkness, waiting with
a pounding heart, fearfully I wondered what was going to happen, fearfully I knew what was going to happen, "three" whispered Marjorie, quickly and clumsily we pulled our bathing
pants down, and up, and far away, in the outside world, came a
sound of crunching gravel, I wanted to cry Wait! Wait! for I
did not know what I had seen, but far away came a sound of
crunching gravel, suddenly below the raised door I saw a pair
of angry red knees, in terror I held my breath, I was lying in
the water in the sun, I was turning slowly round and round
on the black inner tube, I was trailing my finger in the water
and drawing black wet-marks on the dry part of the tube, high
overhead the hot blue sky burned down, lazily I lifted my weary
head and far away, high among the pines, I could see the four
folding chairs, the cluttered table, the orange-and-white beachball, the blackened grill leaning against a tree, then mother began
to wave and suddenly I bent forward gasping, in the brown
dusk Marjorie's dark eyes stared, but nothing happened, the
knees passed on, moments later I stepped outside, squinting in
the painful light.

5

ONE SUNNY DAY, about a week later, we were playing in Marjorie's upstairs room, wallpapered in robin's-egg blue with pink-and-silver rocking horses. Through the open window we could hear the voices of the grownups down in the back yard. Marjorie's toys were not very interesting—she went in for marvelous toys that quickly lost their marvels, like her magic coloring book whose pictures turned various dull colors when you applied a moistened brush—and we soon grew bored. For lack of anything better to do we decided to have a tickle-fight. Climbing onto her large bed, with its pink ribbed spread and its sky-blue headboard on which was pictured a bright yellow bear in a bright red cap, we faced one another on our knees and were soon tumbling about, shrieking with laughter. She liked to tickle wildly all over, under the arms, on the sides, on the backs of the legs, whereas I preferred to concentrate on a single sensitive place: sitting on her legs, with my knees clutching her sides, I would tickle her lower ribs very softly and methodically, with swift soft motions of my fingertips, while she shrieked and squirmed and clawed at me with her little hands. I was quite a skilful tickler. I would never let her relax, but I would let her begin to relax, before suddenly increasing the pressure and bringing her to a new pitch of gasping hysteria, refusing to stop though tears of laughter, of anguish, spilled from her eyes, leading her carefully to a state of tingling, stinging, swooning numbness as shock after light shock coursed through her delicate and tormented skin and she gulped for air, and her head moved back and forth on the bed, and her eyes filled with terror, and suddenly a voice from the yard cried: "Hey, you two, what's going on up there!" and I scrambled off, and she instantly sat up, alert and gasping. There was no sound of the screen door slamming. Soon the adult voices continued their murmur. Still panting, Marjorie climbed down from the bed and walked across the room into her closet.

It was a large, deep, dark closet, cluttered with shoes and toys. I could see nothing in either of the dark corners on my left and right. "Marjorie," I whispered, and listened intently, but the sounds of quick breathing were my own. Slowly, with a kind of dreamy excitement, I pushed my way through a thick mass of dresses. The wire hangers scraped, a buckle clutched my sleeve; as I stepped into the darkness of the other side my foot landed on something soft that gave out a rubbery wheeze. "Marjorie," I whispered again. And there in the blackness I heard an oddly familiar sound, a repeated snapping sound that I could not quite... "Marjorie," I whispered, moving toward the right with difficulty as the soft tight row of dresses pressed against my side. All at once I stopped. Shrouded in shadow, she was standing in the corner with her back against the wall and her playpants draped about her ankles in a black heap. Darkly she snapped the intimate elastic band against her stomach, and as I stood there listening I knew that I should return at once to the sunny room... if I could make it through that tight mass of clothes... but what if I drowned among those dresses, in that soft sea of cloth... and I knew that somehow it was far more sinful this time, even though... dreamy and forbidden freedom...

6

I HAVE ALWAYS BEEN ATTRACTED to the forbidden. Shortly after mother forbade me to die (I had been fooling about in the medicine chest) I first attempted to commit suicide. I knew that Marjorie and I were doing something wrong, something for which we would certainly be punished if anyone found out, and yet I could no more stop myself than I could stop myself some years later from reaching into the fan. For now whenever we met we took ourselves off to some dark or dusky corner, where without laughter, with a never diminishing sense of excitement and danger, we repeated our forbidden game. And once, when she reached out to touch me, I frowned and knocked away her hand. For what I sought, hidden in darkness with my cousin Marjorie, was not the crude pleasure of sense but the subtle pleasure of transgression, what I sought was the sense of breaking through, what I sought was the dreamlike delight of leaving the bright oppressive world of the all too drearily familiar and entering the dark, deep, boundless realm of the oh so dazzlingly forbidden. And always I would emerge from our sessions feeling that I could look no one in the eye.

Now it may seem strange, but from the very beginning I was deeply shocked by these little adventures into the forbidden, adventures which others, perhaps, took far less seriously than I. For I was an earnest child, and never more so than when feeling myself drawn into dark violation. Often my sense of justice was outraged by adults who failed in their appointed task of vigilance and punishment. Father would sigh, and look hurt, and mother would rage, and slam doors, and forbid me to have dinner, but later she would come into my room with a stern look and a plate of warmed-over food. And all the while I felt that they should have tied a heavy stone to my leg and dropped me into the sea. I remember one afternoon when I was sick in bed. Bored, very bored, I lay drawing in a coloring book. I made the cowboy's face a nice turquoise blue, and his hat a lovely pink, and his lasso a flaming red, but somehow he was still only a boring cowboy, and shutting the book angrily, with a papery softness that seemed to mock my rage, I lay staring up at the ceiling, with its familiar bumps and ripples, and then I turned to look at the wallpaper, pale green with a pattern of silver and dark-green cross-hatchings. Idly I counted the silver lines. And suddenly, for no reason, I was consumed, oh, consumed with an unbearable desire, my heart began to beat painfully, and snatching up the red crayon I made a violent red circle on the pale green wallpaper. Shocked at my crime, feverish with dread, for a long time I lay in fearful silence, waiting. At last mother came in, bearing a cup of soup and a big silver spoon. I said nothing, for I could not speak. Suddenly—as if comically—her smile vanished. Looking from the wall to me to the wall to me she said: "Oh, Arthur, how could you? Why? Why?" Then she looked angry, and left the cup of soup beside me, and went away. Later, when father came in, she showed him the hideous red circle, and spoke in a cold voice. Father rubbed away at it with a piece of tissue paper that he kept holding to a little glass bottle, but the circle would not come out. Nothing more was said to me, nothing at all happened to me, and although I was intensely relieved, for even the mildest frown filled me with terror, still I was troubled by a sense of incompletion, of disproportion, of lack of symmetry, for I felt that my crime should have been balanced by a violent red punishment.

The day came when our secret game took a little turn that filled me with apprehension. I was standing alone in Marjorie's dark closet. We had just completed a somewhat listless version of One Two Three. Marjorie had already pushed her way through the tight mass of dresses and vanished into the sunny room. But I lingered in darkness, for the change to brightness was always difficult for me: the bright sunlight threatened me with its sharp, sudden gaze, and I would long to return to the soothing dark. But at length I pushed my way through the soft wall of dresses, with their dissonant odor of mothballs and sachet, and stepped out of darkness into a shock of light. The gleaming white windowsill, the black shadow-stripes, the burning pink toychest, the flaming dark-blue rug, the sun-shot sun-whirled sun-maddened dustmotes... Marjorie was standing by the pink toychest. Loose strands of her light brown hair glowed sun-yellow. Her dark eyes blazed with sunlight and danger. And suddenly I felt the presence of danger all about me, my heart began to beat violently, I longed to return to the soothing dark. But already Marjorie was slowly counting "wuuuuuuuun," and "twoooooooo," and as I waited for three I wondered how she could possibly think of doing that, out of the darkness, in the bright sunlight, for it was as if she were mingling darkness and brightness, it was as if she were carrying the darkness of the closet into the brightness of the room, it was as if she were announcing our dark secret to the whole sunlit world, it was as if, it was as if, it was as if I didn't know what, and as I stood there in the warm light, half-swooning with excitement, I felt a bright confusion, a warm temptation, a sunny yielding, as if the sunlight itself were wrapping me up in a safe darkness of brightness.

7

AND, IN GENERAL, is there any pleasure or crime greater than that of yielding, yielding . . . that blissful sensation of relaxing some inner tension, of breaking some unknown bond and entering a region of dreamy and forbidden freedom, a freedom for which you shall be punished, destroyed . . . The end came suddenly, one rainy summer afternoon. But I cannot leave the impression that Marjorie and I did nothing but play forbidden games in secret places. Often we spent whole afternoons in innocent play, watching television in Marjorie's brown living room or digging tunnels at the beach. I say "digging tunnels at the beach." But on a glittering beach, beside the shadow of a tilted beach umbrella, under a blue sky where a silver blimp lazily floated, in cold hard sand beneath hot silky sand we dug slow tunnels with burning fingertips, bursting through to a sudden sandpapery touch. We searched the beach for chalky white ashtray-shells with smooth purple linings, rubbery brown seaweed with snappable pods, damp popsicle sticks for weaving into mats, pieces of light-green cokebottle glass smoothed into treasure by artistic waves. We pressed our feet into the dark shine of sandbars, pushing out the shine and leaving pale footprints that quickly darkened and glistened. We rubbed all over our bodies cool oozy mud, squushy squeezy mud, lovely mucky mud, and giggled as it drip-dropped down from behind. Seated foot to foot in warm greenbrown water between two sandbars, we cupped our hands and tried to catch fish-eyes of gold sunlight in our palms. Suddenly we looked at one another and burst into giggles. Auntie Lou, standing a few feet away, turned to mother and said: "I get such a kick out of those two. I'll bet *I* know who Em Eh Are Jay Oh Are Eye Ee wants to marry when she grows up but *we* won't tell, *will* we," winking and winking, but the end came suddenly, one rainy summer afternoon. From the downstairs living room came a soft murmur of grownup voices, punctuated by sharp bursts of laughter that sounded like anger. In the warm yellow glow of Marjorie's overhead light we were assembling all her puzzles on the floor. I wanted to cover the entire floor and so create a universe of puzzles, but unfortunately we ran out of puzzles before we had covered the space between the closet door and the pink toy-chest. In a bored, irritable way we discussed and rejected possible new games, deciding at last, without enthusiasm, on All Fall Down. I climbed up onto the skyblue footboard and fell forward onto the soft bouncy bed. She climbed up onto the skyblue footboard and fell forward onto the soft bouncy bed. I climbed up onto the skyblue footboard and fell forward onto the soft bouncy bed. After a while, for no reason at all, I walked over to the door and turned out the light.

The room was plunged into a sudden and exciting dusk. The window was a bleak rectangle with dark gray at the top and dark green at the bottom. I raised my hands over my head, widened my eyes, and said: "Booooooo." Marjorie held up strands of her hair and said: "Kakabooboo." We both burst into giggles. A game of Ghosts was quickly invented, in which one person had to cover his eyes and listen for the other person, who tried to sneak up on him. But that was boring, so boring, and Marjorie began to sulk and yawn and rub her eyes with the backs of both hands. I suggested ten new games, all of which she rejected with sulky contempt. And because she was bored, and because I was bored, and because it was dusk, and because it was doom, I then suggested, in a half-joking whisper that made my heart beat madly, that we do something we had never done even in darkness: I suggested that we take off all our clothes.

Marjorie perked up at once. She removed her things with casual abandon, tossing her red jeans and her yellow shirt onto a chair and kicking her white undies halfway across the room. Then she stood with her hands on her hips, watching me boldly as I undressed with nervous deliberation, placing my shoes side by side and putting a striped sock in each, draping my pants carefully over the skyblue footboard, and hanging my shirt neatly on the back of a chair. But when it came to my under-shorts, a snug pair that reached almost to my knees, I was over-come by intense embarrassment. With a shyness so fierce that it was a kind of pain I hovered behind the chair, listening for creaking footsteps, and all at once I felt that things were hap-pening too quickly, that we were rushing noisily and clumsily toward disaster, but even as I whispered a cautious "let's stop" I knew that it was too late, that she would never—for there she stood, with her fat little belly sticking out and a frown of impatience on her stubborn face ("Shhh!" I warned). But Marjorie was furious. She made a face, stuck out her lip, tapped her foot impatiently in imitation of Auntie Lou; but nothing in the world, with her watching— "Don't look," I said angrily. She covered each eye with a hand. "Turn around," I com-manded. Contemptuously she obeyed. My temples were pound-ing, my forehead was damp; I was strangely exhausted, and for a moment I felt that I would fall forward in a swoon, a pleasant swoon... With a swoon of painful pleasure I yielded, half-closing my eyes as the elastic band tightened about my knees. Suddenly Marjorie turned around. Blushing angrily I pulled up my clumsy shorts. She called me a name, stamped her foot, and climbed up on the bed, where she lay down on her belly with her chin in her hands and started a conversation with Eeyore, her red donkey. I stood for a while in sulky banishment, looking darkly at Marjorie, who continued to ignore me. Far away I heard the sound of ice cubes in a glass. And I thought how nice it would be to get dressed and go downstairs, I would sit on the brown chair or the green hassock with my hands in my lap and listen to the grownups, perhaps there would be pink lemonade, with ice cubes, perhaps there would be pretzels with loops in them, perhaps there would be a wooden bowl of mixed salted nuts and there, just visible among the boring peanuts and the bland cashews, the brown-and-ivory smooth side of a flawless Brazil nut, but my pants were on the footboard, my shirt was on the chair, my shoes were halfway across the room, it was all too difficult, it was all so boring, angrily I went over and climbed up on the bed and began pulling Eeyore's black tail, which came off. Marjorie continued to ignore me, and with the distinct sense of inviting disaster I picked up Eeyore and tried to make him stand on Marjorie's rubbery behind, but it was no use, and so I made him walk along the bumps of her spine up to her hair, where I turned him sideways and fitted his legs over her neck. And suddenly she was tugging down my elastic band and I was trying to break her grip as Eeyore lay sadly watching us beside his tail. Those mournful oval eyes . . . It was then that the door opened and the light went on; a lesson for all three of us; for I gasped, and Eeyore blushed, and Marjorie began to cry; and then I too began to cry, giving great gasping heaves of anguish, the thick hot tears pouring out of me with a violence that terrified me into hotter tears; and far away I heard the sound of ice cubes in a glass; and I could not see bad Marjorie Grumm alone after that; and Eeyore never did recover his tail.

8

MY GRADE-SCHOOL YEARS exist in memory as a long brown virtuous blur. I did well in everything and was liked by my teachers, and among my schoolmates I made no enemies, no friends. I recall a time when I drew bluebirds, kingfishers, red-winged blackbirds, Baltimore orioles, and black-and-white birds with labeled parts. I recall a bird that sang "Sweet Sweet Sweetie" and "Weet Weet Weet Wee-chee." Soon I was drawing green bluebirds, black-winged redbirds, yellow crows. One day I drew a big fat bird with an egg inside, and a little fat bird inside that egg, and a little fat egg inside that bird, and a little little bird inside that egg, and a little little egg inside that little little bird. Later we drew wigwams and covered wagons, and sang a song about musical instruments of which I recall this line: "The clarinet, the clarinet, sings doodle doodle doodle doodle det." One fine day I was taught the importance of dividing words into syllables: "b-a-c"—pause—"k-a-c"—pause —"h-e," spelled my teacher, but I shouted out the answer instantly, for I was quite smart. My fifth-grade teacher read a story in which there suddenly appeared the words "she did her duty," and the class burst into titters as blue angry eyes, uncomprehending, glared over the tops of pink-rimmed eyeglasses. Each time I finished a book I cut a little book out of red construction paper and pasted it onto a chart beside my name. Soon my row of books was far longer than all the other rows, but this was not at all pleasing to me, and I began to conceal my shameful amounts of reading. I scarcely ever saw my cousin Marjorie any more, for she had become quite a proper little lady. "Heya, Artie," father was always saying, "how's about throwing the old ball around." "I don't feel like it," I would always answer. Often I was sick, and I loved to stay home in bed, reading and dreaming, as the anguish of missed assignments softened to regret, to indifference, to lively oblivion.

Two incidents stand out sharply from the general blur of those years: the incident of the fan and the incident of my attempted suicide. The fan was one of those little ones with a stand and a round wire cage, which mother liked to have blowing on her during hot summer days. I had been warned not to put my fingers in the cage, and perhaps there would have been no temptation if the fan had not somehow begun to appear wherever I looked. I would see the blur of those blades on the green counter beside the sink, on the gleaming white stove, on the dining-room buffet, on the glass table under the living-room window, and I could not help wondering what would happen if by some unforeseen accident a wandering finger should suddenly find itself inside the cage. The bluegray blur intrigued me: it looked so soft, so insubstantial, in comparison with the hard clarity of the four stationary blades, shaped like large flat lima beans. The blur looked like mist, like steam out of a teapot, and it was hard to believe that you could not insert a finger as harmlessly as into a winter breathcloud. I quickly discovered how to work the silver button on the gray bulge behind the cage. I liked to watch the hard blades dissolve into mist: at first they would turn slowly, teasingly, so that you could readily distinguish their shapes, and even as they turned faster and began to multiply you could still see clear outlines flickering past, but all at once they vanished into a soft, trembling mist, which seemed to thicken and grow steady as the speed increased. By turning the button again I was able to reverse the process, and I watched eagerly for the moment when the trembling mist revealed its first edges. I also enjoyed spinning the stationary blades with my finger, for then I could reach in for a harmless touch as the dangerous blades slowed down. "Arrrthur!" mother would call, and I would whirl around, but she only wanted me to come out into the miserable sun.

One day when mother was out shopping I found myself on a stool before the kitchen counter, gazing into the blur. It was a humid, drowsy, dreamy day, and half mesmerized by the whirring blur I watched my slender finger move slowly toward the cage. Somewhere a sparrow softly squawked. I watched my finger penetrate beyond the wire, I watched it move closer and ever closer to the blue, soft blur, in my mind I saw little brown feathers spitting from a fan, suddenly I snatched my tingling finger away. Untroubled, the soft blur murmured on. I was still trembling as I walked over to a white drawer and removed a yellow pencil with a hard pink eraser.

Holding the eraser-end away from me, and tipping my head to one side, for fear that splinters of chewed pencil would be flung into my eyes, I slowly moved the pencil toward the—a sudden clank. I snatched the pencil away. The eraser showed a small dark mark but was otherwise unharmed. I repeated the experiment and proceeded to new ones, turning the fan on and off, introducing the clanking pencil at different places, and above all studying the stationary blades in hope of piercing their mystery. For the first time I noticed the bend: each flat blade was carefully bent in such a fashion that when it was pointing toward the left, its bottom portion was closer than its top portion to the front of the cage. And as I spun the blades idly, poking my finger in and out, suddenly it seemed clear to me that the blades could not possibly chop off a finger, or mangle a finger, or wound a finger in any way. Now follow my reasoning. The blades turned in a clockwise direction. Therefore they rose at the left of the cage and fell at the right. If a finger were introduced very gently and carefully into the left of the cage, the bottom portion of each rising blade must graze that finger harmlessly from beneath. If a finger were introduced very gently and carefully into the right of the cage, the top portion of each falling blade must graze that finger harmlessly from above. In either case the slicing edge of the blade would not, could not, dared not strike my finger, for in either case the slicing edge was bent safely away. Thus it was when I spun the blades myself, and thus it must be when the blades were spinning in a blur. And turning on the fan, and waiting for the blades to reach their highest speed, I began to insert my right index finger slowly into the left of the cage.

At once I noticed the ominous shadow of my finger on the blur. As I moved my finger forward in minute stages, pausing after each advance, my heart began to beat with an unforeseen violence. Already my finger had penetrated far deeper than I judged necessary, and soon I could force it no farther, but held it rigidly before the loud blur, which seemed to have a hungry, humming force I had not noticed before. And now the tip of my extended finger felt as sensitive and vulnerable as the quivering soft end of a tongue, and I was ready to cry out in anguish and failure. But fixing my attention firmly on the remembered bend of the stationary blades, I gathered the strength with which to force my fingertip minutely forward through vast, throbbing spaces, as the shadow of an unseen bird rippled over the sunny counter and behind the windowpane the blue sky hummed and whirred, and all at once I felt a shock of contact, a first faint shock of contact, a mild absurd tickle of contact, I heard a little sound like the chirr of a cricket, and as terror dissolved in joy, softly, triumphantly, deliriously I pressed my buzzing finger against the mad blur of those blades . . .

My suicide was much less successful. Mother had forbidden me to die, and standing on Mrs. Schneider's upper back porch, gazing on tiptoe over the peeling white rail at the lawn, the swing, the hedge, the stream, the dazzling white side of the body shop, I so intensely imagined myself falling from that height that I felt as you do at the end of an elevator ride, when you feel yourself falling down into yourself, as if you had been stretched through three floors. Father had said that death was like being asleep and never waking up, and many a fine midnight, lying fast awake, I would imagine myself falling into an eternal sleep, while outside my castle the thornbushes rose past my windows, and down in the kitchen the flames of the fire did not stir, and forever and ever no prince came. And I would feel so sorry for the little boy asleep forever in his dark cold room, that sometimes I would feel a sudden sting in my eyes. And many a fine morning, coming out of a dream, I would tell myself that I could not open my eyes, and for a moment I could not open my eyes: my lashes would stick to my skin: drained of all images, and filled with terror, my mind would beat its wings in blackness and fling itself against unseen walls, until suddenly through trembling eyelashes there shone a row of white venetian blinds, and casually I invented the day. And one balmy afternoon when Mrs. Schneider went inside, and I heard the rattle of the bolt on the bathroom door, I climbed over the peeling white rail and stood on the narrow gray ledge with my back to the yard, clinging tightly to the slender white posts. Carefully I turned myself around. I gripped the chalky rail behind me, I pressed my heels against the spaces between the posts, I saw the ends of my shoes stuck over the ledge, and looking down at the sunny green yard, at the red toy truck blazing in the grass, at the tall yellow sunflowers blooming along the wire fence at the side of the house, carefully I began to fall with my arms outspread on the thick soft air, falling swiftly, softly, slowly, dreamily down, now passing the bottom boards of the porch, now passing the rust-stained clothesline pulley, now passing a gray and peeling shingle, and there below, on the bright green grass, my dark green shadow stretched to meet me, and high above, in the bright blue sky, no sound disturbed the summer day, and looking about me, like another Alice, lazily down and down I fell toward soft, balmy, dreamy, drowsy Death, but the telephone rang and the green yard plunged away, the telephone rang and I was standing at the edge of a high white porch, the telephone rang and I called in terror for Mrs. Schneider, who came at last to pluck me from my precipice, while Wynken, glittering beside the rocker, stirred in his white sleep.

9

A WORK OF FICTION is a radical act of the imagination whose sole purpose is to supplant the world. In order to achieve this purpose, a work of fiction is willing to use all the means at its disposal, including the very world it is plotting to annihilate. Art imitates Nature as Judas imitates Christ.

From the very beginning I was an avid reader. I lapped up

books as other children lapped up popsicles and ice cream. Yes,
I had my chocolate books, my vanilla books, my fudge-ripple
books... and best of all were the ones with little surprises in
them, you know, the pistachio books, the maple-walnut books
... On stifling summer afternoons I would lie for hours on my bed
before an open book, beside the closed and glowing blinds, and
slowly raising my word-heavy eyes I would be amazed, amazed,
at the green wallpaper, the gray windowsill, the reddish cracks
in the knuckle of my thumb... It must have been in the sixth
grade that I first began to sense my difference. For some reason
I had been transferred to a new class, where I knew three or
four boys from earlier grades but was otherwise a stranger. The
new girls all seemed large, unattractive, and dimly threatening.
One day, entering the room a few minutes after the others
because I had lingered in the candy store, I had the sensation of
a sudden hush, as if I were intruding on the privacy of the whole
class. But please do not misunderstand me. I am not speaking
simply of my uneasiness in a new class but of an essential difference which my uneasiness first revealed to me. For there they
were, my new coevals, with their frowns, and their smiles, and
their footballs, and their jackknives—and there was I with my
chin in my hand, dreaming of islands and Edens. Oh, I did my
work well, I did my work all too well; I said hi! to everyone.
But it was as if I were a mere visitor among them, sharing in
none of their habits. And perhaps for this reason I began to
suffer a continual dissatisfaction, a yearning, a churning, an I-
don't-know-what of dark unease; and the boredom that had
afflicted me intermittently from the time of my earliest childhood now began to afflict me like a disease of the senses. Moods
of sullen restlessness came over me. I spent a great deal of time
brooding alone. There seemed no reason to do anything at all,
combined with a pressing need to do something at once, at once.
And then, there was my sense of being hemmed in, of being unable to breathe... As if windows were being shut all about me
... Oh, I despair of making myself understood! But it was as if,
can't you see, it was as if I needed things that others did not

need, it was as if they needed things I did not want or need. Those somnolent summer afternoons... In nothing did I feel my estrangement more keenly than in my relation to my cousin Marjorie. We scarcely knew one another any more. She seemed much older than I, though we were the same age, and whenever our families got together we could find nothing whatever to talk about, nothing whatever to do. She was a Girl Scout and was always mentioning her troop. She sat with her ankles crossed and her hands folded on her lap. She bored me silly and I bored her back. So the world went, and even mother, even father, shared in the general distortion; things were increasingly expected of me that I found impossible to understand. Mother thought, for instance, that it was "high time" for me to "help" about the house. I was expected to "help" paint the perfectly good shingles and "help" mow—I!—the perfectly wretched lawn. I pleaded headaches, heartaches, soulaches, and went off to dream of cool civilizations under the ocean. It was all I could do, in that worst of times, to wrest a few hours of revery from the noisy day.

10

I FIRST SAW MY DOUBLE in the seventh grade. He was sitting at the back of the long yellow bus that stopped at my corner on the way to school. The long double row of laughing strangers had filled me with desolation, and as I slipped into the first vacant seat at the front of the bus I fought against despair by thinking of all the others who sat alone. He was scarcely more than a pale blur to me then, for I had shut up my eyeglasses in a brown case in my pocket, but he had struck me more than the others precisely because he was sitting so far away, in the part of the bus to which I myself would never have penetrated. Bright sunlight streamed through the windows across from me, bringing out a dark shine in eyes and shoes, and as the bus turned the corner at the top of the hill and entered a half-strange region where I scarcely ever rode my bicycle, I felt that I was entering a period of my life as depressing as the leathery brown seat-cover beside me, from whose torn center a little yellowish tuft sprouted like a malignant growth.

Under a blue sky bright as glass we passed along maple-lined streets that were sunny on one side and shady on the other, stopping now and then at a corner to let on strangers. A pale fat boy with a pale fat crewcut, through which a glossy pink scalp was visible, sat down next to me. He leaned forward, talking to the boy in front of him and sputtering into giggles.

As I stepped from the bus onto a wide sidewalk filled with knots and masses of strangers, a tall blond boy with a white patrol-boy's belt across his chest shouted and made sweeping motions with his arm, ushering me away from the line of yellow buses toward a central walk. Curving sidewalks between bare lawns led to a long low orange building full of glass. It was nothing at all like the dark brick grammar school with the tall flight of steps in front, and the newness and brightness of it, the glitter and bareness of it, seemed more dismal than darkness. I noticed a few familiar sixth-grade faces in the crowd, but no one waved or shouted to me, and as I moved uncertainly toward a group of laughing boys whom I had not seen since June, I turned to see my double standing on the steps of the bus, holding in one hand a large blue notebook with a rainbow of plastic tabs, and gazing out at the crowd as if he were standing on a beach in summer, pushing his toes into the hot sand and staring out at the blue, flashing, sharp-edged water.

As fate would have it he was in most of my classes, and we proved to have certain habits in common. We were quiet, we were studious, we were smart and unsociable; above all we avoided one another like the plague. But avoidance is only a complicated form of connection, and from the very beginning we watched one another cautiously across near distances. I would be standing at my bench in woodshop, sawing away at a flat bear that was destined to serve as one side of a napkin-holder, and I would look up to see, through sawdusty eyeglasses, my double watching me from a nearby dusty bench. He would instantly lower his eyes and turn away with a redness that seemed less a blush of embarrassment than a flush of anger. Or I would see him in gym class, in his white t-shirt and gray shorts, seated at the far end of a shiny gray mat and listening intently to the tall instructor who was explaining how to climb a thick rope that plunged from the ceiling and ended in a heavy knot beside the instructor's thigh. My double turned to see me watching him, but instead of looking away I shifted my gaze slightly, pretending to examine the horizontal ladder on the wall behind him.

He was a neat serious boy with a faint perpetual frown. His shiny brown hair was carefully parted on the left, forming a white line, and was trimmed so closely around the sides and back that the color faded to ash. At the ends of his ashen side-burns, streaks of blond down were visible. His mouth was held tightly shut, giving him a severe or sullen look, and when he looked at you his eyes would suddenly narrow and two lines would appear at the top of his nose; I learned later that he owned a pair of eyeglasses which he never wore. He wore long-sleeved plaid shirts, dark blue or charcoal-gray pants belted high on his waist, and brown shoes with a pattern of little punc-tures on the toe. In the pocket of his shirt he carried a white plastic pencil-holder in which he clipped a dark blue fountain pen and two mechanical pencils, one glossy red and one glossy green. He was a quiet, hardworking, inoffensive student, and there was nothing at all remarkable about him except his re-semblance to me and the fact that he made no friends.

For even I did not become his friend until that winter, though whether I was ever his friend at all is a question worth asking. It was more than that, it was less than that; he was my brother, my stranger. Meanwhile we watched one another with an inter-est that was something more than idle curiosity. For there were times, there were times—well, there were times when I caught

William Mainwaring looking at me with eyes narrowed in hatred, though perhaps it was only his myopia. It is true we were rivals of a sort, for both of us were A students; and if I floated to the top of the class without effort, without interest, simply because I was more comfortable there, he drove himself to the top with an energy that fascinated and repelled me. But more than that, the accident of faint personal resemblance had joined us indissolubly in our own minds and in the minds of our witty classmates. Now it is not pleasant to resemble someone else, however faintly. Perhaps resemblance threatens that principle of individuality without which—and so forth. But this I know: that suddenly I would see in him a gesture, the flicker of an expression, which reminded me of myself, and a hot wave of revulsion would dash down in me, sending up a poisonous spray. At any rate I watched him, and I watched him watching me; and if I was eager to discover differences, I was not disappointed. And yet those very differences bound us more tightly than likeness.

We were all sitting on the cool gray mats that had been dragged onto the shiny floor of the gym. He and I avoided one another intensely during gym-period, for the ill-fitting uniforms emphasized our mutual thinness. At the same time I was secretly grateful for his presence, for otherwise I would have been as alone in my thinness as the unhappy fat boy in his fatness: that lone sufferer looked no one in the eye, and wore his immense shorts so low on his hips, with some sad notion of seeming tough, that when he bent over you could see the top of the cleavage in his enormous buttocks. Mr. Coolis, a tall instructor in a tight white t-shirt and tight blue shorts with a white stripe running down each side, was standing near a thick rope that hung from the ceiling and ended in a knot beside his knotty thigh. Suddenly he leaped onto the rope and began pulling himself slowly and effortlessly up, pausing now and then to explain a point of technique. At the very top he touched the piece of black metal and looked down at us over one shoulder, and suddenly he came hurtling down hand over hand and leaped to the mat, where he stood breathing heavily before us with his hands on his hips. Only when he pointed to the first boy did I realize that we too were expected to climb the rope.

The first boy was nervous but strong. He pulled himself up onto the thick knot and stood clinging to the rope as Mr. Coolis arranged his feet properly. Then he began to pull himself slowly and grimly up, while Mr. Coolis shouted encouragement. He had climbed halfway up before Mr. Coolis called him back. He came down carefully, hand over hand, and leaped unsmiling to the mat below. Mr. Coolis' gaze swept over us again, and this time he pointed to William Mainwaring.

Narrow-eyed and tight-lipped, frowning straight ahead, he tripped on the edge of the mat. A few nasty titters sounded. Flushed and frowning he stepped quickly to the rope and without pausing leaped up and tried to pull himself onto the waist-high knot. He hung with his feet a few inches above the mat, kicking violently but unable to pull himself up. Several boys laughed and made noises as Mr. Coolis lifted him onto the knot. He stood swaying there, pale and grim, gripping the rope high overhead and straining to pull himself up while Mr. Coolis tried to arrange his feet and said "Whoa, boy, whoa," as if he were addressing a pony. But as soon as Mr. Coolis stepped back, William Mainwaring kicked away the entangling rope and with a tremendous pull drew himself up to his fists as if he were chinning himself on a bar. He hung there with his legs dangling and his teeth clenched and a vein standing out on his neck until, exhausted, he simply let go, jumping out and falling to the mat on his hands and knees. Mr. Coolis motioned him to sit down apart from us and at once chose the next boy, who climbed easily halfway up. William Mainwaring sat alone, frowning down at the mat. He sat in the Indian position, his forearms resting on his thighs and his hands dangling inward, his back curved, his neck slanting forward, and when it was my turn I knew that all I wanted was to do better than William Mainwaring; and drawing strength from his failure I pulled myself awkwardly but successfully onto the knot; and although I could not climb more than a few feet, and later joined my double and the fat boy and four other boys who required special instruction, still I knew that my failure had seemed success compared to his; and in my triumph I felt a burst of affection for William Mainwaring, mingled unmistakably, for life is a curious thing, with faint contempt.

11

GEORGE SZABO HAD SHINY BLACK HAIR that he combed ripplingly back on both sides of his head so that it met at the back in a vertical line. In front, over his forehead, his hair fell in a careful V. When he combed his hair in the lavatory he would comb the left of the V carefully upward, following each motion of the comb with a smoothing motion of his other hand. Then he would comb the right of the V carefully upward, following each motion of the comb with a smoothing motion of his other hand. Then, watching himself carefully in the mirror, he would hold the comb horizontally over his head so that the ends pointed front to back, and with a sudden deft motion he would rake the comb forward, causing the point of the V to topple over his forehead. George Szabo wore shortsleeved shirts with the sleeves rolled up to his shoulders. He wore his collar up and the back of his shirt pulled out. When he walked, looking straight ahead, he held his arms almost stiffly at his sides, away from his body, as if in readiness. When he smiled, forming two dimples, he showed a perfect row of small square bright white teeth.

Richie Twiss had shiny copper-blond hair that he combed straight back on both sides of his head so that it met at the back in a vertical line. In front, over his forehead, his hair rose in a sweeping copper-blond wave that showed the wide teeth-marks of his comb. When he combed his hair in the lavatory he would comb up the wave in elaborate semicircular sweeps from left to right, following each motion of the comb with a smoothing motion of his other hand. Then he would hold the comb vertically against the wave and pull it suddenly forward, carefully disordering his too-perfect wave. Richie Twiss wore long-sleeved shirts with the cuffs turned back over his thin tanned wrists. He wore his collar up and the back of his shirt pulled out. When he walked, looking straight ahead, he held his arms almost stiffly at his sides, away from his body, as if in readiness. He smiled rarely, looking about with uneasy eyes.

George Szabo and Richie Twiss were always together. They walked together on the playground in the morning and during lunch-period; they sat across from one another in the cafeteria; they combed their hair together in the lavatory; they rode on my bus, seated side by side. I carefully avoided them, and to my relief they never bothered me, perhaps because mother had had George Szabo in the first grade.

One day as I entered the bus I noticed that George Szabo and Richie Twiss were seated directly behind William Mainwaring toward the back of the bus. Since there were no empty seats in front I sat farther back than usual, three seats ahead of William Mainwaring in the opposite row. He had seen me enter and had immediately looked away, and now was staring out the window at the dark plate-glass front of a dry-cleaning shop. As the bus started up, George Szabo leaned forward with a smile and said quietly to William Mainwaring: "Hey, Bird." Richie Twiss leaned forward without a smile and said: "Hey, Bird, what's your name, Bird," and I instantly looked away.

That afternoon I was standing on the playground after lunch-period, watching a violent game of tether-ball. As two tough eighth-graders smashed the yellow ball back and forth around the trembling red pole, a third boy crouched on the metal stand beneath the circling ball, waiting his turn. I had noticed William Mainwaring not too far from me, watching the game intensely from the circle of onlookers. When I happened to glance at him again I saw George Szabo standing on one side of him and Richie Twiss on the other. They had their collars up and their jackets tied around their hips. "Hey, Bird," said George Szabo, dimpling into a smile. Richie Twiss said: "Hey, Bird, can you fly, Bird, hey, Bird, I'm talkin-a-you." William Mainwaring stared rigidly ahead. Smiling more broadly, George Szabo placed an arm gently around William Mainwaring's shoulders and said: "Hey, Bird, my buddy's talkin-a-you." Richie Twiss said: "Hey, Bird, can't you talk, shitbird?" George Szabo said: "Hey, don't you know birds can't talk?" Richie Twiss said: "Yeah? What can birds do?" "Hey," said George Szabo, giving a little hug, "what can birds do?" A roar went up from the crowd as the rope of the tether-ball wrapped itself round and round the pole, and when I looked back toward William Mainwaring, several eighth-graders obscured my view. Three rows of boys stood behind me now, and it was a while before I could maneuver myself into a new position. George Szabo and Richie Twiss had disappeared. William Mainwaring was still standing there, staring straight ahead. There was no expression on his face at all. As I watched, feeling that I should turn away, his head turned suddenly in my direction. I instantly turned away, but not before he had flung into my eyes a look of burning hatred.

12

IT WAS MOTHER'S WISH—it was mother's will—it was mother's pleasure—that I should learn how to dance. No sooner had the mimeographed circular arrived, announcing the commencement of weekly dancing classes in the school gymnasium from 7:30 to 9:00 P.M., than she declared herself highly pleased. "It's not at all unreasonable, Walter, if you keep in mind what private lessons cost. And look at this part here: parents cordially invited to attend. It won't be as if we were leaving him all alone. Somebody will always be there to look after him. It's the best thing in the world for him, I sincerely believe."

"Okeydoke," said father. "If he wants to learn how to dance, I won't stop him."

"It's not a question of stopping him, Walter. It's more a question of starting him. You know how he is, never wanting to try anything new. You remember how he absolutely refused to take oil-painting lessons that summer, remember? He said he didn't like oil painting. Didn't like oil painting! Now how did he know he didn't like oil painting if he never even tried it before? That's what I want to know. I want to know how in the world you can know you don't like something till you at least give it a try. It's too much for me. I don't understand it. I must not be as smart as my own son, that's all. When I remember how he absolutely refused to go on with piano lessons, even though Miss Wilcox said he had such promise—you remember— 'he has such promise,' she told me, 'it's really a shame'—and it *was* a shame, a terrible shame. Why, when I remember how he played Anitra's Dance at the church concert. I was so proud. Everybody said he and Judy Walcott were the two best. Of course she was two years older than Arthur. You remember Judy Walcott. That big girl with the funny eye. Rita had her in the second grade. There was some complicated thing about her eye. Personally I didn't think she played half as well as Arthur. Of course with her eye I suppose it was a miracle she could play at all. Be sure and speak to Arthur about those dancing lessons, Walter, lord knows he's past listening to me. Of course I'm only his mother. It's not as if he could trust me. He's only known me all his life. You'll see, he won't want to go. Then when he grows up he won't know how to dance and he'll blame everything on me. Mercy, why not? I'm only his mother."

And so, one chill October night, father and I drove along moonchanged avenues to Jefferson Junior High. My short brown hair was slicked down with water, and the tips of my polished brown shoes shone like little mahogany tables, from which I rose in vivid bloom. I was in a state of high nervous awareness, caused in part by my first white shirt, my first long tie, above all by my first sportjacket, a light-blue tweed thing that had caused mother to clasp her hands to her chest in the clothing store as she smiled at me from all three mirrors. It was either then, or later, when the man said: "This is one of our most popular jackets, ma'am," that an absurd fear swept through me, though in fact I had no idea whether William Mainwaring would be present. Father parked in the lamplit lot behind the school and we walked around to the front, where I noticed in alarm large numbers of boys who were strolling up the walk alone, unattended by parents. Inside, a tall girl with a bouncy blond ponytail told us to go down the hall and turn left to the gym.

Outside the gym a smiling woman with an auburn ponytail directed us down the hall and to the left toward the cafeteria. In the half-lit cafeteria, eerily empty except at the near side, coats lay carefully heaped on three long rows of tables that had been placed end to end. I laid my coat at one end of a corner table and returned along the hall with father to the gym.

A long row of brown metal folding chairs, occupied by only three boys, lined the wall opposite. Along the right wall stood a row of chairs occupied by some dozen girls in pink and green and blue dresses and shiny black patent leather shoes. To the left and right of the entrance the chairs were six deep and half-filled by chattering parents, mostly mothers. An eighth-grader with a blond crewcut and cold gray eyes was grimly unfolding metal chairs from a leaning row of them in a nearby corner. Groups of boys and separate groups of girls stood about, talking and giggling, and glancing from time to time at a mustached man in a dark blue suit who stood talking to a raven-haired lady in a shiny red dress. Father, looking about uneasily, took a seat in a nearby row as I walked off by myself, not wanting to be seen with a parent, not wanting to join a group of strange boys, not wanting to walk conspicuously across the gym and sit down, not wanting to exist. As I stood looking unhappily about, wondering whether scientists would ever master the secret of invisibility, I happened to glance through the open door of the gym. William Mainwaring, dressed in a tan overcoat that concealed his jacket, was being directed toward the cafeteria by the lady with the auburn ponytail. At once I stepped over to father, whispered something about forgetting a comb, and made my way out of the gym and down the hall to the cafeteria.

Big girls and vast mothers were removing their coats. In the dark depths of the room a few boys raced and hooted. He was standing at a corner table with his back three-quarters to me, frowning down as he undid the bottom button of his tan overcoat. I walked at once to my own corner table, on the other side of the room, where I found my coat lying under three other coats. I pretended to search its pockets as I watched my double, who was still having trouble with his button. Suddenly he turned to see me standing across the room in my light-blue tweed jacket, watching him. He started—looked directly at my jacket—and at once turned away, with a distinct flush. Icy and prickly sensations passed over me, I longed to tear off my hideous jacket and trample it to death with my polished shoes, for one mad moment I considered running out the door and down the hall toward the dark part of the building, where I might hide until the dancing lesson was over; and no one would ever find me again; and mother would weep for her lost, dead child; but unable to move, I stared in rude fascination at his profile, as he stood with his head bent over those infuriating buttons, and suddenly a tall girl in a brilliant yellow dress and a shiny black belt stepped in front of me and I leaned painfully across the table to see past her; and intensely ignoring me, but burning under my burning gaze, William Mainwaring fumbled with his buttons until, suddenly done, he gripped the lapels of his coat and pulled them back with a forward thrust of his chest, revealing, in triumph or in shame, a fiery red jacket that practically took my breath away.

13

ODDLY ENOUGH I CANNOT RECALL the early stages of our friendship. He seems simply to have stepped into my life, after a
period of waiting. Mother approved of his existence, for he was
"such a nice boy, Arthur, and so well behaved," although "he's
so shy you can't get a word out of him." In fact he was not at
all shy but simply cautious, and if at first he answered mother
in monosyllables it was only because her own words came out so
easily. He took at once to father, however, for like father he was
a passionate hobbyist. I had known for some time that he often
stayed after school to work in one of the numerous clubs he
belonged to—the Photography Club, the Chess Club, the Stamp
Club, the Science Club—but I had not known that he possessed
a valuable collection of American stamps and a considerable
knowledge of philately; he informed me privately, without
malice, that father was an amateur. He himself subscribed to a
weekly stamp newspaper, and every Thursday he received
from a local philatelic service an illustrated list of all new stamps
issued in the world that week, with the total price listed at the
end. In his serious and assured way he urged father to invest:
"You have the money, sir." "Well," replied father uneasily,
rubbing his chin with the back of a forefinger, "I do and I don't.
If you follow me." "I think I follow you," said William
thoughtfully. "You mean you do—but you won't." "That's it!"
cried father. "I do—but I won't! Say, Marth, did you hear that
one? I do—but I won't! I do—but I won't!" And he began to
laugh so hard that he had to wipe his eyes with his knuckles.

On his next visit William brought over a small black dish and
a bottle of Carbona and showed father how to look at a water-
mark. "That is one smart cookie," father confided to me after
we had driven him home. After that he began to bring over all

sorts of things, including an album of his photographs; as a
patrol-boy captain in the sixth grade he had been awarded a
trip to Washington, D.C., and had taken his camera along. But
recently he had become interested in movie cameras and was
now learning how to edit on a small home editor. Father, who
was a little unnerved by all this, was relieved to learn that my
new friend knew nothing at all about mineralogy, and he
quickly inspired in William a new ardor. William borrowed
from father *A Field Guide to Rocks and Minerals* and *How to
Know the Minerals and Rocks,* and he flushed with gratitude
when father gave him a box of ten minerals from the New York
Museum of Natural History, representing the ten degrees of the
hardness scale. I myself was an indifferent hobbyist but was
willing enough to catch the spirit of an enthusiasm. William
overflowed with admiration for father's Connecticut minerals
and begged to be taken on a rock-hunting expedition; and although father had not undertaken one for years, he promised a
trip as soon as the weather grew warm.

Meanwhile our friendship took its course in a long bout of
indoor winter games. Like myself, William Mainwaring played
to win, and an eager rivalry soon sprang up between us. But
there was this difference, at least to begin with, that whereas my
passion was solely for the sake of the game, and was always in
danger of collapsing into indifference, his was part of his very
nature, and flourished in the empty spaces between games. His
desire to win was so intense that he could not endure a single
loss; losing always put him in a nasty temper and impelled him
to play one more time. But it was precisely his desire to win,
his nasty temper, his need to play one more time, that inflamed
my own desire to win, and soon I found myself longing to beat
him decisively, mercilessly, endlessly. In addition he was such a
passionate follower of rules that he was forever challenging the
simplest move, forever checking the lengthy instructions. When
playing Monopoly, for instance, father and I had always put the
money owed to Chance, Community Chest, Luxury Tax, and
so forth in the center of the board, where it was collected by

anyone who landed on Free Parking. But William insisted that you had to pay it to the bank. "Show me," I demanded, rapping the instructions with my forefinger. At once William snatched up the folded sheet, opened it eagerly, and began scanning the lines in hungry haste. "Here it is," he said, thrusting the sheet before me and holding in place his infuriating forefinger. "Look, it says—" "I can read," I said, snatching away the rules and at once seeing that he was right. I shrugged contemptuously, tossing the rules aside as if they were beneath my notice, and began to argue that new rules could be invented so long as both players agreed beforehand. But William was outraged. "You've got to follow the rules, you've got to. You can't just make them up. If the rules say you can do something, all right, you can do it. If they say you can't do it, you can't do it. You can't. It's impossible." "You sound like my mother," I said, as nastily as possible, and he looked at me with hatred. But I wanted to play Monopoly. We paid the money to the bank.

William Mainwaring was an avid keeper of records, and one day he brought with him a special two-ring notebook divided into numerous sections by white tabs on which were neatly printed the names of our various games: Boxes, Canasta, Checkers, Chess, Ghosts, Gin Rummy, Monopoly, Ping-Pong, Salvo, Scrabble, Tic-tac-toe. Each page was divided in half by a ruled vertical line and each half consisted of two columns headed W and A. Final scores were recorded where appropriate (Canasta, Scrabble); otherwise the victories were recorded as tally-marks, ranging down the page in little picket fences of four vertical lines crossed by a diagonal fifth line. A separate page was reserved for Highest Scores, Lowest Scores, Winning Streaks, Percentage of Games Won, Wins per Month. In fact William Mainwaring was a lover of all lists and records, and his mind was an orderly madhouse of precise information concerning lifetime batting averages, the distances of stars and planets from Earth, the dates of famous voyages, the population figures of major countries and cities. He read the Almanac with a frown of interest and he devoured countless books about photography, rockets, reptiles, volcanoes, stars. He seemed puzzled by my love of novels—I was reading books like *The Three Musketeers, Captains Courageous, The Black Arrow*—and tried to interest me in science fiction, which bored me to death. He was enamored of riddles, of brain teasers, of problems and puzzles of every description; and he was delighted when I taught him the old trick by which g-h-o-t-i spells "fish" (*gh* as in rough, *o* as in women, *ti* as in motion).

One day he insisted on taking my photograph. Wearing his heavy camera on a long brown strap around his neck, and snapping up the metallic hood, he pointed the two dark lenses at me from the level of his stomach and gazed sternly down into the viewing screen as he posed me carefully against the maple, the bare hedge, the garbage cans, the shingles, the cold sunflowers by the bent wire fence. "Don't smile," he commanded, making me smile. "Turn your face a little to the left. More. Chin up. Good. Hold it." He took eight outdoor shots, including one aimed down at me from Mrs. Schneider's porch, and four indoor shots with the aid of a flash attachment: in the first I sat in the worn armchair near my bed pretending to read *The Black Arrow*, in the second I stood bent before my brown wooden bookcase pretending to select a book, in the third I sat on the floor before a carefully arranged chessboard with the fingers of my right hand resting lightly on a white bishop, and in the fourth I did not appear at all, for he wanted a photograph of the studious corner of my room, where my maplewood desk joined my brown wooden bookcase. When he had taken the twelfth picture he turned the silver knob on the side of his camera until the film was wound onto a single spool; and removing the camera from its brown leather case, and holding it carefully in his lap as he sat on my bed, he opened the back and removed the dark red roll of film, licking the white seal and then placing the roll in its yellow box. "Well," I said, "I guess you've got me where you want me," and looking up with a frown he said: "What did you say?"

Despite our growing intimacy we continued to avoid one an-

other in public. We still did not sit together on the way to
school, and we sat together on the way back only when he was
coming to my house. An irritable, prickly sensation passed over
me whenever I found myself near him in full view of other
students; his own annoyance was evident in the coolness that
came over him at such moments. Even mother said that we
looked as alike as two peas in a pod—a gross exaggeration, by
which she meant that we both were thin and had brown hair.
And yet I was always fearful that we would come to school
wearing the same shirt, the same pants, even the same belt or
socks. I studied his wardrobe minutely and once refused to wear
a new plaid shirt that reminded me of his plaid shirts. One day
he alarmed me by wearing a yellow shirt but luckily my single-
color shirts were light blue, dark blue, tan, and light green. My
watchfulness made me keenly, indeed morbidly sensitive to his
traits and habits; I became a student of William Mainwaring, an
expert in William Mainwaring. I could not endure the way he
wore his pants, with the cuffs a half-inch over the line of his
shoe; my own cuffs broke on the shoe, as mother said they
should. One day I pulled my belt around as some of the tougher
boys did, so that my buckle was at my side, but I felt embarrassed and quickly pulled it back. At home I practiced combing
my hair in different ways, but did not dare to change my style.
One morning when I entered the bus I saw William Mainwaring
with his hair combed up in a small wave, instead of flat and to
the side. I looked away in embarrassment, in rage.

Sometimes on schooldays he walked home with me from my
bus-stop, and sometimes on Saturday he rode over on his English bike. All during the fall and winter he did not once invite
me to his home, a fact that left me indifferent though it annoyed
mother. On weekdays mother drove home at a quarter to four;
father came home by bus at half-past five; and sometimes before
dinner, and sometimes after dinner, father drove William Mainwaring home. Turning right at the bus-stop we drove past the
field and the front of the body shop and entered a region of
small stores and houses and diners and gas stations all mixed

together, and coming to a corner drugstore we turned left onto a quiet street lined by rows of small two-story houses behind brown hedges and white picket fences. At a white church we turned right and entered a street with larger houses set back from the road. Turning left at the end of the street, and right at the end of the next street, we came to William Mainwaring's porchlit house, set back from the road with no front walk. Below the front windows a flagstone path ran parallel to the house. At the place where the path joined the upsloping drive-way we waited as he strode along the flagstones. We waited as he climbed the six concrete steps of the little front porch, with its ironwork railing and its long black mailbox. We waited as he rang the bell. We waited as the wooden door behind the glass door opened and a tall woman with eyeglasses appeared. Open-ing the glass door, and keeping her hand on the knob, she seemed to lean toward us as we backed away.

14

As the weather grew warm and the first hedge-buds, invisible from the kitchen window, at close range showed bright green against the brown, in the next yard a baseball smacked with two different sounds into the leather of two different gloves. Fat black oily grackles shimmering with blue and purple pecked at breadcrumbs in the dirt-patched grass. Suddenly they flew away with a sound of shaken cloth. A skinny gray cat with sharp shoulderbones and one ear half torn off came crawling up out of the field and skulked under a hedge-arch, waiting. Far away soft hammerthuds mingled with sawscrapes. A dog barked sharply twice. Somewhere a buzzing motorplane went round and round above its wire. And there came over me a restlessness, a discontent... As if the pure air of winter had become filled with a subtle irritant... Or as if a layer of skin had peeled off, leaving me rawly sensitive, morbidly alive. Oh, it was as if the shedding of my heavy wintercoat had left me so dangerously exposed that I could never last until the return of winter, when I might wrap myself tightly tightly in my warm cocoon of fur and wool. And how I longed to fall asleep and wake up in cold white weather . . . How, even then, I looked askance at the trees, the birds, the sky, the sun, and all the little green leaves . . . And girls in their gay spring dresses, laughing girls . . . Their laughter infuriated me. I longed to take them by the shoulders and shout Stop that! Stop that! for their gay, high laughter drew itself across my nerves like the prongs of a fork across the sides of a glass. And walking tensely in the fury of corridors and sitting tightlipped in the violence of buses, I wondered whether my nerves lay too close to the surface and responded to subtle pressures undetected by people safely cushioned in fat. And violence on the playground, violence in buses, violence in the halls . . . There was a boy called Rudy Dietrich who had been in my sixth-grade class. He had been a quiet, polite, unnoticeable sort of boy, and suddenly he cursed out loud, he thrust up his middle finger, he spat white-frothing spitpools on the floor of the bus, he wore a flat peaked cap at an outrageous angle, tilted high in the back and pulled down savagely over his forehead: and his evil laughter, his bony brown arms, his soft brown eyes glittering with rage, filled me with gentle anguish. And that evil laughter, those bony brown arms, those soft brown eyes glittering with rage, seemed somehow connected with the trees, the birds, the sky, the sun, and all the little green leaves—as if, when coats were removed and arms became bare, bodies became more dangerous, restrained no longer by all that weight of clothes.

At the bus-stop each morning, standing alone, was a boy called Hugo who had been in my fifth-grade class. At the time he had been a chubby little boy, but now he was large and silent and heavy and combed his black hair back on both sides. His plump dangling hands had little black hairs on the back, and he had an unpleasant habit of pulling at the wide and faintly shiny back of his dark brown pants, as if continually unsticking himself. We never spoke to one another. One sunny morning when I arrived at the bus-stop Hugo removed from his shirt-pocket a carefully folded piece of newspaper and handed it to Kenny Pearson, who looked at him contemptuously and began reading. After a moment he looked up and said angrily: "Hey, Hugo, you're dirty, you know that?" Hugo grinned suddenly, revealing green-stained teeth. Kenny Pearson stepped to one side and began reading in a low blurred excited voice to John Cusick. It was about a cab driver and a movie star. She was wearing a short white skirt and kept crossing her legs. He had adjusted his mirror so that each time she crossed her legs he could get a good look, all the way up to her pink nylon underpants. "Oooo, dirty Hugo," said John Cusick, looking up with an odd expression. Hugo expelled air sharply through his nostrils in little laughs. Kenny Pearson said: "Yeah, whatta you know about it, Hugo babes?" Hugo looked quickly from face to face. "Jack Bassick seen his sister in underpants. She don't even care." At his thigh he held up a plump hand palm upward with the fingers partially contracted like a claw. Narrowing his eyes he looked from John Cusick to Kenny Pearson to John Cusick and in a coarse-throated voice he said: "Curly black hair." His fingers contracted to a fist and in a mock falsetto John Cusick said: "Oooo, dirty Hugo." Hugo grinned again. With a sudden frown John Cusick shoved him hard in the shoulder. Hugo fell heavily against Kenny Pearson, who pushed him angrily away. "I don't want it," said John Cusick, shoving Hugo back. Kenny Pearson shoved him furiously away and John Cusick shoved him back and for a moment Hugo was leaning awkwardly to one side, standing on one foot and trying to keep his balance with one outflung arm. His plump cheeks were mottled with pink, his mouth was crooked and partway open, on a peaceful side-street the leafy shadow of a maple reached halfway across the mica-sparkling tar, in the black rear window of a shady parked Oldsmobile dark green leaves showed rents of blue, in the shady back seat of a yellow taxicab a movie star leaned back languorously with half-closed eyes, drowsily uncrossing her legs, "Oooo, dirty Hugo," said John Cusick, "Oooo, dirty Hugo," said Kenny Pearson, "Oooo, dirty Hugo," said John Cusick, and I felt myself filling with a strange anguish . . . Modestly I averted my inward gaze.

And girls in their gay spring dresses, laughing girls . . . And girls in white blouses, those indolent smiles . . . And how shall I explain the oppressive afternoons . . . the peaceful afternoons . . . dark languors of the sun . . . One morning at the bus-stop Kenny Pearson told John Cusick that Joanie Kovacs was going down to the shack in Domizio's Lot to take it all off. And suddenly I felt that I was trembling on the verge of an overwhelming secret, which nevertheless eluded me. In shocking detail I imagined a dark, crumbling shack, the dusty sunbeam coming through a single broken window, the weedgrown dirt floor, the crushed rusty can in the corner, the upturned silent faces, and Joanie Kovacs standing there, looking about nervously, trying to smile but breathing quickly, breathing violently, her nostrils going in and out as she tossed back her head in feigned indifference and smoothed back her thick black hair, and now with a weary and indifferent motion she removes from her waist a wide black belt, dropping it to an outspread piece of newspaper on the ground, and now, breathing more quickly, she lifts her black eyes to the upturned silent faces but at once looks down as a dark flush rises in her tanned cheeks, and now with slender fingers she begins to undo the top button of her white blouse as a slight trembling begins, the blouse is trembling, the floor is trembling, the walls are trembling, the upturned silent faces are trembling, the belt, the blouse, the walls, the sunbeam all quiver for a moment and vanish, leaving only the brown telephone pole with its black oilstreaks and white chalkmarks, the prickly concrete sidewalk, the broken weedstalks and grassblades, the dusty curbstone, and I longed to talk to someone but I knew only William Mainwaring, who was not the right person. But that afternoon as we knocked a ping-pong ball back and forth in my dank cellar I said casually, as if I did not notice what I was saying: "Hey, I hear Joanie Kovacs is going down to the shack in Domizio's Lot to take it all off." Even as I spoke I knew that it sounded wrong, and that for some reason it was my destiny never to be allowed to say: "I hear Joanie Kovacs is going down to the shack in Domizio's Lot to take it all off." Under the weak light of the dusty bare bulb the dark green table dully shone. William said nothing at all. He concentrated intensely on the game, pretending not to have heard, while in a shady taxicab a movie star leaned back languorously with half-closed eyes. Kenny Pearson never mentioned Domizio's Lot again. The weather grew warmer, William and I began playing whiffle ball in my back yard, one day after school as I was walking in line toward the row of yellow buses Rudy Dietrich suddenly began shouting, as if he had gone insane: "Don't lookit the face! Grab the knockers! Don't lookit the face! Grab the knockers!" And although I had never heard that funny word before, I knew at once what it meant, and suddenly I remembered seeing Gene Masso standing on the playground with his arm around Mildred Schipul in an awkward way, so that his hand hung over her chest, and suddenly I became clearly conscious that Joanie Kovacs, like a lady, had breasts, and as the knowledge came to me I felt, mingled with terror, the sort of intense satisfaction that I experienced whenever I solved a mathematical problem concerning one train moving East at sixty miles per hour, another train moving West at eighty miles per hour, and two cities one thousand miles apart.

15

THE DAY OF OUR EXPEDITION was a warm blue lovely day, perfect for staying home. It was the sort of day I would have liked to spend in the cool depths of my room, reading about Jody and his yearling, or in the wicker rocker on the shady front porch, gazing through a frame of maple leaves at the sunny black street. Instead I would have to climb hills and lug heavy shovels and picnic baskets all over the place. I had slept badly in anticipation of an early rousing, and my head was thick with the vapors of evaporated dreams. I was in a sour mood and could think of nothing less likely to put me out of it than a jolly family jaunt into the dewy day. I sat sulking in the bright living room as mother noisily wrapped sandwiches in the kitchen. "Goodness, do you have to wear those rags? What will your friend think?" she had said when I appeared in my battered old shoes, my faded blue dungarees with a dark blue rectangle where the right back pocket had been, and my brown jacket with the grass-stained elbows. She herself wore a bright yellow dress full of purple flowers, ideal for the Easter parade. Father, in clean rumpled khakis and a checkered green-and-black flannel shirt rolled up to the elbows, walked back and forth between the living room and the kitchen, rubbing his hands together and saying: "Any day now, Artie, any day at all, we're bound to get moving any day of the week. Hey, this is some weather, huh? What a peach of a day." "I prefer October," I said wearily, and father turned to me with a face about to become angry. "I mean," I added quickly, looking away with a frown, "all months are nice in their own way." "Okay," he said, "but I don't see what that's got to do with the price of eggs in China." "China?" called mother from the kitchen. "Are you two making remarks about the new china?"

Father began to load the car and before long we were backing out of the garage over the hard dirt tracks of the grassy driveway and rolling merrily along toward William Mainwaring's house. Through six different windows I watched the bounded day. Shiny, framed, and blue, it reminded me of a glossy picture-postcard divided into four parts with the words "Scenic Connecticut" stretching from the lower left-hand corner to the upper right.

As we turned the corner onto William Mainwaring's street I saw him seated on the cement steps, gazing with a frown in our direction. The moment he saw us he rose, picked up his gear, and began hurrying down the steps toward the driveway. He reached the bottom of the drive as we pulled up on the street before him. He wore a light-blue zippered jacket, stiff dark-blue dungarees rolled up high to form thick cuffs, and an immaculate pair of high white sneakers topped by thick white socks. In general he looked like a sky. On the upper left-hand side of his jacket was a round red baseball-patch with white stitching that imitated the seams of a baseball. Across the baseball, in plump white script, stretched the word BILL. Around his neck he wore a leather-cased camera, and over one shoulder he wore a green cloth carrying-bag. In his right hand he clutched *A Field Guide to Rocks and Minerals.* "Don't you look fresh and nice," said mother pointedly as he stooped into the back seat beside me, and without enthusiasm William said: "Thank you very much, Mrs. Grumm." With a look of contempt I said quietly: "Don't you look fresh and nice." William turned to me with tight lips and flaming cheekbones. "Beg pardon?" said mother, straining her head around. "Nothing, nothing, forget it," I said, looking out the window with a frown.

We drove back the way we had come, passing the body shop and the bus-stop, and as we continued toward the center of town I lay back against the warm seatcover and watched through shut lids a ripple of red brightnesses, red darknesses. Now and then I suddenly opened my eyes to admit images. A row of glossy triangular pennants, alternately orange and green, hung fluttering against the rich blue sky above the bright white top of a gas station. A pile of red-orange pipe-sections, their open ends facing me, formed a pattern like a honeycomb. Behind a nearby wire fence, which rushed past my window from post to post, a far brick factory slid slowly, lazily along. Mother chattered away with William as she folded and unfolded a loud roadmap, and at a mass of route-signs, one of which had an arrow pointing to heaven, father made the turn that led out into the country.

Swiftly we drove along a sand-colored parkway with a grassy divider and occasional stone bridges stretching across. Through approaching bridge-arches shaped like half-circles I would see bright blue, then bright blue and dark green, then dark green. On both sides stretched a monotonous blur of trees broken now and then by a precise gas station with dazzling yellow or red pumps. From time to time there rose out of the trees a little turret-shaped water-tower on tall silver legs and once there was a vast spherical gas-tank with a comma-shaped stairway winding to the top. At last we turned off the parkway onto a gray road full of leafshadows and bits of sun. We drove past white houses shaded by tall elms, past fields with cows in them, past white chemical plants and long tan factories and tall sunny pylons hung with high-tension wire, past striped barberpoles and red fire departments on miniature Main Streets in miniature towns, and coming at last to a granite monument we turned onto a narrow black road. After a while the tar ended and we found ourselves bumping along a rutted dirt road between fields of tall grass. In the distance, where the road came to a point, a dark wooded hill rose up.

We parked on marshy ground at the edge of the wood. Across the road a field of grass, higher than my head, stuck up into the blue. "What a day, what a day," said father, hooking his thumbs into his belt and taking deep breaths. William frowned and narrowed his eyes; and resting his hands on the unopened leather-covered camera that hung at his stomach, he swept his stern gaze slowly along the horizon. At the end he nodded gravely twice. "Well?" I said, but turning to father William said: "I should have loaded with Ektachrome." Father, inhaling deeply, slapped himself once on his plump chest, and let out his breath with a "Hwoooo, you said it, Willy, yessiree Bob." "His name isn't Bob," I said, but no one laughed, and mother said: "What's that about Bob? Since when do you know anybobby called Bud? Anybubby called Bod? Anydobby called—well this is just plain ridiculous."

Father opened the trunk and removed the short shovel, the long shovel, the rock-hammer, a ball peen hammer, a claw hammer, the brown picnic basket, the red-and-silver thermos jug, his old khaki-covered tin canteen, mother's yellow-and-white aluminum folding chair, three cardboard cartons, a folded brown army-blanket, and mother's bag of knitting. He was about to shut the trunk when William said: "Hold it." Moving back with his camera, and asking us to step aside, he carefully photographed that pile of rubbish beside the back bumper, before the open trunk, against the wooded hill. Father then shut the trunk-door with a thump, distributed the items apologetically among us, and marched us back along the road toward the place where the trail began.

Father led the way up the hard dirt path that wound, now in sun and now in shade, between high rows of sun-patched trees. It was a flickering world of green sun and brown sun, green shade and brown shade. Carrying the long shovel and the rock-hammer in one hand and the short shovel and the heavy picnic basket in the other, and wearing around his neck the bouncy canteen, father took long strides and kept stopping to look back at us. William came next, leaning to one side as he lugged the red-and-silver thermos jug; in his other hand he carried mother's bag of knitting, and around his neck he wore his camera and his green cloth carrying-bag, into which father had placed the two other hammers and the book. From time to time William stopped, switched the jug and the bag of knitting to opposite hands, and then continued, leaning the other way. I came behind William, burdened with the army blanket and mother's aluminum folding chair, which I sometimes allowed to scrape on the path. Mother came last, embracing the three cardboard cartons one inside the other, with her big straw pocketbook in the middle. "You people go on ahead," she would call breathlessly, pausing every ten steps. "I'll catch up. Please don't wait for me." Father would then stop and turn around, saying: "How's everybody doing? Need any help?"

Gradually the hard dirt path became littered with sparkling bits of mica and small rocks of all sizes, many of them white and smooth, with flat glossy surfaces. "What are these shiny white ones, Mr. Grumm?" asked William. "Cleavelandite," I answered.

William looked at me over his shoulder with a frown and turning back to father said: "Is that right, Mr. Grumm?" "Cleavelandite it is, Willy. Common as dirt here." After a pause he added: "Artie's been here before." The path turned, changing from shade to sun, and as I stepped into a sudden glitter of mica I felt a tremor across the back of my brain, it was as if I were about to recall or forget something, great masses shifted in my mind, but father cried "How's everybody doing?" and a dim world vanished among the white stones and the thousand bits of sparkling mica.

Suddenly, around another bend, the abandoned quarry-pit came into view. To the right, great dark walls of stone plunged far below to a dazzling greenblue pool. It looked like the glossy Swiss lake on an old puzzle-cover of mine. Here and there the mineral-stained water formed patches of dark blue and purple, and where the shadow of the walls cut across the pool, the color darkened to greenblack. In the middle of one cliff-face, in large white dripping letters, loomed the words: ANTHONY WAS HERE. As we waited for mother, William stood at the edge of the cliff beside the red-and-silver thermos, looking down into his camera. Over the bottom lens he had fitted a big black lens-shade. Father sat on a sunny boulder with the long shovel across his knees, looking at William. "Some day for pictures, huh Willy? What a day, what a day, what a peach of a day." I unfolded mother's chair and sat in the hot shadow of a decaying oak. Picking up a white pebble, I flung it far over William's head and heard with pleasure the delayed splash. "Hey," said William, turning around excitedly, "there's a fish or something down there." Finally mother came around the bend in a burst of yellow, and I had to abandon my shady chair, where for five minutes she sat wiping her forehead with a lavender hanky, sipping ice-water from father's canteen, and fanning herself with the folded road-map, which she had carried along by mistake.

Soon we continued our merry climb. William, perhaps affected by the heat, began chattering away to father's back. "That was cool, Mr. Grumm, the cliffs, the green water down there—green from mineral deposits, I'd say. Sure. That must be where they dug up the ore. Wonder how much per day they could mine out of a place like this. Cost a pretty penny to operate, I bet. Brought the trucks up from the road, I guess, and shipped it all down this trail. Cool. Wish I'd brought color. I think if I— holy mack'rel!" A thick black snake, shimmering like oil, slid swiftly away under a bright bush into the shadows. "Did you see that? Man! Did you see that?"

"Almost there," called father at last, turning out of sight to the left. William next turned out of sight, and I heard a loud "phew" of surprise, imagining at once the comic-book bubble above his head. Breathing heavily, I came up behind them. Twenty feet away a hill of white rocks rose towering into the blue air. On the grassy dirt before the rock-hill, white-and-black boulders lay scattered about. A patch of oak and maple stood to the right of the clearing, and I quickly walked over to the sun-pierced shade, where I unfolded the aluminum chair and sat down. William was already adjusting his camera. "Lovely, isn't she?" said father. "Shame all the good stuff's gone by now. Used to be beryl for the taking, back when they were working the quarry. Man I met here, Jim Murray, 'member him?, found a pink tourmaline crystal I swear that big. It's mostly little bits of things, now. Still, you never can tell. Artie, be a good fella and go give mom a hand with those boxes, huh? I'm bushed."

Later, as mother sat knitting in the shade, father and William and I climbed the sunny white hill. Bending over like monkeys, stumbling as we climbed, we dislodged rocks that tumbled downhill in miniature landslides. Halfway up father stopped and said: "Well, I guess this'll do for now." Laying his rock-hammer on a flat slab behind him, he began digging into the rock-hill with the short shovel, examining with his fingers each shovelful of stones and sand and then carefully spilling the load to one side. "I'm after beryl, men," he said, in the special voice he used for adventures. "Keep your eyes peeled for anything green or yellow. Here, Willy, give this baby a whack on the head, let's see what she's got inside." After a while I grew bored, and moving off to one side, so as not to kick rocks down at them, I began to climb toward the top, where I remembered a nice view.

Below me I heard the rasp of father's shovel and the knock of the metal hammer against stone. To the left and right the landscape dropped away. Over me the white rocks flashed in the sun. And as I slid and climbed, again a ripple passed across the back of my brain, the white rocks flashed in the sun, and suddenly I was climbing a slippery green hillside where silver dimes and quarters glittered among tall blades of grass. White gulls shrieked above, somewhere a bulldog barked, in my right hand I clutched a bloody knife, and far below, beside the sparkling blue stream, William Mainwaring lay twitching in the sticky grass, and as my dream melted back into the black night it had come from, once again I was climbing the sunny white rocks, breathing heavily in the hot, dusty light. At the mound-like top of the hill I stood looking down at father and William, bent head-to-head over their rocks like two conspirators. Then I turned to look at the tracts of light green and dark green, light brown and dark brown, stretching away toward a line of bluegreen hills.

Lunch was served at the foot of the white hill. I sat on a shady boulder, nibbling at a ham sandwich without enough mustard and sipping lemonade not cold enough from a blue tin glass that tasted of metal. William ate his sandwich standing up, with one foot resting on a shade-patched boulder of white cleavelandite streaked with black tourmaline. Father sat on a sunny boulder, holding his sandwich in both hands and leaning forward to take enormous bites, while mother sat upright on her shady chair, eating carefully over her piece of waxpaper, and occasionally urging someone to sit on the useless blanket. After a while William stopped eating. Wrapping his half-sandwich neatly in its piece of wrinkled waxpaper, he laid the folded part carefully down upon his boulder. Then taking up his camera he said: "I'd like to take a few pictures if nobody minds.

Just be natural and don't pay attention to me." Father said: "Shoot." Mother said: "Oh, but I'm such a mess," and at once picked up the large straw pocketbook leaning against her chair. Pulling out her long white comb and snapping open her gold compact with its round mirror, she began to comb up loose strands of her hair, fastening them with black bobbypins. William said nothing, though he could not repress a frown; and after a polite shot of mother, who smoothed her lap, pulled back her shoulders, and grandly smiled, he turned his attention to father, who looked up with a startled expression as William dropped to one knee before him and aimed upward. "Oh, William," said mother suddenly, "do you know what? We don't have a picture of you!" And brushing aside his protests, she rose from her chair and began to arrange a picture.

Standing with the heavy camera around my neck, I gazed down at the bright square of the viewing screen as I carefully turned a silver knob. William stood rigidly between mother and father, glaring at the camera as if it had just accused him of something; the line of his jacket kept spilling over a rim of perfect focus. "Come on," said mother, lifting William's arm up behind her waist, "I won't bite you." William, looking as if he did not believe her, suffered his arm to be positioned there. And really he looked ridiculous: one arm was pressed rigidly to his side, one arm was at right angles to his body, and over his lifted shoulder his blue jacket-shoulder stuck up grotesquely. Still dissatisfied with the focus, I swung out the little magnifying glass attached to the black metal hood and concentrated my attention on his red baseball-patch, until the miniature white letters of his name were as beautifully precise as the cuts of a razorblade in balsawood. Meanwhile mother put her arm around father's shoulder, pulling him toward her, and father put his arm around mother's shoulder, pulling her toward him, until they leaned over William like the sides of a triangle. "Say cheese," I said wearily. "Cheese," said father. "Cheese," said mother. She gave a little giggle, hunching up her shoulders and covering her mouth girlishly with a hand. And as if someone had said something unbearably funny, the corners of William's mouth began to twitch, and suddenly he began to laugh. Clinging to mother, he gave forth high giggling whoops of laughter, his shoulders shaking, his eyes screwed shut, his nostrils pulled wide by the stretch of his mouth, and as he laughed mother began to laugh, throwing back her head and shaking with great gusts of mirth as gleaming lines of wetness streamed down her cheeks, and all at once father began to roar with laughter, now leaning back and thrusting out his stomach, now bending forward and showing the top of his head, and as the torrent began to die down, and mother, gasping, began to wipe her streaming cheeks with the back of a hand, William cried "Cheese!" and they were all off again, howling and shaking and weeping and rocking with laughter but always standing in place and clinging tightly to one another, like an animated monument, William with his arm around mother's waist and mother with her arm around father's shoulder and father with his arm around mother's shoulder—quite a happy little family, one could not help thinking.

16

AND IT WAS, it was, a happy little family. I watched them chatting and laughing together at the dinner table as I ate in indifferent silence. Make no mistake about it, William Mainwaring had a way about him; mother was charmed. Besides, he cleared the dishes from the table and loved to help mother dry. Alone in my room I listened to a rattle of dishes and a hum of talk, and later William would poke his head in and invite me into the dining room to play canasta with the whole family. When I entered the dining room I would see that the place-mats and the bowl of ivy had already been cleared away, and on the maple table, ashine in the glow of the frosted lightshade, a triple deck of cards lay in an open box: three blood-red backs trimmed with gold.

And now every Saturday we went on trips together, sunny greenblue trips smelling of pine trees and lakewater and charred frankfurters dripping with the sweet relish William endlessly devoured. He loved the dank old bathhouse at Lake Sassacus, where Marjorie and I had once counted to three, and he loved the pine-shaded picnic area, with its brown carpet of pine-needles and its sun-flecked wooden tables. From my folding chair in the shade of a lakeside pine, ten feet above the lake, I would look down at the three of them below, father in his dark blue trunks, mother in her white rubber bathing cap and her immense black-spotted white bathing suit with its tiny skirt, and William in his baggy brown trunks, his green goggles, and his green rubber frogfeet. "Come on, Artie, join the crowd," father would gaily cry, splashing about like a great pale seal while mother stood in the water up to her shoulders, brushing her arms about, and William rose sputtering beside her with his hair flattened down and his goggles streaming. But I preferred my high shady perch between the pines, where at any moment I might lower my eyes from the vague lake to a vivid book, whose black letters dissolved magically into precise landscapes. And there is also the reverse process, when startled by a shout, confused, half-drugged with revery, blinking in the sudden light, you look up blindly from your book and try to understand where exactly, what precisely . . . To everyone's surprise, William seemed never to have been anywhere at all. He had never been out in a rowboat, he had never gone walking on trails, he had never seen a blackberry patch. He had never even been to Reese Park, a large wooded park at the north end of town, with babbling brooks, stone bridges, winding paths, a duckpond, and a small zoo that featured a sagging elephant. William ignored the monkeys and the elephant but stood for a full half-hour feeding the boring geese with little balls of bread that he tossed through the wire fence. To father's disappointment he did not photograph any of the animals, but instead asked the ice-cream man to open the black door at the top of the ice-cream cart, and proceeded to photograph the frosty rows of popsicles and fudgicles and ice-cream sandwiches.

One Saturday father drove us to a distant lake where wooded hills were reflected in dark water. At the end of a white metal pier we stepped down, far down, into a peeling white boat with water sliding about in dark puddles on the floor. Mother sat on a pillow at the stern with her arms folded across her chest and father took the oars. But soon he allowed William to row, and in memory I retain a distinct picture of the two of them standing up awkwardly in the swaying and slowly turning boat, father repeating softly "It's all right, Marth, don't worry now, it's all right, it's all right" as slowly and clumsily, like a man groping in the dark, he felt his way around frowning William until, safely past, he bent over suddenly to steady himself with spread fingertips against the bow-seat and slowly, slowly began to turn himself around, becoming rigid at one moment and alive the next, as if he were playing Statue—and suddenly losing his balance he sat down heavily, with a look of bewilderment that changed to a cautious smile. William meanwhile had quietly taken his place at the oars, and after some trouble keeping them in the oarlocks he began to row in his earnest fashion, straining back with a tortured grimace and bending grimly forward as the gray blades lifted from the water like slender dripping wings. We stayed close to shore, gliding past gloomy pines and black metal trashbarrels and a beached red canoe on a patch of sand. I was in a somewhat dreamy mood, less bored than usual, but still pretty bored, and I sat trailing a finger in the dark and rather dirty water, through which the tops of underwater grasses were sometimes visible. At one point we passed a few lilypads, which I had thought existed only in movies where women in straw hats were rowed by men in white dinner jackets, and which with their tough and rubbery look entirely failed to resemble the delicate dreamflowers that floated in the blue lake of my mind. As I gazed into the dark water, where pine needles floated above rippling pine trees, the man in the white dinner jacket raised his oars and allowed the boat to glide smoothly, soundlessly, beneath rich overhanging boughs. The tip of his boat floated out of sight behind a bushy bank, followed by the smiling man, and last of all by the woman in the straw hat, who was leaning back dreamily in her frothy dress, smiling with half-closed eyes, and now there is nothing at all except the bushy bank and the bushy green silence, a silence that swells and swells until it bursts into a piercing scream, followed by a different silence, and soon the tip of the boat glides into sight, followed by a man no longer smiling, rowing hard in his empty boat, rowing furiously . . . "Honeydew," said mother, completing an unknown sentence, and I looked up in terror, but she hadn't seen anything.

17

ONE DAY WILLIAM invited me to his house. He came up to me on the playground, where I was standing alone in the warm shadow of a wall, gazing out at the alien crowd, and asked with a kind of brisk aloofness if I wanted to "drop over" that afternoon. To my surprise I felt so flattered and excited that it became necessary to affect an absolute indifference. With a weary shrug I replied that I would "see." That afternoon as I rode past my bus-stop with William I felt a foolish thrill of fear, as if I were violating a law; and I could not help wondering, as we rolled along, what part in all this his mother had played.

But she was not there; no one was there. At the end of the upsloping black driveway William put down his books and with both hands pulled up the white garage door at the side of the house: in folding sections, noisily, it was swallowed up. Together we entered the big empty garage. The walls were neatly lined with garden tools and sacks of peat moss and folded lawnchairs, and the cement floor was divided by a long strip of wood, on each side of which lay a large dark oil-stain. At the dark red inner door William again put down his books, climbed onto a cluttered toolbench, and removed from the top ledge of the doorframe a small penny-colored key. The door opened onto a rising flight of gray steps covered with black rubber treads; to the left I glimpsed the corner of a ping-pong table in a yellow room, to the right was a closed door. William led me up the steps and at the top opened a second, unlocked door. Directly ahead rose a second flight of steps, carpeted in dark blue; through archways on the left and right I saw a piece of dark living room, a piece of sunny kitchen. For a moment I did not know what floor I was on. We were standing on a strip of translucent plastic that covered the portion of rug before the stairs. Suddenly William lifted his left foot onto his right thigh. Clutching his books in his left arm, and balancing on his right leg, he swiftly unlaced his shoe. Then switching his books to his other arm he lifted his right foot onto his left thigh and unlaced his other shoe. Still standing in place he removed each shoe with the aid of the opposite toe. "Wait here," he said, and in brown-and-yellow-striped socks he stepped into his living room. Standing with the tips of my shoes at the edge of the plastic mat, I bent forward and peered after him into the dark room striped with sun. A dark couch was flanked by mahogany end-tables, each with its white lamp. Across the ceiling stretched a pattern of venetian-blind slats. Against one wall stood a dark glossy piano with a neat pile of yellow music-books at one end, a slender blue-glass vase of pussy-willows at the other end, and a piece of intensely white-and-black music standing open against the dark curves of the music-rest. William headed straight for the piano and for a moment I thought he was going to sit down and play. But instead he examined with one hand a pile of mail that was lying beside the pile of yellow music-books. "Good," he muttered, plucking out a thick white envelope, and striding back toward me he picked up his shoes between thumb and forefinger and began to race up the stairs two at a time. "Should

I," I began to say, but he was already turning out of sight at the landing. Bending over I unlaced and removed my shoes, and with my books in one hand and my shoes in the other I climbed the stairs. When I reached the landing I turned left, climbed two more steps, turned right, and found myself facing a carpeted hallway. At the end of the hallway a mahogany-framed oval mirror hung above a small brown table with a black telephone. The first door on the left was partway open, and with a curious feeling of intrusion I stepped inside.

It was as if I had stepped into an underwater grotto. The room was bathed in a deep-sea glow of aquamarine. The dark aquamarine rug was bounded by pale aquamarine walls, and through the translucent aquamarine window-curtains, lightly streaked with swirls and bubbles of green, aquamarine sunlight poured. Undulations of aquamarine sunlight lay on the long, undulating aquamarine curtain that hung from a silver pole. Under a long fluorescent light, enclosed in a shade of frosted glass, the aquamarine curtain was reflected in the wide silver of the sliding mirror; and under the windowsill, in a niche of gleaming black, a roll of aquamarine paper hung. A furry oval of dark aquamarine covered the closed seat. Softly I stepped forward, curling my toes against the rug, and suddenly a voice behind me said: "What are you" and I whirled around. William stood frowning in at me from the hall, clutching in one hand a cellophane packet of stamps. As if I had been caught at something I said quickly: "I thought it was your room." William frowned more deeply. "Mine! Are you crazy?" In a changed voice he added: "Did you want to . . ." "No no," I said, stepping toward him. Quietly he said: "You didn't have to take off your shoes," and proceeded to lead me down the hall to the last door on the right.

It was a serious brown room with dark brown curtains, dominated by a large brown bed and a large neat desk. The door opened against the left wall and the bed was immediately to the right of the doorframe: the mahogany headboard with its black metal reading-lamp stood against the wall and the big bed stretched forward into the room, leaving narrow passageways on three sides. On the other side of the bed, under the right-hand window, loomed the desk. Upon it lay a green blotter in a dark brown frame, behind which sat a shiny brown fluorescent lamp. It was as if you could do nothing in that room but study or sleep—and both choices were matters of the utmost importance. The only other pieces of furniture were the bureau and a small brown bookcase, filled partly with books and partly with magazines, and topped by a large whorled seashell, a piece of yellow-and-red petrified wood, and a display of minerals collected on our trip. Each stone sat behind a neatly printed label. The walls were painted light brown and were bare except above the bureau, where three black-and-white photographs hung in white cardboard frames. One showed the Washington Monument through a frame of leaves, one showed a telephone pole silhouetted against a mass of stormclouds, and one showed the pile of equipment beside the back bumper, before the open trunk, against the wooded hill. On the bureau were a square black clock with white numerals, a wooden hairbrush with a black comb sleeping among the tan bristles, and a glass-covered photograph of William at the age of five or six: it had been touched up with color, and his ghastly blue-white cheeks were flushed rose-orange.

On the sunny windowsill above the low bookcase stood a small glass globe about two inches in diameter, such as I had seen in a science class. Within the globe was a turning apparatus: at the ends of four horizontal arms mounted on a slender vertical rod, four flat lozenges, silver on one side and black on the other, tremblingly turned and turned; and as they turned, a shadow trembled on the sunny windowsill.

William sat on the bed in his striped socks before some dozen little packets of stamps and a printed list. He had plucked a mechanical pencil from his pocket and was adding prices on the margin of the list, erasing furiously from time to time and brushing away the eraser-dust with short sharp sweeps of the side of his pinky. I placed my shoes and books on the dark green oval rug beside the bed and then straddled the wooden desk-chair, resting my forearms on the back with my elbows pointing out and my hands dangling inward. After a while he muttered: "Three seventy-two. Never make it." At once he began adding up figures again. I gazed about the room, wondering what I was doing there, and after a while I cleared my throat and said: "Hey, tell me, where's your mother?" "My what? Oh, she's out. Forty-five, fifty-one . . ." "Does she work?" "Does she what? Js a sec'n. Forty-five, fifty-one, fifty-eight, sixty-seven, seventy." He looked up with a frown. "Seventy-two. No, she's just a housewife."

After he had finished with his stamps he sat frowning to himself and then he said, with a trace of annoyance: "Since you're here I might as well show you my complete collection." At once he went over to his bureau and from the drawer above the bottom drawer he removed six albums, which he spread carefully over the entire bed. There were an American album, two foreign albums, a United Nations album, a miscellaneous album for countries poorly represented in his foreign albums, and a special album for mint sheets, plate-blocks, and first-day covers. He was especially proud of the mint-sheet album, a slender booklet with transparent pages between which colorful sheets of stamps were held like pressed flowers. "Look," he pointed, "the Ryukyu Islands. I paid three eighty for it a year ago and it's selling now for twelve and a half." After that he showed me the two missing places in his United Nations collection and after that he showed me two sets of "investments" in transparent packets. "Yes," I said, "uh huh, yes." When at last I suggested Monopoly, he looked at me first with surprise and then with amusement and said: "But my set's at your house. Remember?" So was his chess set; so were his ping-pong paddles; so was his box of dominoes. He didn't even own a pack of cards. He had nothing at all I would have called a game, and as he put his albums away I could not help wondering why I had been invited there.

William sat down on the bed and looked off with a frown.

After a while he snapped his fingers sharply and said: "I've got it." Scrambling from the bed, he opened his closet and removed from a hook a noisy contraption consisting of two long parallel silver springs attached to red wooden handles at each end. He stationed himself before me, gripping a red handle in each hand, and began to pull them apart, straining and growing flushed as his arms spread wider; and shutting his eyes and twisting his lips over clenched teeth, he completed his crucifixion. He released the springs with a great clatter and stood taking deep breaths. "I didn't know you could play the accordion," I said. "Listen," he said with a frown, "it's not that easy. You try it." I tried it, and to my annoyance I could not do it, and to my greater annoyance he did not smile in triumph but said earnestly: "Don't worry. I couldn't do it either when I first started. It takes practice. You have to start with one spring and work your way up." Moments later he plucked from his top desk drawer a green wooden hand-exerciser, which he invited me to squeeze, and from another drawer he removed a black notebook, in which he had recorded the exercises, the number of times per day, and the size per month of each muscle. According to his record, his chest had increased by one-half inch in six months. "It may not seem like a lot," he said, "but actually . . ." "Look," I said, suddenly furious, "where's your mother?" William looked startled. "She's out somewhere. I don't know. What difference does it make?"

For the rest of the afternoon he showed me things, without much enthusiasm, and without much enthusiasm I looked. He showed me a dark blue folder in which Indian-head pennies lay scattered among neat rows of penny-shaped empty spaces, and he showed me a leather-covered scrapbook in which newspaper photographs illustrated the damage caused by a recent hurricane. He showed me a book that contained black-and-white photographs of pinwheel galaxies and furry nebulae, and a color photograph of an eclipse of the sun in which sixteen suns stretched diagonally across the page. He showed me a book that contained colored drawings of gigantic black segmented ants with beady black eyes and bristly bodies, plump green larvae that looked like little accordions or collapsible cucumbers, and a great praying mantis with upraised prickly forelegs and two big red eyes. He showed me a mountain on the moon, the digestive system of an amoeba, the cross-section of a volcano, a camera obscura, and the magnified spinning-glands in the abdomen of a spider. He showed me a dark brown Egyptian in a white loincloth, measuring the height of a pyramid by means of a stick and a shadow. His most recent treasure was a large glossy book depicting on the cover a fat pink hemisphere of sun setting or rising behind a bright red ocean of molten lava from which dark brown crags rose up. The book's special feature was the full-color fold-out, displaying against detailed backgrounds great swarms of extinct plants and animals, with many printed names along the bottom border. There were titles like "The Morning of Life," "The Seas Grow Crowded," "The Land Is Clothed in Green," "Reptiles Inherit the Earth." On pink, rocky earth studded with ferns, broken tree-trunks, and a few tall trees bursting into fernlike or pompom-like foliage, sluggish scaly creatures squatted. Great spiny crests sprouted from lizard-like backs, in the background jagged pink cliffs thrust up, and in one corner a great red-brown reptile with high hind-legs and little forelegs and a row of teeth running along his back stood bent over a furry mass of white flesh stained with bright red blood. Another fold-out showed a great black woolly mammoth with a raised black trunk and long curved tusks, standing in a pleasant autumnal setting of red and yellow trees against a backdrop of snowy crags. In stately poses on both sides of him were a mastodon, a saber-toothed tiger, a musk-ox, and a megatherium. Except for the snowy crags and the shaggy monsters it looked like a picture postcard of rural Connecticut in the fall, as I pointed out to William, who did not smile. He showed me a book about space travel, and a book about home movies, and a fat blue Scott catalogue, and as the afternoon wore on I could not overcome a growing sense of betrayal. There was so obviously, so abundantly nothing at all to do that it was as if William were trying to prove to me my mistake in coming. If in fact he was trying to prove something, he had succeeded triumphantly. I wanted to go home. At four o'clock he reminded me to call mother and tell her where I was, and when I returned from the hall I wondered how we would manage to drag our weary way through the rest of the wasted afternoon. But this time William brought from his closet an object I had never seen before.

He placed it on the floor near his bureau and we sat down in front of it. From each end of a foot-long wooden base rose a vertical support about eight inches high. At the top of each support was a handle that looked like the handle of a pencil sharpener. In the middle of the wooden base was a little viewing screen, and attached to the back of the viewing screen was a rubber cord ending in a plug. As I idly turned one of the handles, William opened the bottom drawer of his bureau and brought out a flat round silvery-gray tin, about three inches in diameter. When he took off the top I saw a little roll of movie film on a gray plastic reel. Fastening the reel to one of the handles, and an empty reel to the other, he drew the film under the viewing screen and onto the empty reel. Then he plugged the cord into a wall outlet; in the suddenly illuminated viewing screen I saw the front of William's house and the black driveway. A little to the right of center a black line came down and on the other side of the black line the same picture appeared. As William slowly turned the handle I watched the little pictures passing in the screen. He turned more quickly, and through a blur of swiftly passing frames I saw a black car turn onto the drive. William stopped: the car-door was open and a tall woman with eyeglasses, dressed in a dark blue coat and a white kerchief with red flowers on it, was stepping out of the car. One hand was on the door and one foot, in a dark blue high-heeled shoe, rested on the driveway. He turned faster and stopped again: the woman, in profile, now stood frozen on the flagstone walk, her legs parted in the midst of a stride. He turned fast again, stopping her on the bottom step; at the top step; at the door; and when he next stopped there was nothing at all but the white front door behind the glass door, and the deserted concrete steps with their black iron railing. He turned slowly; the same picture kept repeating itself, separated by black lines; and suddenly the scene shifted to a shiny purple-black bird perched on a wooden bar before a red-roofed birdhouse. "That was your mother," I said softly. William said: "Now you can watch me splice." Opening the bottom drawer he brought out another strange instrument and a bottle of fluid, and proceeded to attach his mother to a second roll of film.

At five o'clock William looked at his clock and said: "Well, I guess it's time for you to go. Can you get a ride?" I was about to become furious when he added: "Otherwise I can ride you home on my bike." "No, that's ridiculous," I said, and went into the hall to call mother. "I don't know," I whispered into the receiver, "he says she's out," and when I returned to the room I saw William sitting crosslegged on his bed, bending forward over two rows of transparent packets of stamps.

We waited outside, by the open garage, glancing at occasional passing cars. "I didn't know you played the piano," I said in the warm silence. "I don't," he said, and shaded his eyes as he frowned off at the road. Suddenly he cried: "Here she is!" and I whirled to look, but it was only mother. We hurried down the driveway and reached the street just as she pulled up. William went over to her window, smiling hello and saying: "I'm sorry you had to go out of your way, Mrs. Grumm. But my mother was out. And my father doesn't get home till after six." "Oh that's all right, William," said mother in a voice much too jovial, "it was no bother at all." William stood watching us with a frown as mother turned into his driveway and backed out, pointing the other way. Then he walked swiftly back down to the garage. As we drove off I caught a last glimpse of him standing in his garage, disappearing from top to bottom as the big white door came down.

18

THE SUMMER WAS BORED TO DEATH. It sat with slack jaw and parted lips, gazing dully from beneath drooping eyelids. It stretched out its arms, squeezed its eyes shut, gave a slow, widening, shuddering yawn—and voluptuously collapsed, leaning back wearily with half-closed eyes. And again it stretched out its arms, squeezed its eyes shut, gave a slow, widening, shuddering yawn . . .

On burning afternoons, that boring summer, William and I played ping-pong in the dank shade of my cluttered cellar. We contrived elaborate tournaments, witnessed by invisible audiences, in order to stimulate our exhausted interest. With sickening precision we knew all of one another's serves and spins, our strengths, our weaknesses, our little unlovable habits—as when, after a serve of mine had missed the table, he would try to catch the ball with his paddle and bat it back to me without touching it with his hand, or when, instead of picking up the ball as it rolled flatly along the table, he would pry it up with the end of his paddle, or when, before a serve, he would dart a conspicuous glance at one corner of the table, in order to make me think that he would serve to the other corner, or when, mistakenly convinced that the ball was cracked, he would rub it round and round on the table with his paddle, tilting his head to listen, frowning intently . . . With Monopoly we fared no better, for we had overplayed it to death, and all our card games seemed as weary and sullen as the dirty, sticky, exhausted cards themselves. And I was so bored with it all! And it was all so boring, so boring! And I longed to lie down, and close my weary eyes, but I was so restless . . . Unable to stand any of our old games, we began to search for new ones. One day William brought over his paperback Hoyle and for a week of stifling afternoons we played exotic card-games that soon became quite domestic. With a brace of BB pistols we shot at paper targets and orange-juice cans in the hot shade of the cleared-out garage. One afternoon in the dirt-patched back yard father stretched a tight green net between bright red poles. It was father and Auntie Lou versus Uncle Manny and me, William and Uncle Manny versus Marjorie and father, William and Marjorie versus father and me, and later that evening William and I practiced serving under the darkening sky until the dim white shuttlecock was visible only high above, in the dark air to which a last lightness faintly clung; but when at last we had to stop, our passion stopped as abruptly as the faint twang of the racket against the rubber of the bird. And again we returned to the white one-dollar bills, the pink five-dollar bills, the yellow ten-dollar bills, the green twenty-dollar bills, the blue fifty-dollar bills, the tan hundred-dollar bills, the orange five-hundred-dollar bills . . .

One day father drove us to the old department store in a nearby city that had seemed hundreds of miles away when I was a child. Taking an elevator to the fifth floor while father shopped on the third, William and I stepped into a formal and well-trimmed garden of girls' dresses and coats. Pink and yellow and green and blue, in long shoulder-high rows they hung from parallel silver poles. As I walked between flowering hedges of cloth I held out both hands, brushing the soft dresses with my fingertips and making the hangers scrape, while William, walking in front of me, looked over his shoulder with a frown. Turning and turning at the ends of aisles, we came at last to a dark green rug, where making our way past gleaming mahogany tables, upholstered chairs, bronze standing lamps with curved necks, couches dark brown and dark green, we turned a corner and found ourselves in a hushed world of glass counters filled with white boxes showing flouncy blue nightgowns and shimmering white slips. On top of one counter a pair of pink legs stood in a gleaming black girdle. One leg was raised slightly, with the knee turned toward the other knee, and a heavy frowning woman with massive calves, wearing a dark red dress and holding a white coat over her arm, was slowly lifting from an open box on the counter a lacy black nightgown. A salesgirl with blue eyelids and a yellow pencil stuck in her hair stood watching with a frown as William and I walked past with downcast eyes, and as I turned the corner I suddenly glanced up at the lifted heel, the smooth wooden calf, the shimmering buttocks, the frowning salesgirl, and turning another corner we entered a miniature zoo, where yellow birds and green birds chirped in their cages and orange fish and black fish swam in bubbling green tanks while beside a cash register a smiling man with a white crewcut and black eyeglasses handed to a frowning boy with upstretched hands a small white cardboard box that dripped and swayed beneath its wire handle, and passing among blue rubber bones, gray cloth mice, green porcelain mermaids, red pagodas, we turned another corner and came at last to the department of toys.

For almost a month I had saved up my allowance. We were going to chip in for a new game. "There they are," said William, jerking his chin in the direction of the board-games; he strode around an aisle. "You check 'em out," I called, "I want to browse a little, I'll be with you in a . . ." And how I had once longed for a two-thousand-piece puzzle, a ten-thousand-piece puzzle, a million-piece puzzle that would cover the floor of an entire room, an entire basement . . . an entire back yard . . . and I had dreamed of a puzzle of puzzles as large as an entire town, so that you could cover the grass with grass-pieces, the sidewalks with sidewalk-pieces, the floors of the rooms of all houses with rug-pieces and linoleum-pieces, and roofs with roof-pieces, and parks with park-pieces, and hills with hill-pieces . . . and ocean floors with ocean-pieces . . . But the puzzles before me could not even cover a little table, and the boxcovers showed not the storm-tossed ships and gloomy forest cabins of distant summer afternoons but only a white lighthouse at the end of a gray reef, a bowl of pink flowers beside which lay one curling pink petal, a droopy-eared cocker spaniel looking over the edge of a wicker basket, a white kitten with one paw resting on a ball of blue wool. Beside the puzzles rose a series of brightly boxed games. There was a word-game consisting of lettered dice that you shook in a cup, a question-and-answer game in the shape of a bowling ball with a little window where the answers appeared, a game of three-dimensional tic-tac-toe, an electrical football game with a metal playing-field that vibrated when you plugged it in, causing the little players to move. And it was all boring, so boring, as boring as the display of toy trains on a nearby counter with tunnels and trees and cute little underpasses, as boring as the rows of golf clubs and hockey sticks in the boring sports department, as boring as the model cars, the toy tele-phones, the walkie-talkies, the log-cabin sets, the wind-up roller coaster with its shiny red cars, the yellow tin parking garage with its blue tin pumps and its white tin ramp. Glossy boxcovers were coated with faint layers of dust, streaked to a shine by un-known fingers, and it seemed to me that the glamor of games was nothing but this shine, this dust. With my forefinger I wrote my shiny initials in the dust of a game. I looked at the darkened pad of my finger. Scornfully I remembered my ache of envy only last summer, when I had seen a quiz program on television in which the winner was allowed to keep everything he could throw into a shopping basket during three mad minutes in the toy department of a towering New York store. It was all dust and shine, dust and shine, and by the time I joined William at the board-games I felt as shiny and dusty as the piece of wet red candy I had seen on the white-enameled towel machine in the mothball-smelling men's room; dark yellow urine on frosty white camphor-chunks. I wanted to leave but William had already sorted out the games in his efficient way, rejecting first the games that required more than two players, and second the games that were variations of games we already owned, and third the games without instruction booklets, whose too-simple rules were printed on the inside of the boxcover. From the remaining games he had settled on four: a mystery game, a newspaper game, a financial game, a world-war game. I was bored to death with it all but grasped at his enthusiasm in a kind of despair. I wanted a complex game with long difficult rules and as many accessories as possible—metal pieces, wooden pieces, scorepads, penalty cards, play money, spinners, diceboxes, red dice with white spots, white dice with black spots, hourglasses with white sand—but William argued that too many accessories was a sign of inferiority: the secret was in the rules. And so we studied the rules, we examined the pieces, we compared the boards. We rejected the mystery game and the financial game, took back the mystery game, argued over the world-war game, and settled on the newspaper game. On the way home we sat in the back seat, studying the instructions and trying to work out the moves on the bouncing board. At home we hurried into my room. In a fever of impatience I set up the board while William read the rules aloud. At last we played, clumsily at first and then with passion, and after dinner we played again, and then again, but by the middle of the fourth game I could no longer conceal from myself the faint feeling of disappointment that had been present from the beginning, and later that night, waking from a dream that I could not remember, I suddenly remembered a domed game of my childhood with three steel balls and a clown's red-and-blue face, and with a feeling of panic I wondered what had happened to all those vanished games.

19

AT THE AGE OF THIRTEEN my cousin Marjorie was a plain, dumpy, motherly sort of girl, with boring light-brown hair that was always changing its style. Sometimes she had bangs and a ponytail; sometimes she had masses of tiny curls all over her head; sometimes she had thick bouncy rolls weighing on her shoulders; sometimes she wore her hair short and a little wavy, with a black velvet band holding everything in place. She had one bathing suit like mother's, with a little pleated skirt attached, and another bathing suit that ended in shorts. Otherwise she wore plain shirt-like blouses with the sleeves rolled above the elbows, bermuda shorts, and white socks with red or blue sneakers. Her favorite books were *The Swiss Family Robinson, Hiroshima,* and *Rebecca of Sunnybrook Farm.* She also owned a set of abridged classics (*The Count of Monte Cristo, The Last of the Mohicans, Two Years Before the Mast*) in red and green and blue bindings with titles in gold, which Auntie Lou had purchased for her one by one in a supermarket. She liked magazines about rock-and-roll stars, glossy black-and-white photographs of movie stars signed "Love" and "Best Wishes," and big shiny record albums on which were pictured sleek-haired singers in pink shirts or gold dresses. William treated her kindly though he could barely endure Uncle Manny and Auntie Lou. They were sometimes about on the weekends and would accompany us on our expeditions, after which William and Marjorie and I would play Monopoly in my room. William even added a special supplement to his record-book, with columns headed M and W and A. I always chose the racing car, William always chose the battleship, but Marjorie always chose the old shoe. "Look," I once said to her, "how come you always take the shoe? Why don't you take the hat? I hate that crummy shoe." Marjorie flushed faintly and took the handsome hat. But halfway around the board she threw it back and took the shoe, saying: "Oh, Arthur, it just doesn't feel right." "Let her take the shoe if she wants to," said William, which infuriated me for some reason.

One fine day the whole pack of us went to Lake Sassacus. Marjorie and William and I rode with father in our car, while mother got stuck with Uncle Manny and Auntie Lou. I had seized the vacated front seat but immediately became annoyed when Marjorie and William began talking in back. From what I could hear of it, their conversation was appallingly boring and stupid, all about school. William wanted to know what books they used in Marjorie's school, what time classes ended, what clubs she belonged to, that sort of garbage. When he asked her what her favorite subject was, she said: "Oh, I dunno. I guess I kind of like hiss tree." "I prefer pine trees, myself," I said, turning around, but no one was amused, and I felt fairly stupid and wretched and decided to ignore those two boring people. A little while later William brought out his pocket chess set and began to explain the moves to Marjorie. "That doesn't look like a castle," she said. "Actually," said William. "Hey," I said, "I know, why don't we all play Geography? Mexico. Your turn, Dad." "Right-o," said father: "Oregon." There was a pause. "Well now, come on now, Willy, Marge: Oregon." "Norway," muttered William. "Yalu River," said Marjorie, who always said Yalu River or Yangtze River. "Red River Valley!" I cried. "Yosemite National Park!" cried father. "Kalamazoo," muttered William . . .

We changed in the old bathhouse, father and Uncle Manny and William and I on one side, mother and Auntie Lou and Marjorie on the other. I began to change quickly, for William and I liked to make a race of it, and as I changed I listened idly to the shuffle and thump coming through the wall from the women's side. And as I idly listened, all at once I was consumed by curiosity, a curiosity so powerful that it took the form of a physical sensation in my stomach, and checking abruptly to make certain the door was locked, with a violently beating heart I approached the damp brown wall, through which, in the brown gloom, three needles of sunlight pierced at sharp angles. Crouching over and holding my breath I moved my eye slowly toward a tiny aperture at the base of a rotting knothole. At once, quite clearly, I saw an enormous drooping double-chinned buttock above the thick, bruised, and blue-veined thigh of Auntie Lou. Pulling back with an odd mixture of self-loathing and sadness, I turned the block of wood in the door and stepped outside. A moment later, two doors away, William stepped out, frowning in the bright light. I noticed that he was holding his clothes so that they hung down in front of his bathing suit. He noticed that I noticed. I bent over and picked up a dusty rock and began tossing it up in the air and catching it, tossing it up in the air and catching it. Father stepped out, making a face as he put his large pale foot on the hard pebbly dirt, and Marjorie came around the corner in her new bathing suit, an all-white one with a white pleated skirt. Father smiled and said: "Oo la la." Marjorie lowered her eyes. William looked away. I kicked a stone. William coughed. "Oof," said father, "this stuff is murder on the old feet," and sitting down in an open doorway he began to put his shoes on over his murdered feet. A door swung open and Uncle Manny stepped out with a smile, drumming three fingers on his hairy belly. He frowned suddenly and slapped his shoulder. He looked quickly at his palm and then up at the sky. He frowned again at his shoulder, pulling the skin forward and trying to peer at his back. Looking up he said: "Tell ya, these horseflies. They eat me alive. Mmmm mmm. Lo, Beautiful. Heya, Arthur Parthur" (rumpling my hair). "Lo, uh, what's-your-name? sorry I . . ." "Betcha can't catch me," said Marjorie, suddenly breaking away and running with plump swiftness toward the far end. William made and repressed a motion to follow, and then he and I were running wildly side by side after her as father was saying "can run on this" and Uncle Manny was saying "crazy kids they."

We rounded the first corner neck and neck but William was on the inside. As we rounded the second corner and started along the ladies' side he was a whole stride ahead of me. Marjorie was some six doors ahead of William, running with surprising swiftness over the hard pebbly ground, her little skirt going up and down, up and down, and her heavy brown hair bouncing on her neck. Halfway along she glanced quickly over her shoulder with a frown, and a moment later she stopped; turned; and disappeared into one of the rooms.

And at once a strange thing happened: William, who by now was three doors ahead of me, suddenly slowed down. Two doors away he stopped, and I came running triumphantly past. Stopping at Marjorie's door I glanced for a second at William, who was glaring at the ground. Then I climbed into the little room.

Marjorie stood in a corner with a hand on her stomach, taking great breaths. She gave a little gasp as I stepped in. "Oh, Arthur," she said in a whisper, "you can't come in here! What if anybody ..." And suddenly I became intensely embarrassed, for what if anybody ... And turning to the partly open door, I quickly closed it, twisting the block of wood. And as I turned that block of wood I felt a small block of wood turning in my mind, and I began to blush, but the darkness protected me. Marjorie stood in the corner with a hand on her stomach, breathing less loudly and watching me. The outside world had shrunk to a patch of sunlight under the door. It seemed to me that this must be the very same room, with the very same pattern of dark dampness on the walls. And as I stood there with my heels in sunlight and my toes in darkness, and remembered counting to three, a vague, troubling excitement came over me, and I scarcely dared to imagine that she, that I ... In the brown darkness Marjorie stood watching me. And everything was as I remembered it: the damp walls, the darkness, the sounds of rapid breathing ... I took a step forward. Marjorie seemed about to speak, but said nothing. Her lips were parted slightly. And everything was as I remembered it: the damp walls, the darkness ... Marjorie was breathing more rapidly now, as though she had been running again. And I remember thinking, what am I supposed to ... The pirate captain with the red bandanna and gold earrings grasped the dark-eyed gypsy dancer around the waist. Bending forward as she bent back, he kissed her on the mouth. And I tried to remember that scene in all its detail, but I saw only the red bandanna, the gold earrings, the dark gypsy eyes ... In the darkness Marjorie stood watching me. And I remember thinking, if only she ... but that boring girl just kept standing there. And I remember thinking, but what if she ... and besides, she was my cousin. And I remember thinking, but what if I, but what if we, if only she ... And everything was as I remembered it: the damp walls, the darkness ... With sudden fury I turned, twisted the block of wood, pulled open the door, and stepped into the fierce sunlight.

I was not a moment too soon. As I glared at William, who was still standing two doors away, the next door opened and Auntie Lou stepped out, dressed in a shiny green bathing suit with orange flowers on it, and clutching in one bent arm a mass of clothes and underwear. "Well hello there, boys," she said, tugging up the top of her suit. "What's cooking?" "Nothing," I answered. "Nothing," said William. "Nothing," I added.

20

BORED TO DEATH with our indoor life, for William too was becoming restless, we began to take long bicycle trips to unknown destinations. Starting early in the morning, before the air became heavy with its accumulation of light, we would strike out toward unknown parts, William on his shiny black English bike and I on my dented red American one, with its one black handlebar-grip and the broken odometer that I had purchased in the fourth grade for two boxtops and fifty cents. Each day we set off in a new direction. As we approached some familiar boundary I would feel a ripple of adventure that swelled to a toppling white-capped wave that crashed as we passed beyond, into undiscovered territory. And how I loved that sudden plunge into strangeness, when for a moment a wire fence, an attic window, a black puddle, a yellow hydrant all quivered with a mystery that quickly vanished, as when, in the morning, waking in an unfamiliar room, calmly and drowsily you open your eyes to a door, a chair, a wall, a white curtain all threatening you with their strangeness, till recognition tames them. At first the simple passing of a boundary was enough, but soon we were less easily satisfied, and began to judge severely the new scenes we passed among. In no time we had progressed from eager amateurs to jaded connoisseurs of Nature. Increasingly we sought wild, uninhabited regions, and one day we came to a houseless section of town I had never seen before.

To the left of the curving road a bright yellow sign with a black backward S on it stood before a dark depth of evergreens. To the right, beyond a ragged strip of weeds, rose a crumbling yellow-brown cliff with little bushes growing in crevices and a scattering of trees on top. "Let's take a look at the view from up there, men," said William, who sometimes addressed a band of whom I was the sole visible member. The rock-face was too steep for us to climb, but riding farther we came to where the stone sloped down in a clump of trees. Parking our bikes among the pines, out of sight of the road, we penetrated the little forest and began to climb the tree-grown rocky slope, pushing away springy bush-branches and clutching carefully our brown paper bags with their egg-salad sandwiches and their heavy oranges. Over one shoulder William wore father's canvas-covered canteen. At last the slope leveled out and we entered a thicket at the rather disappointing top of the cliff. Through the trees we looked down at the far half of the road below and the tops of the dark evergreens, beyond which, in a square dirt clearing, sat a bright orange tractor. Turning our backs on the view we began to make our way through the thicket, stepping over a fallen log, ducking under branches, and avoiding the shiny sumac leaves that threatened here and there. William was a few steps in front of me. Suddenly he stopped, holding his hand out behind him with the palm up, like a policeman.

I came up to him and saw that he was standing at the top of a bushy slope that plunged invitingly far down. Beyond, another slope rose steeply and leveled out among trees. We were looking down into a miniature valley—a valleyette between hillocks—a secret wild-place at the edge of nowhere. There were splashes of yellow and white and orange-brown; I counted six shades of green. At once we headed down, clinging carefully to the tough roots and branches of massive bushes, scraping our legs on thorns and prickers, and supporting ourselves against occasional small trees. At one point William picked up a crooked knotted stick that he found under a bush. "You look like Huckleberry Finn," I said. "Huckleberry Mainwaring," said William.

"Tom Mainwaring and Huckleberry Grumm," I said. As we clambered down I recognized the coppery shine of sumac leaves, a solitary blackberry bush, the dark frond of a fern, but mostly we passed among green shapes I had never seen before, nameless and mysterious as the suddenly remembered pictures in a vanished book of my childhood that showed, in pen-and-ink sketches twisting over an entire page, the tall, spiked, dangerous vegetation of the moon. The farther down we went, the larger and greener everything became. At the bottom we pressed through two thick bushes with spiky dark leaves, and came to the sudden edge of a slow brown sun-sparkling stream.

A small dark-spotted green frog, sitting on the dry gray back of a rock in the stream, leaped into the water with the sound of a dropped pebble. Under the water lay an upside-down ankle-sneaker that seemed dimly familiar. The submerged canvas rippled slightly in the moving water. On the opposite bank, great bushes grew at the edge of the stream, trailing their leaves in the water. Taking off our sneakers and socks, we rolled our dungarees up to our knees and began to step across the stream on the backs of dry pale stones and wet dark stones. William was ahead of me, using his crooked stick like a cane. His pale hairless legs, his reddish heels, his bony anklebones, the tendons rising from the back of each heel, filled me with sudden anger; we were such an unlikely Huck and Tom. "Come on," I said, "hurry up, why don't you throw that piece of junk away," and William looked over his shoulder with a frown. "I need it for balance," he said, but my good spirits had returned and I wasn't listening. William sprang from the last stone onto the bank, in the space between two great bushes. "Hey," he said, pushing aside some leaves, "look at this." I sprang onto the bank beside him and bent to see.

He had pushed aside a curtain of little leaves, revealing a small sloping hollow between the base of the bush and the overarching branches. Together we entered the green secluded space. The ground was bumpy; here and there a piece of twisted root poked through. We were crouching in a little green room, a leafy grotto, a living bush-house at the edge of a secret stream. Bright broken bits of sunlight lay all about. William sat down against the central mass of multiple stems, with one leg stretched out and one leg raised at the knee; I sat below him, close to the curtain of leaves. They were little maple-green leaves, shaped like slim ovals, edged with little sawteeth and fringed with tiny hairs. Where the sun struck them directly they became translucent, revealing a skeleton of veins, and I was suddenly reminded of the machine in the shoe department that had fascinated me as a child, where I could see the bones of my feet floating in green light. The bottommost leaves hung in the brown water and were pulled with the current. Glistening, they bumped lightly on the surface of the stream. Under the water, Friday's lost sneaker gently stirred. "This is neat," said William, unscrewing father's canteen; the top knocked against the side with a canvas-metal thump and a click of chain. "Hey," he said, "look."

Annoyed at all this racket, I turned impatiently to look. William was holding out his hand and staring at the back. "Well," I said, "what's all the noise about, I don't see anything." "But look," he said, "it's green." Then I saw that the back of his hand was glowing with green sunlight. There was a faint shimmer of green under William's eyes, on his chin, on the top of a cheek. I looked quickly at my own hand, and saw with a pang that it was mere flesh and shadow. But raising it to some translucent green-glowing leaves, I saw green light shimmering on my skin. "Your face is green," William then said. And I was happy to be green, yes, happy to be green. For there we were, my friend and I—green and innocent as two boys in a book. Sitting in that little Eden, bound in green brotherhood in the secret heart of a secret wilderness, I felt I could have been content to stay there forever. Indeed, anything less than forever would not have suited me at all.

21

UNFORTUNATELY WE COULD NOT STAY there forever. We could not even stay there all afternoon. And I suppose it was just as well, for by the time we left I had begun to grow somewhat bored. And to tell the truth, I had begun to grow somewhat bored with all our riding around; for to tell the truth, Nature is nice, but books are better. William too was increasingly restless, and in fact I had noticed that during our short friendship—but then, no one forced him to do anything, no one forced him to become bored to death. And again we returned to the white one-dollar bills, the pink five-dollar bills, the yellow ten-dollar bills . . . I felt lost in a monstrous maze of boredom. And this was strange, really, for I suffered from no obvious lack of free-dom. It was as if life itself were a restriction, a form of mon-strous dullness from which there was no escape, except one. Of course I had not yet tasted the joys of love, whatever they were, but even in advance I seemed to know that they would not—and how I despair of making you understand, you smug ones, you smilers! And sometimes it seemed to me that if only I were an artist, if only I could create a world superior to this world, which would annihilate it and replace it. For you see, it was as if my mind outran this world at every point. And although in a sense it may be true that my boredom was the boredom of the sensualist, weary of commonplace pleasures and forever seeking new and strange ones, in another and far truer sense my bore-dom was the boredom of the ascetic, for I looked askance at the pleasures of this world, I longed for something far better. The blue fifty-dollar bills, the tan hundred-dollar bills, the orange five-hundred-dollar bills . . . and how I longed for them to go on and on, oh! how I longed for them, the black one-thousand-dollar bills, the silver five-thousand-dollar bills, the crimson ten-thousand-dollar bills . . .

22

As THE WEATHER GREW HOTTER I began to suffer from a sense of oppression and suffocation, as if all the light of summer were pressing heavily against me. An irritable languor took possession of me: for hours I lay exhausted in my darkened room, brooding darkly over nothing in particular, and resenting the sound of William's voice or of mother's clippers in the yard. Only at dusk was I able to find some measure of relief, for I rejoiced in the death of the stifling day, yet a restlessness remained, indeed grew stronger as the night advanced. I longed to be free of my body, which seemed the source of only unpleasant sensations. I longed to escape, to dissolve, to die, to feel some marvelous dilation of my entire being that only my body prevented. Oh, I felt stifled, crushed, if you only knew . . . you stupid reader . . .

One oppressive night I sat up in bed and pushed aside the cool blinds. Beyond the dark shine of the glass, where I saw my transparent face, it was one of those colorful blue nights that you see in technicolor movies, when the nightworld resembles a deeply dyed version of day. The maple rose into a glowing blue sky where a round and piercingly white moon, light-blue-shadowed, seemed to have burned all blackness away. Lazy clouds left over from the afternoon still floated here and there, now stained a luminous blue-gray. An intense blue-white light poured down from the moon into the mystery of the yard. From one horizontal branch of the maple, black against the blue sky, the two ropes of the swing hung clearly down, and on the wooden seat, shining in the moonlight, a design of leafshadows was clearly printed. The lawn was a checkerboard of luminous grass and dark leafshadows, stirring. The nightworld looked so cool, so blue, that it seemed a shady blue hiding-place under the dark blue leafshade of heaven. Under the cool blaze of the blue-shadowed moon, I felt myself melting out of blackness into a dark radiance of blue...

With a clatter I released the blinds. I remained sitting up in bed, hugging my knees in the excitement of a sudden longing. And for a long while I sat like that, fearfully listening, for the very desire seemed a noisy intrusion into the hushed domesticity of the dark. The dark walls, the dark windows, the dark quiet of the slumbering house, seemed to press upon me from all sides, in a gentle conspiracy against adventure. Even my clock ticked out the soft measures of its disapproval: tsk tsk, tsk tsk, tsk tsk, tsk tsk... With sudden revulsion I flung the covers off and began to dress quickly.

Softly, expertly, I crept from my room into the moonlit kitchen, where magnified shadows of five-lobed maple leaves lay in the gleaming sink, on the metal cabinets, on parallelograms of moonlight on the walls. Softly I slipped the bolt of the windowed wooden door, softly I turned the fluted glass doorknob, softly I turned the dented metal doorknob of the wooden screen-door and stepped out into the warm blue air of a radiant summer night. O blue summer nights with your moons of snow... O blossom of the moon in your dark blue garden... For a few moments I stood on the leafshadowed porch beside the silvery milkbox and then tiptoed down into the yard, passing through shadows that rippled over me; and I myself seemed to ripple as I passed through rippling shadows, as if I were dissolving under the moon. A racket of crickets sounded from beyond the dark hedge. Ghostlike I glided—oh, insubstantially—over to the blossoming swing and sat down. I looked both ways to make certain that the windows of both neighboring houses were black. Then softly, softly, I began to swing, kicking off on the bald patch and sweeping through the familiar arc of my childhood, leaning back with my feet straining upward, rippling through leafshadows and twigshadows into the clearness of the moon, swinging higher and higher to the higher and higher top of my arc where, for one feathery moment, I rested, before falling swiftly, softly, swooningly back, swinging higher, and higher, and higher, and higher, until suddenly I let go: and as in one of those newsreels where the motion suddenly stops, and the basketball player stands frozen in the air with his back arched, his arm straining upward, and a heavy basketball fastened to his extended fingertips, so for a moment I seemed to hang suspended in the thick blue medium of that painted summer night: behind me the empty swing had not yet fallen back: motionless in moonlight I lazed in air, the merest feather of a Grumm: but the basketball spills from live fingers, the player drops down, with a rush I plunged downward, hitting the earth heavily with both sneakers and breaking my fall by bending my knees. I fell lightly forward onto my outspread palms and then rolled over onto my back. The swing was jumping crazily in a silent jerking arc. I stared up at the dazzling moon, which seemed to be rushing in a vast arc through bluegray wisps of clouds. Though flat on my back I held on to the grass to keep from falling off. After a while I stood up. For a moment I hesitated. Then slowly, heavily, I started back toward the house.

At the steps I stopped, turned, and walked swiftly back across the lawn.

Squeezing through the narrow space where the hedge joined the wire fence, I made my way down the slope and out into the moonlit field, following the dim path between rows of leafy bushes where things rustled and crackled and shushed and hissed. At the concrete ledge of the stream I leaped down onto the hard grassy dirt at the edge of the moongleaming mud. On the lifted backs of stones I stepped across the mud onto the hard weedgrown dirt of the opposite bank. Gripping the scratchy concrete ledge, which was level with my neck, I gave a leap and pulled myself up, hooking a leg over and scraping my knee. Then scrambling up the

steep dirt slope I made my way across the cinder driveway at
the back of the body shop, passing moonlit black trashcans
and the wheelless husk of a car, and continued along the back
of a shut-down gas station and a car-wash and a dark diner,
catching glimpses of red and green traffic lights between
buildings. Onward I went with swift dream-ease, a ghostly
glider, a merry moonlit doppelgänger, passing garbage cans
and heaps of crates, climbing over stiff wire fences, squeezing
through hedges, until climbing over an old wooden fence I
entered a slumbering back yard, where on a clothestree before
an old two-family house a smiling Raggedy Ann doll hung
by her wild red hair, and fleeing across to a tall hedge I
pressed my way scratchily through and entered another yard,
where in a sandbox an upside-down pail cast a long shadow
among moonlit sanddunes, and fleeing across to a ragged row
of forsythia I crawled into another yard, where two green
eyes glowed beside a garbage can at the back steps of a store,
and climbing over a bent wire fence I entered another yard,
where from a second-story clothesline a pair of stiff dungarees
hung upside down beside a sleeveless undershirt while on the
moonlit rail of a high porch an empty flowerpot sat beside a
hanging gray rug, and as I fled from yard to yard, pursued
by frowning windows, I felt that each dark house was waking
up behind me and that each black window was bursting into
light, and ducking under a low clothesline and leaping over
a lawnmower-handle I came to a high pricker-hedge that
barred my way. Fearfully I made my way along the narrow
sideyard, ducking below the black windows. At the edge of
the house I paused. Across the street a row of dark stores
reflected a streetlamp and a mailbox. I made a dash across the
little front yard, but a headlight appeared on the right, and
throwing myself down before a low pricker-hedge I waited
for the car to pass as the house stared at me. Then leaping the
hedge and scratching both legs, I crossed the street to the row
of stores. At the drugstore I turned left and entered a quiet
street. Gliding along past small one-family houses that sat

behind hedges and moonwashed picket fences, I came to a glowing blue-white church and turned right, onto a street with larger houses set back from the road. Turning left at the end of the street, and right at the end of the next street, I came at last to William Mainwaring's house, set back from the road with no front walk.

Softly I crept along the moonlit black driveway in the company of my shadow, stretching to the left. When I came to the glowing blue-white garage door at the side of the house, my shadow leaped up and towered over me. With laborious care, inch by halting inch, almost soundlessly I pulled up the dangerously grating door to the level of my knees. Holding it painfully in place, I slipped underneath into the gasoline-smelling garage, where two dark-gleaming cars huddled side by side. I lowered the door carefully and felt my way along the side of a car to the dark inner door. Climbing onto the cluttered toolbench, I patted my fingertips slowly along the dusty top of the doorframe until I felt the sudden metal of the key.

The door opened with a creak that startled me; for a moment I stood at the bottom of the black stairs, listening. Then slowly, on tiptoe, I climbed the wooden stairs, and slowly I opened the next dark door. I stepped onto the plastic mat and softly closed the door behind me. In the dark living room on my left, edges of mahogany and bits of glass were polished by moonlight. In the dark kitchen on my right, a moonlit patch of lawn was visible through half a window. Bending over, I unlaced my sneakers and placed them side by side in the center of the mat. Slowly, on the thick dark rug, I began to climb.

The stairs were silent but a creak on the black landing made me hold my breath. In the intense silence I became aware of a familiar mechanical humming sound that suddenly stopped. Faint watery plumbing noises were audible from the bathroom. Turning left at the landing I climbed the next two stairs, and at the top I turned right and faced a toneless blackness from which there slowly emerged blacker blacknesses: a black doorjamb, a black piece of wall, a black molding, and far away, at the very end, a faint black shimmer that puzzled me. Holding one hand before me with extended fingertips, and placing one foot gingerly ahead of the other, I made my way warily along the dangerous hall, and as I advanced through a silence that grew more and more threatening I longed to stamp, to run, to shriek out a magnificent booooooooooo, to crash into a sudden table: a bed would creak, footsteps would sound, a bright yellow light would flood the hall: but in flawless silence I continued along the hall toward the black shimmer of the suddenly remembered mirror until with absurd, comical ease I reached the last door on the right. Gently I gripped the knob. With absurd, comical ease I silently opened the door. A few feet to the right, William lay on his cheek, facing me with closed eyes. As I stepped into the room his eyes opened and he sat up in bed as if he had been expecting me. "It's me—Arthur—shhh," I whispered, closing the door softly behind me and sounding to myself like someone in a movie. In a stagey whisper I added: "Don't worry. No one heard me."

"Shhh," hissed William, playing his part to perfection. Even in the dark I could tell that he was upset, and with a throb of nervousness I felt my moon-mood slipping away. Quickly I whispered: "Don't worry, I . . ."

"Shhh, I said. Shhh." In a low, intense voice he asked: "Are you in trouble? Is anything . . ."

"Oh no, no," I whispered, somewhat relieved, "nothing like that. It was so hot in my room . . . the moon was out and I thought . . . I can't explain it but I thought . . . don't you want to come out and . . . go for a walk or . . ." Even to me the words sounded foolish to the point of insolence, and now a clear sense of what I had done began to come over me, and I longed to be back in my bed, in the safe darkness of my room. And again I felt my lovely moon-mood slipping away, twisting, changing, losing its force under the stern gaze of the hushed and listening dark. William's eyes were blazing and in a furious whisper he said: "Shhh. Don't say anything. Just get out, all right? Shhh. Just get out of here. Will you? Shhh. God, what a rotten—shhh. Just go. Make sure you lock the door. And put the key back. God, what if you—don't say anything, I said. Just go. And be careful. Just get out of here. Shhh. Shhhhhhhhhhhhhhhhh."

With a sudden motion William swung out of bed; jerking back my head I raised my arm to my face. But ignoring me he stepped to the door and listened for a moment with his ear against the wood. Then straightening up he whispered: "Okay. I'm going down with you. Just in case. Shhh." Opening the door quietly, he stepped into the black hall. Meekly I stepped after him. I had begun to creep uncertainly forward when suddenly the light went on.

It was only William. Standing in his blue-and-white-striped pajamas, glaring fiercely at me and holding a finger to his tight angry lips, he jerked his head toward the well-lit stairway. Then he tiptoed ahead of me to the top of the stairs. He waited there as I tiptoed after him, imagining my back retreating deeper and deeper into the oval mirror, and when I came up to him he turned out the light and for a moment all was blackness. Slowly the landing emerged, and behind William I tiptoed down the stairs. My sneakers were visible on the mat below. At the bottom I put them on, and suddenly the mechanical humming stopped again, and this time I recognized the refrigerator motor. William insisted on accompanying me down the next flight of stairs and into the garage, where he skilfully climbed up on the toolbench and replaced the key. With infinite care he raised the garage door to waist-level and held it while I slipped beneath. Then slowly, silently, expertly, he lowered the door.

Outside I stood up and dusted myself off. The night had changed. The too-white moon in the too-blue sky threatened me with exposure and punishment; I longed for the far darkness of my room. Against the bright blue-white garage door my shadow stood up taller than before. Stepping over to the row of shiny black windows, I leaned forward—and sprang back, for William's pale face glared out at me. Softly, swiftly, on winged rubber feet I ran down the driveway to the sandy crunch at the side of the street. Softly, swiftly I fled past large houses set back from the road, turning right at the end of the street and left at the next street, until coming to the blue-white church I turned at the precise moment when, I imagined, William was opening the first dark door. Softly, swiftly I ran past smaller houses behind hedges and picket fences. Turning at the drugstore as William opened the second dark door, softly, swiftly I ran along the well-lit deserted sidewalk, past stores and houses and gas stations and shut-up diners, under an ambiguous sky that had already begun to lose the quality of night without yet achieving the quality of dawn, and crossing the street as William stepped into the black hall, I ran up behind the body shop, scrambled down the dirt slope, leaped over the concrete ledge into a puddle of mud, pulled myself up on the other side, ran along the path between rows of bushes, scurried up the slope, squeezed between the hedge and the wire fence, ran across the yard where a dead swing hung from a gloomy tree, leaped up the back steps, opened the screen door, opened the wooden door, and saw my angry father seated at the kitchen table; but it was only an apron on the back of a chair; and fastening the bolt and removing my muddy sneakers I crept fearfully through the kitchen and into the hall to my beautifully still-dark room, just as William entered his own dark chamber.

23

WILLIAM DID NOT COME the next day, or the next day, or the next day, or the next day. I thought of calling to find out whether he was sick, but I had never called before, and some-how... "Where's William?" mother persisted in asking. "Oh,"

I would answer, "dead I guess," and return to my book. I would begin reading at the sunny breakfast table, when the pages were barred by slim bright rectangles of summer light, as if the lines of print were wandering through a sun-pierced shady wood, and I would continue all the long morning in my cool but warming room, while from the yard came the faint scrape of mother among the zinnias, and from the street came the happy shouts of young hoodlums at play, and from above, at irregular intervals, came a sudden ripple of muffled thumps mingled with a sound of torn paper: old Wynken galloping across the linoleum. By lunchtime I was headachy and sluggish. Nevertheless I continued to read all the long afternoon, moving from my hot room to the living-room armchair before the leafy window, flowing smoothly from one book to another as from one chapter to another in an enormous book, watching from time to time the green reflections of leaves in my eyeglasses, and starting nervously at a sudden dark motion in the corner of my lenses: the quick dark flight of a bird past the window behind me. Occasionally I would rest, lying on the puffy couch-cushions with my eyeglasses on my stomach and my arm over my eyes, listening to the oppressive sounds of summer: the scissors-sound of a hand-mower, the plump smack of a baseball into a catcher's mitt and the sharp smack of a baseball into the unpadded pocket of a fielder's glove, the rock-and-roll of a distant radio ... "Where's William?" father would ask as he jingle-jangled among the coat-hangers. "Oh," I would answer, trailing off with a weary shrug. After dinner I retired to my room while father sat in his chair with his feet up on the red leather hassock and a moist can of beer in his hand and watched a bluish ballgame on the hot, flushed, screaming television. Sometimes he and mother played pinochle with Mrs. Wakeman, who taught third grade, and Mr. Wakeman, a used-car salesman who always left behind him, in at least three ashtrays, olive-colored wet cigar stumps, large bluegray cylinders of ash, and crumpled, faintly crackling cellophane wrappers with bands of gold. From the fortress of my lamplit room I would listen to their jovial noise, waiting for it to disappear so that I might enter the kitchen in peace, and later, as mother and father prepared for bed, I would hear snatches of conversation: ". . . William . . . just have to learn to . . . room all day . . ." At last, weary and irritable, I would turn out my light and in the oppressive darkness close my eyes, just as my dull body, so empty during the crushing day, filled slowly with its restlessness.

One hot night I sat up in bed and pushed aside the cool blinds. The jaded moon, half dead with boredom, continued to shine down into the same old yard. The same old maple rose into the same blue sky, where the same old clouds, exhausted, floated; and the same old swing, too tired to complain, hung listlessly from the same bored branch. Even the crickets fiddled wearily, wiping their brows with their pocket handkerchiefs. For a long while I watched, intently but without interest, admiring the infinite banality of Heaven and Earth. As I gazed, finding in the scene a quiet consolation, my attention was caught by a sudden motion at the left-hand corner of the hedge, where it joined the wire fence. The dark branches moved to one side, and silently, eerily, William Mainwaring squeezed into the moonlit yard.

Slowly he crept forward, in moonlit sneakers, with the exaggerated tiptoe of a cartoon villain. Halfway across the lawn he stopped, looked sharply to the left and right, and stood frozen for a few moments before continuing. As he approached the back steps, I could see quite clearly his neat brown hair, his dark eyes, the cleft between his nose and mouth, the white rim of the dark red baseball-patch on his jacket . . . and then he passed beyond the range of my peephole, and I sat up in bed, listening fiercely.

I could barely hear the pad of his rubbery footfalls on the porch. Straining to hear, as if my ears were muscles that could be tensed, I discovered a hidden clamor in the heart of the hush of the motionless summer night: the faint squeal of distant brakes, the rustle of a cat in a bush, the tick of a clock, an attic creak, the bump of a moth against my screen, a gurgle of plumbing, a soft swish of distant highway traffic, those fiddling crickets; and always, behind and beneath it all, a faint and steady ringing in my ears, as if the very intensity of my listening were itself a form of commotion. A sudden creak outside my door made me suck in my breath with a foolish hiss. But it was only one of those mysterious sounds that a house makes for no reason at all, out of sheer boredom—no doubt the floorboards, cracking their knuckles. And now I could hear quite clearly the faint creak of the opening screen door, the jiggle of the glass doorknob, the clamorous silence, the jiggle of the glass doorknob, the soft closing of the screen door, the pad on the porch, a creak, a pause, a sound as of wood sliding, what was that sound as of wood sliding, a scrape, a rub, a sound of cloth against wood, a creak, a quiet thump, a sudden metallic rattle—and at once those ghostly sounds, so eerily disembodied, took shape around that metallic rattle, for I saw the knives and spoons in their little box at the end of the dishrack, and I knew that he was coming in through the kitchen window. That footfall in the sink . . . a sudden silence. Or rather, stillness that trembled on the threshold of the audible, heard silences, mirages of the ear. And now with slow precision I saw him emerging backwards from the sink, reaching down gingerly with first one leg and then the other, I saw him turning around slowly, pulling down his pushed-up jacket, smoothing his hair, tiptoeing slowly across the moonlit linoleum toward the open doorway, stepping carefully from the linoleum to the rug, making his way slowly, slowly, along the short dark hall to the door of my room, turning carefully, carefully, the bronze doorknob, pushing slowly, slowly, open the door . . . But the dark door failed to move. And so with a renewed effort of imagination I retraced his progress, attempting to duplicate, with inartistic completeness, the exhausting precision of reality: I watched him place one foot slowly before the other as step by cautious step he tiptoed across the dangerous linoleum, placing each sneakered foot carefully, from toe to heel, down onto the floor, now pausing to listen for sounds in the dark, now casting a look behind him at the windows of the wooden door with their translucent checkered curtains filled with moonglow and the dim shadow of the distant maple, now approaching with mad slowness the dark open doorway before him, and as I saw his sneakered toe swing slowly across the line dividing the linoleum from the narrow strip of wood before the hall rug, and hover uncertainly before daring to descend, suddenly my dark door moved, a dark shape appeared, the real William entered, and as he crept toward me in dark reconcilement, bearing on his face an expression of fierce triumph that mirrored my own, out in the hall the imagined William continued to hover between the linoleum and the rug, abandoned forever in that exhausting stance.

24

WILLIAM'S DARK VISIT was the bright beginning of a new intimacy between us. It was as if he had chosen me over—well, over something; and for the last days of that summer there was the feeling that we were secretly in league. In league against what, I scarcely know. We never discussed it. That night he sat silently in the dark armchair as I quickly dressed, and together we crept out of the house and down to the concrete stream. After the first flush of triumph he had begun to worry so much about getting home that I accompanied him part of the way; it was as if his own audacity had frightened him. And after all it is not surprising, for it was his very first venture into the forbidden. The next day he came over as usual, and when mother said: "Why, William. Where on earth have you been?" his eyes shifted to her left shoulder and he said somewhat clumsily: "Oh, sort of ... sick, sort of ..." Mother gave him a sharp look and then pretended to have noticed nothing. "Well!" she said brightly. "I'm certainly glad you're better. We were all worried about you, around here. Arthur, have you seen my trowel, by any chance? It's not in the pail. I've looked high and low. I can't seem to find it anywhere. Have you seen it, by any chance?" Poor William looked intensely miserable; events seemed to be forcing him into these nasty little concealments.

But in the last days of that summer our friendship blossomed. We dreamed, we yawned, we did nothing at all; we returned with gusto to our abandoned games. We planned long bicycle expeditions that never materialized, and rejoiced in the sense of arduous efforts we did not have to make. We became bored to death, but our boredom now had about it an air of revelry. And always our intimacy was strengthened by that special quality of the end of summer vacation, you know, that troubled sense of freedom that is quite different from the serene freedom of July, for unlike the early days of summer the final days do not have room to expand lazily into an infinity of hot blue summer afternoons. Crushed into a little space, the days press out a pungent essence of freedom that pains as it intoxicates. Those are the days when the schoolyear seems too greedy to wait its turn, and reaches hungrily backward into the end of summer. One hot day mother dragged me off to the clothing store, where I was measured for three pairs of oppressively new pants; the next day she came home with a package of pencils, a three-ring binder, and a bottle of blueblack ink. It was as if the future were invading the present, and establishing itself physically there. Mother herself seemed to become busier and more formidable with each passing day, as if the approaching end of her own vacation, like the end of a prolonged illness, were producing in her a series of physiological changes that would soon result in all the dangerous signs of aggressive health. In the face of all these forces, William and I were practically hurled together.

On the Saturday before the Wednesday on which the eighth grade began, father took us on a farewell expedition. It was not a success. A red Volkswagen was parked at the foot of the wooded hill, and as we turned a bend in the mica-sparkling trail, where the abandoned quarry-pit plunged to the pool of green and purple water, we came upon two people walking ahead of us. The man wore baggy khaki bermuda shorts and a shortsleeved white shirt, and was puffing away on a glossy pipe whose brown bowl was visible beyond his right ear. Behind his back he held a horizontal rock-hammer which he twirled slowly. The woman, in black slacks and a white blouse, wore a large brown leather pocketbook over one shoulder and held in one hand a rock-hammer of her own. It was she who turned around with a smile and said: "Morning," tugging meanwhile at the man's sleeve. To my dismay, father stopped and at once struck up a conversation. We were soon old friends. The man, it turned out, taught general science in high school. The woman taught fifth grade and was a den mother. Both had been rock-hunting for years. I muttered a few surly nothings and glanced at William, who was not at all happy. At last mother huffed into view, and everyone said hello, how are you, and we all finished the climb together: father walking in front with Mr. Oliver ("Call me Jim"), mother in back with Mary Ann, and I in the middle with William. "Basically," Mr. Oliver was saying, "there's no such thing as a juvenile delinquent. There are only boys. And all boys love machines. Now, the problem isn't so much . . ." "Ted, Joey, and Mike," Mrs. Oliver was saying. "Joey gets A in absolutely everything but Ted—well, Ted is going through a phase right now. He seems to have some sort of grudge against the world. Sometimes I—he's really such a good boy, it's awful to complain like this. You know, Ted must be about your son's age. He's entering seventh grade."

At last the narrow path ended in the boulder-strewn clearing before the hill of white stones. I set up the folding chair for mother in the patch of oak and maple, and William came after me with the jug of lemonade. A rough grassy path at right angles to the main trail was visible beyond the trees. Mother was reluctant to let us wander off by ourselves, for she feared that we might get lost, or fall off a cliff, or be attacked by Indians, but Mr. Oliver assured her there was no danger at all. "Let 'em go," he advised, puffing sagely on his pipe. "They're big boys now. Got to learn sometime." We disappeared through the trees and followed the curving path to a small heap of stones no higher than our heads. Without much interest we poked about and wondered if we should pretend to have gotten lost. Suddenly there was a crackling noise behind us. I whirled around. Shoulder to shoulder with their smiles and rock-hammers, father and Mr. Oliver stood on the sunny path. "Say, boys," said hearty Mr. Oliver, "mind if we join you?" A bit later Mrs. Oliver came tiptoeing up, asking what we menfolks were up to and darting apologetic glances at William and me. At last mother appeared, carrying her aluminum folding chair and her bag of wool; and seating herself with a great "Oof" in a patch of tattered shade, she began clicking and clacking and chattering away, looking up sharply from time to time to assure herself that no one had fallen into an abyss.

Lunch took place on the other side of the trees. Mother spread her blanket under a shady oak, and father and the Olivers sat down in the midst of waxpaper sandwiches and blue tin glasses and a small silver thermos that came from Mrs. Oliver's pocket-book. "Come join the party, boys," said father, patting a corner of the blanket, and when I hesitated Mrs. Oliver said: "Oh heck, they don't want to join us old fogies. You do just what you like, kids. Don't worry about us." And so, William and I joined them on the blanket. William sat between father and Mr. Oliver, staring at the blanket and saying nothing; I sat next to Mrs. Oliver, who kept addressing me in a hushed voice, accompanied by a special look, as if she and I were secret friends. "I was wondering, Arthur," she would say. "Do you have a—you know, a certain time set aside for homework each day? You don't have to tell me if you don't want to." "Oh," I would answer cheerfully, "I just work all the time," and she would grow thoughtful and sad. Mother, meanwhile, reigned sublimely over us on her throne, urging everyone to have another pickle, praising the weather, bursting into laughter, and chattering away with girlish exuberance. After the sandwiches and lemonade, Mr. Oliver lit up his pipe and leaned back against the oak with his hands clasped behind his head, puffing away and making

little popping sounds with his lips, and only then did William
and I glance at one another and proceed to stand up together,
slapping the crumbs from our laps. "Why, William!" cried
mother in a melodramatic voice, placing a hand on her chest
and looking at him in horror. Terrified, William flushed and
said sharply: "What's wrong?"

In the brief silence Mr. Oliver looked over, father glanced up,
and Mrs. Oliver, who had been looking at me, turned to stare at
William. Looking at him severely, mother said: "Oh, William.
How could you? How could you? Oh, how could you? Do you
know what you've done?" She paused dramatically. "You've
forgotten your camera!" Father chuckled, Mr. Oliver gave a
little snort of amusement into his pipe, causing smoke to rise
from the bowl, and even Mrs. Oliver smiled. But William, lowering his eyes, stood motionless and unsmiling.

25

ON THE TUESDAY before the Wednesday on which the eighth
grade began, William stayed for dinner. It was not a success.
Mother was tired and irritable, for she had taught a full day,
and father had not yet recovered from his own exhausting day,
and sat slumped at the table in weary silence. William and I had
spent the day playing ping-pong in the cellar, watching half a
movie on television, and lounging about on the wicker furniture
on the shady front porch. We were both bursting with boredom
and energy, which seemed disgraceful in the presence of so
much praiseworthy exhaustion. We lost no time in retreating to
my room. But even there the spirit of work pursued us, and in
order to escape it we decided to take a walk. "Don't be too
long," mother said, "you know you've got to get ready for
tomorrow," as if putting a pencil in my pocket required three
hours. Outside, in the hot and dusty end of the day, in the hot

and dusty end of the summer, there was nowhere to go. We strolled down my street past the wooden porches of old two-family houses where half-familiar older boys sometimes sat together on the steps, and turning left at the bus-stop we walked past a shut-up grocery store and a vacant lot to an open drugstore, where there was nothing to buy. We walked another block and stopped. On the other side of the street a tall boy with wavy yellow hair stood leaning against a corner mailbox, smoking a cigarette so that his cheeks were sucked in. He wore a black leather jacket and dark blue pants with pink side-stitching. He turned to look at us, placing both hands in his jacket pockets and narrowing his eyes as the line of smoke from his short dangling cigarette poured upward and broke into a wavering plume. With a sudden motion he reached up, removed the cigarette, and with his thumb flicked it over his shoulder. Tumbling over and over, it traced a graceful arc and hit with a faint thump the shut black window of a parked car behind him, shooting off sparks and dropping swiftly into the gutter. William and I turned left, onto an alien street flanked by tall horsechestnut trees. I glanced over my shoulder, but no one was following. The sounds of rock-and-roll pouring through a kitchen window mingled with a rattle of plates and a splash of tapwater. A tall frowning boy in dungarees and an unbuttoned shortsleeved shirt stood polishing the black hood of a Mercury. He had copper hair and a darkly tanned chest. A pair of large soft dice hung down behind the windshield, which reflected dark green leaves and a brown telephone pole, and from a small red radio on the roof of the car came the shouts of a ballgame. As we drew near he straightened up, placed a hand on his hip, and glared at us with narrow eyes. Holding my breath I walked by in silence, staring at the ground. At the end of the block we turned left, glancing back to see if we were being followed, and two blocks later we turned left onto my street. Two small boys with glossy black hair, who looked like miniature hoodlums, glared at us from the steps of a porch. When we reached my house we did not immediately enter. I half-sat on the gray rail, leaning against a post, and William sat in the wicker rocker. "Well," I said lightly, "here we are again." But William said nothing, and sat without rocking, as if he were lost in thought, or as if he had no thoughts at all.

26

AND AT LAST THE EIGHTH GRADE, that stifling grade, began. From the very beginning I was barely able to breathe. And perhaps if I had simply stopped breathing, everything would have been fine. And perhaps in any case everything would have been fine, had not William, to my keen disappointment, plunged into schoolwork with his usual fervor. He labored over his assignments with depressing zeal, and by the end of the second week he had joined three clubs. We now rode to school side by side on the yellow bus, and ate across from one another in the cafeteria, and strolled together on the playground, but the business of school, like a rival friend, seemed always to come between us. It was as if, for William, summer boredom had been bred merely by the absence of school, and not by the hideous inadequacy of the universe. Our science book seemed to set his mind ablaze. He pored over the weather map with its isobars and isotherms, and at last wrote to the Weather Bureau in Washington, D.C., from which he received a large weather map with an elaborate table of symbols, a pamphlet describing the technique of cloud-seeding, and a cloud-chart showing twenty black-and-white photographs of clouds above the correct names. He read library books that contained star charts, diagrams of atoms, and shaded drawings of lunar eclipses, and for his first science project he presented a thick sheaf of notebook pages covered in black construction paper and bound with brass fasteners, in which he discussed the major theories of the origin of the moon. He was equally ambitious in Math, in

English, and in American History, where in early October he
began to prepare for his project on The Thirteen Colonies, due
on December first; and even in the less important subjects that
met once a week he showed excessive industry, laboring over
the correct use of the India-ink pen in Art, and in Metal Shop
making a careful mold in the foundry, into which a frowning
teacher wearing a green leather apron poured hot liquid metal
that cooled into a perfect ashtray-map of Connecticut. His
manner toward others was much relaxed. Perhaps because many
faces were now familiar, he no longer held himself entirely
aloof; he even joked occasionally with the brightest girls. In
gym he changed quickly, concealing his growth of darkening
blond hairs, and he showered with downcast eyes. But to my
surprise he climbed the rope halfway; and although he was not
very good at tumbling, and could not perform the backward
roll at all, he was an aggressive volleyball player and was able
to walk the parallel bars, unlike five other boys in the class. And
sometimes it seemed to me that all of William's activity was
only a fierce effort to shield himself from my dangerous restlessness.

For I was restless, I was restless, I was unbearably restless.
And can't you hear that hiss in *restless,* that coiled snake waiting to strike ... My restlessness began on the first day of class
and grew steadily worse until by the end of September it was
clear that something would have to be done. Schoolwork had
never interested me much, and my classmates all seemed pecu-
liarly disagreeable instances of the brutal and the bland. Girl-
friends were a matter of dates and dances, which I instinctively
despised. It was as if I were carrying within me an insatiable
monster of boredom, feeding on everything. Sometimes I was
able to breathe easily in some splendid spacious book, which
affected me like a burst of fresh air in a stifling room, but increasingly I found my attention wandering from the page. Odd
fancies took me. I imagined myself buying a gun and shooting
a classmate in the foot. I imagined myself running about and
biting people, like a mad dog. One day I bit down on my finger,

to see how hard I could bite. My rather sharp teeth pressed in until my finger throbbed, and still I had barely begun to bite, my jaws had the power of a machine, I forced them more tightly together until suddenly my teeth itched and I had to let go. There were deep red-blue marks in my finger, but I had not even drawn blood, no, I had not even begun to bite.

And then, one bright September morning, as I was walking along my street toward the bus-stop, I happened to glance to the right, where at the end of a long dirt driveway stood an open, empty garage. And at once, as if without my collusion, a plan took shape, a secret plan that soothed my secret fever. Oh, it was nothing much, my plan, but to me it was all in all. The odd thing was, I had passed the Chernaks' garage daily without giving it a thought. And now each morning as I passed the open garage a secret thrill would ripple through me as I darted a glance at its conspiring depths. And perhaps I hesitated for so long simply because of that sweet secret thrill. Old man Chernak worked all day in a machine shop. No one ever saw Mrs. Chernak. The windows of the neighboring house showed no signs of life. The real danger was from the houses across the street, from any one of which someone might happen to glance out as I suddenly turned into the driveway. And for a long while I could not solve the problem of the houses, until one day I thought to walk on the other side of the street and found that the long narrow driveway, flanked by high two-family houses, was only partially visible from the two nearest opposite houses. And one sunny morning as I strolled casually toward the corner bus-stop where two boys were standing with their backs to me, I glanced to the left, where the houses were shady and silent, and suddenly I turned into the Chernaks' driveway, walking swiftly, but not too swiftly, along the grassy strip between the hard dirt ruts, glancing up at the dark windows to the left and right, giving a start as I saw the sudden motion of my legs in a cellar window, holding my breath as I came into view of the ominous back yards, but all was deserted, all was peaceful, all was dead, a gray steel chair sat emptily on its porch, two empty brown milkbottles sat in a wire basket, a hand-mower stood against the side of a chestnut tree, and entering the shady garage I stepped to the left and stood flat against a narrow piece of wall with my back against a shovel and hoe. Breathing heavily I stared at my new watch with its black leather band, a present from mother for my thirteenth birthday. Several times I was tempted to step out of the garage, walk back along the driveway, and rejoin my usual life. It was not too late, it was never too late, even if the bus had arrived I could run back along the driveway to the sidewalk and shout, and wave ... And how strange it was to imagine the door of the bus folding shut without me, and William frowning in his seat, how strange it was to imagine the bus driving off into the distance, growing smaller and smaller until at last it turned out of sight, leaving behind the curb, the sidewalk, the indifferent telephone poles ... I waited until ten minutes beyond the usual time of the bus's arrival. Then stepping cautiously from my hiding place with my weight of books, I walked to the back of the garage, climbed the broken picket fence, and stepped into the weeds and bushes of the slope. Crouching awkwardly I made my way along the top of the slope beside the broken picket fence. The pickets changed to a bent wire fence and then to a ragged row of forsythia and at last to the tall hedge of my back yard. Peeking through I saw Mrs. Schneider's empty rocker on the upper back porch. At once I pressed through the hedge. Avoiding the highly visible porch I hurried to the sloping cellar door beside the garbage cans, where lifting the tin-covered wooden flap, descending four concrete steps, and quietly lowering the flap over my head, I was safe in darkness. I placed my heavy books on a step and sat breathing heavily. But almost at once I picked them up and descended the last two steps to the wooden door with the loose doorknob. Before the door was a bristly doormat. Under the bristly doormat was a green-stained key. Opening the door softly, replacing the key, and closing the door softly behind me, I locked it from the inside and made my way past the rusty white boiler to the gray wooden steps. At the dark top of the stairs I opened another door and stepped into the bright silence of the kitchen.

The little china dairymaid with her little brown buckets looked at me from the windowsill. Two white plates bordered with red apples sat hushed in the yellow dishrack. On the checkered red-and-white oilcloth of the kitchen table sat a glass saltshaker, a sugarbowl with red apples, and a brown radio. One chair was pulled out slightly from the table. And how strange it was to imagine my empty desk in homeroom, my empty desk in English, my empty desk in Art... Carefully, ever so carefully, I tiptoed from the kitchen, across the deserted dining room, and into the sunny brown living room. Father's chair was watching television. The shadow of a branch lay across the green screen. Quietly, ever so quietly, I walked across the room and let myself down into the softness of father's chair. I placed my books on the floor beside me and removed from among them a library novel. But for a long time I could not read, and sat in stillness, with my hand pressed to my pounding heart.

27

MY MILD CRIME went entirely unnoticed. When mother came home from school she found me in my room as usual, lazily reading a library novel, and the next day, when my homeroom teacher asked for the required note, I reached into all my pockets and could not find it. "Oh," she said, "well, don't look so glum, heavens, you can always bring it in tomorrow." And with her hand she made a gesture of dismissal, as if to say that such rules were not meant to apply to a person like me. The next day I forgot to bring my note, and thereafter the matter was forgotten. I confessed the truth to William, however, fearing that he might mention my absence during his next visit, and wondering a little what he would say. To my annoyance he seemed annoyed. "I don't get it," he said with a frown. "What's the point of that?" "Oh," I said, in a bored manner, and shrugged. Yet it must have troubled him in some way, for the next day he mentioned it again. "I don't get it. You have to make up the work anyway. What's the point?" "Oh," I said, and shrugged again. With sudden vehemence William said: "I wish you wouldn't do that: shrug like that." I shrugged again, and William looked away with a frown.

Boredom is exhausting. My little deed, far from assuaging my restlessness, acted as a further irritant. A vague desire to disrupt my life took possession of me, combined with a curious paralysis of the imagination. I could think of nothing whatever to do. Images of self-destruction flapped their wings in gloomy caverns of my mind, but the idea of death was far too fictional for me to take it seriously. Shiny black guns, shiny silver knives, bright red blooddrops were illustrations on the jackets of mystery novels, and mystery novels bored me to death. And perhaps it was simply that I feared for myself, and longed to protect myself against the harm to myself I cruelly sought. And perhaps it was simply that I was tired, tired . . . for there is nothing, O innocent and bustling reader, more exhausting than boredom. I would wake each morning with a feeling of heaviness, as if I had scarcely slept, whereas in truth I had been sleeping more and more. I seemed to have barely enough energy to force myself through the tedious motions of my day. Home from school, I would lie down on my bed and dream away the time over some novel or other, and after dinner I would "do" my homework, and then I would read some more, and suddenly I would open my eyes in drowsy confusion, wondering where I was, wondering about that gray piece of wood which made no sense at all, wondering what was happening to me, until all at once I felt a motion in my mind, comprehension, like a muscle, tensed within me, the gray wood became the bottom of my windowsill, and all about me rose another morning.

And then one morning as I opened my eyes the joyful knowledge dawned upon me that I would not have to go to school at all that day because it was summer. Hot sunlight soaked through my shut blinds, outside in the sunny green world the robins and sparrows were swaying on the leafy hedge-branches, plump bees hummed among blossoms of honeysuckle, somewhere a panting dog circled round and round and lay down in dark green shade, lowering his head sleepily onto his paws, reading and dreaming I could while away all of the long slow lazy summer day, but something was odd, something was wrong, there was the windowsill, there was the window, some piece of knowledge was about to burst within me, something I had to know at all costs, something to do with the brown rubber cord of the heater by my bed . . . and at once my mind filled with the chill knowledge that it was a sunny autumn morning.

And I was so tired! When I opened my eyes, how I longed to lie there drowsily forever, listening to the busy sounds of the morning, to the hiss of water in the bathroom sink and the thump of the turned-off hot-water tap, to the clash of the brass loops as father opened and closed the drawers of his bureau, over and over again, for reasons I could not imagine. And I was so tired, so tired! How I longed to close my eyes forever, to sleep, to dream, to drift away, to drown, to die . . . but far away I could hear a slap of slippered footsteps coming closer and closer, all at once there was a terrific banging, "Up and at 'em!" cried father, the door flew inward, I felt on my neck an unpleasant breeze, and I saw the blue-white-and-black tail of father's checkered bathrobe lifting in the wind of his hurried passing.

And I was so tired, so tired! As I walked to the bus-stop, drowsily in the mornings, I took pleasure in the evidences of decay. Under a summer-blue sky I passed beneath branches of rich green leaves brightened with patches of yellow. A shiny dark-red leaf, streaked with green, lay flat on the black windshield of a tan station wagon, its red stem trapped beneath the rubber of a slightly raised wiper. The summery sun gleamed on a yellow hydrant, on a silver fender, on the black roof of a garage, and suddenly, before me, a large green maple-leaf fell from a dark branch. It dropped swiftly and as if heavily, with scarcely a flutter, and landed with a faint smack at my toes. At the side of a house, a sunny strip of earth contained a row of blossomless stems. I felt myself becoming a connoisseur of decay, and I dreamed of starting an autumn garden, composed of rows of ruined summer flowers. And always, behind the violins of summer, faintly I heard the dark flutes of autumn... One night the wind howled, and the next morning many yellow leaves lay about. Under a bare hedge I saw a stiff sparrow. Stooping over, I touched the delicate hard beak, I stroked the sleek, cold back. Through the chill feathers, with a shudder of delight, I felt the little nubs of bones, like bumps of a disease. That afternoon the sky darkened over. And how I loved those gloomy autumn skies, those dark brooding clouds that drained the luster from the colors of things and brought out tones unknown to summer: the damp melancholy browns of tree-trunks and telephone poles, the gloomy pallor of sidewalks, the doleful darkness of grass...

28

I FIRST SAW MY TRIPLE at the end of October. He appeared in homeroom one melancholy day, a languid and dreamy William with brooding heavy-lidded eyes. His dark brown hair was parted on the left, forming a white line, and faintly in his forehead, as if the skin were translucent, you could see the pale blue outline of a vein. The backs of his hands were soft and cream-colored, except where the knuckles rose up, forming rednesses that looked painful. At the ends of the second and third fingers of his right hand, dark yellow stains were visible. He sat drowsily in his chair with his cheek resting against the back of a hand, gazing off through eyes that seemed perpetually half-closed. There was about him an air of illness, of exhaustion, of precocious decadence, and from the very beginning William fiercely avoided him. And perhaps I too would have avoided him, had not William remained so busily inaccessible. Not only did he fail to ride home with me more than once or twice a week, but he no longer rode over on his bicycle every weekend. He was always busy busy busy with some wretched task or other. He would explain impatiently that he had to attend a meeting of the newly formed Mineralogy Club after school; he had been elected Secretary and had to write up the minutes in detail. It was all very stupid but it had to be done; besides, it was good practice. Practice for what? Oh, practice for later life; that sort of thing came in handy. One boy had brought in a rock-tumbler. Had I ever seen one? I ought to stop by sometime and have a look. No, that Saturday the club was going into New York to visit the Museum of Natural History. He didn't know when he'd have time for all his homework. He envied me . . . Often I would look up from my desk in study hall to see him bent over his work with a frown of angry concentration, writing ferociously in his three-ring notebook, erasing with loud rubbing sounds, and flicking away the eraser-dust with vigorous sweeps of the side of his pinky. There was something unpleasant about it all, as if he were engaged in an act of destruction. Then I would shift my gaze ever so slightly to a quiet desk two rows away and one seat back. And for a long while I would gaze at that dreamy boy, with his pale blue vein and his brooding heavy-lidded eyes.

Often you would see him sitting drowsily in his chair with his cheek resting on the back of a hand, gazing off through eyes that seemed perpetually half-closed. If at these moments he caught you looking at him, two spots of red would appear in his pallid cheeks, and his lips would curl in a faintly mocking smile.

And yet he was not simply an effete William, a wilting William, a William in watercolor. Rumor had it that he had been expelled from a private school, though no one knew why, and his classroom behavior, though always correct, carried with it the faintest suggestion of insolence. It was as if the effort of enduring it all required in him a constant painful tension of the will. His schoolwork was oddly erratic. He would do his work like everyone else and then, without offering an excuse, he would fail to hand in an assignment. He would promise politely to bring it in the next day but the next day he would again fail to hand it in, without offering an excuse. But his failure to offer an excuse was not in the spirit of blushing evasion or open rebellion, it was far more in the spirit of indifferent frankness: he had no excuse. He had simply chosen not to do the assignment. And this angered teachers far more than if he had uttered a transparent lie, for it revealed his terrible remoteness from their world: it was as though he had sudden lapses of interest in their lives. You would see him sitting quietly at his seat, looking as if he had just dreamed himself into being, or looking as if he had not quite made up his mind to go that far, looking in fact as if he were not quite energetic enough to exist but not quite bored enough not to, and something in the manner of his stillness would begin to attract the irritated attention of the teacher, who would suddenly turn on him with a sharp question, as if to reprimand him for interrupting the class. Yet if there was about him that air of pale exhaustion, as if he were melting in the sun, at the same time there were hints of secret strains and excitements. He would be reading drowsily in his chair with his cheek resting on the back of a hand, gazing at the page through eyes that seemed perpetually half-closed, and in the blue-shadowed hollow of his temple you could see, like a miniature heartbeat, the faint and rapid throbbing of his pulse. Once, as he sat brooding over some volume of verse or book of tales, I saw his lips twist into a sudden grimace. He shut the book instantly, not slamming it but closing it with quick ominous quietness, and sat staring at his desk, the very picture of idle dreaminess except that one hand was clenched in a tight pale fist. But it was not only while reading that he seemed to reveal the other side of drowsiness. Sometimes, when he sat motionless at his desk, gazing at the back of the chair in front of him while a teacher talked and talked, you would become aware of a sudden quickening, a sudden tautening, a sudden tensing—and the poise of his head and the angle of his shoulders suggested not languor but a strained alertness, as if he were listening to distant music. At such moments I had the sensation that, in him, sensitivity had been developed to the point of corruption. And sometimes, as he sat with an expression of calm weariness on his face, he would frown suddenly to himself. Then lifting a hand to his forehead he would rub the smooth space between his eyebrows with two fingers, stroking from his forehead down to the hollow at the top of his nose.

Always among his schoolbooks you would see, like a brooding stranger at a boring party, some alien book, with a scrap of white paper sticking out.

William fiercely avoided him. William did not merely avoid him, William despised him; and he carried avoidance to the point of impudence. He seemed to quiver with hatred if Philip came within ten feet of him. Once, as William and I were strolling on the playground, we came upon Philip sitting alone on a cinderblock beside the wire fence at the side of the parking lot, with a pile of schoolbooks by his leg and a slender faded volume in his lap. Philip, shocked out of a revery, glanced up with a start. At once William turned around and strode off with his back to Philip, I skipping to keep up with him. Another time, in the cafeteria, William and I were sitting across from one another at a table where only one other boy was sitting. The two chairs on William's side were empty, and there was an empty chair between the third boy and me. Philip emerged from behind the cash register at the end of the silver rail, holding his tray awkwardly against his stomach and looking vaguely about for a seat. At last he came to our table and sat down on William's side, two seats away. William, who had been talking vigorously about the birth of the moon, plunged into stormy silence. I asked him a question, which he shrugged away. For a while he chewed angrily on his hamburger, and then, raising his head, began to look around with a frown. A moment later he said: "Good. Let's try that table over there," and at once stood up and carried his tray to a nearby table with two free chairs. I was annoyed, for I preferred to have an empty chair beside me when I ate, and I felt it was rude for William to abandon our table without consulting me. As I rose, I glanced over at Philip, as if in apology; but he was frowning down into the pages of a dark book that he had tucked under an edge of his plate.

29

IT WAS NOT TOO LONG after his appearance among us that an incident occurred in English class which made Philip generally disliked. Our class had received the assignment of committing to memory any poem by an American poet. A mimeographed list of suggested poems had been distributed, and each of us had to recite his poem in front of the entire class. It was the sort of assignment that made me sick with foreboding, for I could not endure standing in front of everyone and being examined by those keen, shrewd, merciless eyes. I could not even endure having my name called out, for exposed to that hushed multiplicity of hearing, I experienced a sensation of audible nudity. I had scarcely slept at all the night before, and as I sat waiting at my desk for the torment to begin, I could do nothing but repeat over and over again, in silent desperation, the opening lines of my poem: "This is the ship of pearl, which, poets feign, Sails the unshadowed main. This is the ship of pearl, which, poets feign, Sails the unshadowed main. This is the ship of pearl, which, poets feign, Shails the unshadowed sails the unsadowed this is the sip of pearl"—for I clung to the belief that if only I could manage to recite the first lines flawlessly, even though they no longer possessed any meaning, the remaining lines would be sure to follow, even though I no longer remembered them.

With ominous cheerfulness Mrs. Barlowe seated herself at an empty desk at the back of the room. Opening her green leather grade-book, she called the first name. Mary Schuyler strode briskly to the front of the class, stood firmly before us, and glancing coolly from face to face recited "Annabel Lee" in a brisk, efficient, rather cheerful voice. I glanced over at William, who was frowning down fiercely at his desk. Two rows away, Philip gazed idly out the window, with his usual expression of heavy-lidded languor. Mary Schuyler paraded back to her seat and Beverly Mason gave a throbbing recital of "To a Waterfowl," looking off mistily into the distance. Tony Lutka, flushing darkly, angrily muttered "To Helen." Judy Lee began to recite "Annabel Lee," gave a little giggle, suddenly forgot everything, and miserably jumped to the last stanza. Valery Jarzynski recited "Old Ironsides." William, in a grim monotone, recited "The Concord Hymn." Gene Masso recited "Annabel Lee." Someone recited the opening lines of "Hiawatha." "Well," said Mrs. Barlowe, "we have time for one more," and suddenly I could not remember my opening line, I could not remember the name of my poem, I could not remember the name of my poet, but she chose Philip Schoolcraft.

Slowly, dreamily, he walked with lowered eyes to the front of the room, where at the central desk he turned to face us. And as he turned, he lifted for a moment his heavy-lidded eyes, throwing a quick dark excited glance over the seated faces. At once he lowered his eyes, and for a few moments he stood silently in front of us. Then abruptly raising his face to the map at the back of the room, he began to recite in a soft, quick voice: "The Red Death had long devastated the country. No pestilence had ever been so fatal, or so hideous. Blood was its Avatar and its seal—the redness and the horror of blood. There were sharp pains, and sudden dizziness, and then profuse bleeding at the pores, with dissolution. The scarlet stains upon the body—" Mary Schuyler was whispering to Bonnie Pearson, William was frowning, Mrs. Barlowe was rapping her knuckles on the desk. "That will do. That will do nicely, thank you.

Now suppose you tell me exactly what you think you're doing, mister. I would sincerely like to know. And let's get one thing straight, mister: I don't like wise-guys. You are supposed to be reciting a poym." Philip said nothing, but stood in silence with lowered eyes; and as the whispers grew louder and Mrs. Barlowe shouted for him to sit down and see her after class, two spots of red glowed in his pallid cheeks, and his lips curled in a faintly mocking smile.

30

HE INVITED ME TO HIS HOUSE, one dark November day, when a few last withered leaves hung from bare branches like pieces of old tinsel on abandoned Christmas trees, and dead brown leaves, curled into cylinders, lay in the gutters like old cigars. He lived at the end of the bus-route, in the old part of town, on an avenue of ancient elms. At the end of a weedgrown cracked front walk I saw two rows of black-shuttered windows, and high above, in the sloping black roof, three dormer windows with peaked black roofs. On both sides of the house rose tall dark chimneys covered with trailing vines. A thin line of smoke, mixed with sparks, twisted from the chimney on the right. In the high dark grass of the unmown lawns lay scraps of old newspaper, a brown paper bag, a garbage-can cover, and a rusty rake; and a long faded lawnchair, pierced by tall grassblades, lay half-buried beside a fallen doe. On each side of the walk a great elm rose up, forming an archway of intermingled branches, and as we passed between the noble pair I could not help noticing the mushroom-like growths on the knobbed and peeling bark. "Blighted," said Philip, catching my look, in a tone of grim satisfaction. Dark untrimmed bushes lined the front of the house and grew up above the windowsills, and as we approached the house a broad appearance of whiteness gave way to specific images of soilure. The weathered clapboards were flaking badly, and the two round wooden pillars of the small portico were streaked with lines of soot and rust. The two brick steps were crumbling at the edges, and a faded red-and-black doormat, crookedly placed, revealed rusty rods of metal where the rubber was torn. Beside the doormat sat a large earthen flowerpot, packed with hard dirt, from which blossomed a tilted gray stick with a piece of white string tied to it. On both sides of the peeling white door with its big black knocker rose tall narrow strips of glass, on one of which lay the scraped remains of a Red Cross sticker. To my disappointment Philip did not bang the big black knocker but removed from his pocket a cordovan keycase at the end of which dangled a nickel-colored key. When the door opened I stepped after Philip into a dim high-ceilinged front hall. Straight ahead a dark-carpeted stairway rose to a dusky landing. To the left was a dim room in which I saw part of a dark table with part of a cut-glass bowl beneath part of a hanging candelabrum that held brass candles with flames of glass. Through an open doorway on the right I saw a dim, almost dark living room. Over a great fireplace in the right wall loomed an enormous brown painting set in a deep tarnished-gilt frame. Beside the fireplace stood a stiff-backed faded-dark-red armchair with little mahogany lion-heads sticking up at the corners. "Philip?" came a quiet voice, and I stepped behind Philip into the dusky parlor.

Against the left wall stood a faded-dark-red couch with little mahogany lion-heads sticking up at the corners and little fat lion-paws sticking out below. At the far end a thin pale woman in a white dress half-sat half-lay against a lamplit corner. Her feet were tucked under a slanting couch-pillow and on the floor beside her lay two white sandals. Her eyes were closed. Her straw-colored hair was combed so tightly back that it seemed to be pulling her head back against the couch. One arm was raised so that the pink-flushed elbow rested against the couchback and the pale forearm lay pressed against her forehead with the palm outward. Upon her white stomach rested a blood-red book with the pages facing inward; a pale, slender hand, lax at the wrist, lay drooped over the cover. Bluish shadows lay beneath her closed eyes, and faintly in her forehead, as if the skin were translucent, you could see the pale blue outline of a vein. "Mother," said Philip, in a neutral tone. Slowly her eyes opened, and for a moment she cast upon us a brooding heavy-lidded gaze. But almost at once her eyes fell closed, and Philip, motioning vaguely with a hand, murmured: "My mother." In a hushed voice I said: "How do you do." Without moving, without opening her eyes, Mrs. Schoolcraft said: "It's so nice, so very nice . . . Philip, haven't I asked you . . ." "It's all right, Mother, he's . . . all right. Would you like me to fetch your pills, Mother?" "Yes, that would be nice, Philip, you may fetch, as you say, the blue ones in the brown bottle, and really, Philip, you are sounding more implausible every day. You go up now and I'll . . . and I'll . . . and really, Philip, I am not in the mood . . ." "Yes, Mother," said Philip, placing his pile of books carefully on the slanting couch-pillow. Swiftly he left the room as the pile toppled softly.

I looked about uncertainly for a place to sit down, and chose at last the stiff-backed armchair beside the fireplace. Carefully I placed my books on the dark faded rug with its dim pattern of brown branches and yellow leaves and brown-blue-and-yellow birds. I faced Mrs. Schoolcraft, who took no notice of me but continued to sit with her eyes closed and one arm pressed across her forehead. There was a damp warmth in the room and a smell of woodsmoke. All the long curtains were drawn. Against the drawn curtains at the right-hand end of the room an old piano with yellowing keys stood beside a curve-necked standing-lamp upon whose dark yellow shade dim green birds were fly-ing. Tattered music-books lay scattered over the piano-top, and on the dusty music-bench a long white glove lay beside a paper rose. Beside me, in the fireplace, a small smoky fire seemed about to die. The painting over the fireplace showed a stormy landscape, all grays and browns except for a luminous pallor in one corner that threw a watery brightness over a solitary bent black tree.

Between the long-curtained windows of the left wall a mahogany rocking-chair seemed to be leaning back too far, as if it
held an invisible grandmother, and above it hung an irregular
arrangement of small oval portraits covered with glass. Across
from me, over the faded-dark-red couch, hung a painting of a
raven-haired lady in a white dress, wearing a black mask. She
sat indolently on a dark blue couch with one arm thrown over
the back and one hand clasping a lacy black fan. Mrs. Schoolcraft said: "But then, don't you find it all so very ... I suppose
I should really make an effort to say something, though frankly
... Philip has told me so much about you, Charles. But what an
absurd lie, of course he never tells me anything. Forgive me,
I ... These dreadful headaches ... Let's talk about the weather,
shall we? I loathe weather, don't you? Adolescence, I imagine,
must be quite a bore. Those dreadful little boys with their
ghastly little secrets ... and all the sad girls ... And you know,
when I was a girl, Father would bring me apples ... lovely red
apples ... Of course this is all too impossible, you realize that
under no circumstances ... But then, what does it matter, after
all ... And one is so drowsy, so very drowsy ... after all ...
And it was always so drowsy, in the evening ... on the verandah
... when I was queen of the apple blossoms ... It was always so
drowsy, in the evening. The four of us would sit outside, on
the verandah. Henry—that was our dog—would bring Father
the paper. One day—I can still remember it as though it were
yesterday—I climbed the apple tree. Everyone was very upset,
of course. Mother was very angry. She said I was a bad, bad
girl. But Father only smiled and said ... my little princess. Then
with his napkin he made me a paper crown. Mother was very
angry but Father put the crown on my head and said my queen,
my queen of apple blossoms. Then mother went inside, she was
very angry, Father said Mary, Mary, I could hear them through
the glass door, mother was crying and saying You always thwart
me, you do, you do, you always thwart me, I hate you, and
Father said Mary, Mary, and I took off my crown and I tore
it into a thousand shreds. But how my mind wanders! ... and

how one meanders ... on a November afternoon ... And one
feels at times so very like a parody ... so very, very like a
parody ... and if only one knew, if only one knew ... if only
one knew ... then it would all ... it would all, it would all ...
but then, you know, the most interesting people ... and really,
you know, the most fascinating people ... and don't you think
the most memorable people ... are always parodies ... take
Proust, for example ... which reminds me of that dreadful ass
in the bookstore who told me she was reading Prowst. Oh but
Mrs. Ostheimer, I said, surely you mean Proast. And oh, God,
it's all so ... and the irony, and the mockery ... say something,
why don't you say something ... Philip is in the throes of Poe,
the poor darling. Imagines himself to be a sort of Poe-ette.
Surely, Charles, you have heard of monsieur Poedelaire ... this
dreadful generation ... and then, one day, there was no one to
bring me apples ... Is that you, Philip? I thought I heard a foot-
step. And how does it go, in that old story, don't you remember, oh I have it: it's only the wind. Be a dear and stir the fire,
Charles, I feel chilled through and through. And I feel, you
know, so cold, in this drafty old house. And you know, when I
was a girl, Father would bring me apples ... lovely red apples ... Ah, Philip, Charles and I have been having a delightful,
an absolutely delightful ... thank you, thank you, such filial
devotion is really ... and really, Philip, I am simply not in the
mood ..."

Swiftly Philip gathered his fallen books. Gathering my own
fallen books and nodding to Mrs. Schoolcraft, whose eyes, briefly
lifted, had already closed, I followed Philip out of the living
room to the dark-carpeted stairway, where a dark brown wooden
globe sat upon a four-cornered post. The thick balusters consisted
each of a squarish top and bottom that held a central piece
shaped like a bowling pin. At the top of the stairs we came to a
dusky hall stretching away on the left and right. The faded wallpaper showed a repeated pattern of faded green willows shading
a faded brown pond where a faded boy in blue sat with his faded
fishing pole. Turning right, we walked past two white doors to

a dark brown door with a peeling brown knob. Shifting his books to the other arm, Philip opened the door and led the way up a dark uncarpeted flight of creaking wooden steps. At the top we entered a dark cluttered attic with sloping beams. A tall muddy mirror on short curving legs with a dark zigzag crack down the center reflected in two unmatching parts the black-and-pink painting of a vase. Beside it stood a torso with smooth nippleless breasts and smooth blank loins balanced on a pole. Around the headless neck hung a frayed extension-cord and scattered on the floor beneath it were a red glass Christmas-tree ball, a dented fencer's mask, and a stiff white glove with curved fingers that lay palm downward like a hand resting on a table. By my feet a blond-haired doll's face with rosy cheeks and little red lips and glassy blue eyes stared up at me. Beside it, in a torn white nightgown with faded pink bows, lay a headless doll from whose open neck poured gray clumps of stuffing. Making our way past a dark chest of drawers with one missing drawer, a hooded black baby carriage from which a blown-out umbrella protruded, cartons of dusty pink dishes, piles of fallen paper-backs, a black rubber plunger with a yellow handle, we came to an unpainted wooden door with a bronze knob. Shifting his books to his other arm, Philip tugged at the door and at last jerked it open with a wooden squeak. We stepped into a short dim hallway ending in a dusty round window. The wallpaper showed faded ballerinas in green, pink, and lilac skirts, pirouet-ting, leaping, and bowing among faded bouquets of green, pink, and lilac flowers. At the end of the hallway Philip stopped be-fore a tall white door on the left with a loose brown doorknob. Placing his books on the floor, he turned the doorknob carefully and began pushing against the door with his shoulder. At last he knocked his hip against the door, which suddenly flew open with a rattle of its knob.

It was a small smoky room with a beamed sloping ceiling. The ceiling plunged to a strip of wall that opened into a small space at the end of which was a dusty dormer window composed of many small panes. One pane was black and opaque, as if the window had a patch over its eye. The window was half-covered by one of two faded blue curtains hanging from a bent metal rod; it looked out at the upper reaches of an elm, one of whose branches came twisting almost to the sill. Along the sloping left and right walls, bookshelves reaching from floor to ceiling were lined with dusty faded sets of leaning books. Against the bookshelves on the right stood a small bed without a spread. On the rumpled yellowish sheet lay a scattering of books, a dark blue bathrobe, and a chipped coffee cup with a pattern of red cherries and green leaves, half-filled with smashed cigarette butts. At the foot of the bed stood a brown wooden chair holding a small open phonograph, on which sat a dull black record with a bright black scratch. Against the remaining wall, near the door, stood a dark brown chest of drawers with two pale circles where knobs were missing. On top of the chest of drawers stood an empty coffee-jar, a dark green winebottle half full of black-looking wine, and an aluminum photograph-frame without a photograph. On the wall above were three black-and-white illustrations. The first showed a man in a stovepipe hat holding a smoky torch before an opening in a wall of stone. Behind him stood a wide-eyed man with his mouth open and the back of one hand pressed to his forehead. In the wall-opening stood a long-haired corpse with a black cat perched on its head. Under the picture were the words: UPON HIS HEAD SAT THE HIDEOUS BEAST. The second illustration showed a man sitting on the fat black branch of a tree. Below him, where the landscape dropped away, two very small figures stood at the edge of a cliff. At the twisting end of the branch was a large grinning skull. Under the picture were the words: THE CLIMBER WAS SOME SIXTY FEET FROM THE GROUND. The third illustration showed a plump lady with stringy black hair and one partially bared breast, standing in a white robe before a dim four-poster bed. One arm held high a corner of her robe and the other hand rested on the back of her head. Under the picture were the words: IT WAS THE LADY LIGEIA. The only other piece of furniture in Philip's room was a white wooden chair, on which sat a crumpled pack of cigarettes and an open silver matchbook, displaying wide white matches with a red inn printed on them. The threadbare maroon rug, full of dark stains, was littered with rumpled underwear, open books turned face downward, and empty coffeejars. In one corner a dusty pile of uncovered records stood beside a tarnished bronze lady on a round black base; she had bare bronze breasts and broken arms, and the bottom half of her body was draped in thick bronze folds. Nearby stood a large empty aquarium with dusty green sides, containing white and pink pebbles among which lay a fallen coral cave, a ruined temple, a dark green mermaid, a bent teaspoon, and a dirty black sock draped over a school copy of *Johnny Tremain*. At my feet stood another statue. He was about eight inches high and made of white marble. He was entirely naked, with a little white marble penis and little white marble testicles. One hand, bent at the wrist, lay languidly against his chest, and the other arm was raised so that the elbow pointed upward and the hand rested behind his head. Leaning back dreamily with closed eyes, the head nearly touched one shoulder. There was about him an air of languid, swooning, sensual abandon, as if he were a woman posing seductively, and it was with a mild shock of surprise that, stooping over, I read the metal plaque on the base: THE DYING SLAVE.

Philip offered me a cigarette, which I refused, and as he lit his own he looked away with the trace of a mocking smile. He then proceeded to show me his books. He was particularly fond of two different sets of the complete works of Poe: six black volumes with dull gilt titles that said THE WORKS OF POE, and five gray volumes with faded black titles that said POE'S WORKS. He removed one gray volume, blowing dust from the top, and carefully opened it to the yellowing frontispiece. The black-and-white illustration showed a man sitting in an armchair and staring up at the top of a tall white door. Upon the lintel sat a white bust, and upon the bust sat a black bird that cast a large black shadow on the wall behind. Under the illustration was the word: NEVERMORE. Philip also owned the complete works of Stevenson, a flaking crimson set with gilt titles that stretched on and on across one long shelf. "Have you read Stevenson?" asked Philip, carefully removing a flaking volume, as if it were made of glass. The cover left red marks on his palms and fingers. "Have I read Stevenson?" I said in confusion, for no one had ever asked me whether I had read an author, but only whether I had read a particular book. But at once I added: "Oh yes, I've read *The Black Arrow, Treasure Island, Kidnapped*..." "But that's nothing, everyone reads that. But have you read *The Suicide Club?*" "*The Suicide Club!* No, I didn't know, I never, it sounds..." "It's in *The New Arabian Nights*," said Philip, and opening the volume very carefully, he turned to the table of contents. "You see," he said, pointing with a yellow-stained finger to the words "The Suicide Club." Then holding the book carefully in his left hand, he turned several pages swiftly and carefully with his right hand, resting his long thumb lightly against the page and turning with his yellow-stained index finger delicately from the top. He stopped at a page entitled THE SUICIDE CLUB. Beneath the title was a curious subtitle: *Story of the Young Man with the Cream Tarts.* Pointing with his finger, in a low voice Philip began to read: " 'During his residence in London, the accomplished Prince Florimel of Bohemia gained the affection of all classes by the seduction of his manner and by a well-considered generosity. He was a remarkable man even by what was known of him; and that was but a small part of what he actually did. Although of a placid temperament in ordinary circumstances, and accustomed to take the world with as much philosophy as any ploughman, the Prince of Bohemia was not without a taste for ways of life more adventurous and eccentric than that to which he was destined by his birth.' " Looking up abruptly Philip said: "You can always tell by the first three sentences." He paused, and I had a confused impression that I was supposed to say something, but after some moments of silence he continued, somewhat impatiently: "But you should read it yourself. I can't lend you this copy, though. But wait, I have another one." And abruptly closing the book, and replacing it carefully among its flaking companions, he reached up to the next shelf and removed a dull red volume. "Here," he said, clutching the book tightly, "let's bring it over to the bed, you have to be careful with these old volumes..." And with a distinct air of excitement he carried the book over to the bed and placed it on the rumpled sheet. "Here," he said, "why don't you open it? Don't pick it up, though, just open the cover, these old books are very fragile..." And although I had been warned by his air of excitement, still I was somewhat shocked to see, when I carefully opened that dull red cover, a black revolver lying in the hollow book.

31

AND NOW I BEGAN TO GO about increasingly with Philip School-craft, much to the evident disgust of William, who directed at me from increasing distances frowns of furious disapproval. He refused to sit at the same table with Philip and me, and on the playground he strode off in the opposite direction whenever he saw us coming. Philip, for his part, was equally contemptuous of William, whom he referred to as "that scientist" or "that illiterate" or even "that Philistine," a word that at first I thought had to do with philately. Indeed for so delicate and languid a boy Philip was surprisingly full of hatreds and bitternesses. He mocked our classmates with continual soft savagery and referred to school in tones of quiet viciousness. He spoke with contempt of "schoolbooks" and "schoolboys" and "teachers and their problems." Once, to my puzzlement, he described school as "inartistic." At any rate it was, for him, less a form of active misery than a form of boredom carried to the point of pain. He seemed mildly content only in his room, and day after day I would ride home with him and climb stair after stair to his remote attic cave, where lighting a cigarette and stretching him-

self languidly on his bed he would bend an arm under his neck
and blow streams of smoke softly at the ceiling, while I sat
rather uncomfortably across from him on the threadbare rug
with my back against a bookshelf. Often there were long silences, during which I would listen to soft exhalations of smoke
or glance over my shoulder at the dark leaning rows of faded
flaking books. Sometimes, without a word, Philip would sit up
effortfully, and bending over the record player he would place
the needle on the dull black record with the bright black
scratch. Then he would lie back as if exhausted by his effort as
the phonograph emitted a brief loud scratchiness followed by a
sudden silence. And there rose from that silence the dark, doleful, solitary tone of a flute, which seemed to come from far
away and filled me with a restless sadness. I longed to halt the
music there forever, I longed to be penetrated by that tone as
wood is penetrated by water until each of its living particles is
replaced by a particle of stone, but almost at once the tone
rippled dreamily downward, pausing for a moment and then
climbing upward to its first perch, only to ripple dreamily
downward again, pausing for a moment and then climbing upward and with a lazy burst of energy fluttering to a higher
perch in an arch of three notes, before falling with a swoon
below, where clinging for a few moments it fluttered in another
arch of three notes and instantly dissolved in a shimmer of harpstrings, through which, in the distance, an echo of horns was
sounded; but through the whole drowsy, dreamy, dissolving
world of that faun-music, with its shimmering heat-waves and
dark green leafshade, its sudden violences dissolving into languor, I listened only for the return of the dark, doleful, solitary
flute, which seemed always about to appear, as if the entire
piece were nothing but the continual shattering of an image in
a pond, an image that scattered into a thousand flashing trembling bits that slowly, tremblingly, began to coalesce, only to
be flung apart again, while with softly beating temples and exasperated nerves I waited and waited for the dark, doleful,
solitary flute, waited and waited for that always imminent mo-

ment which with each passing heartbeat seemed less capable of satisfying the desire it was always creating, always increasing, until it seemed as if the very pressure of my desire were itself the force that prevented its satisfaction, waited and waited with softly beating temples, with exasperated nerves, with a patient excitement bordering on pain, so that when at last the instruments ceased and in the sensual silence I heard again the dark, doleful, solitary flute, I was pierced with a painful sweetness, a rapturous sorrow, a wild tranquility, a serene despair. O restless listless yearning-unyearning, drowsy delirium, fevered oblivion ... When the piece ended there was a revolving sound of scratchiness on two different pitches. After a while Philip sat up laboriously, without a word; and lifting the needle-arm, and turning off the phonograph with a dull click, he would lie down once again, and again there would be silence.

Sometimes we talked; or rather, he talked and I listened, adding a word hesitantly here and there. They were like nothing I had imagined, those murmured monologues, intensely literary and obscurely dangerous, utterly remote from the bookish conversations I had dreamed of having with a kindred soul. It wasn't so much the things he talked about as the tone of voice in which he talked: a low rather musical murmur with an undercurrent of tension, reminding me of a softly humming overhead wire with its dangerous burden of electricity. Perhaps for this reason I can scarcely remember a specific syllable of what passed between us. One thing is certain, that I quickly realized he was not interested in anything I had to say; in fact he seemed bored by everything in the universe except fiction and death. On these two subjects he would reveal signs of a hidden animation that left me excited and uneasy. One of his favorite notions was of a secret kinship between fiction and suicide. Both, he said, refused to accept the world as it was. Both were forms of murder: their victim was the universe. Far from being pale dreamers who longed to escape from an oppressive reality, the artist and the suicide were dangerous killers from whom reality, poor old reality, fled in vain. They were no more escapists than was a revolutionary who murdered a tyrant. Stevenson, in his Suicide Club, had invented a pleasant and clever game, but he had completely failed to understand its higher implications. He did not take suicide seriously; hence the curiously unsatisfying air of the story, with its odd mixture of comedy and moral indignation. In a true suicide club the members would spurn the notion of assistance, just as an artist spurns the notion of assistance in his works. The difficult act must be performed in solitude. But just as the artist takes consolation in the knowledge that other artists are struggling alongside him in his despised and solitary task, so the suicide is strengthened by the knowledge that he belongs to a band of brothers. A true suicide club is not a league of cowards but a society of soulmates dedicated to a secret cause. Thus Philip, lying on his back and blowing soft smoke-streams at the ceiling; and I across from him, listening to that dangerous hum. And always, as I listened, I would be filled with a strange, dreamy, fearful excitement, as if I were penetrating deeper and deeper into a dark forest from which I planned at the very next moment to turn back.

One dark afternoon we climbed the many stairs to Philip's room as usual. I sat against the bookshelves, as usual, and as usual Philip lay down wearily on his bed with one arm bent behind his neck, exhaling smoke with quiet blowing sounds and tapping with faint slapping sounds dark showers of ash toward a coffee-stained saucer on the floor. There seemed to be nothing much to say. Indeed I had noticed, as the afternoons passed, that there was increasingly little to say. Philip's range of talk was far narrower than at first I had imagined, and all his habits and gestures were intimately familiar to me. Even his brooding silences had come to seem unmysterious. There he lay, gazing up dreamily at the ceiling through long-lashed heavy-lidded eyes, while above him the thick smoke clung drowsily to the ceiling like some thick, soft, slowly undulating animal. Somewhat bored, I gazed over at the small half-curtained window, through which I could see a black branch against a gray sky. "This is boring," said Philip quietly. "Would you like to play a game?" And at once my heart began to beat faster, for Philip did not play games, and I said: "What kind of a game?" "A dangerous game," said Philip, blowing out smoke at the smoky ceiling. Then he turned his head drowsily in my direction and cast at me his brooding heavy-lidded gaze. "Oh," I said, avoiding his eyes, "I don't know, it all depends. What kind of dangerous game?" And at once the corners of his lips curled in faint mockery, and without answering he turned his face away and gazed up at the ceiling. There followed a long silence, during which I felt I had failed in some way, but still I felt a tightness in my stomach and a dryness in my throat. I stole a glance at the dark green wine-bottle on the chest of drawers, at the cup of cigarette butts on the white wooden chair, at the dark rows of flaking books, at the naked white statue, at the black sock in the aquarium, and I wondered what I was doing in this dangerous place, while in my warm room my cozy armchair sat emptily beside my standing lamp, and far away William sat frowning at his big dark desk, and Philip said: "Why don't you get down the old volume I once showed you—you remember—and bring it over to me. But be careful. Those old volumes are very fragile." And as if I had not heard a word I continued to sit with my back against the bookshelf while Philip continued to blow out smoke at the smoky ceiling. For a long while we stayed that way, I sitting there, he lying there, as if we were listening to music. Then I rose, as if to say good-bye, and when I turned I suddenly saw that book, as if his library consisted of a single volume or as if, searching among his books in vain, suddenly I had come upon it, long after giving up hope. But avoiding its gaze, I began to run my eyes along the shelf above, removing a dusty volume and opening to a page that began "ing with her face to face, in this very garden, basking in the" but at once I shut it with a dusty thud and thrust it back into place. Then I ran my eyes along a higher shelf, but as if my vision had expanded I was unable not to see the dull red volume which stood slightly pushed in between a slender black book and a thick gray book, so that a shadow was cast on the illegible gilt title, the crumbling spine. And as if I were anxious to improve the appearance of Philip's shelves, I pulled forward slightly the dull red volume so that it was flush with the black book and the gray book, and then I began to tip it out slowly. I removed it carefully. It was much too heavy. Carefully I carried it over to the bed.

Stretched out on his side, Philip leaned up laboriously on his right elbow, so that his right shoulder was pushed up beside his right cheek. With his right hand he opened the book and removed the revolver. It looked like one of my old cowboy pistols except that it was black with a dark blue sheen. It looked very black and dark-blue-shiny against Philip's pink-flushed pale hand. I stood before him, uncertain whether to sit down; finally I dropped to a squat before the bed. "You see," said Philip, holding the gun in his right hand and spinning the cylinder with his left. Almost at once he stopped the spin. "Now look," he said, swinging out the cylinder so that I could see the five black holes and the small brass circle. He tipped up the gun and a small bullet fell out onto the bed. It had a blunt leaden nose and a brassy body. It looked like a miniature bomb. Philip picked it up in his left hand and held it out in his palm. He gave it a little toss in the air, catching it in his palm, and then offered it to me. "No thanks," I said. "Well, let me just"—and taking it between thumb and forefinger I held it for a moment as delicately as I had once held a hollow, fragile, eerily weightless red-blue-and-gold egg. I had longed to crush that egg with a sudden contraction of my fingers, my palm had itched with the smashed sharp bits of the still smooth and unbroken shell, carefully I had placed the dangerous egg in my teacher's outstretched palm; and placing the bullet carefully in Philip's outstretched palm, "I've never," I murmured as I watched him slip the bullet back into the cylinder. He pushed the cylinder back into place. Still leaning up on his right elbow, and holding the gun in his right hand, with his left hand he gave the cylinder a terrific spin. Grasping the side of the bed I watched the spin grow slower and slower and stop. At once Philip raised the barrel to his right temple. "Don't!" I cried. He pulled the trigger. I jerked my head away. There was a loud click.

When I looked up, Philip, breathing heavily, was gazing off dreamily with half-closed eyes.

Looking suddenly at me he said: "Now it's your turn," and held out the gun handle-first.

Still crouching beside the bed I leaned away, thrusting one palm to the floor behind me. "My turn! But I can't, I've never, I don't have the faintest . . ."

Frowning, Philip continued to hold out the gun. After a few moments he said: "But you knew what I was going to do. Didn't you."

"No, I . . . yes, I . . ." Blushing, I lowered my eyes. Philip continued to hold out the gun, but after a while he let it fall from his fingers onto the bed. Lighting a cigarette he lay down on his back, bent an arm under his neck, and blew a thin stream of smoke softly at the ceiling.

"But I can't, I've never even, you can't expect . . . and besides, I don't know anything about it. Of course, it doesn't look too different from a cowboy pistol, except for the color, not that you'd ever . . . for one thing it looks . . . just let me . . . it certainly feels heavier, much heavier, I'm really surprised at how heavy it feels," and standing up I held the gun at my side with the barrel carefully pointing down and swung my arm slowly back and forth. Philip meanwhile had turned his head toward me and lay gazing at me with heavy-lidded eyes. In a curiously excited state I began to walk about the room with the heavy gun in my hand, stepping over books, dragging old socks about, brushing against statues. "Of course," I heard myself saying, "I could never imagine doing it your way, lying down like that, as if it didn't matter at all, the mere idea somehow makes me feel odd all over, a person should stand at attention, if you know what I," and stopping suddenly I raised the gun to my temple so that the barrel was an inch away and instantly lowered the gun. "Of course," I said, beginning to pace again, "I suppose a person would have to be careful he didn't miss, by accident, I remember reading something... I can't remember exactly, but anyway, he pulled the trigger, there was a loud bang, a horrible sound, just thinking about it gives me goose-bumps, he thought he was dead, but then he realized he had missed completely. And think how he must have felt, standing there, holding the gun in his hand... I realize I'm speaking a lot of nonsense, I can't help it though, I never imagined I would ever be holding a gun like this, it's such a strange, such an eerie," and stopping again I raised the gun and pressed the barrel against my temple, shuddering at the cold pressure of steel and quickly removing it. But at once I forced the barrel against my temple, holding it in place as a pulse beat against the steel. In a dreamy voice I heard myself saying: "It reminds me of being sick, when the doctor comes, and you have to take off your shirt and undershirt and then he puts the two plugs in his ears and leans forward and presses that ice-cold circle against your chest, and takes it away, and presses it again. And each time he takes it away, you can see a white circle on your skin before the blood rushes back. It's awfully hot in here, I can hardly breathe, all this smoke... everything is so strange... and my finger feels so odd, on the trigger, so weak, so strong," and I began to pull slowly on the trigger and relax, pull slowly and relax, as long ago I had pulled slowly on the trigger of my cowboy pistol, trying to find the exact point of balance before the hammer sprang forward, and as I pulled slowly I felt my finger moving slowly through great spaces, I felt myself breaking some unknown bond and entering a region of dreamy and forbidden freedom, suddenly there was a loud explosion, and as in a dream of falling, when plunging at last onto the sharp spike of rock you experience with intense lucidity the knowledge that you are dead, but already your eyes are opening, already light streams through your parting lashes, already you see before you the bright white cord of the venetian blind with its little bell-shaped grip and a fluffy knot sticking out of the bottom, so for a moment I knew quite clearly that I had died, but already the explosion had shrunk to a loud click, sweat streamed from my armpits, smoke clung to the ceiling, and gazing at me with heavy-lidded eyes Philip was saying: "... ulations."

32

In the dark days that followed I murdered myself many times, swooning toward death with a fierce, pounding, sensual excitement, and tearing myself painfully awake. And at once I would be filled with languor and sorrow, and stretching myself out on the hard threadbare rug before one of the two orange-glowing heaters I would lie with one arm bent behind my neck and stare up drowsily at the brown gloom; or sitting in the cluttered window-space with my back against the wall I would stare out at the black elm-branches against a whitish sky. Sometimes I would half-inhale on a cigarette, bringing the hot smoke lower and lower into my throat as the pulse in my temple quickened and my brain filled with soft flames. And always there was a sense of fading light, of thickening shadows, of objects draining into dusk; and slowly the orange heater-glow became brighter and brighter in the darkening winter afternoon. In the night-time of five o'clock mother would pull up with a noisy crunch at the end of the front walk. Then wearily I would wrench myself from the warmth and dimness of Philip's cozily gloomy room, lit by a single dusty bulb in a lamp whose yellow oil-paper shade showed dark brown scorch-marks; and making my way through the cluttered attic and down the two flights of stairs I would step into the dark living room and whisper good night to Philip's mother, who lay on the couch watching the orange embers, and then I would step out into an ice-cold shock of night. At the end of the walk the car trembled as if with impatience, pouring from its tailpipe plumes of wintry breath. The sudden cold, the fidgety car, mother's frown of effort as from inside she bent toward me to open the door, her inquisitive glance, her robust words of greeting, filled me with sullen rage; I longed not to be disturbed, never to be disturbed, I longed to lie brooding forever in languor and sorrow in some warm, cozy, gloomy place. But the car-door slammed, the gearshift thumped, mother creaked in her seat—and while my temple still felt the cold pressure of steel, down went the gas pedal, spin went the wheels, the car lurched forward, and she roared me home in a torrent of chatter.

At dinner I was silent and sullen, and after dinner I retired to my room, where I asked not to be disturbed.

And yet, and yet—but how shall I explain that sense of disillusion, that secret disenchantment? It was as if, in the very center of my excitement, I detected a nuance of the familiar. Even during the second time I had not failed to notice a faint dilution of the thrill of terror—a slight infection of the strange by the known—a contraction of the never-before to the once-again. By the third time, despite the increasing danger, I could no longer ignore a troubling sense that my terror lacked something, as if the sharp edge of it had become blunted by repetition. Philip's behavior encouraged my disenchantment, for he liked to affect an ostentatious indifference: he shot himself the second time while turning the pages of a book. The third time, deliberately, he pulled the trigger in the middle of a yawn. And I, in uneasy emulation, held an open book in one hand and the gun in the other. I felt myself in danger of becoming a roué of suicide, a jaded debauchee of death. This in itself was frightening, for I felt that the impurity of my terror made me far more vulnerable to the lurking explosion that perhaps only the pressure of my fear had held back; and sometimes, at night, I would picture myself in the act of casually pulling the trigger, and a shudder would pass over me, not of fear only but of intense revulsion. It was as if my attitude toward death were becoming flippant and cynical; I longed to be healthily afraid. It was in this mood that the next time I instantly agreed to a sinister variation of our game proposed by Philip. Sitting on the bed beside him, I watched him spin the cylinder, and as it slowed to a stop I felt my heartbeat quicken. Slowly he raised the gun. I shut my eyes in pleasurable anguish, shuddering as the barrel touched my temple; after the space of a long breath he pulled the trigger. When it was my turn I lowered the gun slowly to Philip's temple, but as soon as the barrel touched his skin I yanked it away, as if I had pricked him with a needle. Under his scornful gaze I gently and fearfully touched the barrel to his temple; my finger began to squeeze; but it was impossible; and as I lowered the gun and prepared to meet his scornful gaze I saw, beneath the pallid skin of his temple, the swift and delicate throbbing of his pulse.

One afternoon Philip was lying on his bed beside the gun, and I was sitting with my back against a bookshelf, idly turning the pages of a book, when there came the sound of a closing door, followed by quiet footsteps in the hall. I glanced at Philip, who frowned, shrugged one shoulder, and swiftly tucked the gun under his pillow. "Your mother?" I whispered. "Never," said Philip. The footsteps halted outside the door. There was a sharp double knock. "Who is it," muttered Philip. The knock was repeated. "Come in," said Philip irritably. The doorknob turned, and there was a sound of pushing. A series of three sharp knocks followed. " I said come in," said Philip more loudly. The doorknob turned angrily, and the door seemed to buckle as a hip or shoulder was flung with a heavy thump against it. The thump was repeated, the door, coming unstuck, opened suddenly inward, and there in the doorway, with one hand resting on the knob—

"Well," said Philip, "if it isn't William Wilson."

"Mainwaring," said William. He looked about with a deepening frown as he continued to stand on the threshold. When he glared down at me I glanced at Philip, who lay blowing out soft streams of smoke with one arm bent under his neck and one ankle resting on his raised knee. "Come in," I said uncertainly, but William did not move. Looking down at me he said stiffly: "I was in the neighborhood." There was a pause. "Well," I said, "come on in." Angrily William said: "It's not your room." "Oh," said Philip, "you can come in, if you want to." William took one step into the room and said: "God, it's smoky in here." He began to wave a hand quickly in front of him. Turning to me he said: "I was in the neighborhood, I thought I'd stop by." There was a pause. "I can ride you home," he added. "Thanks," I said, "but the old lady picks me up at five." William raised his eyebrows in surprise. "What old lady?" Flushing I said: "My mother. It's just an expression. Anyway, don't just stand there, why don't you come in, we were just, we were just..." "Playing a game," said Philip. "A game?" said William. "No," I said, "we weren't really, we were just talking, and besides, it's getting late, what time is it, does anyone have the time, why doesn't anyone have the time?" William flung out his left hand as if he were tossing a coin and then looked at his bared wrist. "It's six minutes of four," he said. "Well," I said, "my 'mother' usually picks me up at five. I guess you could ride me home. I don't know." Turning to Philip, William said: "What game?" I threw a warning glance at Philip, who had turned up onto his side and was gazing at William. "Oh," he said, "just a game. Why: do you like to play games?" "Sometimes," William said sharply. He coughed suddenly, raising a fist to his mouth and bending forward slightly. "Can't you open a window?" he said angrily. "In the middle of winter?" said Philip. "It isn't winter," said William. "It's December," said Philip. "Winter starts on December twenty-first," said William. Philip looked over at me and smiled. I began to smile but savagely repressed it, lowering my eyes with a fierce frown. When I raised my eyes I saw William looking down at me, his eyes filled with anger and pain. He jerked away his eyes. Enraged I said: "What difference does it make? Don't just stand there. Are you coming in or aren't you?" William flung out his left arm again. "Well," he muttered, "it's getting late. Guess I'll have to get going. See you around." And turning abruptly he walked out of the room and down the hall. I heard the attic door open and after a while I heard the sound of footsteps descending the wooden stairs. Far away I heard another door close softly. "Exit the scientist," murmured Philip, but I shouted: "Why did you tell him! Why!" But looking at me in surprise, Philip said: "But I didn't tell him."

33

AND AT LAST, one rainy winter afternoon, in the double orange glow of the electric heater, Philip announced that he was weary of games. With a curious mixture of sudden excitement and profound unsurprise I listened as he proposed a suicide pact. Eagerly, tranquilly—as if I were shedding a secret burden—I agreed. Philip seemed disturbed by my abrupt acquiescence, and with a trace of annoyance he asked if I knew exactly what I was getting myself into. "Oh yes, yes," I said, with an impatient nod, and added: "When?" Philip frowned at the ceiling and blew out a long slow stream of smoke. At length he turned his head slowly toward me, and casting upon me his heavy-lidded gaze he murmured: "But first, you know, we have to take the pledge."

And so, that rainy winter afternoon, Philip and I took the pledge of death. The instruments were the dark green winebottle, a silver needle, and a dusty glass. One by one, at Philip's drowsy direction, I brought them over and placed them on the white wooden chair, which I had moved beside the bed. Philip leaned up on his elbow and I sat down on the floor with my shoulder against the bed, watching closely. Frowning down, Philip struggled with the winebottle cork. As he turned it from side to side with a woody squeak I held my head away, waiting for the sudden explosion. Suddenly the cork slipped out soundlessly. Still leaning up on his elbow, Philip tipped the green bottle over the rim of the dusty glass, and a dark red liquid came smoothly flowing out. It rose slowly in the glass, casting on the white seat a trembling pale-red glow. When the glass was half full he tipped back the bottle and placed it on the chair. A few drops ran down the sides of the bottle in shiny black stripes; when one stripe touched the seat it formed a little bright-red pool. Philip next picked up the silver needle. He pressed his left thumbnail against the tip of his left forefinger, causing a rosy flush; and holding the needle poised above his rosy fingertip, and frowning intently down, with a sudden quick motion he pricked his finger. At once a bright red blooddrop appeared, like a little blossom. Holding his fingertip carefully upright he moved his hand over the glass of wine and quickly turned his finger over. The bright red drop clung upside down for a few moments but slowly gathering weight it began to pull downward and at last fell into the dark red wine, where it formed a little cloud. Philip squeezed his finger again, forcing out a second drop, which he squeezed into the glass. Then he sucked his finger, wiped the needle on his wrist, and asked me to strike a match. Slowly he moved the tip of the needle into the unflinching flame. Suddenly he sucked in his breath with a hiss and dropped the black-tipped needle, shaking his hand. "Stupid of me," he murmured. From his pocket he removed a wrinkled yellow handkerchief, which emitted bits of dust, and grasping the needle with the handkerchief he held it in the flame of a new match. He blew out the flame, and after a few moments gingerly felt the needle. Then squeezing off the black deposit between two fingers he handed the needle to me.

I pressed my thumbnail against my fingertip as Philip had done. Tightening my lips I touched the needle gently to the rosy skin. Slowly, slowly, I began to push, feeling that at any moment I would burst through the tight rind into a soft red pulp— suddenly I felt a prick of pain, and jerking away the needle I searched eagerly for the bright blossom of blood. I saw only a little red pitmark in my fingertip. "Not like that," said Philip, "like—so," and he made a little quick darting motion in the air. Again I pressed my thumbnail down, and gripping the needle tightly and holding my breath I made a little quick darting motion at my fingertip. The needle pushed painfully against my tough skin and sprang off. "Well," I murmured, "this is just plain ridiculous," and I heard mother saying: "This is just plain ridiculous." Clenching my teeth and squeezing my finger until it hurt, I made a sudden determined jab and felt a throb of pain. And as I watched, a tiny spot of blood appeared and grew into a small smear. Squeezing and squeezing, I held my throbbing finger over the glass and with my thumbnail pushed toward the faintly bulging blood until a droplet fell into the wine. "That isn't enough," said Philip, with an expression of distaste, as if my inelegant blooddrop had offended him. "Why don't you try another finger." But I kept squeezing my wounded finger, until a much larger smear had spread, and again holding my finger over the glass I pushed in a larger drop. "Well," said Philip, "I suppose that will do," and looked away, as if asking to be spared the sight of my inartistic wound. As I anxiously sucked my throbbing finger I imagined the shiny black gun, the pale blue-veined hand, the sudden silence, and a small, round, perfect blooddrop on Philip's throbbing temple. When I looked up suddenly, Philip was gazing at me with his brooding heavy-lidded eyes.

Still leaning up on his elbow, Philip picked up the glass and gazed down into it, shaking the liquid gently. Then raising his eyes to mine he lifted the glass to his mouth and slowly drank, continuing to gaze at me through eyes that grew narrower and narrower as he tipped back his head. Lowering the glass abruptly from his glistening lips he gazed at me with eyes that were unnaturally bright. Then he held out the half-drained glass. I took it and raised it to my lips, but hesitated as the sharp odor of wine streamed upward into my nostrils with the force of feathers, bringing tears to my eyes. And although I felt it was wrong to disturb the solemn silence, I could not overcome a sudden fear, and in a whisper I asked: "Will it make me drunk?" Philip shook his head slowly. At once I tipped back the glass and took a small swallow; after a pause I quickly finished the wine. "Well," I said, setting the glass gently on the chair, "is that all?"—and I felt a warmth sliding through me as if I had swallowed a flame. "Your blood is in my body and my blood is in your

body," said Philip. "Now we are blood brothers, Arthur." And
at the sound of my name I was darkly, wildly moved.

34

WE AGREED TO PERFORM the act one week from the day of our
pledge, and we passed the dull dark intervening days in a cozy
brotherhood of death. No longer did we play our dangerous
game, but met drowsily in Philip's sloping room, where sometimes he read aloud, softly, passages from his favorite works.
"During the whole of a dull, dark, and soundless day in the
autumn of the year, when the clouds hung oppressively low in
the heavens, I had been passing alone, on horseback, through a
singularly dreary tract of country . . ." Oddly enough I did not
think about the moment itself but only of our proud, our
secret bond. Nor did I abandon my usual routines, but plunged
into homework with grateful ardor. Sometimes a smoldering
fear would burst into sudden flame in some distant corner of my
mind, but I would quickly beat it out, leaving only a black,
charred place. Often I would imagine Philip lying on his bed,
pale and cold, and beside him, on the white sheet, the black,
warm gun. I myself was carefully absent from this artistic com-
position, with its touching clutter of statues and books and, on a
chipped saucer, a crushed but still-warm cigarette from which a
last thin line of smoke feebly curls. A neglected schoolbook lies
beside a dark green winebottle, and a thin beam of watery winter
light pierces the brown gloom. One night I dreamed that I was
clinging to father's hand as we descended the steep path beyond
the hedge. Leafy weeds brushed my bare legs, a black-spotted
red ladybug seemed to crack in half as she rose in flight, father
said: "You wait! I'll get you for that!" and there, lying among
tall weeds, fast asleep and very pale, was Philip Schoolcraft,
with a small red hole in his temple. I bent over to examine that

wet red hole, in which little white globules seemed to be floating, but when I thrust my finger in I woke with a throbbing headache.

As the days passed I began to notice a curious change in Philip: a distinct gentleness came over him, which I had never felt before. Gazing at me with those brooding heavy-lidded eyes, he seemed at times to lose his perpetual mild air of pride and scorn and to be taken with a quiet tenderness. One afternoon, after long silence, as he lay on his back blowing streams of smoke softly at the ceiling, he said in a quiet voice: "You know, I've been meaning to say, if you have any second thoughts about this..." But I almost shouted: "No! Never! Why would I—after that day—" "All right, all right, you don't have to get upset about it, you know, I was just wondering... Because if you do, you know..." This little conversation upset me profoundly, in part because I was hurt that my blood brother should seem to doubt my devotion. And yet there was something else that disturbed me, something elusive and dangerous that would not be named. From the moment of that conversation I was seized by a gentle nervousness. Philip's tenderness oppressed me like hatred; I longed for the faint, familiar scorn. One night, unable to fall asleep, I imagined quite vividly Philip gazing at me with those gentle, compassionate eyes, and I felt myself filling with terror, it was as if my breast would burst, the room seemed unbearably hot, and sitting up in bed I pushed aside the blinds and pressed my burning forehead against the icy glass.

As if suddenly, the fatal day arrived. It was an oppressively usual day of calm gray skies and thin winter light, of gray shadowless streets beneath motionless black branches, and as I passed along the yellow corridors with their rows of shiny green lockers or sat chin-in-hand at my glossy desks in English and Math and American History, I could not understand why Philip and I were not the center of frenzied attention. How I loathed them all, those dull, cheerful people, who had no idea that Death was stalking among them. Pale and scornful, doomed and proud, He gazed upon them with his brooding heavy-lidded eyes. I felt that Philip and I were carrying among them a dangerous secret, which would explode in their smiling faces if they were not careful. At the same time I scrupulously avoided thinking about that secret, nor did Philip mention it as we strolled together, pale and doomed, on the cold, loud, indifferent playground.

Then I found myself walking beside Philip past the towering elms of his long front walk. I watched as he removed from his pocket a cordovan keycase at the end of which dangled a nickel-colored key. Dreamily I followed him into the dim living room, where on the faded-dark-red couch Mrs. Schoolcraft sat in a black dress with one arm over her eyes and one hand resting upon a yellow book. "Mother," said Philip, slowly she began to raise her heavy-lidded eyes, but already we were climbing the dark-carpeted stairway to the dim hall with its faded green willows, its faded brown ponds, its faded boys in blue with their faded fishing poles. Then a door opened and we climbed the creaking wooden stairs to the dark attic, where beside a muddy mirror a headless dummy searched in vain, in vain, for its missing head, and passing the broken dolls, the fallen books, the dusty pink dishes, the black rubber plunger, we entered the little hallway with its whirling and leaping and bowing ballerinas. I watched Philip struggle with the white door, which suddenly came unstuck, and I followed him into the dim smoky room. And everything was so exactly as it had always been that I wanted to smile, but I dared not smile. Philip lit a cigarette, and lying down on his bed with one arm bent under his neck he blew soft streams of smoke at the ceiling, while I sat on the threadbare rug with my back against a bookshelf. I looked about the room, wondering what it was doing there, and all at once, quite vividly, I imagined Philip shooting himself in the head, and I began to tremble violently, but when I looked at my hands they were quite still. After a while Philip sat up effortfully, without a word, and placing the needle on the dull black record with the bright black scratch he lay back as if exhausted by his effort as the phonograph emitted a brief loud scratchiness, followed by a sudden silence. And there rose from that silence the dark, doleful, solitary tone of a flute, but it was all quite useless, quite dead. When the record ended there was a revolving sound of scratchiness on two different pitches. After a while Philip labored up and lifted the needle-arm and turned off the phonograph with a dull click. Then he lay down once again, and again there was silence. After a while he said: "Why don't you get down that book now, and bring it over to me. But be careful. Those old volumes are very fragile." And although I had begun to tremble again, I could not repress the flicker of a smile.

At once I rose, turned, and removed from the shelf the heavy book.

I sat before him on the white wooden chair, with my knees pressing into the soft bedside. Leaning up on an elbow, Philip opened the dull red cover and removed the black revolver. "You see," he said, swinging out the cylinder and showing me two brass circles sitting cozily side by side. But at once I lowered my eyes, murmuring "Yes, that's all right." I felt a keen rush of affection for Philip Schoolcraft, the pale doomed boy who was going to die, and I longed to say something passionate and memorable, but flushing slightly I murmured: "Well . . ." Philip pushed in the cylinder with a startling clack. I looked up abruptly. A quiet panic started in me but I crushed it to death. On the chipped saucer beside him, a smashed cigarette gave off feeble spurts of smoke. I forced down my eyes, for I felt it was indecent to look, but they sprang up despite myself, and pressing back in my chair I moved a little away. But in my mind I continued to move slowly backward in my chair, sliding across the room, sliding through the wall, sliding out into the gray winter sky . . . Philip took a deep breath and exhaled slowly. In the blue-shadowed hollow of his temple I could see, like a miniature heartbeat, the faint and rapid throbbing of his pulse. As if to himself he murmured: "The time has come." Then gazing up at me with those long-lashed, brooding, heavy-lidded eyes, he said decisively: "The time has come." At once he held out the gun handle-first.

"What," I began, and started to smile, but my throat and fore-head were aflame, I could not breathe, and scraping back in my chair I breathed out the words: "I thought . . ."

"What's wrong?" said Philip sharply. Scornfully he added: "You've changed your mind."

"Oh, my mind, but I thought . . ."

"You thought . . ."

"I thought that you, you first . . ."

"Me first! Don't be a fool. How can I be certain that you . . ."

"But that's not fair!" I cried. "How do I know that you, that you . . ."

Our eyes met and jerked away. A horrible suspicion fluttered across my mind, flew out into the room, and flung itself madly against the dusty window. Frowning to himself, Philip contin-ued to hold out the gun handle-first.

After a while he let the gun fall from his fingers onto the bed. Then he lit a cigarette and lay down on his back, and bending an arm under his neck he blew out a long slow stream of swirl-ing smoke.

For a long while I sat there, waiting for him to speak. When he finished his cigarette he lay in silence and then lit another cigarette. After a while he sat up, turned on the record-player, and leaned back. As the flute-melody melted into a shudder of harpstrings I said: "Shall I go?" I cleared my throat and said more loudly: "Shall I go?" Philip said nothing, but continued to blow smoke at the smoky ceiling. He did not call to me as I opened the door. He did not call to me as I walked along the hall. He did not call to me as I passed through the attic and down the wooden steps and along the hall and down the car-peted steps and out the front door into the chill gray air, and as I walked down the long front walk, past the littered lawns and the decaying elms, he did not call to me from the high black window.

35

HE DID NOT CALL TO ME from the high black window; and after a tense pause, lasting several weeks, during which I watched William, and William watched Philip, and Philip turned the pages of various books, suddenly William and I once again rode to school side by side on the yellow bus, and ate across from one another in the cafeteria, and strolled together on the playground. And once again we returned to the white one-dollar bills, the pink five-dollar bills, the yellow ten-dollar bills ... I was happy to immerse myself in the strange world of the usual. At William's urging I attended a meeting of the Mineralogy Club, where William solemnly read the minutes of the previous meeting and Mrs. Shipley described the six kinds of crystal, drawing on the blackboard six diagrams in which dotted lines indicated the principal axes, and removing in turn from her brown leather pocketbook six small crystals wrapped in tissue paper twisted at the top. At the Photography Club, where on tall cork boards mounted on wheels, glossy black-and-white photographs were displayed above title, student, and homeroom number, I watched William work at one of the metal contact-print machines on the long counter at the back of the room. William explained a point of technique to a serious seventh-grader, and when the boy turned to me with a question I stammered out an "Oh, I don't know, I'm just a friend, I don't know anything about it," and looked away with a fierce embarrassment that surprised me. One day father drove us to a distant museum. In a towering room with tall arched windows, row after row of long glass cases contained colorful minerals and gems. From there we stepped into a room filled with the yellow skeletons of dinosaurs, and passing through a room of frowning Indians and dark totem poles we entered a room where smiling ladies in hoop dresses stood with tasseled parasols, and from there we stepped into a room full of clay bowls and bone buttons and stone tools, and all these rooms reminded me of something, as if I had been there before, and coming to a silver escalator we floated down to a gleaming cafeteria that resembled a miniature museum, where slices of red roast beef and plates of Boston cream pie were carefully displayed behind glass windows. Later, at a little gift shop overflowing with postcards and booklets, William bought a bush of white coral mounted in a dab of plaster, a small box containing a slag-like mineral pressed into white styrofoam and bearing on the boxcover the words: "Atomic Trinitite: this silicate was fused by the heat of the First Atomic Bomb Explosion at Alamogordo, New Mexico," and a black card the size of a postcard, entitled SHARK TEETH: *Captain William E. Smith*, upon which, in two rows, six ivory teeth were glued: TIGER, BLACK TIP, BROWN, DUSKY UPPER, NIGHT, DUSKY LOWER. "If only you could buy the stuff on display," said William as we walked out to the car, and suddenly I remembered what the museum reminded me of: a department store.

At my house we played ping-pong in the cellar and Monopoly in my room. But sometimes, in snowless weather, we played harmless versions of dangerous outdoor sports: in the cold back yard we practiced throwing a football wobblingly back and forth, and one mild winter day father attached to the garage an orange metal hoop with white netting, and William and I practiced standing at various distances and seeing how many shots we could sink in a row. One rainy day William landed on two houses on St. Charles Place. As he held out a five-hundred-dollar bill he asked me what game Philip Schoolcraft and I had been playing. As in a movie melodrama, my reaching hand paused; then the motion continued. "Oh," I said, handing him three hundreds, two twenties, and a ten, "I don't remember. Just some game." I shook the dice and dropped them loudly on the board. That night there was a knock on my door and William entered. He looked at me with hatred, and as he advanced he reached into his fiery red jacket and removed a gun. "Please don't," I whispered, but he pulled the trigger, and as the bullet burned into my chest I woke in blackness.

One cold blue Saturday I accompanied William by bus to an old brick building beside a factory. In a dark damp room full of long benches and dark green lockers, William and I changed silently into our bathing suits. A few benches away, two tough-looking boys flicked one another with heavy white towels. One of them wore a dog-tag on a chain around his neck and had oily black hair combed back on both sides. The other had a little sharp peak of hair pointing down over his forehead like the prong of a beercan-opener; and down the back of each forearm, from the elbow to the wrist, ran a long and faintly swelling vein. Pale and wary, visible and vulnerable, I followed William out of the dark room along a dismal hall into a sudden warm room with a translucent green pool set in the middle like an enormous crystal of beryl. The yellow board was trembling in the air. A slick head rose from the water. At the side of the pool a red metal ladder rippled gently. A dark muscular boy gripped the white ledge of the pool and pulled himself easily up. He had curly black hair on his dripping thighs and he wore a tight turquoise-blue bathing suit with black trim. He stood on the ledge with his hands on his hips, breathing heavily as water streamed from him; and as he breathed, a tiny bright gold cross moved on his streaming chest. A few other boys flashed and splashed in the green pool. William walked over to the deep end beside the diving board and stood for a moment staring grimly at the water. Then he held out his arms, lowered his head, and dived stiffly into the pool. No one laughed. I lowered myself cautiously into the shallow end, and as I did so the two tough-looking boys entered. Striding springily, sticking out their chests, laughing and snapping their fingers and shoving each other in the shoulder, they advanced to the edge of the pool. Suddenly the one with oily black hair gripped his crotch, twisted his features into a look of pain, and cried: "Aw, they got me." He began to stagger along the band of white marble at the edge of the pool, tottering at the rim, moaning loudly; and lifting his eyes, and throwing out an arm, he fell stiffly sideways into the water with a great splash. The other boy leaped after him, hugging his knees to his chest and landing in the water with a loud sitting splash. I stayed quietly at my end, keeping my eye on the dangerous friends, and later, as William and I stood on a darkening streetcorner, waiting for a number 7 bus, I felt myself filling with despair at the thought of the dismal locker room, the flicking white towels, my narrow shoulders, William's clumsy dive ... But after dinner, in my cozy room, playing Monopoly safe in lamplight, I recalled with a sudden burst of pleasure the green pool with its rippling red ladder, the warm voluptuous water, the sharp green scent of chlorine ...

William had begun to come over nearly every day, and our friendship throve in the warm yellow lamplight of cold gray winter afternoons. This was friendship's temperate time, and only sometimes did I long for a deeper comradeship, of the sort that happened in the pages of books of adventure, as among D'Artagnan and the sword-fighting musketeers, or among Robin Hood's band in the shady greenwood. Sometimes we made plans for the coming spring. I was excited by the prospect of long expeditions to unknown places, of green adventures in secret shade, but at the same time I preferred not to think ahead to the warm, dangerous season, with its troubling twilights, its sudden breezes, its little sharp-edged bitter-tasting leaves. One night I was sitting at my maplewood desk, bent over a list of very black questions at the end of a chapter in my American History book. I was writing the answer to the third question on blue-lined bright-white paper. My dark blue fountain pen was poised in preparation for pressing down onto the next word, and suddenly I was lacerated with restlessness, if I did not do something at once, at once, I would burst into tears of anguish, but there was nothing to do, there was nowhere to go, rage and despair fluttered wildly about the room until, exhausted, they lay down in a corner and were still, and quietly my fluent pen ran on.

36

SPRING CAME, that famous season, and with it a sense of dark withdrawal, as if I sought protection against the growing violence of light. I found myself longing to return from school each day to the cool peacefulness of my room, where on days when William did not come over I would change quickly out of my belted pants, my polished shoes, and my oppressively neat schoolshirt into grass-stained sneakers, faded jeans, and a rumpled playshirt with a torn elbow. Bringing in from the kitchen a tall glass of chocolate milk and a saucer of red pistachio nuts, I would close the blinds and pull out the metal wall-light, and lying down on my stomach on the light-brown bedspread crisscrossed with dark brown and dark green, I would open a book. And as in one of those black-and-white movies that begin with the image of some dusty old-fashioned book, which a mysterious hand opens slowly, with intensely crisp papery sounds, to a page of words so large and thick that they are not real words but cunning imitations, and a mysterious voice that is not a real voice but a British voice begins to read, and slowly, softly, you sink through the page into a sudden street where men in tall hats and bushy side-whiskers stride briskly along: so I too sank through soft pages, down, deep down, into other streets and universes.

Twice a week father drove me to the distant stone library, where I borrowed armfuls of books from the teenage section. I looked for familiar names, like Stevenson and Poe, but I was far more attracted by the completely mysterious and unknown. At times I felt I was searching for a book so violently satisfying that a deep calm would come over me, my internal itching would cease, and at last I could stop reading forever. In the high brown room, under the yellow light, I loved to open some dark old novel with a faded title and many dates stamped in crooked columns on the paper slip in back; and leaning against a shelf I would eagerly read the opening sentences, in the hope of coming upon a phrase that would possess me. My needs were imperative and had nothing to do with taste. What I searched for, what I demanded, was a certain mysterious power of annihilation, of dissolution—and behold! on a sudden street, men in tall hats and bushy side-whiskers stride briskly along.

And yet, that spring, I could not conceal from myself a growing fretfulness. Often, as I read, the men in tall hats would waver and grow dim, and I would see only a page of precise black print, upon which there sometimes lay, like a white scratch, a slanting line of space formed by a hazard of typography; and shutting my book unhappily I would grow sullen with disappointment. Sometimes I felt that I was tired of teenage fiction, and asking father's troubled permission I would look at books in the adult section, in a high brown silent unfamiliar room. I would choose a book and ask him to take it out for me, and he would open it with a frown and turn the pages uncertainly and cough into his fist and push out his lips and scratch his neck and at last, with a sigh, oblige me. At home mother would glare through the bottom of her reading glasses as she turned the pages grimly and asked what in the world I hoped to accomplish by reading adult books before I was an adult. But adult books always bored me to death in the first two pages; and I began to wonder whether I had reached an age for which no books were written. And perhaps it was simply that I longed for the remembered mystery of the vanished books of my childhood, rendered in language not for children. Lying indolently on my lamplit bed, gazing down at a page of print, I would recall with sudden vividness a picture in some forgotten storybook: a green hill where plump watermelons grew on watermelon trees, an orange-and-brown tiger holding in his tail a dark green umbrella, a yellow brick house with a bright red roof. One day I brought home from the library an armful of children's books. In my room I began reading feverishly, with a shock of delight, but my eagerness quickly gave way to boredom and despair. And once, in a dull adult novel, a man and a woman went into a room. The woman sat down on the edge of the bed and began to undo the buttons of her blouse. There was a white space, and the scene changed to a vicarage, and I felt strange and anxious, but they never returned to that troubling room.

As the warm weather continued, a discontent came over me. In my games with William I was impatient and irritable, and longed to return to the solitude of my books. But as soon as he left I felt lonely and abandoned, and became furious at William for his cruel absence. On my lamplit bed, before the upward-slanting blinds, on afternoons heavy with held-out sunlight, I could not read, and would lie half-dreaming, leaning my cheek on my bent-back hand. A queerness seemed to have seeped into the universe, leaving me strangely troubled and oppressed. Home from school, one sunny afternoon, I let myself in with my key as usual, and as I stepped into the cool brown living room, with its faint odor of furniture polish, I felt a sudden ache of sadness that seemed somehow to be composed of polished mahogany surfaces, brown cloth, a heavy drooping cluster of purple lilacs above a scattering of tiny brown-edged petals, and a blazing window printed on the worn brown carpet. In my room I lay down in a swoon of sadness, listening to distant outdoor sounds, but after a while I felt restless and bored, and twisting from my bed I hurried from my oppressive room into the kitchen and out onto the shady-and-sunny back porch; but when I stepped out of the warm shade into the hot light of the sun, I felt all the hot bright irritating afternoon scratching against me with its prickly points of light.

Those weary schooldays, those troubling afternoons . . . And the purple evenings, odor of lilacs and gasoline . . . And after dinner, in the darkening air, the soft shouts of strangers, faint cries of rock-and-roll . . .

It was a warm spring night. I was sitting at my desk before my open notebook, brilliantly white in the faintly tremulous glare of my fluorescent lamp. Through the dark screen came a warm moist smell of freshcut grass. To the right of my notebook lay a neat pile of six dark library books. Behind my notebook, partially obscuring the upper part of the page, a seventh book lay open. Somewhere a radio played softly. A car-door slammed. The light from my fluorescent lamp trembled faintly. A motor sounded, and became softer and softer and disappeared as I waited in vain for a sandy crunch. Frowning in annoyance, I began to copy in quotation marks from the open book, and suddenly I became enraged at the trembling light, the glaring white page, the gleaming yellow pencils, the stifling universe, and scraping back noisily in my chair I stood up. My temples were throbbing, the walls were throbbing, the ceiling was pressing down on me. Striding across the room I pulled open my door and walked swiftly to the end of the dark hall, where to the left, in the dim living-room beyond the dark dining-room, a mahogany table shimmered and flickered in the light of the invisible television screen. I turned right, into the bright kitchen. Mother was standing before an open white cabinet with a pencil and a piece of paper. From the blazing lightshade came a tinkle of little glassy sounds, made by some hardshelled insect. "Where are you going, Arthur?" said mother, turning with a frown. "Just out," I muttered, with my hand on the fluted glass knob. "Out? Out where?" said mother, looking at me with intense concern. "Can't you leave me alone!" I cried, slamming the screen door behind me. In rage I strode across the dark back yard, pushed through the hedge, and walked through the scratchy field to the concrete stream, where I jumped down into black, sharp weeds. Clenching my teeth and fists until I trembled with the effort, I held back the hateful tears. Then I plunged among the weeds, along the stream-edge, heading nowhere, and I heard myself mutter: "What's wrong with me?" After a while my eyes narrowed and I said more loudly: "I don't care." Then taking a deep breath I turned around and went back.

37

Spring came, that famous season, and in the languorous and restless air I walked the purple evenings in an odor of lilacs and gasoline. Hands thrust in pockets, jeans slung low, watchful and without eyeglasses I walked tensely and alone, alive to dangers that seemed to press upon me from all sides. And perhaps it was only danger that I sought as, passing the familiar wooden porches, I wandered into alien realms, where sunbrowned old men stood raking in backyard gardens, where among garbage cans at the back of a stucco house a dark green grapevine grew on a secret arbor, where in a weedgrown lot behind a crooked wire fence a dirty goat lifted its head and stared. At a drugstore counter two killers in black leather jackets sat eating doughnuts and coffee. In the dirt of a darkening baseball diamond a flung bat spun in a cloud of dust. Once, turning a shadowy corner with its shut-up grocery store, I came upon a row of trashbarrels and empty wooden cartons. In a line against the wall two tough boys in dungarees and high-school jackets stood beside a wavy-blond-haired girl in a tight black skirt and a tight pink blouse. The back of her pink collar was turned up and her pointy-looking breasts stuck out of the tight-stretched pink cloth like small hard funnels. One boy was smoking a cigarette with his eyes narrowed and his cheeks sucked in, one boy held his hands in his jacket pockets so that they touched in front of his stomach, and the girl, leaning her head back drowsily against the bricks and gazing through half-closed eyes along the slopes of her cheeks, held her arms folded tightly across her stomach with the elbows in both hands, as if she were embracing herself. In the dangerous silence I walked past with lowered eyes. Suddenly a beer-can came bouncing and scraping across the sidewalk and rolled off the curb into the gutter. No one said a word . . . And seeing myself through those mocking eyes I despised my weakness, I despised William Mainwaring and all the tribe of the smart and weak, the pale bright boys who had no girls. And I longed to be tough, I longed to be one of the boys in black jackets, lords of the sidewalk with their bitter eyes. And as I walked in the dangerous air, in the dust, in the dusk, in the threatening streets, I too was one of the boys in black jackets, lord of the sidewalk with my bitter eyes. Often I wondered why I never saw any girls from school. I wondered if they all stayed indoors after supper, I wondered if they gathered at some place known to everyone except me. I wondered where they all were, the girls of 8-12: Diana Marsilio and Barbara Santino and Mildred Schipul and Judy Lee, Marilyn Marcinko and Valery Jarzynski and Linda Gulowski and Paula Gruszecki and Bonnie Carson and Judy Henderson and Carol Schurig and Irene Banks. I thought how nice it would be if a girl I knew, even slightly, lived in my neighborhood. As I strolled by with my hands in my pockets and my jeans slung low she would call to me from the porch. I would go over and stand talking with one foot on the ground and one foot on a step. She would invite me inside, she would put on records, we would dance, slowly it would grow dark, and in the warm and melancholy dusk, heavy with languor and the sharp scents of greenness, her face would turn to me, slowly her eyes would close, and I would press upon her lips a tender kiss.

38

THE FOURTH OF JULY was a big, bustling, boring family affair. William arrived on his English bike in the sunny middle of the morning as father and I were setting off striped one-inchers on the ledge of the back porch, and Uncle Manny and Auntie Lou and Marjorie arrived after lunch, bearing crisp packages of firecrackers, boxes of sparklers, punks, snakes, bottles of soda, hotdog buns, and bags of powdery marshmallows. Uncle Manny shook father's hand and at the same time put his hairy arm around mother's waist, saying "Heya, Martha Partha," while Auntie Lou, exclaiming at my height, lifted a powdered cheek for me to kiss. William shook hands with everyone and said nothing. Marjorie, wearing red sneakers, turquoise-blue bermuda shorts, and a white blouse with sleeves rolled above the elbows, stood to one side, holding over her arm a tan sweater, and pushing from her eyes the hair that she now wore in movie-star fashion, combed down wavily over one eyebrow. After the helloing and the how are youing, I had to stand back to back with mother to show that I was nearly a head taller than she, and then I had to stand back to back with father to show that I only seemed taller than he, because I was so thin, and then Marjorie and I had to stand awkwardly back to back while everyone said My! and How he's grown!, and then William and I had to stand back to back while everyone tried to decide who was taller, Auntie Lou thinking William was taller but mother saying no, the lawn was crooked, and "Don't fidget so, Arthur. Stand up straight and tall, now. I don't know where he gets his posture from, it's really a crime." Finally Uncle Manny placed on our heads a package of sparklers, which fell off, and everyone laughed, and there followed a great setting up of lawnchairs under the shady maple, but no one sat down except mother and Auntie Lou. Uncle Manny and father and William and Marjorie and I set off firecrackers in turn, to ooh! and aah! from under the maple, and then Uncle Manny led mother, protesting and giggling, to a little half-inch firecracker resting on the porch ledge. Holding her face away, and frowning fiercely, mother slowly moved the flame of the wooden match closer and closer to the upward-curving wick while father, pretending to be amused, watched anxiously. Suddenly mother snatched back her hand and stepped away. Father flinched. The firecracker sat there with its little tail sticking out. Everyone laughed, and mother blushed faintly. Lighting another match she thrust the flame boldly under the wick, and Uncle Manny shouted "Step back! Step back!"—whereupon mother snatched away her hand but remained motionless, and as the firecracker exploded she gave a terrified start and said angrily: "Well, I hope you're satisfied. I nearly blew my head off." "Ah, Martha-girl," said Uncle Manny, "you're beautiful," and father said: "You're not burned, are you? You're all right, aren't you?" "Of course I'm all right," said mother, tossing back her head and placing her fists on her hips; and glancing at the place where the firecracker had been she said: "Lord! I certainly blew it to kingdom come." And everyone laughed, and laughed, and the grownups sat down on the lawnchairs, and William and Marjorie and I excused ourselves, while Uncle Manny, lighting up a fat cigar, began telling father about his new outboard engine, and Auntie Lou, moving her chair into the sun, began to unscrew a dark brown bottle of suntan lotion.

At the front of the house we set off a few more firecrackers, but soon grew bored. "Let's kill ourselves," I suggested. "Oh, Arthur," said Marjorie. William frowned. Marjorie suggested ping-pong. We went inside and creaked our way down into the cool, damp cellar. Marjorie no longer served in her old way, dropping the ball on the table and then hitting it over the net; she now held the ball correctly on the flat of her palm, gave it a little toss in the air, and delivered a fast, spinning serve that was difficult to return. When William and I played she sat on top of a paint-stained stepladder with her elbow on one raised knee and her chin in her hand, watching intently. Her intent stare, her big, dry-looking knees, William's frown of concentration, the glare of the overhead bulb, all this annoyed me, and after a while I said: "This is boring. Why don't we do something else?" "I'm not bored," said William. "Oh," said Marjorie, "everything bores him." "That's right," I said, "everything bores me," and threw my paddle on the table. It hit loudly, making Marjorie start, and went skidding into the net. "Hey," said William, "take it easy." "Tough guy," said Marjorie. For a while I sat scowling as they played, and suddenly I gave a short, abrupt laugh.

"What's so funny?" said William. "Nothing," I said. "Oh," said Marjorie, "don't pay any attention to him." "That's right," I said, "don't pay any attention to him." A short while later Marjorie said: "I've just about had it." "I'm pooped," said William, pushing his hair out of his eyes and placing his paddle on a slant over the ball. And so, we all went upstairs. In the warm shade of the front porch we sat on the wicker furniture, drinking pink lemonade and talking about nothing in particular. Marjorie, it turned out, had been on the Student Council. William told about his clubs. I became intensely restless. "The Student Council," I said wearily. "I don't see how anyone can stand any of that junk." "Oh, Arthur," said Marjorie. William looked angry. "Listen," I said, "I don't see what everyone's so annoyed about for Christ sake. It's a free country. I have a right to my opinion." "That isn't an opinion," said William, "it's a prejudice." "He's right," said Marjorie, "and watch your language." I said: "You people ought to get married." There was an abrupt silence. "Anyway," I continued, "cheer up, Marge, I did join a club this year, so don't give up hope, all is not lost, the honor of our race and so on and so forth amen." "You did?" said Marjorie. "That's right," I said, and paused. William said: "I didn't know you joined a club." He frowned and said: "You didn't join a club." I said: "Oh, didn't I?" "Was it the Art Club?" said Marjorie. "No," I said, "it was the Suicide Club." There was another silence. Then Marjorie gave a little giggle, and I began to chuckle, and Marjorie began to laugh, and William, who at first had thrown me a sharp glance, gave a congenial snort or two, and after a while we strolled to the drugstore, where Marjorie bought an ice-cream sandwich, and William an orange creamsicle, and I a toasted almond, and later it was William and mother versus Auntie Lou and me, and Marjorie and father versus mother and Uncle Manny, and William and Marjorie versus father and me, and later William chose the battleship, and I chose the racing car, and Marjorie, hesitating between the shoe and the hat, finally chose the flatiron. The sun was low but the sky was still bright blue when we were called outside for supper. More chairs had appeared and were grouped haphazardly about the smoking grill, on which lay four hissing frankfurters with black stripes and little beads of moisture. On a round metal table there were paper plates, paper cups with paper handles that folded out like wings, yellow napkins, and a plate of silverware. On the folding card-table stood a jar of dill pickles, a bowl of sauerkraut, jars of mustard and sweet relish, unopened packages of hotdog rolls, a pitcher of pink lemonade, a bowl of potato salad sprinkled with parsley, and a basket of potato frills. William sat on a wooden lawnchair with his plate carefully balanced on his knees, Marjorie sat by father's legs at the foot of a long aluminum lawnchair, and I sat on the blue canvas seat of a wooden folding-chair. Uncle Manny and father took turns at the grill, and mother kept pouring pink lemonade into half-empty cups and asking if anyone needed more ice. After a while Marjorie put on her sweater. "Come on, come on, one more won't kill you," urged Uncle Manny, pressing his long chef's fork into a plump frankfurter that sputtered more loudly, and mother looked up in terror as somewhere a cherry bomb exploded. When the sun went down behind the body shop I went inside to get my light jacket. As I stepped back out I saw William standing over the grill with the long fork, at the end of which was a flaming black marshmallow. In the darkening blue air father lit a punk for Auntie Lou. Far away, more and more firecrackers were exploding. "More lemonade?" said mother. "Don't be shy, now."

When supper was over and it was almost dark, except for a gloomy grayness where the sun had set, father nailed a pinwheel to the trunk of the maple while the rest of us sat in a row on the open back porch, holding our punks and slapping at mosquitoes. "Okey-doke," said father, "that should just about do it. Everybody ready?"—and striking a match he leaned forward and stepped quickly away. Round and round it spun with a whooshing sound, shooting out orange-yellow flames; and all about it, in the almost-dark, little glowing particles moved through the air and went out. "Oh," said mother, clapping her hands once and drawing them to her throat, "I just love Catherine wheels." "Who is Catherine Wheels?" I said. "And now," said Uncle Manny, "ta-tum ta-tah," and raising an arm he held up a long stick with a slender red rocket attached. He went down to the yard and set it up on the lawn, thrusting the stick into the ground so that the rocket was pointing over the hedge toward the field. Kneeling on one knee, he struck a match and held it to the wick. The rocket made a sizzling sound and shot not very high over the hedge, bursting feebly into blue and white dust. "A dud," said Uncle Manny bitterly. "Oh," said mother, "I thought it was just lovely anyway." "I wonder," said father, "can you get your money back." "Maybe it's down in the field," I said, turning to William. On his chair lay a box of sparklers. I glanced at Marjorie. Raising her eyebrows and lifting her shoulders, she turned both hands palm upwards and crossed her eyes. "I think he went to the bathroom," said Auntie Lou. And so, we all went down onto the lawn and lit our sparklers. I held my finger in the harmless sizzling spark-spray that had frightened me as a child, and then I wrote my dissolving name in the blueblack air, and then I made a complete but slightly lopsided orange circle by making my sparkler go round and round in quick small circles. After the sparklers Uncle Manny and father and I opened the last packages of fire-crackers and began setting them off on the porch ledge. "I need another punk," said Marjorie, wandering off. The screen door slammed. Auntie Lou sat down in the long aluminum lawnchair, waving her punk, and mother sat on the swing with her arms bent around the ropes, gliding back and forth very gently and trailing one foot in the dirt. "I don't know about you folks," said mother, "but these bugs are eating me alive. Isn't that a light in the cellar?" "I think the damn punks attract 'em," said Uncle Manny. He lit a cigar and strolled over to the dark maple, where he stood leaning back against the trunk. From time to time a glowing orange circle appeared at the end of his cigar. Father stood near Auntie Lou with his hands in his pockets. "Here," said Uncle Manny, "let's give you a hand with that," and bending over he gave mother a little push. "Careful, careful," said father. "Oh, for mercy's sake," said mother, kicking off a little on the dirt, "you're talkin' to a country gal." Uncle Manny sang: "Country gal, won't you come out tonight, come out tonight, come out tonight . . ." The rope creaked slightly. Far away a string of firecrackers went off. Auntie Lou yawned loudly and suddenly slapped herself on the arm. In the cellar window a dim light shone. "When I was a kid," said father. "Excuse me, I have to go to the bathroom," I said.

In the dark kitchen the cellar door was partly open. I tiptoed down the steps in darkness and made my way quietly toward the far side of the cellar, where a bookcase and a broken chair were dimly illuminated by an invisible bulb. With a curious feeling of panic I stepped around the corner. Under the glaring yellow bulb a red paddle and a green paddle lay overlapped at one end of the dark green table. At the other end a dark blue paddle was slanted over a ping-pong ball. "Hello?" I called softly, and peered around the next corner into the darkness. Then I turned out the light, made my way back to the stairs, and climbed into the dark kitchen. Through the window I saw father standing with his hands in his pockets beside Auntie Lou, and suddenly mother's outstretched legs came swinging into view. Her dress billowed lightly, paused, and then lay down as her legs swung back. I walked quietly down the hall to my room, where the door was closed. "Hello?" I said softly, and tapped on the door, but there was no answer. When I opened the door the room was black. Reaching inside I patted the wall and found the lightswitch. The dark room burst into light. On the floor, the Monopoly board lay as we had left it. On the bed beneath the closed blinds was a white shuttlecock with a black rubber tip. I turned out the light and made my way down the hall and turned left into the dark dining room and passed into the darker living room, where light from a streetlamp made dark bits of glass shine. "Hello?" I said softly, but there was no answer, and opening the front door I stepped out onto the warm night of the front porch. To the right of the door was the wicker sofa. Marjorie was sitting with her back to me and her legs up on the seat. Her frowning face was turned to me over her shoulder. To the right of the wicker sofa was an empty wooden chair. To the right of the chair, in the dark corner formed by the side-rail and the house, William sat in the wicker rocker, looking at me without expression. "We were just talking," said Marjorie. "That's nice," I said. William said nothing.

39

THAT WAS AN UNSATISFACTORY SUMMER; an indolent and oppressive summer; a summer of sudden angers and dark indifferences, of yearnings and exhaustions, of hot sunny rooms on hot blue afternoons and hot yellow lightbulbs in the muggy dark. I had looked forward to long slow days of lazy summer freedom but within two weeks I realized there was nothing to do. William and I played ping-pong in the cellar, and badminton in the back yard, and Monopoly in my room. We went to Wednesday and Saturday matinees, we took a hot bouncing bus to a hot boring beach, we sat sprawled on the wicker furniture on the shady front porch, playing blackjack and sipping lemonade; but really there was nothing to do. It seemed as if, the older I got, the more there was nothing to do. And I longed for something, for anything to do, but at the same time I did not want to do anything. I longed to be left alone, by everyone, forever, and yet I could not endure being alone, I could not endure anything. Stubbornly, for no reason, I refused to go on family expeditions.

"Now, Marth, the boy is getting too old to tag along after his fat old decrepit dad, let him be, Marth, let him be," and in rage I saw, through father's genial smile, the keen signs of disappointment on his face.

"I don't see why you have to tell me to let him be, Walter.

Heaven knows I don't want him to do anything he doesn't want to do. I certainly won't force him to have a good time, if he doesn't want to. So far as I'm concerned he can sit on his backside till the cows come home. But let me ask you this, dear: what does he do all day? Nothing. Not one little thing. He sits in his room. I've never heard of anyone who sits in his room so much. If he's going to sit in his room all summer long the least he can do is go on a picnic. It's not asking too much. I've never seen a boy with so much time on his hands. Dorothy Zilko's son has a paper route and works weekends in the store, and Tommy Ryan. Don't talk to me about Tommy Ryan. Little Tommy Ryan who doesn't have as many brains in his whole head as Arthur has in the end of his little finger made four hundred dollars last year mowing lawns and selling hotdogs at Little League games."

"Oh, Jesus," I said.

Her nostrils widening, her cheek-ridges aflame, her neck moist above her cool green voluminous summer smock, thrusting her flushed face toward me mother said: "How dare you curse at me young man how dare you."

Inflamed, trembling, sick with rage, I stalked from the room, I slammed my door, I threw myself down on my bed and decided to kill myself, but already my rage was dying, already I was sinking into a stupor of languor . . . soft indolence . . . images of distant cool-green islands . . .

And I was so bored with it all! And it was all so boring, so boring! The blue sky bored me, and the green grass, and the yellow sun. The moon bored me, and all the little twinkling stars, and the black spaces in between the stars. The wind bored me, and the rain bored me, my boredom bored me, it all bored me, and I longed to lie down, and close my weary eyes, but I was so restless . . . Even William seemed bored and restless. As we played our games, our boring little games, irritable expressions would flit across his face, and once or twice he flared into anger for no particular reason. At such times I became furious and contemptuous and vowed never to see him again, but the next day he would arrive as usual, and again we returned to the white one-dollar bills, the pink five-dollar bills, the yellow ten-dollar bills . . . I don't mean that we didn't have our little enthusiasms, our little exuberances. One day we hammered two short iron posts into the back yard, initiating a few feverish days of horseshoes, and one day William came over with a shiny block of wood full of little holes, and so began a week of cribbage. One day we took a long hot bus-trip to Marjorie's. When we arrived we discovered that the ping-pong table was broken, and so we all sat around in the living room with nothing to do. William and I had not brought our bathing suits and besides, no one wanted to go swimming. There was a ballgame on television but Marjorie hated baseball. Her old Monopoly set was missing the Chance cards and half the properties. After a while we all went out back and sat on the grass in the warm shade of a crab-apple tree. William stretched out his legs, leaned back on one elbow, and plucked at pieces of crabgrass. I asked after Uncle Manny and Auntie Lou, who were out clamming. Marjorie kept jumping up to check something in the oven. After a while William and I glanced at each other and stood up. On the way home he stared out the dusty bus-window with a frown, and at my house we returned to the white one-dollar bills, the pink five-dollar bills, the yellow ten-dollar bills, and I began to feel that nothing would ever happen, that everything had already happened, that the entire universe was turning into a cliché, and I longed, I longed, I longed, I longed . . . Oh, it was a peaceful summer, an idle, evil, eventless summer, a shimmering and too-silent summer, like the fallen electric-wire I had seen one day, just sitting there, so peacefully . . . And the melancholy sun, and the white-hot moon . . . And my pains, my dreams, my sudden stiffnesses, night-nakedness between cool sheets . . . And as the days dragged on, and nothing happened, I had the sense that I was simply waiting: waiting for high school, waiting for the end of summer, waiting for adventure, waiting for death—oh, anything would do.

40

BORED WITH OUR BOREDOM, angry at our anger, in the last weeks of that summer William and I began to make long expeditions by bicycle. With surprising ease we surpassed our youthful voyages, and quickly found ourselves on familiar streets in neighboring townships. It was becoming harder and harder to get lost. William seemed intent on extending the range of the familiar, whereas I sought the ever-receding territory of the unknown; but it came to the same thing. Sometimes I longed for my earliest sense of things, when a pond with reeds, a stucco house, a grape arbor, a baseball diamond were detached landmarks floating like remote and shimmering islands in the dream-geography of childhood, not pieces of a vast jigsaw puzzle that increasingly fit in. In no time we completed the neighborhood around Reese Park. We attached it to a familiar row of stores bordering Philip Schoolcraft's part of town, and then we attached the park and the stores to a four-lane road from which a series of smaller streets wound their intricate and lazy way suddenly to William's neighborhood. I shared with William a certain pleasure in joining the green piece with a splash of red on one knob to the red piece with a knob-shaped hole in its side—but at the same time I felt uneasy, as if we were using up the universe. One day on the outskirts of town we passed a small bushy lot with a few leafless trees and a rippling hillock. There was something dimly familiar about it all, and suddenly I recognized the spacious countryside where I had gone blackberrying in some other life. At the end of the street we turned left onto a curving gray road and soon we came to a yellow-brown cliff with little bushes growing in the crevices. Across from the cliff was a bright yellow sign with a black backward S on it—and the sudden conjunction of that yellow-brown cliff and the old field of blackberries filled me with a curious anguish.

Leaving early in the morning, and returning in time for dinner, each day we traveled farther; and one day we discovered an island.

We had come to an unfamiliar region of dark wooded hills and long riverlike lakes. As we rode along a black winding street on which the blacker shadows of telephone wires lay in long parallel curves we saw, through sudden rents in the green-black pines descending on our right, sunny pieces of blue lake-water tipped with dancing points of light. It was almost noon, by William's watch. Around the next bend a narrow road appeared in the trees. We turned onto that road, lightly littered with pinecones and brown needles and prickly brown pine-twigs, and went rippling down through shadows torn by holes of light. A stone wall rose higher and higher on our left. On our right the water was no longer visible. After a while the road turned sharply, an old railroad track appeared, suddenly below us lay a forlorn grassy field and a dusty parking lot aflash with cars; beyond the field was a thinner stand of pine, among which little brown picnic tables were scattered; and clearly through the pines we saw the still-distant lake, now sparkling gray, and the wooded hills of the opposite shore.

From the parking attendant in his white shed we learned that rowboats and canoes could be rented by the lakefront in the more thickly wooded region to the right of the picnic grounds. There, before a tilting shack, we found an old wooden pier with gray rowboats tied on both sides, in water that was now dark brown. A rusty red canoe speckled with sun and pine-needles lay on its side upon the half-bared roots of a pine. In the brown twilight of the shack, pierced by bars of dusty sunlight, a frowning older boy, wearing faded dungarees and a white t-shirt with the sleeves rolled up to his shoulders, removed from a dark corner two upright gray oars. There was a clear line on his upper arms where the tan ended and the white began. He accompanied us out onto the pier and waited with spread legs and folded arms as we looked at the double line of gently moving rowboats, all of which contained dark puddles. Slowly by turns we stepped down into a peeling boat and watched the dark water rushing at our shoes. Clumsily we fitted the heavy oars in the clanking oarlocks and at once the attendant untied the boat, gave us a push, and shouted "Put in your oars!" as the oars banged against the sides of neighboring boats. He stood frowning at us on the edge of the pier, his arms folded across his chest. Slowly the gray pier floated away, growing smaller and smaller until suddenly it was shut out of view by a bend in the wooded shore. At first William rowed close to shore, among the dark brown shadows and bright yellow-brown sun-spaces, but soon he rowed out just beyond the shady fringe, into the bright gray depthless water.

It was a bright hot day. William took off his shirt. Across the lake a little red canoe with two little people in it flashed in the sun. A breeze stirred a distant part of the water, changing it from glass to quartz. Far away, on the other side of the lake, a motorboat appeared. After a few minutes the calm lake began to heave, our boat rocked in a storm, small waves slapped the bank, then all was calm again. In the bright distance a shadow appeared on the water. It came sweeping toward us, and suddenly we were rowing on a grim gray lake, among gloomy trees, in a dark and lonely region, but already in the distance a patch of brightness was growing, it was sweeping toward us, it was coloring the trees with lighter green and putting flashes on the dead water, suddenly the dark gray boat was radiant light-gray cut with black shadows, bright drops sparkled on the lifted oars, William frowned in the fierce light, and in the distance, on the opposite shore, strangely remote from the blazing summer day, a dark house sat in mournful shadow.

After a while I took the oars. William sat on the seat facing me and replaced his shirt to prevent sunburn. He took a long swallow from the canteen, tipping his head far back and suddenly bending forward. He wiped the back of his hand across his dripping mouth. "Aach," he said, "I needed that." Then he unrolled his brown paper lunchbag, unfolded loudly the wax-paper wrapping of an egg-salad sandwich, and took an enormous bite. The day was bright and clear. Everything stood out sharply. It was a precise day, a detailed day, the sort of day that is painted not in broad brushstrokes—a dab of green for foliage —but leaf by leaf and leaf-vein by leaf-vein. The dripping oars, the prickly black-green reflections of the pine branches, the fresh, faintly sour water-smell, the bits of boat breaking apart and coming together in the water, all seemed to quiver with a rich significance, as if the day were about to break into speech. Despite my laziness and love of shade I felt oddly happy in the hot sun, with my hands on the warm round wood of the oars. The oars pulled through the water with a pleasing tension, lift-ing with sudden lightness into the unresisting air, and as I rowed I leaned forward and pulled back, leaned forward and pulled back, leaned forward and pulled back, it seemed, all the gliding pines and the flowing shore.

Around a bend the island appeared. It was a solitary wooded island, nearly halfway out across the water. And at once I felt an unbearable yearning, as when, on somnolent summer after-noons, I had longed to melt into pictures in storybooks, and turning to William I said in a bored, weary voice: "I guess we could make it out to that island there, if you think it's worth it. I don't care, myself. I bet they don't allow it, anyway. Besides, it doesn't look all that interesting."

"I don't see why they wouldn't allow it," said William, gazing at the island with a frown and narrowed eyes. "Myself, I could use a rest. But if you think it's not worth it . . ." He shrugged.

"Oh, I don't say it's not worth it. It might be worth it. Who knows what we'll find out there? Doubloons, pieces of eight, a skull, Robinson Crusoe's hat . . . Besides, you're right. We need a rest. Yes, we ought to go out there . . . explore the territory . . ."

William took the oars, for by now my hands were stinging and my back ached, and at once we headed toward the island, out over the deep water. Glancing over my shoulder I was startled to see the shore floating back and back and back and back. The water had become a thick wet gray. The rowboat seemed to be sitting too low in the dangerous water, and on the floor a heavy puddle rolled loudly from side to side. The oars slid dangerously in the jumping and clanking oarlocks and all at once I remembered a movie in which great waves came crashing down onto the ship's deck. A man in a hooded yellow slicker stood glistening beside the tipping rail, and down below, in the narrow cabin, a lantern swung wildly from the ceiling, and suddenly William lost hold of an oar. It went rushing through the oarlock, a man with streaming hair and staring eyes fell through dark water, at the last moment William seized the oar, and over his shoulder, not too far away, dark-green individual leaves were visible on the separate and enlarging trees.

As we came closer I scanned the dark water for the dangerous tops of rocks, but nothing appeared except bits of floating grass. The island was a thicket of trees that seemed to come right down to the water. Suddenly through the brown water I saw flat black rocks with clumps of grass growing between them. Just ahead, the tops of grassblades stuck up through the water. With dreamlike ease we floated right up to the island, tearing through yellow mats of dead grass that lay composed in intricate swirls. We dragged the boat up onto a tree-shaded crescent of damp earth. A black barkless log with green fur growing on it lay partly in the brown water. To the left and right of the little shore, and directly before us, a shady wood rose up. Several trees came right down to the water, exposing fat bunches of twisting mossy roots. Here and there grew little four-petaled yellow wildflowers. "Well," said William, "this is okay." He stood with his hands in his back pockets, frowning and looking around and nodding in silent approval. Then he turned to me and said: "Let's give it a look." And jerking his head in invitation, he stepped into the trees.

There was, in fact, nowhere to go but in, and as the shade closed over me I felt, in the midst of a vague excitement, a little sharp burst of disappointment, as if I had expected to disappear. Stepping on snapping twigs, ducking under branches, I followed William through the moist clinging undergrowth. Through the thick foliage overhead, dark blue pieces of sky looked down. Suddenly, between dark trunks, the sunny lake appeared. The trees thinned out on this side of the island; a few brown rocks rose from the water. Sunny pine trees lined the opposite shore. "So that's it," I said, looking around as if I had missed something, and William said: "Look at that, Crusoe, you lowdown varmint. An island." He stood with his legs spread and his thumbs tucked into his pants. He took a deep breath, putting his hands under his ribs and thrusting out his thin chest.

Later, in a shady clearing near the edge of the lake, William carefully laid himself down in the high grass, parting the blades to check for stones and insects. He crossed his arms under his head and lay staring up at the overarching leaves. Then he rolled over on his side, leaning on an elbow. Reaching over to a long slender weedstalk, he plucked it with a sound of breaking string. He placed the weed in his mouth, turning it between his fingers as he frowned through the dark trees at the sunny lake. Here and there on his shady dungarees, on his plaid shirt, on his bare forearms, bits of sunlight moved. "You look like Davy Crockett," I said, sitting nearby against a rather hard tree. "I'm hungry," I added, plucking a weed of my own. "Reckon there's any bar in them thar woods, Davy?" "Tain't likely, Dan'l." I settled back against my tree. My shoulders ached and my palms throbbed faintly. Far away a buzzing motorboat cut across the lake. I began to think of the long trip home. After a while ripples began to fall on the shore. "Man," said William, sweeping up an arm, "this is the life." "Oh," I said wearily, shrugging one shoulder, "this is the life, I guess."

41

HIGH SCHOOL OPPRESSED ME: the dreary brown corridors, the dark rows of lockers, the dusty window at the turn of the stairs ... And shoes in the corridors, the dreary brown corridors ... Never had I seen so many shoes. The polished brown shoes, the dusty brown shoes, the scuffed brown shoes, the creased brown shoes, the pointy brown shoes, the blunt brown shoes, the dark brown shoes, the light brown shoes, and the red-brown shoes and the purple-brown shoes, and the big brown shoes and the little brown shoes, and the fat brown shoes and the thin brown shoes and the laced brown shoes and the smooth brown shoes, and the polished black shoes and the dusty black shoes and the scuffed black shoes and the creased black shoes and the blue suede shoes and the flat red shoes and the fuzzy tan shoes and the dull white shoes ... But really it is difficult to say what I mean. And perhaps it was only the prickly crewcuts, and the bouncy ponytails, and the shiny waves. And really it is impossible to say what I mean. But high school oppressed me: the dreary brown corridors, the dark rows of lockers, the dusty window at the turn of the stairs ... And shoes in the corridors, the dreary brown corridors ... With my chin in my hand I would gaze through tall windows with dark yellow shades coming partway down. From one room I saw a lawn, a thin maple, a thick flagpole, a gray road. From another room I saw a strip of dark asphalt that fell to a green field ending in towering tiers of empty gray benches, and behind them a wire fence, railroad tracks, the red-brown backs of stores. Some of the windows were raised slightly, and between the sill and frame were sharp, bright images of the dusty, faded, faintly rippling scenes above. Sometimes a train passed, shaking the windows, and I would imagine a stranger seated in that train, leaning back and looking out at the dark school with its rows of tall windows. Wearily I walked in the dreary brown corridors with their rows of olive-green lockers. Wearily I climbed the foot-hollowed stairs, sliding my hand on the nicked brown banister. Wearily I sat down and leaned my elbow on the glossy blond writing-surface of a movable desk-chair—and as the arm suddenly collapsed, I watched my heavy algebra book slide with dream-slowness toward the rim. I liked putting all the x's on one side of the equation and all the boring numbers on the other side. I liked the black, plump, prickly German letters, the soft, dreamy, drowsy sound of schön, and the mysterious dark change that took place when fire became Feuer. On the glossy red-and-white covers of my school-books I liked to trace dark blue outlines around each letter with my ballpoint pen. In one room there was a toylike object consisting of eight shiny steel balls hanging in a row and touching one another. When one ball was pulled away and allowed to strike the remaining seven, one ball from the far end would swing out. When two balls were pulled away and allowed to strike the remaining six, two balls from the far end would swing out. When three balls were pulled away and allowed to strike the remaining five, three balls from the far end would swing out, and when four balls were pulled away and allowed to strike the remaining four, the four remaining balls would swing out. But when five balls were pulled away and allowed to strike the remaining three, then not only those three but two of the original five would swing out, preserving a mysterious symmetry. Wearily I walked in the dreary brown corridors with their rows of olive-green lockers. Wearily I climbed the foot-hollowed stairs, sliding my hand on the nicked brown banister. Wearily I sat down and leaned my elbow on the glossy blond writing-surface of a movable desk-chair . . . I scarcely saw William any more. For some reason he was in none of my classes and we now rode to school each in a different bus. Once or twice he rode home with me after school, but in my room he seemed anxious about his homework, he kept looking at his watch, we had little to say to each other, and I felt relieved when he went away. A school-remoteness seemed to have come over him. And how strange it was to see him walking tensely along the dreary brown corridor, with his hair combed up in a wave and brushed back on one side, looking neither left nor right, but wary, wary, and smiling abruptly—as if unwillingly—and passing on.

Perhaps because there was nothing better to do, I was working fairly hard. In school I ignored everyone, concentrating on class-work and writing away efficiently at my desk, and home from school I would change quickly into my playclothes and go at once to my desk. Closing the blinds, and pushing the button of my twin-bulb fluorescent desk-lamp, I set to work solving the algebra problems at the end of the chapter, copying out the solutions neatly on a new sheet of notebook paper and writing in the upper right-hand corner my name, and below my name the course-name, and below the course-name the date. Then I turned to German, reading over the new selection, memorizing in order the neat lists of dark black vocabulary words with their pale black definitions, answering carefully the questions at the end of the chapter, and memorizing my half of the conversation between Herr Meyer and Herr Schmidt. At dinner I was silent and sullen. After dinner I returned at once to my room, and pushing the button of my twin-bulb fluorescent desk-lamp I would lean forward to read a chapter of general science and work out the problems at the end. Then I would read the assigned pages in my world-history book and answer at great length the tedious questions at the end, and then, for I was still not done, I was never done, I would read two chapters of *Ivanhoe*, study my vocabulary and spelling list, and diagram ten sentences. Sometimes there would be a knock at my door, and with a stern frown I would look over my shoulder and say: "Yes? Yes? What is it?" Then the door would open and mother would appear, holding a small white plate on which stood a glass of milk half-circled by overlapping chocolate-chip cookies. "I thought you might be hungry, Arthur. You've been working so hard. It's so hot in here . . ."—and I would suffer patiently this interruption of my work. Sometimes I would grow suddenly weary. Then I would think of William, at his large dark desk, bent over with a frown of concentration as he wrote out the math problems in small, neat, slanting numerals. And at once I would bend over my work with renewed energy.

   At night I found it difficult to fall asleep, and I would wake up weary and heavy-headed, but by the time I arrived at school I felt a tense, strained alertness.

   One rainy afternoon toward the end of September I was sitting in German class, waiting for the bell. I had finished my silent seatwork and had read ahead in the next lesson and now there was nothing to do but wait for sixteen minutes. There was a scratching of pencils, a hissing of radiators, a dripping of rain. High overhead, one of the fluorescent light-fixtures, resembling a long, luminous ice-cube tray, flickered faintly. From time to time people coughed softly, as if they were at a play. I was gazing idly about the room, thinking of nothing in particular, when my attention was arrested by an empty desk in the middle of the row beside the windows. There was nothing unusual about an empty desk, and yet there was something oddly familiar about it that I could not quite grasp. It looked exactly like all the other desks in German: dark brown and old, it was screwed into the yellowish lacquered wood of the floor. Vaguely I recalled that it had been empty the day before. I had no memory of the absent student, and as the dreary minutes continued I kept glancing over to the window-row—lowering my eyes abruptly as a girl looked up with a frown.

At last the bell rang, and gathering my books wearily, wearily I walked along the dreary brown corridor to World History, where I sat down and leaned my cheek on the back of my hand. The thick, black-covered book, the double columns with their fat black titles, the small, blurred, grayish photographs, made me think of World History as a gray-haired grandmother in a black dress with a gray shawl over her shoulders, sitting drowsily in her rocking chair in the parlor before the fire, dozing off as she dreamed of her lost youth. On the margin of my notebook paper, as a thin voice talked about ancient trade routes, I drew shaded cubes, striped beachballs, cups with handles, apples with stems. At last the bell rang, and gathering my books wearily, wearily I walked along the dreary brown corridor, down the brown stairs, and along another corridor to my study hall. There I completed all my algebra homework, looking out from time to time at the blurred, trickling field and the wavering bleachers. But at last the bell rang, and gathering my books wearily, wearily I walked along the dreary brown corridor, up the brown stairs, and along another corridor to my homeroom class, where I sat down wearily to wait for another bell. As I waited, I looked at the green blackboard with its white scribble of obscure formulas, at the long pale-green chalktray with its white dust and its shapeless stub of white chalk, at the black carvings on the top of my old brown desk, and when I turned and glanced across the room at the dark sky, I saw an empty desk in the middle of the row beside the windows.

And perhaps that would have been the end of it all, but the next day the absence appeared again. I noticed it instantly when I entered homeroom, nor was I surprised to see it repeated in my morning English class. It appeared again in my afternoon German class, and when I entered homeroom at the end of the day it was waiting for me in the row beside the windows. All that day I tried to recall the absent student, but I had so little noticed him when he was present that I could form no impression whatever. Suddenly, as I rode home on the bus, there came into my mind the startlingly clear image of a red-headed boy with piercing blue eyes; with annoyance I realized that I was recalling a face I had seen in the cafeteria. I had no name for the missing student, for in homeroom and in both classes attendance was taken silently. The next day, when I entered homeroom, I saw at once that he was absent. With strange elation I watched as two people sat down casually, indifferently, leaving between them an empty desk. That afternoon in German I was troubled to see a familiar boy sit down at that desk—but at once he rose, realizing his error, and moved to the desk behind. With secret pleasure I looked forward to the end of the day, when I might watch it take shape again in homeroom. For already I was looking forward to it, my absence, already I felt that it was attending me. At the same time I felt that I was only waiting, and the next morning, as I entered homeroom, I did not look immediately at the window-row, but glanced first at the green blackboard, and next at the teacher's desk—and suddenly, with a sharp intake of breath, I flung a glance at the window-row. I thought of asking someone, but for some reason I hesitated. And perhaps, I thought, it has always been empty, perhaps no one notices except me.

42

ONE WEARY, melancholy, and oppressive morning, when the sky was gray but dully luminous, and the world was nothing but a long brown corridor, I hung up my coat, took out a book, banged my locker shut, and stepped into homeroom, where glancing first at the blackboard, and next at the teacher's desk, and then at the row beside the windows, I uttered a faint gasp, raised my hand to my chest, and instantly lowered my eyes. With fierce, feverish calm I walked to my desk in the middle of the second row from the door. For a few moments I sat without stirring before slowly raising my eyes and turning my head. She was sitting motionless at her desk with her face turned toward the window. Her ankles were crossed and her hands rested lightly in her lap: the back of one hand in the palm of the other. Darkly her shoulders fell forward, giving her back a curve. The windowsill was at the level of her eyes, and her pale, mournful face was lifted slightly but already she was fading, already there was nothing but an empty brown desk . . . She was always absent. Or rather she was so often absent that absence seemed her element, from which she would emerge suddenly with dreamlike vividness—only to fade away again. I seemed to see her fixed in a pose: sitting motionless at her desk with her face turned toward the window. Her ankles were crossed and her hands rested lightly in her lap: the back of one hand in the palm of the other. Darkly her shoulders fell forward, giving her back a curve. The windowsill was at the level of her eyes, and her pale, mournful face was lifted slightly as she looked out at the gloomy sky with eyes narrowed against the light. She wore a black skirt, a white blouse, and a dark green sweater buttoned at the throat but hanging loosely over her shoulders like a cape. Her black, wavy hair was parted on the side and came rippling down over her ear and a little below her shoulder. Through her dark sweater pressed the faint outlines of her shoulderblades, and on her white leg, below the knee, but again she was fading, again there was nothing but an empty brown desk ... Often when she appeared she would seem deeply weary, drained of energy as her cheeks were drained of color. At such times her pallor, intensified by the blackness of her hair, had about it a touch of the ghastly. And indeed there was something of the phantom about her; and secretly I called her The Phantom Eleanor. I would see her sitting very quietly at her desk before her open German book, staring fixedly at the page, but there was something too rigid about her pose, as if her attention were absent, and sometimes when she was called on she would give a sudden start, and with a crimson blush on her white, too-white cheek she would say: "Oh, I was ... I'm sorry, what did you ..."

Through her dark sweater pressed the faint outlines of her shoulderblades, and on her white leg, below the knee, was a small purple-yellow bruise.

She did not hold herself deliberately aloof, but neither did she seek out friends. Rather she passed among her classmates as among so many ghosts, casting upon them a vague and intermittent attention. You would see her talking to some girl, smiling and nodding, but slowly a vacant look would come into her eyes, and although she still smiled, still nodded, her smile would lack a certain tension, her nods would seem slower and somehow inaccurate. Or she would be writing away at her desk, pausing and then scratching on. She would be frowning in concentration, and all at once her frown would fade, her gaze would float to the edge of the page, her pencil would still be scratching on, and suddenly she would look down at the page, and with another frown she would begin to erase. She was always like that: drifting off, floating away ... or knocking into things. She was always knocking into things. You would see her walking along the aisle with downcast eyes, so wearily, so mournfully, like a sad, sad queen in a high, high tower, and suddenly she would bend over, frowning and rubbing her knee. The next day there would be a dark purple bruise on her white leg. I would watch the purple turn slowly yellow as the days passed, and sometimes, with a strange feeling, I imagined that she must be covered with bruises, on her arms, on her hips, on her breasts, on her thighs ... like some ripe, soft, damaged fruit. And always there was that air of carelessness about her, as if her attention wandered even from herself. Her very clothes, which gave a general impression of dark neatness, revealed little flaws of inattention that sprang to my notice. There were, for example, her flat, black, soft-looking shoes. The left one had a faintly collapsed look about it: she had worn it down in such a way that her foot rested half on the bottom and half on the inner side. When she walked, in her shuffling and rather indolent fashion, leaning back slightly from the waist as she hugged to her stomach an upward-slanting notebook and an uneven pile of books, then her left heel, shiny and reddish, kept rising from the shoe, which went slapping with odd vigor against the floor; and when her heel descended it would crush down the soft back, which would begin to unfold slowly as her heel lifted again. And that slow unfolding, that sudden crushing, that slow unfolding, that sudden crushing, impressed themselves so forcefully upon me that riding home on the bus with my neck resting against the leather seat or sitting at my desk with my forehead leaning against the outspread fingertips of one curved hand I would see quite clearly, when I closed my eyes, that sudden crushing, that slow unfolding, that sudden crushing, that slow unfolding. Then she had a dark green skirt that buttoned in back. One day the black zipper below the button was partway down, exposing a bright inch of silky blouse. The girl behind her leaned forward, whispering, and rather wearily she reached back, trying now to look over her shoulder, now to peer around the side, and finally, without looking, she pulled up the zipper and pushed down the little metal part with a forefinger, and placing her hands in her lap she looked out the window. But the zipper was still not closed, for it had caught on a bunched-up piece of blouse, and again the girl leaned forward, whispering, and again she reached back, with a frown of annoyance, trying now to look over her shoulder, now to peer around the side . . . Often she would forget what she was doing. As she sat at her desk in English class, reading in our book of classical myths, she would wind a black strand of hair slowly about a finger, and then she would stop, leaving her finger bound in her hair; and as she turned the page and absently began to lower her hair-bound hand, she would wince with sudden pain. And different parts of her would often seem to go their own way, as if she failed to watch over all of them at the same time. Once, as she gave one of her stifled yawns, with shut quivering lips and tense under-eyes, she bent a fist up to her shoulder, and slowly, languorously unfolding her arm until it was stretched all the way out, she opened her fist and spread her fingers tightly, tensely, a ripple passed through her arm, her fingers wiggled, suddenly it was over, she returned to her book, leaving her arm oddly suspended for a few moments, as if she had forgotten it.

She was always absent. Sometimes for a day, once for two weeks; I did not know what was wrong with her. Only, she was so tired, so inattentive, so absent even when she was present. Often I would see her sitting with her hands in her lap, her shoulders falling forward and her face turned toward the window. Once, as I watched, I saw her head turn slowly from the window. I saw her mournful gaze fall on the brown radiator, on the edge of her desk, on the next aisle, and I knew I should turn away, but I did not turn away, and when she saw me seeing her she flushed and lowered her eyes, and I jerked my eyes away, feeling in my neck a hot flush. But often, when I glanced at the window-row, I would see only her empty desk. There it sat, with its three round slats under a curved chairback and a ridge of black metal running down the side and screwed into the floor. And as I watched the desk take shape in homeroom, and in English, and in German, and in homeroom, I felt not elation but discontent. And perhaps it was only that the absence was no longer like the old absence, which had been an abstract absence, an absence of nothing, the absence was now a specific absence, an absence, for example, of crossed ankles and two hands resting lightly in a lap: the back of one hand in the palm of the other.

One rainy day when, having hung up my dark dripping coat in the locker, and thrown in my wet earth-smelling rubbers, I entered homeroom shortly before the bell, I saw at once that she was absent. An intense annoyance came over me. I sat down at my desk, in the second row near the wall, and looked across the room at the gray, dripping windows. The attendance sheet was passed around. I scribbled my name, and finally someone was sent with the sheet down to the principal's office. Then we stood up, and recited the Lord's Prayer, and pledged our allegiance, and sat down. There was a click, and a student's voice came into the room, announcing an assembly and urging everyone to buy tickets for the Thanksgiving game. The voice ended, and quiet conversation was allowed. I began drawing shaded cubes on the blue, faintly bumpy cover of my notebook. A pocketbook clicked shut, or open. A desk-chair creaked. Someone laughed softly. A door opened, and when I looked up, and saw Eleanor Schumann striding breathlessly and a trifle awkwardly across the front of the room, I felt a sudden bursting sensation in my stomach, and at once I lowered my eyes, as if in pain.

43

AND NOW A STRANGE LANGUOR came over me, a physical sorrow, a dolor of muscles, a desolation of the blood. Home from school, I would change out of my schoolclothes and lie down with a book, and after a while I would notice that I was still on the same page. I would frown down at that page, imagining as I did so the pale, serious youth, lying on his bed before an open book, under the pulled-out wall-light. There he lay, the pale, serious youth, in his faded dungarees and his dark blue flannel shirt. There he lay, the pale, serious youth, with his slender hands, his dark, tousled hair, and his frown of stern concentration. There he lay, the pale, serious youth, in his gloomy room, in his mournful house, on a cold and silent darkening autumn day; and suddenly I would be stirred by a tender melancholy. And at once I would imagine, on his face, a look of tender melancholy. Then I would turn over, and placing my hands behind my neck I would look up at the shadowy ceiling; and anyone watching, secretly watching, would have seen that look of tender melancholy. And I would be so stirred by that look of tender melancholy that sadness, like a disease of the nervous system, would ripple through my skin. Pale as death he lay, the pale, serious youth, while far away there came the sound of an opening door. Gentle footsteps sounded. Suddenly, on his cheek, he felt a gentle hand. And closing my eyes, and raising my hand to my cheek, I would press the palm softly against my skin, shuddering in an ecstasy of desolation. At dinner I was silent and sullen. I sat staring at a white paper napkin with a satiny pattern of swirls and mother said: "Twice and I'm not going to ask you again," and when I looked up I saw with surprise her angry face. After dinner I returned to my room, where sitting down at my desk I would push the button of my fluorescent lamp. First one bulb would flicker on, and then the next, and as I pulled from my pile of books my orange German book, suddenly I would be seized by a feverish sorrow, my heart would beat painfully, and raising my hand to my forehead I wondered whether I had a fever.

In the morning I was silent and sullen. As I rode to school I would look out the window at a curb, a branch, a grocery store, a garbage pail, and suddenly my chest would contract, a feverish sorrow would seize me, wearily I closed my eyes, but already I was taking off my coat, already I was entering homeroom, already I was looking at the empty desk in the middle of the row beside the windows. And at the sight of that empty desk a prickly sensation rippled across my arms and chest, my temples throbbed, and I felt so ill, so weary, so unable to pull myself through the thick brown clinging day, that for a moment I could not move, blood drained from my temples, and I wondered whether I would faint, or die. Then I sat down heavily at my desk, wondering how I could pull myself through the thick, brown, clinging day. There were twenty-four hours. If I concentrated my attention very carefully on my work, then I could go from class to class, from desk to dinner, from dinner to bed, and finally I would fall asleep, I would wake up, I would step into homeroom, and she would be there, she would be there, sitting with her hands in her lap and her face turned toward the window. But at the thought that tomorrow she would be there, I cast another look at the empty desk, and only then did I seem to feel the full force of her absence, which struck at me and bruised me with its hard brown edges. Yet even then I wondered whether she might still arrive, for the bell had not yet rung. But when I looked up, and saw that there were only two minutes before the bell, I felt as if I had been struck in the chest, and I abandoned all hope, in order to spare myself. And at once I began to feel relief at her absence, for if she appeared, then I would have to suffer the sudden shock of her arrival, but if she did not appear, then I could remain in desolate peace. And at once a sad calm came over me, and I thought how soothing it would be to walk through the peaceful brown day, knowing she would not be there. And I became so reconciled to the smooth brown image of her absence that when at last she did appear, hurrying in breathlessly before the bell, I felt a shock of such desolation that I cast at her a look of pain.

Then sometimes in the morning, when she was there, suddenly and unaccountably I would refuse to look. Grimly I would open my general science book, or else I would stare with a slight frown at the green blackboard at the side of the room, with its scribbled white formulas. I would refuse to look as I stood starring at the flag with my hand on my pounding heart, I would

refuse to look as I stared down at my loosely folded hands. I
would refuse to look as I rose from my seat and walked along
the aisle and into the corridor, and when I entered Algebra and
sat down in my glossy desk-chair, all at once I would realize
what I had done, and I would look about me in a desolate daze.
Then I would imagine her sitting mournfully with her hands
in her lap and her face turned toward the window, or staring
absently at the back of a chair as her long thumb and forefinger
played with one of the white and faintly iridescent buttons of
her plain white blouse, and I would envision her so intensely
that when at last, seated in English class with a pounding heart,
I saw her enter with another girl, holding her bookheap against
her stomach and nodding briskly and almost cheerfully, rage
and disillusion would well and break in me, and I would look
away savagely, as if I had been betrayed.

Mournfully I watched her walking with downcast eyes to the
front of the English class, where at the green blackboard she
reached up to write the first of five sentences in her wavering,
collapsing script, and as she reached up she rose slightly on her
toes, so that her bare left heel rose from her flat black shoe,
and just to the right of the blackboard I noticed the edge of
my brown wooden bookcase with the frayed red cover of a
dictionary, and William said: "Your move." His eyebrows were
close together. I shook the dice and dropped them on the board.
Mournfully I watched them turning over and over to the front
of the English class, where at the green blackboard she reached
up to write the first of five sentences in her wavering, collapsing script, and as she reached up she rose slightly on her toes,
so that her bare left heel rose from her flat black shoe. As she
wrote the sentences she kept stepping away from the board,
checking to see that the lines did not slant, and at the end she stood
back and read them over with a frown, holding her left elbow
with her right hand and resting the side of her tilted face on
her upraised left forefinger. Sometimes she stepped forward to
enlarge the loop of an l or e, and at last she dropped the chalk
with a click into the tray, rubbing her chalkdusty fingers to-

gether, and rising from her desk she walked with downcast eyes to the front of the English class, where at the green blackboard she reached up to write the first of five sentences in her wavering, collapsing script, and as she reached up she rose from her desk and walked with downcast eyes to the front of the English class, where at the green blackboard she rose from her desk and walked with downcast eyes to the front of the English class, where at the green blackboard she rose from her desk and walked with downcast eyes to the front of the rose from her desk and walked with downcast rose.

One day as I sat gathering my books at the end of German I heard the soft slap of a shoe and a rustle of cloth, and clutching the sides of a book I stared darkly at the back of the desk in front of me. To the right of the desk I saw a fluttering edge of black skirt, and suddenly she said: "Did she say to write out the answers to the Fragen?" "Yes," I said abruptly, violently, glaring down at my books, and when, lying on my bed with my arm over my eyes, I tried to reconstruct that scene in all its detail, I could see her round wrist with its loose circle of dark silver, her wide dark-red belt with its square copper-colored buckle, her long slender thumb with its flat, blunt, bitten-down nail, but I could not see her face.

44

FIVE AFTERNOONS A WEEK at precisely 1:59 I would raise my eyes to the big round schoolclock above the green blackboard. I would gaze anxiously at the long brown minute-hand, which looked away wearily, stifled a yawn, and began to close its eyes. Suddenly it sprang forward, a bell rang, books banged, chairs creaked; feverishly I walked along the dreary brown corridor to my homeroom class. And five afternoons a week at precisely 2:04 I would raise my eyes to the big round schoolclock above the green blackboard. I would gaze ironically at the long brown minute-hand, which looked at me insolently, twirling its mustache. Suddenly it sprang forward, a bell rang, chairs creaked, and Mr. Girolomo, raising his head abruptly from his desk, swept his black eyes across the room with a flash of challenge. He would pause just long enough for his authority to be asserted, but not quite long enough for his tyranny to be defied, and turning his head majestically to the first person in the row beside the windows he would nod once, very lightly, pausing at the bottom of the nod and lowering his black eyelashes briefly before lifting his head. Slowly and without a word the six people in the row beside the windows would rise and file out into the hall. Each row was supposed to return before the next row was dismissed, but because Mr. Girolomo was a wavering tyrant who desired to be loved as well as feared, often the second row was allowed to leave before everyone in the first row had returned, and sometimes the third row was allowed to leave after one person in either of the two preceding rows had returned. And every afternoon as I sat in homeroom, observing carefully the slow procession of rows, I would watch for her return. She was very slow. She never returned until after the second row had left, and sometimes she returned as people from the second row were returning and people from the third row were leaving, and once she came hurrying in as I rose trembling from my seat in the fourth row. And once she did not appear in the doorway until with throbbing temples I had turned left at the end of my row. Then I quietly stepped aside in order to let her pass, and as she passed she glanced at me, but not directly, allowing her gaze to brush across my cheek. And as she passed I felt on the backs of my fingers the breeze of her passing, I inhaled from her coat-collar a faint odor of fur, and I heard, beneath the slap of a shoe and the bang of a bracelet, beneath a soft flutter of cloth, faintly, very faintly, as if it were coming from far away, the delicate quick silky sound of one knee brushing past the other.

One day Mr. Girolomo seemed preoccupied. He sat with his

right elbow propped on his desk, the forearm raised, the thin wrist rising from the falling jacket-sleeve, and the long forefinger, bent upward at the tip, pressed against his right temple. He was frowning down at a piece of paper that lay on the desk before him and that he held up at one corner with his other hand. People from the second and third rows had begun to return but she had still not appeared. Raising his eyes, but not his head, to the fourth row, Mr. Girolomo swung his right hand outward at the wrist, so that the fingers were pointing toward the front seat; and with the second and third fingers he made two swift brushing motions. Then he lowered his eyes, swung back his hand, and replaced his long forefinger against his temple. As I rose from my desk I kept my eyes lowered. Rigidly I kept them lowered as I turned the corner, suddenly I raised them to the door, but it was someone else. Before me the brown-blond corkscrew curl at the bottom of a ponytail bounced up and down before a white sweater, I longed to plunge through that white sweater as through white smoke, suddenly I stepped on something and the girl before me hopped forward on one foot, bending nimbly sideways and slipping her red shoe over her upraised bare heel without breaking her stride. "Sorry," I murmured, and as I passed through the doorway and stepped into the cool brown hall I felt as if I had just passed softly through a wall. She was standing before her locker, buttoning the top button of her dark green wintercoat. Her locker door was open. At her feet lay a notebook and a fallen pile of books. My locker was separated from hers by seven lockers, and between us stood another girl, gripping her locker door with one hand and reaching up on her toes for a book on the top shelf. I looked at the little white numbers on my silver-and-black combination lock, trying to understand what they were doing there, I looked at the word RUDY scratched in the olive-green paint of the dented metal door, I looked at my notebook slanted against my hipbone, and none of this made any sense at all, for there she was, seven lockers away, and as I stood frowning before my locker in the brown hall it seemed to me that something intimate, mysterious, and impossible was happening, as if she and I were sitting alone on my back porch in summer, sipping lemonade and gazing through the slender white balusters at the bright green lawn with its dark green shade. As we sat together on my back porch in summer, sipping lemonade and gazing through the slender white balusters at the bright green lawn with its dark green shade, a warm-cool breeze ruffled her loose blouse-sleeve, bits of sun and shade moved on her legs and lap, her long white straw darkened as she drank, somewhere a locker banged, in the brown odor of corridors shocked with sadness I bowed my beating head, and suddenly I became enraged, but then I felt drained and weary. Beside me the girl banged her locker shut. Seven lockers away, Eleanor Schumann was sitting on her heels before her books with her legs pressed together and one knee higher than the other knee. As the girl brushed past me, Eleanor Schumann rose without her books and gazed up at her locker with a frown. Somewhere a door closed. In a weary monotone, not looking directly at me but brushing my cheek with her gaze, she said: "You're tall, would you mind getting down that book?" And vaguely, indolently, she pointed toward the top shelf of her locker. Lowering my eyes, I instantly stepped over. Without a word I reached up to the top shelf. The book was wrapped in brown paper and on the front was printed, on ruled pencil-lines, her name, the subject, and her home address. "Thank you," she said, lowering her eyes, but the next morning at the lockers as she spoke to another girl I saw her suddenly raise those eyes, exposing to my startled gaze, briefly before she lowered them, her large, piercingly black pupils, her gleaming mahogany irises, and the moist, faintly glistening whites, with their moist-pink tear-ducts and their delicate little red slashes.

45

AS THE WEATHER GREW COLDER she was more and more absent. She would be out for three days and appear for two, out for two days and appear for one. She seemed to be fading as the weather faded: blue into gray, green into brown, brown into white. Now when she appeared faint shadows showed below her eyes, and between her eyebrows were two small vertical lines. She seemed wearier and more mournful as she sat with her hands in her lap and her face turned toward the window. Now she wore heavy pullover sweaters, and folding her arms across her stomach she would hold both elbows, as if she were cold. One afternoon, glancing into the hall mirror, I saw faint shadows below my eyes, and between my eyebrows I noticed a look of strain. "Yes," I said softly, "that's all right," and suddenly I bent forward with a fierce stare that startled me. One cold day she appeared in a straight black skirt and, over a white blouse, a black jacket with small plump buttons that looked like faceted globes of glass. With her black hair, her black eyebrows, her black eyes, her black nostrils, her white face, her white neck, her white legs, her white hands, she seemed one of William's black-and-white photographs, retouched with not quite the correct shade of red in the flush of her mouth and the flush of her fingertips, not quite the correct shade of delicate blue in the backs of her hands, in her temples, at the sides of her neck. And as she sat at her desk with her white hands lying listlessly in her black lap, and her black lashes weighing down her white eyelids, beneath which lay blue shadows, it seemed to me that she was visibly fading.

One afternoon when I was sitting in German, gazing at the book spread open on my desk, I had the sensation that she was looking at me. My heart began to beat painfully, and I concentrated intensely on the page, frowning fiercely at the lines of print which seemed to be saying the same thing over and over again, over and over again. I felt a warmth in my cheek, and as I bent intensely over the page, frowning fiercely at the lines of print which seemed to be saying the same thing over and over again, over and over again, it seemed to me that her gaze was burning into my cheek and setting it aflame. And because I had only imagined her gaze it seemed to me that all I had to do was raise my eyes and look across the room to see whether she was looking at me with her imagined gaze, but because I had imagined her gaze I could not raise my eyes and look across the room for fear of meeting the gaze I had imagined. Strange ripples passed across my heart, I felt that my head was beginning to tremble slightly, I held myself rigidly over my book, I thought that perhaps I would raise my trembling head very slowly and turn my gaze very slowly and very casually in her direction, but suddenly I jerked my head in her direction. And I was so shocked to see her sitting at her desk with her hands in her lap and her face turned toward the window, that it seemed to me that she was only feigning, and that seconds ago she had whirled around and was now sitting with a pounding heart as she pretended to sit calmly, calmly, with her hands in her lap and her face turned toward the window.

It came over me, as she faded away, that I scarcely saw her at all. Even when she failed to be absent I would see her only in brief glimpses, which left long brown empty spaces only sometimes interrupted by sudden and as if supernatural appearances, as when, one morning as I made my way wearily up the brown stairs and turned onto the second-floor corridor, I saw her vanishing slowly into a distant room, or when, one afternoon after school, glancing out the bus-window with its crack shaped like a spiderweb, I saw her standing on the steps in a glow of autumn sunlight: and I had become so used to seeing her indoors, in a setting of brown walls and dusty windows, that her sudden freedom produced in me the effect of one of those portraits in old-fashioned stories, in which a mysterious change takes place, filling the observer with dread.

Then once, in the auditorium, she sat in the row before me. She sat not directly in front of me but one seat to the right. Up on the stage three seniors with blond crewcuts were talking about democracy and communism. She was wearing a wide leather belt, and as she breathed I could hear a faint creaking. I stared at her left shoulder in its dark green sweater, at the delicate black hairs on her cheek below her ear, at the edges of her black lashes which seemed to be trembling slightly, at the faint tensings in her neck as she minutely moved, and as I stared I felt in my neck the tensings of her neck and in my lashes the trembling of her lashes, I felt my arms flowing within her arms until my fingers slipped within her fingers, and stretching myself inside her until my skull rubbed against her skull and my toes wriggled within her toes I felt my shoulders within her shoulders and my knees within her knees and my breasts rising and falling faintly as I breathed, and as I breathed I felt my stomach pressing in and out against the wide leather belt with a faint creaking. Then I felt a drowsy, swooning languor, my heavy eyelids half-closed, suddenly she bent forward and I felt a shock of pain, as if she had torn herself out of me with loud ripping sounds.

And once, at the lockers, she put on her dark green wintercoat. With a sudden motion she reached up behind her neck and lifted her trapped hair from beneath the gray fur collar: and her falling hair, and the sudden stillness of the spread-out strands of her hair, reminded me of the wildly falling pick-up sticks of my childhood and their sudden stillness on the rug.

One dark afternoon as I sat in homeroom, wishing I had brought my umbrella and listening to the loud rain that hurled itself with three different sounds against the windows, the street, and the top of a car, I turned with a slight frown to look across the room at the noisy sky. She was looking directly at me. And I was so startled to see her looking directly at me that I forgot to take my eyes away, and continued to stare with parted lips long after she had jerked her eyes away, long after the pink flush staining her neck had seeped into my own.

That evening I resolved to walk home with her the next day after school. The mere desire to walk home with her seemed the violation of a law, and my chest contracted and a prickly feeling came over me as I carefully imagined, in slow detail, the long dreamwalk through lonely autumn landscapes, beneath black branches, in pools of yellow leaves. The next morning, after a sleepless night, when with pains in my stomach and with feverish vague expectations I climbed the stairs to the second floor, I saw her standing at the locker. And at once I felt a motion of annoyance, for I had not expected to see her standing at the locker but had carefully imagined her sitting at her desk with her hands in her lap and her face turned toward the window. As I went up to my locker I gave her a curt nod, noticing with displeasure the sloping tendon in her neck. All that day I angrily ignored her, she herself seemed tired and remote, and when I arrived home, and lay down on my bed with my arm over my eyes, I felt desolation spreading in me like an infection.

And at last she faded completely away, leaving behind her an empty desk. Each morning I hesitated before stepping into homeroom—where I would see, in the row beside the windows, her empty desk. I would see her empty desk in English in the morning, and German in the afternoon, and homeroom at the end of the day. One afternoon a watery November sunbeam trembling with dust came slanting across her chair, and as I gazed at that watery November sunbeam, trembling with dust, the empty air of her empty desk became so filled with her absence that it trembled on the verge of presence, and she seemed to be shadowily seated there, with her hands in her lap and her face turned toward the window. One afternoon in German the large blond boy with black eyeglasses who sat in front of her turned around and placed on her empty desk a blue three-ring notebook and two books. They remained there during the entire period, even though I observed them with a frown of outrage. The next day, as he turned to do it again, the teacher said: "Your books don't belong there, Donald," and I felt, in my chest, a sudden expansion, as if a bronchial congestion had been cleared. And morning after morning, as I stepped into homeroom, I would see her empty desk. I would see her empty desk in English in the morning, and German in the afternoon, and homeroom at the end of the day. And as the bleak days passed, and nothing happened, perhaps, I thought, perhaps it would be possible. But for a long while I hesitated.

46

ONE DARK AFTERNOON as I sat in German class, waiting for the bell, I was gazing across the room at the window above her empty desk, and as I stared through white reflections of fluorescent lights at the dark sea-like sky, at the bending top of a tree, at the wind-tossed flagpole rope knocking against the silver pole, clashing and clashing against the ringing pole, I felt a sudden motion in my mind, and suddenly I was cast deeply back.

As a child I was often sick. I would wake up with a mild pain in my throat and a faint burning in my eyes and I would listen to the sound of father rattling the hangers in his closet and mother stepping softly along the hall. She would tap on my door as she swished into the bathroom, but I would lie without a sound, listening to the bathroom door close softly, listening to the clash of the brass loops as father opened and closed the drawers of his bureau, over and over again, for reasons I could not imagine. When mother came out of the bathroom she would knock more loudly on my door, opening it a few inches but not looking in, before hurrying into the kitchen to put up the breakfast while father strode heavily along the hall to the bathroom and slammed the door. In the kitchen I could

hear the clash of pots and the heavy closing of the refrigerator
door. When father came out I would grow tense, for sometimes
he would fling open the door of my room, so that I would have
to lie there fully exposed to view, but usually he would cry
"Up and at 'em!" as he gave a loud rap that would cause the
door to open only a little more, and then he would stride down
the hall to his room, slamming his door. Again I would listen
to the clash of the brass loops, and then I would hear mother
hurrying along the hall. This time she would open my door all
the way and look in, holding her red robe at her throat and
saying with a frown: "Hurry up, Arthur, don't make Daddy
angry," which meant "Hurry up, Arthur, don't make Mommy
angry." With a faint voice I would whisper: "I don't feel well,"
which sounded to me far more serious than "I don't feel good,"
and at once a subtle change would take place beneath the
surface of mother's frown, so that her expression, outwardly
unchanging, showed not annoyance but intense concern. "What
is it, Arthur?" she would say, stepping toward me, "do you have
a fever?" and before I had a chance to answer she would bend
over me and touch to my forehead first one cheek and then the
other. Then she would draw back and stare at me with grave
sadness. And although I was pleased to see in her eyes a reflection of my suffering, for now I was justified in having stayed
in bed, at the same time I felt a shock of fear, for I wondered
whether I would die. And suddenly I longed to be well, I
yearned for school, I shuddered at the thought of falling behind
in my work. But now mother became very brisk and efficient,
and called for father, whose job it was to take my temperature.
I would hear the drawer of his bureau open and close, and he
would enter with the slender brown leather case of the thermometer, from which he withdrew the delicate glass rod with
its dark red lines and its secret column of quicksilver. Unlike
mother, father would seem quite cheerful, for although my
slightest indisposition filled him with alarm, he loved nothing
better than to take my temperature. Shaking the thermometer,
and holding it up to look at it with a frown, he would try to

place it in my mouth, but I would take it from him and place it delicately under my tongue, with the silver tip touching the sensitive gristly piece. "Under your tongue now, that's the fella," father would say as he began to time me for three minutes, frowning importantly at his watch and rubbing his thumb and forefinger nervously together. We all understood how important those three minutes were, for if the quicksilver failed to rise I was not really sick, I was practically well, perhaps I would even have to go to school. But the idea that I would have to go to school was now unbearable to me, for I had begun to grow accustomed to the idea that I was ill, and health, like a disease, threatened me with a loss of privileges. For although I disliked intensely the sick part of being sick, I loved to distraction everything else about it. At the end of three minutes that seemed like ten, father would remove the thermometer and, holding it up to a light or window, would study it with a frown as mother and I watched anxiously. And sometimes I wondered whether she too, despite her fears, secretly desired the quicksilver to rise, so that she might lavish upon me the full burden of her attention and affection, which only in illness was I strong enough to bear. Sometimes father would have trouble finding the quicksilver, and mother would say: "Well? Well? What's the matter? What does it say? Can't you tell us what it says? Do you have to keep us in suspense all day?" "Just a, hmmm," father would say, and suddenly: "Ninety . . . ninety . . . I can't seem to . . . no, there she is . . ." and turning triumphantly to mother he would cry, bursting with joy and pride: "Ninety-nine and a half! The boy is sick." "I knew it," mother would say, "I knew it, he's burning up." And she would cast at father a look of bitter reproach, as if by reading the thermometer he had caused my temperature to rise. Things began to happen very quickly then. Mother would begin making telephone calls, first to school, for she always stayed home with me on the first days of my illness, and then to the doctor, while father would go in and out of rooms bringing me things to ease my suffering: from the living room he would carry first the piano bench, which he covered with a white towel, and then the television, with its tail of wires, and then a metal folding tray, black with pink flowers on it, on which he placed a glass of water and a metal bell. It was just like a holiday. Meanwhile I would lie very quietly, trying to look like someone who was burning up, trying to conceal my pleasure, looking forward with tense excitement to the long days in bed when father would come home with a new present every day, and books and puzzles would pile up all around me, and school would recede farther and farther as day after day I roamed, a glittering and troubled king, in the golden halls of illness.

And even then I knew there was something not quite proper about being sick, for as I lay enthroned in bed, in the palace of my sickroom, strewn with the treasures of disease, I would recall from time to time the lines of children walking home from school with their books and assignments, or I would hear, somewhere beyond my window, the sounds of cars and buses taking people home from work. At once I would brush them from my mind and plunge feverishly into a jumbo jigsaw puzzle, but as the days passed and health began to threaten I found it harder and harder to banish the bright world from my dark paradise. The very afternoon soaked through my closed blinds and lay heavily against me, tickling me with the dusty pressure of its light. I would feel a tremor of shame as I heard mother crunch into the driveway on her return from school, heard her hanging up her coat in the front hall with angry metal sounds, heard her talking to Mrs. Schneider in the living room, heard her stride toward me across rugs and wooden floors until the door swung open, propelling toward me an unpleasant breeze, and she entered in her dark blue jacket and frilly white blouse. Casting at me an affectionate look, but one no longer brimming with anxious concern, as if only illness were completely lovable, she would say with a smile: "Well! How's my big boy? You certainly look better today. I suppose you'll be ready for school in a few days." Had she said "in a few weeks" I would have been plunged into despair, for it would have implied an

end, however distant, to my pleasant life of eternal recupera-
tion. But "in a few days" was so terrible that it was as if mother
had announced that I had only a few days left to live. She would
notice the change in my face, and at once the look of concern
would appear on her own face as she asked: "What is it?" I
would turn my face to one side, for I did not trust myself to
speak, and mother would come forward anxiously, asking:
"What is it, Arthur? Aren't you feeling well?" And from the
depths of my despair, with absolute truth I would whisper:
"No." At once mother would bend over me, touching to my
forehead first one cheek and then the other, and shedding over
me a flowery scent of powder, as if she were a blossom. "You
don't seem to have a fever," she would say doubtfully, "still, as
soon as Daddy gets home," for mother could never find the
quicksilver, "we'll take your temperature." And even though,
when father came home, I failed to have a temperature, I knew
that I would not have to return to school "in a few days," for
a new note of doubt had been introduced, and with a last effort,
with secret guilt, with a shudder of dark delight, I abandoned
myself voluptuously to the crime of illness.

47

ONE DREARY AFTERNOON in the winter of the year, when the last
bell had rung and the final shuffle had begun, I found myself
lingering in the loud brown corridor, which soon became silent
and empty. From time to time as I paced the deserted hall I
stopped at a brown bulletin board to examine the mimeographed
notices that hung at many angles and gave off a damp, sad,
purplish smell, and then I resumed my wandering, past rows of
dark lockers broken by shiny maple doors, behind which I
sometimes heard bursts of quiet laughter, and coming to a
brown landing, where a copper-colored fire-extinguisher hung

on the wall above a brown radiator, I looked quickly about and peered through a dusty window at the row of yellow buses, pulling away slowly one by one. Soon the buses were gone and the sidewalk was deserted. Behind me, on the stairs above, a little old man in a baggy brown suit appeared, frowning down at me over dusty lenses. Shifting my books to the other arm, and only then realizing that my shoulder ached, I began to hurry down the stairs as if I were being pursued. At the bottom of the stairs I hurried along another brown corridor, past rows of dark lockers broken by shiny maple doors, past a shadowy white drinking fountain in its niche, past a display of burnished silver trophies behind glass, and coming to the hot and hissing front hall, where a yellowish bust of Lincoln had been turned sideways on its pedestal, I stepped out into the icy shock of a snowless winter afternoon. My cheeks tightened in the cold, and for a moment I stood on the deserted steps, gazing at the bare brown trees and the gray, almost white sky. Across the street two students with breathplumes coming out of their mouths turned to look at me with a frown. At once I descended, feeling darkly visible against the pale steps, and turning to the right I began to walk swiftly along the sidewalk. Soon a high wire fence rose up, dropping suddenly to a low stone wall where a purple-and-silver soda-can stood beside a fluted white cupcake wrapper lined with dark brown crumbs, then a dark hedge rose up, a big white building with black shutters appeared, I turned left, the road dropped down and I found myself approaching a black iron railway trestle, beyond which rows of stores were visible. Under the black trestle a sharp oilsmell mingled with a smell of damp stone. On the other side the center of town began. Through my transparent image passing in dark glass I saw a tower of dusty soupcans beside an open box of cigars, a barber in a white apron lazily drawing a long razor back and forth along a thick brown strop, a smiling cardboard lady in a white bikini holding up a green cardboard soda-bottle, a stern wooden man in a gray suit holding up his arms in an exhausting pose, a red-haired lady in a blue nightgown standing in a graveyard with her hands pressed to her ears and her mouth wide open, a white wall covered with pink and blue and green eyeglass frames, a watch rising and falling in a glass of water, a row of notebooks and a display of pens, a smiling lady in white boots and a cheerleader's costume standing with one knee raised and a baton held over her shoulder, a yawning man in shirt-sleeves with a yellow tape-measure around his neck, a panda sitting in a red wagon, a girl in red bermudas and a pink sweater sipping a strawberry milkshake at a green counter, a set of flat silver wrenches growing smaller and smaller and smaller and smaller and suddenly the stores ended and in the middle of the street, on a grassy mound, three iron soldiers were raising an iron flag. Then the road widened, a grassy divider with bare elms appeared, on both sides of the street loomed large white buildings with black windows. A few flakes of snow began to fall, and soon the sidewalks were covered with a translucent whiteness. A glass-covered sign on a lawn announced an evening of Bingo, behind it a gray Catholic church rose up, and turning left I began walking along a quiet street of small pale houses and large black trees. Under a darkening sky I walked in gently falling snow that now slanted toward me, and looking over my dark-coated shoulder lightly dusted with snow I saw a wavering line of footsteps following me along the deserted sidewalk. At a small old grocery store, where behind a black cash register a crooked calendar showed an autumn scene with pumpkins, I turned right, onto a street of dark bare hedges and dark-windowed houses, and as I walked I looked up at each corner street-sign at the top of its silver pole. At the third pole I turned left and found myself on an old-fashioned street of two-story wooden houses with porches and narrow sideyards. Detached garages were set far back at the end of dirt driveways lightly covered with snow. Dark thick twisting trees grew between the sidewalks and the road, softly the snow came down, and I walked more slowly, glancing at the numbers of the houses across the street and noticing how the widening bottoms of the trees, where root-top melted into trunk, resembled the fat-toed feet of elephants. My heart began to beat faster, a feverish weariness seized me, suddenly I saw a gray house with the number 86 in white iron numerals on the door, and although I was across the street I began to walk faster, glancing out the corner of my eye at the front porch on which an old brown rocking chair sat beside a green metal chair with a faded pink cushion. On each side of the steps from post to cornerpost a row of thin balusters supported a flaking handrail, below the level of the porch was a pattern of gray latticework, in the dark window to the right of the door, black reflected branches were entangled in a palely glowing lamp, then a dirt driveway appeared, at the end of the driveway stood a closed gray garage with two garbage pails on the side and a yellowish bare willow rising behind it. A wire fence emerged from behind the garage and ran along the back yard, which came into view as I continued to walk away, bare ragged bushes grew in an uneven line before the fence, behind them rose up the back of another garage, soon the driveway was shut out by the dark green corner of the next house. Slowly the dark green corner advanced across the gray porch, now sliding over the upright post, now touching the edge of the lamplit window, as the white corner of the next house moved across the driveway of the dark green house, and now the brown corner of the next house moved across the driveway of the white house and the white house moved across the porch of the dark green house and the dark green house moved across the lamplit window, the door, the next upright post, suddenly the gray house was swallowed up and crossing the street to the other sidewalk I began walking slowly back, past a yellow house, past a brown house, past a white house as the dark green house began to withdraw from the post, the door, the lamplit window, and as I stepped into full view of the gray house my heart began to beat painfully, my cheek felt flushed, a feverish weariness seized me, I longed to lie down, and close my weary eyes, but looking straight ahead at the faintly falling snow, the dark street, the pale houses, the gray sky, swiftly I walked past, and as I gazed into the

blurred distance, where the street and the sky and the softly
falling snow came together, I had the sensation that the street
would end, the sky would stop, the world would disappear, as
when, long ago, reading about the boy Columbus, who believed
that the world was round, suddenly I had imagined a flat world
shaped like a plate, from whose nightmare edge you could
plunge into blackness, wet snow ran along my cheek, in weariness I bowed my head, for a moment I could not imagine what
I was doing on this strange street, in this strange part of town,
on this snowy afternoon that looked like dusk. Then I stopped,
and turned, and did not move. For a few moments I stood there,
holding my heavy books while snow fell on my dark coat-arm.
Then with a sigh I turned again, and began to walk away, but
suddenly I turned, and began to walk back, faster and faster I
strode through the gentle storm, and as I came into view of the
gray house with the number 86 on the door my heart began
to beat painfully, a feverish weariness seized me, lowering my
eyes I walked swiftly past. When I was several houses away I
stopped, and turned, and did not move. "This is ridiculous," I
said aloud. Behind me a door opened. A little girl in a blue coat
and white mittens appeared, looking at me with a frown. Jerking my eyes away I began to hurry along the sidewalk, on my
right I noticed a gray house, swiftly climbing the five gray
steps I rang the bell. It was a loose black button in a gray oval.
It sounded like a telephone. I stamped my feet on the stiff fuzzy
mat. And suddenly I felt that my body had deceived me, that
it had rushed ahead of me before I had known where it was
going, and I could not understand what I was doing here, on
this strange street, in this strange part of town, on this strange
gray porch with its brown rocker, its green metal chair, its dark
window in which I could see a glowing lamp on a dark table,
high above I heard the sound of footsteps on stairs, suddenly I
realized that I was standing on a strange gray porch, on a
strange street, in a strange part of town, then the door opened
and there appeared before me a tall pale gray-haired woman in
a black dress. She glanced vaguely at me and then looked off at

the falling snow, which was coming down more swiftly now. Slowly returning her gaze to me she frowned suddenly, as if she had forgotten I was standing there, and raising to her throat a long, dry hand she said: "Yes?" And perhaps because of the long silence a constraint had come over me, and turning my head in the direction of the falling snow, but not all the way, I said: "It's coming down much harder now." When I turned back she was frowning at me, whether in anger or puzzlement I could not tell, and lowering my eyes I murmured: "Eleanor . . ." And at once I stopped, for I had not intended to say "Eleanor," I had intended to say: "My name is Arthur Grumm." "Eleanor . . ." she murmured, as if helpfully, and at once I said, raising my eyes: "My name is Arthur Grumm." And as if from far away I heard myself saying: "My name is Arthur Grumm," and I thought: I will turn now, I will run down the steps and across the snow, past the silver poles, past the iron soldiers, under the black railway trestle, but she said, in a coaxing tone: "Yes? Are you a friend of Eleanor's?" "Oh," I said, deeply relieved, "yes, yes, I mean no, I mean yes, but you see, I thought I'd bring a list of assignments, in case she, I've written them all down, where are, I have them here somewhere, I can't," and I began to fumble at my notebook, which was crushed shut by the weight of my books. Then I felt a book sliding from the center of the pile, it was too late, the book fell loudly onto the porch, yellow papers came out, and as I bent over another book fell, kneeling swiftly I began to gather my papers, above me I heard: "But isn't that sweet of you, Arthur. Please come in. Eleanor will be so pleased." And stepping back, and holding open the door, she waited as I hastily gathered my books and stepped over the threshold into the lamplit parlor. "Please sit down, Arthur," she said, taking my coat, "you must be tired," and gratefully I sank into a pillowy dark armchair that wheezed faintly as it let out its breath. "Yes," I said, as I listened to a sound of scraping coathangers, "it was a long walk here, then it started to snow," and wearily I closed my eyes, but opened them at once. Mrs. Schumann was gazing down at me with a dark, doleful gaze. "You poor boy," she said, "you must be very tired." I lowered my eyes and in a softer voice she said: "Eleanor will be so pleased." "Oh," I murmured, raising my eyes, but she had turned away, and striding swiftly across the room she began to climb the dark stairway that rose along the left wall. I watched her disappear at the top of the stairs, wearily I closed my eyes, but again I forced them open, and gazed about with heavy eyelids as overhead a door softly opened and closed. I was sitting beside the glowing lamp, facing an empty fireplace. Before the fireplace sat a large white porcelain cat whose yellow glass eyes gleamed in the lamplight. In the center of the cluttered mantelpiece stood an old brass clock housed in glass. Below a round brass clockface with black numerals and lacy black hands, a pendulum was swinging slowly back and forth above a silver key that lay on its side, fast asleep. Scattered about the mantelpiece were a number of glass-covered oval photographs showing men with white mustaches and women with black shawls, a faded pink-blue-and-gold religious triptych, a small cabin with a little man and a little woman standing in front, a brown porcelain shoe with a red chimney and a little old lady looking out a window, three little ivory monkeys sitting side by side one with his hands over his eyes, one with his hands over his ears, one with his hands over his mouth, and crowds of little porcelain people: a Dutch girl with yellow braids and a white apron and wooden shoes, a pilgrim in a black hat and buckle shoes who was holding a brown musket over his shoulder, a white angel with gold-tipped wings who was holding a singing-book and looking up to heaven with her mouth shaped like an O, a man in a white wig and black knickerbockers and white stockings who had his arm tucked into his coat, a smiling red-cheeked man in baggy blue breeches who was playing a fiddle, a grinning gnome sitting on a barrel. Then I noticed that all about the room, on table-tops, on shelves, on the wide window-sills, little glass and porcelain figures were watching me. A red-and-white fox stood with his forefeet on a rock and his face turned toward me, a Scotsman in a kilt looked sternly at me as he played his silent bagpipes, a hunchbacked squirrel eating a nut gazed at me with wide staring eyes, a panther looked at me over his shoulder. Wearily I closed my eyes, a red fox walked across a table-top, a smiling red-cheeked man began to play his fiddle, a white cat with yellow eyes curled up in front of the fireplace, "poor boy," said the cat, and when I opened my eyes I saw Mrs. Schumann standing before me. "You poor boy," she said, casting down at me a dark, doleful gaze, "you must be very tired," and wearily I murmured: "You see, I haven't been sleeping well." "Yes, yes," she murmured, gazing down sadly at me, and suddenly I felt deeply sad, it was as if something terrible had happened, I longed for her to bend down and place her cheek against my forehead, but in a changed voice she said: "Eleanor will see you now." And turning toward the stairs she raised her arm in a vague, indolent gesture, saying: "At the end of the hall, the last room on your right." "Thank you, Mrs. Schumann," I murmured, pushing myself heavily to my feet, and as I pushed myself heavily to my feet I seemed to be struggling upward against a force pulling me from behind. Mrs. Schumann stood with her arm out, indicating the way, but her eyes had drifted down, she was staring absently at the foot of the lamp-table, wearily I began to climb the steep stairway, pulling myself up by the dark brown banister. At the dusky landing a faded glass-covered view of Venice hung above a faded glass-covered picture of a man in blue lying beside a haystack with his straw hat pulled over his eyes. In the wall-angle a corner-shelf held a little copper kettle, a little glass elephant with upraised trunk, and a porcelain soldier in white pants and a blue coat and a three-cornered hat, beating a drum. Two stairs rose to the right of the landing, and as I turned I happened to look back down the stairway, where I saw Mrs. Schumann standing at the bottom with one hand on the post, looking up at me with her dark, doleful gaze. "Yes?" I said softly, but she continued to gaze up at me without a word, and I wondered whether I was visible on the dusky, really quite dark landing. Then I turned away, climbed the two stairs, and found myself in a dusky hallway. A narrow strip of maroon carpet with a little wave in the middle ran along the floor. The dim yellow wallpaper showed a repeated pattern of bunches of faded purple grapes and faded green vines, with little faded foxes looking up. At the end of the hallway a high narrow mirror rose from the floor and leaned slightly forward. As I walked slowly toward the leaning mirror I watched my legs coming toward me, but in the mirror I was descending a steep slope, it was as if I could barely keep from hurtling forward, and as I advanced I strained back on my heels to keep from plunging down the slope, but when I glanced down I saw my straining feet walking lazily forward on the flat, rippling rug. Then I remembered riding with mother and father on the parkway, in the distance the sand-colored road rose steeply between dark trees, I imagined the car straining and straining toward remote heights until at last a dazzling view would appear and we would plunge down the other side, but somehow the hill never began, the road seemed to flatten out under the weight of the car, and I gazed out the window in confusion and disappointment at the road's rushing shoulder and the more slowly sliding-away trees. The last door on the right was slightly open, and placing my outspread fingers lightly on the wood I gave a gentle push. The door did not move. Snatching away my fingers and glancing down the hall toward the landing, as if I had done something wrong, I stood for a few moments considering what to do. In the mirror I saw myself standing with my hand still raised and the fingers outspread in the form of a claw. Instantly lowering my hand I leaned back for a while against the wall-angle between the mirror and the door, enjoying the cool dimness, suddenly I stepped forward, grasped the doorknob firmly, pushed the door inward—it opened with startling swiftness, as if it had been pulled from the other side—and softly I stepped into the dim, almost dark room.

The door opened near the right wall; the room stretched to the left. I was facing a narrow passageway between the mahogany footboard of a bed and a dark vanity table against the right wall. On the wall opposite the doorway, heavy dark curtains were drawn across what appeared to be two windows. Below the curtains was a dim desk littered with paper and notebooks, among which two soft dolls sat side by side with their feet turned out and their heads leaning together. In the middle of the desk loomed a big black typewriter, before which a soft doll sat with her head leaning against the keys. On the pulled-out desk-chair a large dim doll sat leaning back. To the left of the desk stood a high dark glass-covered cabinet with curving feet. The shelves were crowded with small stiff dolls facing different ways. I could see stiff little outspread arms, flashing eyes, pieces of red velvet and white satin, a raised sword, gleaming jewels in high-piled hair. To the left of the cabinet, in the angle of the wall, was a small high table with downturned end-leaves and a central post ending in three outcurving legs. To the left of the table, against the adjoining wall, was a low mahogany bookcase filled with small objects that I could not distinguish in the half-darkness. In the corner formed by the bookcase, the table, and part of the glass cabinet, a dark chair faced the bed. The dark high headboard stood against the wall to the left of the bookcase, and the large bed stretched past the glass cabinet and half the desk, almost to the door. Pale and shadowy she lay, propped on two pillows, her eyes closed and her arms resting on the quilt. Her white hands emerged from wide black silky sleeves. Her face was turned a little to one side and black hair streamed across her cheek and along the pillow onto the quilt. To the left of the bed was a second bookcase, identical to the first but filled with books. On the floor in front of the bookcase a flung white sock lay upon a fallen wooden doll. Against the wall immediately on my left stood a high bureau with carved drawers each of which had two keyholes. On top of the bureau a soft doll sat slumped forward, her legs apart and her head pressed against one leg. Just past the bureau was the doorway in which I stood. Against the remaining wall, facing the low dark footboard, stood a vanity table with a mirror-tray holding faceted glass vials. Before it sat a padded bench. The glass vials were reflected in a wide high mirror with mahogany curlicues that rose on the wall behind the vanity table. The mirror also reflected a piece of the desk and a corner of dark footboard. "I wondered whether you would come," I heard in the half-darkness, and turning abruptly I saw her looking at me with half-closed eyes. "You can sit over there," she added. And vaguely, indolently, she raised her left arm toward the dark chair that sat facing the bed. She dropped her hand swiftly, as if heavily, to the quilt; and slowly the black sleeve fluttered down about her wrist, and was still.

Closing the door gently behind me I walked on tiptoe between the footboard and the vanity table, watching myself pass in the dark vanity mirror. Turning left I began to make my way slowly past the desk, catching my foot suddenly against the chair, which made a short sharp scraping sound. Softly the big doll began to slide, the flat round head moved slowly down the chairback, the plump whitish legs slid over the front of the seat and suddenly bent at the knees, quickly I reached forward, grasped a soft shoulder and pulled the doll back up onto the chair. When I let go, the head began to slip sideways but stopped against a slat. In the half-darkness I was able to make out the long yellow strings of hair, the round blue painted eyes, and the curving black mouth-line that was shaped like a smile but gave an impression of sly malice. Cautiously I made my way along the narrow passageway between the bed and the high glass-doored cabinet, where a slender doll in a crimson dress lay fallen among stiff indifferent dolls, and when I reached the chair I saw, seated upon it, a small and gaily smiling Raggedy Ann doll. She had red woolen hair growing in a circle around her face and she wore a crumpled blue dress with a white apron. From beneath the apron emerged cotton legs that were striped red and white, ending in black cotton feet turned toe-outward. Each of her arms consisted of two stuffed pieces of cotton sewn together like joined sausages. One hand lay in her aproned lap and one arm hung loosely down. I glanced at Eleanor—her eyes were closed, her head was turned partly away—

and picking up the doll I let myself gently down onto the chair. It was an old chair with a cracked leather seat and a leather back and thin wooden arms and brass buttons running along the edge of the leather. I put the doll on my leg and looked vaguely about, but when I glanced down I saw Raggedy Ann lying painfully on her stomach with one arm twisted and one leg lying up along her back, and picking her up and looking in vain for a place to put her, at last I sat her carefully on my thigh with her head leaning against my ribs and her arms lying neatly in her aproned lap. Then glancing again at Eleanor, who seemed to be fast asleep, I began to examine the objects in the bookcase beside me. They appeared to be toys of some sort, intricately carved toys such as I had never seen before: a merry-go-round three inches high with white wooden horses and red wooden horses and a seat shaped like a swan, a green circus wagon with silver bars behind which a furry black bear stood in real-looking straw, an angry organ grinder standing before a little monkey holding a cap, a smiling Gepetto holding on his knee a sad Pinocchio, a wooden spinning wheel with a little three-legged stool on which sat a beautiful lady with long yellow hair, a mustached magician in a black cape and a tall black hat standing before a black-draped table on which lay a wand, a cube, and a glass. But my attention was caught by a lacquered black box about four inches square that sat on top of the bookcase beside a hand-puppet consisting of the wooden head of a monkey over dark blue cloth. On top of the box lay a beautiful glass key, two inches long. It was an old-fashioned key, shaped not like a housekey but like one of those heavy iron keys used by stooped jailers to open the grating iron doors of stone dungeons in dank passageways in moldering castles. At the front of the box near the bottom was a large keyhole shaped like a circle on top of a triangle. Glancing once again at Eleanor, who lay with her eyes closed and her hands rising and falling gently on her stomach, softly I picked up the glass key. In the palm of my hand it felt heavy and delicate. Softly I leaned to the side and softly, very softly, I fitted the glass key into the keyhole.

Gently, very gently, I began to turn. There was a soft click, slowly the top of the box began to open, and a melody began to play. It was a sad, glassy, tinkling melody, a ghostly, midnight, moonlit melody, a melody such as marionettes, glass animals, or leprechauns might dance to. And as the top of the box slowly opened there rose slowly into view a pale ballerina three inches high. Her glossy black hair was pulled tightly back and under the haughty arches of her eyebrows dark eyes coldly stared. Her little red lips were parted slightly. She wore a dark blue leotard that showed her tiny hard breasts and on her feet were glittering silver shoes. When the platform reached the top of the box there was another click. Then slowly the ballerina rose on her toes, and as she rose her arms rose slowly and somewhat jerkily from her sides until her tiny fingertips met high over her head. Slowly her right leg rose out behind her as she bent forward slightly from the waist. Slowly on the slender point of one silver shoe she turned as the music played. When she had completed her circle she stood motionless for a moment, leaning forward with her leg out behind her and her arms over her head. Then slowly her leg came down and her body straightened up, until she was standing erect on her toes. Slowly and somewhat jerkily her arms came down to her sides, slowly she lowered herself from her toes, and staring off under the haughty arches of her eyebrows, slowly she began to descend. As she descended the top began to come down, and when she was below the level of the box the top closed over her and the music abruptly stopped. Then a sadness came over me, and in the half-darkness I bowed my head. I thought of toys, of circuses, of ferris wheels in winter, of an old music-box with a red wooden handle. Day after day I had turned the handle faster and slower, faster and slower, now so fast that the tune was a glassy blur, now so slow that the music vanished into solitary and unconnected bits of bright tinkling noise. One afternoon when I was alone in my room, and mother and father were away, I pulled off one of the cardboard sides. And as I watched the hard black bumps of rubber striking the wires I was thrilled

and disappointed, thrilled and disappointed, "Well?" said Eleanor. I looked up abruptly. She was gazing at me with a slight
frown. "Well?" she said rather sharply, "did you like it?" "Oh,"
I said, "I'm sorry, did I wake you, I didn't mean, but it was so,
I've never . . . of course I'm very tired. And it feels so strange,
sitting here, all these dolls, at first I put Raggedy on her stomach
but she looked twisted, then I saw the black box and the glass
key, I hope I, I'm sorry if, your mother said . . ." "Oh, what are
you saying, you're giving me a headache, what's he talking
about, Raggedy, I can't understand a word . . . But if you like
toys, I have much better." And leaning up a little she motioned
vaguely and indolently at the bookcase of toys, saying: "That
green box, on the bottom there." Then I saw, on the bottom
shelf, a green satiny box with silver stars on it, about the size of
a large chessbox. Picking it up carefully I handed it to Eleanor,
who was now half-sitting up in bed. With a long forefinger she
slid back the top of the box and removed a man six inches
high. He was dressed in a shiny dark-blue pajama-like costume
with silver spangles all over it. His face was white, like a clown's,
and there was a round blue spot on each cheek. He had a small
blue serious mouth and his nose was a blue triangle. A little tuft
of blue hair sprouted from the center of his white skull. His
small black eyes had little eyelids fringed with tiny black lashes;
at the slightest movement his eyelids trembled. In the box lay
four transparent glass balls larger than peas but smaller than
marbles: one red, one yellow, one blue, and one green. "Now,"
said Eleanor, looking vaguely about, "if you can bring over that
little table, over there . . ." Quickly I rose, tucking Raggedy
under my arm, and moving the leather chair to one side I
brought over the small high table with downturned endleaves,
which I placed beside the bed. The central post of the table
ended in three outcurving legs tipped with paws of brass. With
a weary gesture Eleanor directed me to open the leaves. Then I
sat down on the chair with Raggedy on my thigh and watched
as Eleanor placed the man carefully in the center of the table.
He stood with his legs spread slightly, facing me. His elbows

were pressed to his sides, his forearms were extended, and his white, cupped hands were held out palm upwards. The small black eyes gave his white face an expression of intensity that seemed at odds with his clownlike appearance. A white lever one-half inch long protruded from his back. Leaning forward, Eleanor placed in his right hand the red glass ball. Then in his left hand she placed the yellow glass ball. Then reaching around to his back she pushed the lever down. A faint whirring was audible. His head turned to its left, and with a movement of his lids he looked directly at his left hand. Then his head turned to its right, and with a movement of his lids he looked directly at his right hand. There was a pause, as if he were thinking. With a sudden motion he jerked up his right hand, tossing into the air the red glass ball. At once he jerked his left hand to the right, leaving in his right palm the yellow glass ball. He tossed the yellow glass ball into the air and jerked back his left hand to receive the falling red glass ball. He caught the falling red glass ball and jerked his left hand to the right, leaving in his right palm the red glass ball, which he tossed into the air as he jerked back his left hand to receive the falling yellow glass ball. He caught the falling yellow glass ball and jerked his left hand to the right, leaving in his right palm the yellow glass ball, which he tossed into the air as he jerked back his left hand to receive the falling red glass ball, and in this manner he kept one ball always in the air; but what was most remarkable was the movement of his head and eyes. With close attention he followed the motion of each ball from the moment it fell into his left hand to the moment it rose from his upward-jerking right, and glancing at the uptossed ball he at once looked back at the hand about to receive the falling ball—all in a startlingly lifelike manner, enhanced by the movements of the lids and the intense look of the jetblack eyes; but a lifelike manner which, far from obscuring the mechanical elements, served only to emphasize them, as if the very effort to overcome the artificial drew attention to the glassiness of the eyes, the jerking motions of the arms, the white wood of the cheeks; so that it was difficult to say whether the pleasure of the observer lay more in the lifelike illusion of the performance or in the perception of the deceiving artifice itself. "Oh," I whispered, "I've never—" "Shhh," said Eleanor, who was leaning toward the table, watching intently, and holding between her thumb and forefinger the blue glass ball. As she watched she began to move her hand slowly toward the upward-jerking palm of the white-faced juggler, until she held the blue glass ball just beside his hand. He tossed up the red glass ball, and suddenly she dropped into his right palm the blue glass ball, which he at once tossed into the air. As he tossed the blue glass ball into the air he caught in his left palm the falling yellow glass ball. At once he jerked his left hand to the right, leaving in his right palm the yellow glass ball. He tossed the yellow glass ball into the air and jerked back to receive the falling red glass ball. He caught the falling red glass ball and jerked his left hand to the right, leaving in his right palm the red glass ball, which he tossed into the air as he jerked back to receive the falling blue glass ball. He caught the falling blue glass ball and jerked his left hand to the right, leaving in his right palm the blue glass ball, which he tossed into the air as he jerked back to receive the falling yellow glass ball. He caught the falling yellow glass ball and jerked his left hand to the right, leaving in his right palm the yellow glass ball, which he tossed into the air as he jerked back to receive the falling red glass ball, and catching the falling red glass ball he jerked his left hand to the right, leaving in his right palm the red glass ball, which he tossed into the air as he jerked back to receive the falling blue glass ball—and as he tossed the red, blue, and yellow glass balls in a red, blue, and yellow circle he followed their movements quickly with his white intense face. And as I watched his white intense face, his quick precise movements, his jetblack eyes beneath their trembling lids, it seemed to me that he was straining under the pressure of the relentlessly falling red, blue, and yellow glass balls; and the dark blue spots in his bright white cheeks seemed hectic blue flushmarks erupting from a feverish whiteness. But again Eleanor was leaning toward the table, holding between her fingers the green glass ball, and now a nervousness came over me and I whispered: "Oh, do you think," but "Shhh," she whispered, moving slowly toward the upward-jerking palm, and suddenly she dropped into the palm the green glass ball, which he at once tossed into the air. And as he tossed the green glass ball into the air he caught in his left palm the falling yellow glass ball. At once he jerked over his left hand, leaving in his right palm the yellow glass ball, which he tossed into the air as he jerked back to receive the falling red glass ball, and catching the falling red glass ball he jerked his left hand to the right, leaving in his right palm the red glass ball, which he tossed into the air as he jerked back to receive the falling blue glass ball, and just catching the falling blue glass ball, which rattled in his palm, he jerked his left hand to the right, leaving in his right palm the blue glass ball, which he tossed into the air as he jerked back not quite in time to receive the falling red glass ball, which struck the edge of his hand with a click and fell to the table with a sharp glassy sound, bouncing toward the edge in a series of short sharp hops as his empty left hand jerked to the right, leaving nothing at all in his empty right hand, which tossed nothing into the air as he jerked back not at all in time to receive the falling yellow glass ball, which fell to the table-top and began to bounce sharply along as the red glass ball bounced loudly along the floor and the empty left hand jerked to the right, leaving nothing in the empty right palm, which tossed nothing into the air as the green glass ball and the blue glass ball fell to the table with the sound of spilled frozen peas and the left hand jerked back under empty air, and now the yellow glass ball plunged to the floor and rolled loudly away as the green glass ball and the blue glass ball hopped rattling across the table-top and the empty right hand tossed nothing into the air and the white hectic face followed intensely the movements of the empty hands and the invisible glass balls, and I longed to turn away but stared in fascination at the jerking arms, the empty palms, the jetblack eyes beneath their quivering lids—"How ugly!" exclaimed Eleanor, snatching him up by the stomach, and as the green glass ball and the blue glass ball plunged to the floor and rolled rattling away she thrust him into the satiny green box and slid the lid over him. Far away a single glass ball bounced sharply along the floor. It struck a surface and began to roll loudly, then striking another surface it rolled softly and suddenly stopped. In the intense silence a faint whirring was audible, and muffled thumps. Eleanor pulled herself down under the covers and pulled the quilt up to her neck. She gazed at me with a dark, irritable expression, as if she were about to burst into reproachful speech, but she remained silent, and avoiding her gaze, as if I had done something wrong, I leaned forward wearily, placed my forearms on the table, and laid my cheek on the back of my crossed hands. But almost at once I sat up, for I had felt Raggedy falling over, and straightening her once again on my leg, I leaned back and half-closed my eyes. "Well?" said Eleanor sharply. "Don't just sit there. Say something." "Oh," I said, avoiding her gaze, "say something, yes, but it's not that easy, and besides, I feel tired, my thoughts are so heavy all they want to do is lie down and sleep, but they can't sleep, so they turn over and over, that makes them even more tired. And it feels so strange, sitting here, of course I've never seen anything like that before, it puts the ballet dancer to shame, the way he seemed to follow each ball with his eyes, it was as if he knew what he was doing, of course he's only a mechanical toy. But he seemed so alive, his eyes, the way he followed everything, and then, at the end, it was horrible, I wanted to look away, but I didn't look away, 'How ugly!' you said, and yes, I see what you mean, but to me it wasn't ugly, to me it was embarrassing. Oh, I know that sounds strange, but I was embarrassed, I felt like blushing, and if you want to know what it was like, it was like the knife-thrower in the sideshow. I always looked forward to the knife-thrower in the sideshow, he amazed me far more than the lion tamer or the trapeze artists, after all the lion tamer had his whip, the trapeze artists had their green net, I could see it stretched out under them, and I thought how much fun it would be to fall, closing your eyes, letting everything go ... but that wasn't it, no, that wasn't it. Because deep down I didn't believe in the net, or the whip, or the lion, or the trapezes, because lions and trapezes, lions and trapezes, oh, lions and trapezes were so strange they were magical, they were so strange they didn't exist. But knives, knives were real. And so I looked forward to the knife-thrower, but I could never enjoy him the way I could enjoy the lion tamer and the trapeze artists, which were so strange they didn't exist. Because I was always afraid, oh not afraid he would hit her, the woman on the wheel, that was unthinkable, after the first throw I never gave her a thought, but you see, I was always afraid the knife-thrower would fail, I was afraid he would throw a knife and instead of sticking into the wood it would drop to the platform with a horrible clank. And just imagining that sound was enough to make me blush, I longed to turn away, but I never turned away. And even though he never made a mistake, I could never enjoy the knife-thrower, I was always relieved when it was over. Of course I was secretly waiting for a mistake, I longed for a mistake, and so, when it was over, I was always a little disappointed. And so when the juggler, when the juggler, of course he's only a toy, but when the juggler made a mistake I was embarrassed, I longed to turn away, but also I secretly enjoyed the mistake, I was waiting for it all along. Oh, I can't say what I mean, I don't know what I mean, I'm too tired, and besides, it's all so strange, sitting here, I hadn't imagined it like this. Oh, I imagined it, but I thought ... And then, walking through the snow, the soldiers, the cat with the glass eyes ... I realize I'm speaking badly, I realize it, but I'm so tired, and besides, this may seem strange, but I really don't mind if I make a complete fool of myself, oh, I mind, I mind, I'll never forgive myself, but at the same time I don't mind at all, it's as if, as if, and then ... And really I can't tell you how strange it feels, sitting here, the dolls, the dark, Raggedy, hello Raggedy. And you know how it is, when you're tired, things come into your

mind, you say everything, no, not everything ... Of course I'm
a little nervous, that's understandable, after all, here I am, and
I don't even know how I got here, I think I must have stepped
out of a green box on your shelf, in a few seconds you'll say
'How ugly!' and snatch me up and put me back in my box and
slide the top over me, that's all right. And I can't seem to stop
talking, why is that, I know I should stop and yet I go on and
on. At first I thought no, I can't go there, how can I, it's impossible, but then I thought well, if I just, and then, the snow,
the walk, the dolls, the dark, I feel strange, feverish, no, just
tired, so tired I could close my eyes and go to sleep forever,
and then, when I saw you the first time, it was so, it was so, of
course I'm not really feverish, not really, I'm only pretending,
no, not pretending, only not trying, if I forced myself I could
speak much better, but it's as if, as if, and then, when I saw
you in German, of course I wondered why anyone would take
German, but I myself was taking German, I don't know why,
and it's strange, the word schön for example, the way it sounds,
schön, schön, du bist so schön, I feel strange, feverish, the dolls,
the dark, and then, when I arrived, your mother said 'Please
come in,' and so I came in. And there you were, lying there
like a queen, a queen of dolls, I've never seen so many dolls.
And I can't tell you how strange it feels, sitting here, the
dolls, the dark, and yet, it doesn't feel strange at all, it's as if, as
if, and then ... but this is terrible!" I cried, standing up abruptly
and causing Raggedy to fall softly to the floor, "talking like an
idiot, please excuse me, I'm going now." Then a great weariness
came over me, and passing my hand across my eyes I half-
turned to go. Frowning at me in the half-darkness Eleanor said:
"Don't be a child, you can't go now. You just got here. And besides, you haven't even seen the Childhood Museum. Now sit
down, sit down, sit down ..." "The Childhood Museum," I
murmured, sitting down heavily, as if I had been pulled from
behind. On the floor I saw Raggedy lying on her stomach with
one leg flung out, and bending over I picked her up and leaned
wearily back. Far away I heard Eleanor saying "wondered

whether you," and "Yes," I heard myself saying, "yes, that's all right. And you know, I haven't been sleeping well." Suddenly I felt a violent tug at my sleeve, and opening my eyes I stared at blackness. Then I remembered my long, sad dream of Eleanor, the walk through the snow, the iron soldiers, the cat with the glass eyes, the black music-box, the white-faced juggler, but already it was fading, I wondered what time it was, with a feeling of desolation I made an effort to rise from my bed. Under my hand I felt the wooden arm of a chair. "Don't fall asleep," said Eleanor sharply, and sitting up abruptly I saw her leaning toward me from the bed with a frown. "But this is terrible!" I cried, looking about in alarm, "it must be midnight, my mother will be furious, what time is it," and I made a movement to rise but Eleanor said: "It isn't midnight, it's a quarter to five. Mother will drive you home, obviously." And reaching up she clicked on a dim yellow bedlight. "Oh," I said, sitting back, "a quarter to five, but I thought . . . it felt so strange, for a minute I thought . . . but is it really only a quarter to five?" "Oh, for heaven's sake, what a fuss he's making!" she cried, flinging aside the covers as if she were throwing them at me and revealing for a moment a pale blue nightgown as she swung her legs over the far side of the bed. Tying about her waist the tasseled belt of her silky black robe, she made her way along the side of the bed, turned left, and passed swishingly between the footboard and the vanity table, glancing at herself in the mirror as she passed. On the other side of the vanity table she came to a dim door that I had not noticed before. Opening the door she turned to me with a frown and said: "Well? Are you coming?" "Yes," I murmured, rising heavily, and bending suddenly to catch Raggedy as she fell. As I sat Raggedy carefully on the chair and folded her hands neatly in her lap, I heard a scrape of hangers, a rustling of clothes, a creaking sound. In the dim bedlight I made my way along the side of the bed past the cabinet of dolls and the large desk to the dark opening of the closet door. "Eleanor," I whispered, peering at a dark row of dresses, but there was no answer. I took a step into the closet, whispering: "Eleanor." Breathing more quickly now, I began to push my way into the soft black clothes, inhaling a faint odor of perfume and cloth, and freezing suddenly as my hand touched her arm in its silky robe, but it was only a piece of clothing on a wooden hanger, and pushing through to the other side I came to a black wall. "Eleanor," I whispered, "Eleanor," and in my weariness I longed to lie down among the shoes on the floor and close my eyes. And in my weariness I leaned back for a moment against the firm, slightly yielding row of clothes, and settling softly back and half-closing my eyes I felt myself supported by black softness, then I seemed to be falling backward and I began to struggle to my feet, pushing back against the clothes but floundering helplessly among them, neither upright nor falling I was fixed for a moment in the act of falling by the soft firmness of the clothes, at last I struggled upright, throwing myself lightly forward against the wall. I touched something cold and yanked away my hand as if I had touched a flame. Cautiously I reached forward. My fingers touched a smooth metal protuberance. Suddenly everything became clear, and turning the knob I pushed open the creaking door.

I found myself in a dark, flickering room, dimly illuminated by a single candle in a holder on the floor. In the center of the room stood a large, gabled dollhouse, facing left. Eleanor was sitting before it with her legs thrown under her and her right hand lying palm upward on her lap. The dollhouse roof reached higher than her head. Beside her right thigh sat the candlestick in its holder and on the far wall her enormous shadow rose and fell with the rising and falling candleflame. The room had a stuffy, musty odor, and on the left wall I noticed long, thick curtains that came plunging to the floor. Then I noticed, in the corner made by the left wall and the far wall, a small rocking chair about two feet high. In it sat a large doll with a ball of knitting in her lap and two knitting needles rising above her shoulders. On the floor before her a smaller doll sat combing her hair with one elbow stiffly raised. To the right of the rocking chair, against the far wall, stood a small table with two chairs. Two dolls were stiffly seated. Before each doll sat a little teacup in a little saucer, and in the middle of the table was a teapot with a spout. To the right of the table, in the center of the wall, was a door about two feet high, and to the right of the door stood a dark bookcase about one foot high, filled with three shelves of miniature books. On top of the bookcase was a little model ship with sails. Above the ship a little glass-covered picture, reflecting the candleflame, hung on the wall beneath an upward-tilted nail that cast a long shadow. Before the bookcase a doll sat leaning over an open book. In the right-hand corner a black-haired doll lay in bed with stiff arms resting on the covers; in the darker part of the room, behind the dollhouse, a bureau two feet high was dimly visible; and all about the room, in dim and dark places, wooden dolls and cloth dolls were frozen in attitudes of play. One doll sat bent over a game of solitaire laid out in miniature cards, another doll lay on her stomach with her chin in her hands and one leg bent up at the knee as she stared at a tiny black dog, two dolls sat facing one another with their legs outspread and their bodies leaning forward as they gazed down at a scattering of jacks and a little red ball; and all about the room, leaning back against the walls, cloth dolls with button eyes and wooden dolls with glass eyes stared. "Welcome to the Childhood Museum," said Eleanor, making a vague flourish. "Here you see before you," but her voice faded, her arm fell, she broke off and gazed blankly before her. For a while she remained like that, as if she had forgotten me, then turning suddenly toward me with a frown she said: "Well? Are you going to stand there all day?" At once I came forward, and sitting down beside her, with the candlestick between us, I looked at the flickering façade of the large, many-windowed, mansion-like dollhouse. "Well?" said Eleanor, "aren't you going to look inside?" And lifting the candlestick, so that shadows were thrown about the room, she handed it to me and motioned toward a window on the second floor. Holding the candlestick up to the window, I leaned forward and peered inside.

In the dimming and brightening light of the plunging and

leaping flame I found myself gazing into a dark bedchamber thick with dust. Balls of dust lay on the dusty floor and thick spiderwebs clung to the corners of wall and ceiling. One large dusty web slanted from the top of one wall to the middle of the air, where it joined another web that stretched on a different plane from the top of the opposite wall to the floor. Against the left wall stood a dusty mahogany bureau two inches high. Each of the four drawers had two tiny brass handles, and one drawer was partway open, revealing a dusty white nightgown and a dusty black glove. On top of the bureau an empty brass candlestick, one-half inch long, lay on its side. A circle of clear mahogany showed in the thick dust of the bureau-top, and on the floor beside the bureau a little white candle lay half-buried in the dust. I could see the tiny white wick. To the right of the bureau, in the corner, stood a grandfather clock about four inches high. Its hands, draped with spiderwebs, were stopped at twenty-five minutes past twelve. To the right of the clock, against the far wall, stood an old-fashioned writing-desk, with rows of pigeonholes rising from the back. Tiny envelopes emerged from the pigeonholes, and on the dusty writing-surface, beside a piece of browned and curling paper, a white quill pen one-half inch long lay beside a tiny bottle of black ink. Before the desk stood a wooden chair two inches high which had been pulled back slightly, and over the chair in languid folds lay a lacy, yellowish-white, decaying gown, trailing in the dust of the floor. At the foot of the gown a tiny red high-heeled shoe lay beside a gigantic black green-shimmering fly, lying on its back with its crooked stiff legs in the air. Against the right wall, across from the bureau, stood a four-poster bed. Fluted mahogany columns, four inches high, were crowned by little mahogany pineapples. Stiff crimson curtains hung from tarnished brass rings and were pulled open on one side. Under a crimson coverlet a pale yellow-haired lady, covered with dust, lay on her back with her slender arms resting stiffly on the coverlet. Under the dust her eyes were closed, and her faintly smiling lips were ruby red. A delicate spiderweb, like a piece of knitting, stretched across the diamond-shaped space between her arms. To the right of the bed was a partly open door, and to the right of the door was a small circular table. On the table stood a little glass oil-lamp. Above the oil-lamp hung an oval portrait about one inch high, showing a young girl in a white dress clasping a bouquet of lavender flowers. Beside the portrait, like a large fragile wheel, a daddy longlegs clung to the wall. I then noticed that on the side of the mahogany bureau, along the grandfather clock, on the dusty crimson canopy of the four-poster bed, small white spiders moved. Small white spiders moved across the dusty white nightgown and the dusty black glove, small white spiders moved among the lacy folds of the decaying gown, small white spiders moved on the crimson curtains, on the crimson coverlet, over the streaming yellow hair. Through the partly open door a cobwebbed hall was visible, and part of a shadowy stairway, and "You have to go now," said Eleanor. I turned abruptly and was startled to see an enormous form kneeling close beside me. Her eyelashes were as long as candles, her vast fists, larger than chairs, lay on the thighs of a giantess, her oppressive breasts filled the entire room, pushing the walls outward as she breathed, and I could not move, I could not breathe, then the candle moved and I saw Eleanor kneeling close beside me with her hands on her thighs, gazing dreamily at the dollhouse. "Eleanor," I whispered, but she did not stir. "Eleanor!" I whispered, and turning dreamily toward me she shed upon me her dark, doleful gaze. And held by that gaze I could not move, in the dimming and brightening light of the plunging and leaping flame I stared at the large, piercingly black pupils, the gleaming mahogany irises, and the moist, faintly glistening whites, with their moist-pink tear-ducts and their delicate little red slashes. And as I stared I felt myself melting into black sorrow, I felt like a stone falling deeper and deeper in darker and darker water, I felt heavy and helpless as a slowly sinking stone, slowly I bent toward her but at the last moment she turned her head aside and my lips brushed her warm jaw. At once she rose, her shadow leaped behind her, and when I looked up I saw her staring down at me in anger or sorrow. "You have to go now," she said. "I'm very tired. Give me the candle, please. I'll show you the way out." Wearily I rose, and followed her around the dollhouse; a door opened, and closed; and I found myself standing in the dark hall, alone. I longed to fall down, and press my face into darkness, but wearily I began to walk toward the nearby landing, which glimmered with dim lamplight from the living room; and as I walked I imagined myself in the leaning mirror behind me, trudging heavily uphill. At the end of the hall I descended the two stairs, and when I turned at the landing I saw Mrs. Schumann sitting at the bottom of the stairs with her back to me and her head leaning against the post. "Mrs. Schumann," I murmured, but she did not stir. Wearily I descended, but she did not stir, and when I came to the stair behind her I bent over and murmured: "Mrs. Schumann," but she did not stir, and sitting down across from her on the step above I leaned my head wearily against the wall and half-closed my eyes. Then her head lifted drowsily, and turning toward me she murmured: "Oh there you are, I must have . . ." And shedding upon me her dark, doleful gaze she said: "You poor boy. You must be very tired." "Yes," I murmured, "and you know, I haven't been sleeping well." "We'll have to hurry," she murmured. "Hurry," I murmured. "Oh, but we'll have to hurry," she said, reaching out and grasping the stairpost. "We'll have to hurry," said a loud voice, and when I jerked open my eyes I saw Mrs. Schumann towering above the stairpost, holding open my dark wintercoat.

48

THROUGH THE SNOWING DARKNESS Mrs. Schumann drove me home, and that evening, shortly after dinner, I went to bed and fell into a deep sleep. The next morning I awoke still feeling tired, and during the long schoolday I kept gazing out the window at drifts of dull snow under a dark gray sky. The sunless, bleak, unsparkling snow seemed colder and more dangerous than bright white snow under a bright blue sky, and as I gazed through pallid and transparent reflections of fluorescent lights, a piece of blue map on a piece of brown wall, and my own partially dissolved face at the sunless, bleak, unsparkling snow, I imagined black bootprints sinking into the crust and forming a wavering line as they trudged wearily into the distance, the left one pointing a little to the left, the right one pointing a little to the right, under the black railway trestle, past the barber with his leather strop, past the wooden man holding up his arms, beyond the iron soldiers, onward and onward under a darker and darker sky in the sunless, bleak, unsparkling snow, and dropping my eyes I returned to my book in the soothing fluorescent light of the warm brown study hall. That afternoon I rode home on the bus. Letting myself in with my key I went at once to the hall and with a forefinger turned the notched wheel of the thermostat until the furnace made a gentle thudding sound. Then I went to my room, where changing out of my schoolclothes, closing the blinds, and pushing the button of my twin-bulb fluorescent desk-lamp, I sat down at my desk before the glow of lamplight on my green blotter and set eagerly to work. I had fallen behind badly in school. Tests were approaching, a history paper was due; with intense pleasure I pulled apart the stiff silver rings of my open notebook and removed a fresh sheet of bright-white blue-lined paper with a slender red line running down the left-hand side. Then carefully pushing the stiff silver rings, which suddenly sprang together like snapping jaws, I put aside the notebook and spread my piece of paper at an angle on the soft green blotter. And with intense pleasure I unscrewed the top of my glossy dark-blue fountain pen, fitted it over the bottom, and pushed it into place with a loud creak. Grasping the black grip behind the silver penpoint, so that my forefinger pressed against the ridge, and pressing down the gleaming point with its hard black underside that reminded me of the bottom of an insect, I watched the blueblack letters emerge wet and gleaming from the point. When I heard the crush and crunch of mother's tires in the drive, I went into the kitchen to greet her at the door. Taking from her arms a brown bag of groceries I proceeded to put them away with elaborate care, washing the red-and-green apples, placing one bar of margarine in the butter bin and three bars of margarine on a shelf of the refrigerator, and lining up the plump brown eggs in their row of blue nests in the refrigerator door. Then I returned to the peaceful glow of my desk-lamp, shedding its thickening white light in the darkening room. In my warm room, in the cozy glow of my fluorescent lamp, under the yellow light of my standing-lamp beside my brown reading chair, I felt myself melting into brown and yellow peacefulness.

And in my warm room, in the days that followed, I felt myself melting into brown and yellow peacefulness. After dinner I would sit in the living room with father, watching television and talking, and then the three of us would play hearts or canasta at the dining-room table. Afterward I would return to my room, where I would finish my homework and read myself peacefully to sleep; and sometimes, waking in the night, I would push aside the blinds and look out at the pale blue snow under the dark blue sky. One day, meeting William on the way to study hall, I invited him over. There was a moment of awkward silence. Looking away with a slight frown he said: "Meet you at the locker." "Right," I said. That afternoon we returned to our old games, and as if he himself had not drifted away, as if he had simply been waiting all the time, he now began to appear at my locker after school every day and ride home with me on the bus. "Well," I said, as he sat brooding in silence beside me, gazing out the bus-window, "how're all the clubs? I assume you've been nice and busy, as usual." "Oh," said William, still gazing out the window, "I don't belong to any clubs." "What!" I exclaimed, raising my eyebrows, widening my eyes, and pressing my hand to my heart, "not a single club? Goodness gracious me." William glanced over at me with a frown and then turned back toward the window. "They're nothing special," he said with a shrug. At my house we played Monopoly on the floor of my room and ping-pong in the warm part of the cellar beside the furnace. One afternoon, chasing the ball among trunks and broken furniture, I came upon a pile of stiff round cardboard coasters, on each of which was printed a circular beer-ad in red. Soon William was standing with a bat fashioned from a broken chair as I pitched coasters to him, holding each one upright between my index and middle finger and snapping them toward him in sweeping curves. A single was past the cane-bottom chair with a hole in the seat, a double was past the furnace, a triple was past the cardboard box, a homer was against the far wall. In a burst of high spirits William began tapping the floor with his bat and hunching down in his Stan the Man stance, all the while giving forth a stream of baseball patter: "Two down two on bottom of the third Mays deep in center the infield back two and nothing on the Babe can he do it folks can he do it Cobb edging off third Dimag on second the fans are going wild the big Babe singled on a sharp liner to left first time up but the fans are waiting for the big one folks the fans are waiting for the big one The Big Train in trouble folks the fans are screaming Cobb edging off third The Bambino looking cool as a cucumber the windup the pitch oh! a mile wide three and nothing folks the fans are going wild have a Schaefer folks" and suddenly The Big Train burst out laughing and The Sultan of Swat, frowning, said: "Hey, come on, man, what's so" and exploded into laughter, stopping instantly with a fierce frown but exploding again, staggering back against a rotting chairback as The Big Train held his stomach and laughed and laughed with aching ribs and that night we were still laughing as, wrapped in thick scarves, we stood at the top of the snowy slope behind Jefferson Junior High with our sleds at our hips and suddenly I was flying down past blades of grass that stuck up through the shiny snowcrust while grains of snowpowder blew back into my eyes. William was a little behind me but gaining, gaining, then the slope flattened out and I cut smoothly along iced-over grass, going slower and slower and stopping as William came smoothly cutting past, and as we dragged our sleds toward the tree-fringed side of the slope and began to trudge uphill, the jangle of buckled boots, the shouts of downcoming sledders, the white breath, the sharp scrape of runners, the cold air numbing my cheeks and the clear white moon in the clear black sky made me want to shout for joy but turning to William I said: "I think my runners are rusty." Turning to me with a frown William said sternly: "You ought to go over them with steel wool," and I felt a sudden yearning to confess something to my friend, but I did not know what I wanted to confess.

49

ONE MORNING when I pushed aside the blinds I saw snowdrifts half as high as the hedge. The two parallel swing-ropes plunged into snow. School was called off. William arrived shortly after breakfast and under a sunny blue sky we tramped in jingling jangling jingling boots along a shoveled path of dark wet sidewalk toward the bus-stop. In places the snow had been plowed up higher than my shoulders. From the sidewalk across the street came loud scraping sounds, and suddenly snow flew upward, followed by the edge of an aluminum snowshovel and the blue top of a hat. "Watch it!" cried William, pushing me away and springing aside as something thudded splashing at my toes. When I looked up I saw a glistening dark branch. Snow was dropping everywhere. It dropped in thick clumps from loaded branches, from roofgutters, from the crosspieces of telephone poles; and looking up at the snowheaped telephone wires I saw black spaces in the white snowlines. The air was full of a fine white powder that blew against my cheeks and eyes. A solitary grackle, purple-black, sat on the bright white gutter of a garage. Suddenly it rose into the blue air, flying swiftly away, growing smaller and smaller but not disappearing, and as I watched with my hand shading my eyes I felt myself flying swiftly away, growing smaller and smaller, over the black railway trestle, over the iron soldiers ... Turning abruptly to William I said: "I thought birds are supposed to go south." William said: "He must have missed the train." I bent over and scooped up a handful of heavy wet snow. Pressing and patting it into a hard round snowball furrowed with finger-grooves, I flung it violently at a telephone pole across the street. It hit with a rich wet smacking sound, forming a white spot on the dark brown pole. "What a shot," said William, "what a shot." "Let's do something," I said. "You name it," said William, but there was nothing to do. At the bus-stop we turned left and continued along the tight-packed pale-brown snow at the side of the street. Against high drifts, streaked with brown, pebbled slabs thrown up by the snowplow stiffly leaned. At one corner a narrow strip of glistening dark sidewalk appeared between high banks of snow, and following the sidewalk we came to the open drugstore. In the sudden warmth of the store I dripped and melted. A yellow-haired lady in a pale blue slip was leaning on her elbow on top of a rumpled bed. She gazed down with a faint smile at a pink letter, a cigarette in an ashtray, and a black revolver. An old man behind the counter said: "Well boys, how do you like this weather?" "It's nice," said William. "I'd like to buy a snowball," I said. "Sorry?" said the man, bending forward slightly and turning his ear toward me. "I said I'd like to buy a snowball. I was only kidding." The man drew back and murmured: "Oh." A man in a leopardskin loincloth, grasping a crooked root, leaned out from the side of a cliff and gazed down at a blue line of river and distant white towers. A red-haired lady in a black slip sat on the padded edge of an armchair, holding the back of her hair with one hand and looking into a mirror that she held up in the other hand, while behind her a frowning man in a red shirt was knocking over a card-table and a frowning man in a white t-shirt was rising from his chair with clenched fists. Outside, William said fiercely: "What did you say that for? He thought you were making fun of him." I kicked a piece of ice that went spinning along the sidewalk. "Let's do something," I said. "There's nothing to do," said William. We tramped on in silence. At one corner an olive-green dome was all that remained of a mailbox. A cold blue car parked on a side-street was covered with snow above the door-handles. On bright white snow a coil of excrement, wet dark brown, gleamed like oil-paint. Suddenly, between high mounds of snow, a dazzling yellow hydrant appeared. "Let's do some-thing!" I cried. "There's nothing to do," said William. Foot-long icicles hung like stalactites from the dark green awning of a seatcover shop, and as I stepped into the sunny living room my face prickled, my eyes burned, my temples beat painfully.

That evening after dinner William, mother, father, and I were playing hearts at the dining-room table. I had chosen three cards from my hand and passed them face down to mother on my right. She was frowning at her cards and had chosen only one card to pass to William. I picked up the three cards from father on my left, arranged them in my hand, and glanced at mother, who was still frowning at her cards. "Come on," I said, "let's get going." "Please don't rush me, Arthur. You know I don't like to be rushed. I can't concentrate when you rush me." "I'm not rushing you," I said. "Just don't take all night, that's all." I looked at William, who was frowning at his cards. I heard the loud slow ticking of the kitchen clock and far away I heard the faint faster ticking of the living-room clock. I looked at mother, who was still frowning at her cards. On the skyblue back of each card two rosy-breasted robins sat cheek to cheek on a leafy bough bursting with pink blossoms. Some of the robins were upside down. "Willy," said father, "is this the way to treat an old man?" "Good heavens," said mother, "don't talk like that. An old man! Why, to hear him talk—" "Don't talk," I said. "Play." Mother frowned at me over her bifocals, in which I saw tiny cards. "Don't rush me, Arthur. You know I can't concentrate when you rush me." "Oh boy," I said, rolling up my eyes, "I'm not rushing you. Am I rushing her? Just play first, then talk. That's all I ask." "No hurry, no hurry," said father, pushing out his lips, lifting his chin, and frowning through his reading glasses at the outspread fan of cards in his hand. Slowly lifting a card from one end, he turned it upside down and inserted it into the other end. William coughed lightly. I scratched my neck. "There," said mother, putting down two more cards. Suddenly she covered them with her palm. "No no, now wait a minute, don't rush me, don't rush me," and snatching up one card she put down another in its place. Cautiously she began to push the three cards to William, but suddenly drawing them back she picked up the new card, thrust down the original, and pushed the three cards violently to William, turning her head abruptly away and squeezing her eyes shut. "I'm sure I did the wrong thing," she said, turning back and watching anxiously as William picked up each card in turn without a trace of expression. "Oh well," she said, "it's only a game. It's not the end of the world. What difference does it make? Glory be, it's only a game." She sighed. Suddenly she noticed the three cards lying face down at her left. Placing one finger on the back of the top card she drew it to the table-edge. Slowly she began to lift a corner, tilting her head to one side and leaning slightly away. "Oh!" she exclaimed, "I knew I shouldn't have voided that suit." "Great," I said, slamming down my cards. "Why don't you tell everyone exactly what I gave you. Go on. That'd save everybody a lot of trouble. Go ahead. Go on. I don't care. Go on. Go on. I'm waiting." William raised his eyes and looked at me. Mother turned to me. Father looked over at me with a frown. "Why is everybody looking at me!" I cried. Father said sternly: "Don't talk to your mother in that tone of voice. Either play like the rest of us or don't play at all. Now I mean it, hear? You don't have to play with us if you don't enjoy it." "All right," I said, scraping back in my chair and starting to rise, "that's fine with me. I can't sit around all night playing with madmen. You people are driving me crazy." "I'm sorry," said mother, "but you know I..." "Hey," said William, holding up his hand as if for silence, "come on, sit down, relax, take it easy."

And as if he had cast a spell, for a moment all motion stopped: mother, holding her cards bent forward against her chest, looked at William with slightly parted lips, father, frowning faintly at William over his reading glasses, sat with one hand resting on his turned-over fan of cards and one hand raised to the level of his cheek, the suspended index finger still pointing at me, I remained half-risen from my chair, my body bent forward slightly, one hand resting on the wooden chairback behind me, my feet still hooked around the chairleg. Then father's hand dropped down, mother began to turn her head toward me, a chair creaked, a clock ticked, somewhere water was drip-drip-dripping...

Wearily I sat down and took up my cards.

50

A FEW NIGHTS LATER I was climbing the cellar stairs when I saw a nickel lying in the shadow of a step. As I bent over to pick it up I saw a dime and a nickel on the step above. Eagerly I bent over and picked them up. On the next step I saw a scattering of dimes and nickels, and as I began picking them up and thrusting them into my pockets I noticed in the center of the step a little brown sticky-looking pool. Some of the coins were brown and sticky and when I raised my eyes I saw at the top of the stairs a black dog whimpering on its side as a brown fluid flowed thickly from its broken mouth. Somewhere a door creaked open. Feverishly I began to pick up the remaining coins, which stuck to my fingers and had to be peeled off. Heavy footsteps sounded, faster and faster I picked up the coins, suddenly a heel crushed my fingers, and as I opened my eyes I felt in my hands cold coins that vanished. In the clear darkness I saw my armchair with a black book lying on one arm. On the floor beside the black base of the standing lamp one shoe was stepping on the toe of the other shoe. Under the desk the hot-air vent made faint thumping sounds and the chain clicked lightly in the outflow of air. It was a hot winter night. My throat and the roof of my mouth felt dry; my neck prickled with sweat. My dry lips felt stuck together and as I slowly parted them the stuck lip-flesh peeled apart like sticky pieces of tape. My hand rested on the tickly wool blanket and as I breathed in the hot dry air I felt as if I were drawing into my throat all the hot dry air and all the tiny tickly threads that curled from the hot dry wool. Somewhere a car passed. I imagined ice-cold lemonade in a glass frosted with moisture. The quick muffled ticking of a clock grew louder and louder. Reaching down I picked up a clock wrapped in underpants and saw by the glowing green tips of the hands that it was 11:48. I put the clock down, wrapping it carefully, and turned over on my side. My forehead felt hot and I could hear a muffled ticking. I pressed my finger against my ear-flap until I could hear my finger beating in my ear. Far away I heard a faint ticking. My neck prickled, my face felt hot, in the hot winter night I could not breathe, and when I sat up and pushed aside the blinds I could feel the cold flowing from the glass.

It was a blue winter night. Above the frosted-up bottom of the glass a cold white moon burned in a luminous blue sky above precise tiny maple-twigs striped with light along one side and shadow along the other side. In the blue-white moonlit snow each sunken bootprint stood out sharply, like craters in a photograph of the moon. One wall of each bootprint cast a shadow that entirely filled the hollow but did not spill over. A weedstalk stuck up through the snowcrust. On the swing a sparkling snowmound was shaped like a loaf of bread. The center of the maple began to dissolve in mist, and raising my arm

I rubbed the window with my pajama-sleeve. The trunk returned, but with a slight ripple. A new breathspot appeared, with tiny shimmering threads of pink and green. Leaning forward I breathed deliberately on the glass and with my finger I drew two parallel vertical lines crossed by two parallel horizontal lines. In the central space I made an X, in the upper right-hand space I made an O, in the lower right-hand space I made an X, in the upper left-hand space I made an O, in the upper central space I made an X, and suddenly I pressed my forehead against the cold, moist glass.

I released the blinds with a clatter. For a while I sat up in bed, frowning in the dark. My forehead was burning but when I raised my fingertips I felt a cool spot from the glass. Suddenly I imagined my head smashing through the glass and sharp ice-cold splinters of glass sticking into my eyelids and neck; bright red blooddrops in the snow. Angrily I rubbed the skin of my forehead and lay down with my arm pressed over my throbbing eyes. My temples were beating and the sheet tickled my jaw. I swallowed dryly. Far away I could hear a faint ticking. I turned over on my side and pressed my finger over my ear but through my finger I could hear a faint ticking. Fiercely I pushed my finger down until I felt pain. My neck was pounding, my head was pounding, my brain was bursting, tears burned in my eyes, and flinging off the covers I began to dress quickly.

My boots were in the kitchen by the door, and as I stepped onto the cold back porch I felt as if cool hands were being laid on my flaming temples. On the porch I took deep slow breaths, pulling the clean cold air deep into my chest and expelling long, shimmering, bluegray breathclouds which seemed to contain tiny melting points of ice. The porchrail was covered with a hard crust of snow and knocking off a piece with my gloved fist I bit into the burning-cold snow. Then for a while I stood motionless by the icy rail, looking up at the piercing white moon that burned into my eyes like a frosty sun. The circular side of the nearly full moon was so sharp and precise that it

looked as if you could cut a finger on it. The other side looked
a little soft, as if it were melting. A misty radiance tinged with
red haloed the moon, and beyond the radiance the sky was a
luminous blue which grew deeper and deeper until, far away,
the sky was almost black.

As I stepped across the back yard my boots crunched in the
snowcrust, breaking the hard frosty layer but not sinking
through; and as I stepped across the top of the snow I felt as
if I were striding across the fragile top of a town, stepping
carefully from rooftop to crushed rooftop.

When I pushed through the hedge a cold sprinkle of snow
struck my cheeks and ran in trickles down my neck.

Half sliding down the little slope I stumbled across the snowy
field. Now and then a boot plunged through the crust. I fell;
snow burned my wrists. At the edge of the snowstream I
jumped down into snow that came up to my knees, and as I
climbed up on the other side my cold pantsleg clung wetly
against my skin. I climbed the slippery slope and made my way
across the shadowed and pitted snow at the back of the body
shop, past distorted moongleaming snowshapes from which
pieces of rusting metal stuck out, past the back of a shut-down
gas station, a dark car-wash, a suddenly open diner that cast a
yellow parallelogram on the snow, and climbing over a wire
fence I stalked across the moonlit snow of crunching back yards,
squeezing through snowy hedges, climbing icy fences, until at
last I came to a high icy hedge that barred my way. Turning
left I made my way along the narrow sideyard to the street.
On a slab of snow beside a streetlight a pale red glow changed
to a pale green glow.

At the drugstore I turned left, trudging noisily along the
hardpacked snow at the side of the street; and as I walked,
gazing up through branches at the burning white moon, I swung
my hands together in loud leathery claps, scattering snowspray.

At the cold white church I turned right, onto a snowy street
with large dark houses set back from the road. Turning left at

the end of the block, and right at the end of the next block, I came at last to William Mainwaring's house, set back from the road with no front walk.

As I strode up the shoveled driveway to the moonlit garage door I stamped my boots twice, scattering jingling snow. In a small black window I saw my frowning face. On the black driveway behind me, ghostly white bootprints crept up. Here and there in the bootprints patterns of little x's showed.

Slowly I bent over and placed my gloved fingertips on the silver handle.

When the door was at the level of my boot-tops I paused, watching my breath. Then carefully, very carefully, I lowered the door. At once I rose, turned, and strode down the driveway to the street.

I continued along William's street, glancing up at his dark windows, and as I passed beyond his house I looked up through a white-and-black latticework of branches at the rippling moon. Dark blue moonshadows lay in tangles across the snow. The diamonds of a wire fence were printed clearly on smooth snow like a pattern on a napkin. Suddenly a dog began to yap shrilly. "Silence!" I shouted in a burst of bluish breath; the dog barked once and was still. And looking up with a smile I placed my hand on the buckle of my belted wintercoat and bowed to the dazzling moon. I bowed to my lady moon. I was merry, moon-merry, I was merry as a cherry—I was drunk on moon, I was all moon. And as I strode in the light of the moon I heard mad moonrhymes in my mind: Oh the moon the moon, like a big balloon, he started to croon, in the light of the moon, and the moon the moon, he started to croon, like a big bassoon, in the light of the moon, in the light of the light of the light of the moon, in the light of the moony old moon. And the moon, moon moon, he started to croon, in the light, light light, of the moon, moon moon, oh the moon, moon moon, and the moon, moon moon, oh the moony old loony old moon, moon moon, in the light of the white of the bright of the night of the moon,

moon moon, of the moon, moon moon... The street began to rise and at the top of the hill I turned left and began to descend a street where I had ridden my bicycle that summer, passing houses on my left and a snowy field on my right. At the bottom of the hill I continued for four blocks and then turned right. For a while I made my way along darker side-streets with vivid bursts of white where streetlamps shone on the snow. In the glow of an orange porchlight a snowy porchrail gleamed. I turned left. Above a distant rooftop rose a black corner of the high school.

And the moon the moon, like a big doubloon... I crossed the snowy parking lot at the back of the school. Making my way along poorly lit side-streets I entered a small parking lot at the back of a store. Through a narrow alleyway between two stores I saw the striped barberpole, turning and turning in its tube of glass; and in the bright blackness of the barbershop window the mirrored barberpole turned and turned. Bathed in green light, a stern wooden man wearing a white turtleneck sweater and charcoal-gray pants held up his arms in an exhausting pose. I continued along the backs of stores past snowy steps and garbage cans, gazing through narrow alleyways at a caution light blinking in a window, at a red neon pair of eyeglasses above a blue neon smile, at a glowing yellow word EINGOLD above a dark blue glow of bottles and spigots, and at last I climbed a low wire fence, crossed a back yard, and emerged on a side-street. To the left, a block away, the dark green soldiers were marbled in white snow.

A car passed; snow-waves rose and fell in yellow light and were still.

Over pebbled slabs of plowed snow I gazed at large white buildings with black windows. A few cars passed on the other side of the esplanade. At a gray Catholic church I turned left onto a poorly plowed side-street. On a dark corner, where beneath a dim yellow bulb in the depths of a grocery store I saw a black cash register and a crooked calendar, I turned right. As I passed the moonlit snowcapped silver poles I glanced up at the white metal street-signs with black raised letters. After a while I turned left.

Snowy rooftops gleamed in the moonlight. From the gleaming rust-patched rear fender of a parked car hung little sparkling icicles. On the right a short chimney cast a black hard stripe of shadow down a sloping roof and across the front lawn into the street. On the left a tree threw a tangled and gigantic shadow up along a housefront and across a moonlit roof. Mounds of snow sat on the old brown rocking chair and the green metal chair. In the snowcovered steps dark footprints showed. In the black window to the right of the door stood an icy porchpost. In the windows of the second floor black branches showed pieces of blue night-sky.

Softly I stepped along the icy ruts of the snowy driveway at the side of the house. I gazed at the icy tire-patterns, the ribbed bootheels, the flash of my boots in the narrow cellar windows, the snowheaped windowsills above the level of my head. The moon behind me threw out my long shadow, and as I stepped into view of the back yard I saw, under the deep blue sky, the shadow of the house lying halfway across the snow. Where the shadow ended, the snow was smooth and had a frosty sheen. Dark frozen footsteps showed in the hard snow of the four back steps. Placing each foot carefully in each icy hollow I climbed onto the small roofless back porch. Carefully, ever so carefully, I placed my fingers on the loose doorknob. Slowly I began to turn. The door was locked. On the other side of the rail I saw the sloping cellar door.

I made my way carefully down the four steps and trod with soft crunches along the shadowed snow, leaving fresh bootprints. Carefully I lifted the heavy sloping door. I began to descend the concrete steps, letting the door softly down over my head. At the black bottom of the steps I patted about until I felt the doorknob. The door was locked.

In the blackness I felt myself frowning. Removing my glove I stood on tiptoe and patted along the cold top of the doorframe, feeling bits of grit, a tiny pebble, a chip of wood. Suddenly my boot-toe knocked against the edge of a heavy mat. Bending over swiftly I lifted the cold fuzzy mat and patted the damp concrete. There was no key.

Sitting on the cold steps I folded my arms across my knees and bent my head wearily onto my arms.

I thought of myself standing on William's driveway with my fingers on the silver handle. I thought of the long weary walk home. I thought of myself feeling the sudden cold metal of the key and I thought of myself creeping along the black hall toward William's room. I thought of William creeping from his house. I saw him hurrying down the driveway, leaping into the stream, pushing eerily through the hedge into my back yard... "Of course," I said aloud, and snapped my gloved fingers mutely. Pushing up the heavy door I climbed out and lowered the door softly behind me.

Again I climbed the frozen footprints of the small back porch. Carefully I stepped onto the icy milkbox. Leaning to one side I pressed the heel of one hand against the kitchen window. It rose easily and the thin curtains streamed inward. Climbing carefully onto the narrow icy rail I tried to lift my knee onto the sill, but there was not enough room. Thrusting in my head I pulled my stomach painfully onto the sill and began to crawl in clumsily, gripping the corners of the sink, catching my buckle on the sill, bruising my knee.

In the dimly glowing sink I closed the window quietly and removed my dripping boots and cold shoes.

Softly I tiptoed across the kitchen into the brightly moonlit living room. The yellow glass eyes of the porcelain cat glimmered beside the fireplace. On the mantelpiece the clockhands pointed to 1:16. Softly I began to climb the stairs—and stopped, holding my breath. Then I continued my climb, turning at the moonlit landing, where a little blue-coated soldier gleamed, and climbing the two stairs I began to tiptoe along the hall. Behind a door on my left I heard a slow sound of husky breathing. Softly I tiptoed past, suddenly I saw a motion at the end of the hall, but it was only my black image in the black mirror.

At the end of the hall I leaned against the wall-angle between the mirror and the door, breathing heavily. Far away I heard a gentle breathing. And suddenly I wanted to lie down on the floor and close my eyes. Then I imagined myself lying awake in my room, remembering myself standing in the wall-angle. And for a long while I stood that way, imagining myself lying awake in my room, remembering myself standing in the wall-angle. Then I imagined myself remembering myself placing my hand on the doorknob, turning slowly, and softly pushing open the door. In her dark bed she lay, dark dreamer, with her black hair falling about her. A stripe of moonlight escaping from a corner of the drawn curtains lay across the pale blue-veined hand that rose and fell upon her bosom as she breathed. Softly I sat down on the chair beside the bed and leaning forward I whispered: "Eleanor." Slowly her eyes opened, shedding upon me their dark, doleful gaze, and as I bent closer and closer I saw on the landing the black shine of a glass-covered picture. A piece of moonlight striped the knickknack shelf. I could see quite clearly the blue coat of the soldier and the brass shine of the little kettle. Taking a deep breath I stepped from the wall; and placing my hand on the knob, and turning slowly, softly I pushed open the door.

In the dim yellow bedlight she looked up with a frown. Lowering her book onto her stomach she gazed at me irritably, twisted a piece of black hair round and round a finger, and said in a peevish tone: "Oh, it's you. I wondered whether you were coming back. Is it nice out? You look like a murderer. Move over, Raggedy."

51

"Shhh," I hissed, closing the door softly behind me; that night I sat for an hour in the leather chair beside her bed, whispering my adventure of the moon. "And so, Raggedy," she said, "the prince left his boots in the sink," and in the dark and snowy afternoons that followed I made the long trip to Eleanor Schumann's house, where Mrs. Schumann greeted me with her dark, doleful gaze; and climbing the stairs, and walking along the narrow hallway with the rippling rug and the leaning mirror, I would enter Eleanor's half-dark sickroom. Sometimes when I entered I would see her lying with closed eyes, and softly shutting the door behind me I would make my way on tiptoe to the chair beside the bed. Seating Raggedy on my leg, and straightening her dress, I would gaze at Eleanor's faintly frowning eyebrows, at the black coil of hair lying on her white cheek, at the white blue-veined hand lying on the dark blue quilt with pink four-petaled flowers, until at last I would see a tension in her eyelids, slowly her eyes would open, and gazing drowsily at me she would say, with a slight frown: "Are you a dream?" And leaning forward, softly I would whisper: "Yes." At other times, when I entered, I would see her lying with her eyes half-opened or half-closed. Walking to the chair beside the bed, and taking up Raggedy, I would speak half to Raggedy and half to Eleanor about trifles of the schoolday; and sometimes in the half-darkness she would give a weary smile. And sometimes when I entered I would see her sitting up in bed like a queen, with her dark hair falling about her; and like a queen she would motion me to my place by her side. And like a queen she would be a little bored, a little sulky, a little petulant, so that if I spoke at all she would say "Yes yes yes" and look away with a frown and black-flashing eyes. In fact she could be quite scornful, or "temperamental," as Mrs. Schumann expressed it, who took to warning me downstairs when Eleanor was having "one of her bad days." Of course it was hard for her, Mrs. Schumann would continue, confined to her room like that all day, it was a wonder she bore up so well, and really she was wonderfully good about it, for that matter she had always been an angel, and very smart, in the sixth grade Mrs. Perrano had written that Eleanor was "an intelligent and very mature little lady," those were the exact words, of course Eleanor had always gotten A in everything, except for a B minus last year in Home Economics, but, as Eleanor had put it, Mrs. Whiting only liked girls who carried an American flag in one hand and an apple pie in the other, whereas she, Eleanor, couldn't tell the difference between an apple pie and a pizza pie, they were both round, weren't they, which was just like Eleanor; and really (she continued, leading me to the stairs), it was a wonder how well she bore up, all things considered, and it was so good of me to call on her, it did her a world of good; and I understood, didn't I, how hard it was for her, so that if sometimes she was a little temperamental, I would understand. And as I climbed the stairs I would turn to see Mrs. Schumann standing at the bottom with one hand on the post, gazing up at me with her dark, doleful eyes. When I entered Eleanor's sickroom I would find her sitting up in bed, looking darkly in my direction. With lowered eyes I would walk to the chair and sit down, and taking up Raggedy and straightening her dress I would sit in silence, staring at the black music-box beside the hand-puppet. Once, turning to me as I sat in silence, Eleanor said scornfully: "This must really be boring for you." And flashing at me a black, impatient look she began to twirl a black strand of hair round and round a white finger. "No," I said quietly, avoiding her eyes, "no, actually I feel peaceful, Eleanor." She turned abruptly away, making the bed creak, and I saw a muscle tensing and untensing in her cheek. After a while she turned back to me with a smile and said: "Well, Artoor"—she always called me Artoor, pronouncing my name as in German class—"how was everything heute in der Klasse?" And she continued to smile, but too broadly, and there was a tension about her nostrils. "Oh," I said, "fine, wunderbar, but Eleanor, you seem, do you have a headache? May I get you—" "My head," she said, "is absolutely perfect. There is absolutely nothing wrong with me at all. God would you please stop playing with that asinine doll, you're driving me insane."

But her moods would pass, often quite suddenly, and as if nothing had happened we would talk. She liked to tell me about her grandfather, a very old man with a drooping white mustache who had died when she was a little girl. It was he who had made her dollhouse, and she remembered his mysterious parlor with its many wooden clocks, its big brown model ships with yellow cloth sails, its little hand-carved wooden whales and walruses. Holding her on his lap, and stroking her hair with his dark brown fingers tufted with white hair, he had told her of a cobblestoned street in a village in a forest in Germany that consisted entirely of shops that sold wonderful wooden toys. When you walked along that street you saw in the windows large wooden marionettes hanging from wires, wooden birds that moved their heads and lifted their wings and sang, intricately carved coaches drawn by teams of wooden horses, and clocks, and clowns, and music-boxes, and rocking horses, and jack-in-the-boxes from which there sprang, suddenly as you watched, black-hatted witches with great hooked noses and upward-pointing chins. I liked to hear about Eleanor's grandfather and the street of toys, but Eleanor also liked to talk about things like the lost civilization of Atlantis and life on other planets. She was a great believer in the lost civilization of Atlantis. She was shocked by my skepticism and angered at my indifference; she kept mentioning books for me to read, and I said yes, yes, when I had time. "Time," she said contemptuously, and made a little abrupt gesture of dismissal. As for life on other planets, she expressed scorn for "little green men with radar guns" but believed passionately in highly developed civilizations on other planets in other solar systems. I was bored by the whole subject but argued without interest that there could be complex forms of life which did not resemble anything we knew, had nothing to do with civilization, and were completely unexciting—for instance, a planet of highly developed germs. But this infuriated Eleanor, who looked at me with a mixture of scorn, pain, and pity, and accused me of lack of imagination—a charge she repeated when I confessed that I did not believe in life after death. She herself did not believe in a conventional Hell with "all those little red devils running around carrying pitchforks" or a conventional Heaven with its "boring angels singing Christmas carols" but she believed in "some form" of life after death. I believed in neither Hell nor Heaven nor life after death nor any sort of God—which shocked Eleanor, not so much for religious reasons as for esthetic ones: she considered me unimaginative. And scornfully she would refer to "healthy people."

She did not share my taste in books and writers. When I said that I thought *Huckleberry Finn* was my favorite book, and that I had read it three times, she said that she had begun it three times but could not get beyond the first chapter. She hated books written in "slang." Her favorite book was *The Odyssey,* which I disliked because it had been a classroom assignment. As for Stevenson, he was the most boring writer who had ever lived. Just thinking about Long John Silver made her yawn. Swordfights, pirates, buried treasure, and boys' adventure stories in general were about as interesting as stories about girls who liked to ride horses—and she hated horses, except when they had wings. She thought *Ivanhoe* was ten times better than anything Steven Louis Robertson had ever written, or whatever his name was, and when she asked me what I had thought of *Ivanhoe* I said: "Oh, it was all right I guess, the lists, the Disinherited Knight, Gurth and Wamba and so forth, and the names, Richard Coeur de Lion, Athelstane, yes, and the way he keeps you dangling at the end of a chapter, but it's not—he doesn't—well let's face it, Eleanor, he isn't Poe." "Oh, Poe," she said wearily, making a strained face. "Oh?" I said coldly. "I don't hear you saying anything else. 'Oh, Poe' is no argument. You can't just say 'Oh, Poe' period. That's nothing: 'Oh, Poe.' " "I'm sorry. What I really meant to say was Poe, oh. Is that better? But all those wounds, and pale maidens, and dreary midnights and things— don't you think he overdoes it a little?" "Overdoes it a little!" And looking at me with a kind of sad amusement she said: "I guess I'm not very poetic." "That's not true," I declared, not at first catching the pun. She was equally unimpressed by Poe's verse and could not repress her scorn when she learned that I admired "The Bells," which she referred to as "The Bells Bells

Bells Bells Bells Bells Bells." No, Oh Poe was not a real poet at all, and the way you could tell was that he was so easy to imitate. A real poet, whom you couldn't imitate, was Keats. Her copy of Keats had an urn on the front and was full of under-linings in dark blue ink; she was shocked that I had never read a single poem by Keats, and gazing at me suddenly with a strange expression and raising one hand in the shape of a claw she said: "La belle dame sans merci hath thee in thrall." She would often recite lines of verse that I did not recognize, and sometimes I envied Eleanor her illness, which gave her so much leisure in which to read. The small bookcase to the left of the bed was tightly packed with intriguing volumes: gilt-edged double-column editions of English poets with little ribbons coming out of the bottom like tails, collections of German legends about emperors and devils, a volume of Norse myths with a diagram of the world-ash showing a little dragon gnawing the bottommost root, a collection of Grimm's fairy tales with glossy six-color illustrations covered by translucent paper, an old three-volume set in German about famous legendary mountains and islands, illustrated histories of marionettes, of music-boxes, of circuses, of dwarves; and she had a dark gilt-edged book called *Myths of the Rhine*, with pen-and-ink drawings showing gloomy castles on cliffs, twisted black trees, weeping maidens, and, in one picture, high upon her rock, half-shrouded in mist, the Lorelei, with her long, tangled hair. Looking up from the picture I said with a smile: "She has your hairstyle, Eleanor." At once Eleanor turned away. After a few moments she said slowly: "I have something to tell you." She pressed her fist against her forehead and said: "Oh, God, I didn't want this to happen." I had been smiling but suddenly stopped. She took a deep breath and let it out slowly. Raising her eyes, but keeping her profile toward me, she said sadly: "I didn't want you to know. I was afraid you'd be like the others. I meant to tell you someday. Oh, God, why did this have to happen. You see, Eleanor isn't my real name. Please don't be angry. Every night, at midnight, you can find me sitting on my rock . . ." She was fond of little jokes

like that, and often teased me in ways that I found faintly dis-
turbing.

But if I liked O'Poe and that sort of thing she knew a much
better writer. Bending over, and removing two volumes from
her bookcase, she placed them in my lap. In neat black capital
letters across the front of the top volume were the words:
COLLECTED TALES, VOL. I. Beneath the title, in smaller black
capital letters, was the name: EDWARD OWEN WHITELAW. When I
opened the cover I saw a piece of translucent paper covering a
black-and-white frontispiece. Carefully lifting the delicate,
crackling, clinging paper I found myself looking at a gloomy
photograph of the author. He was a stiff-looking gentleman in a
black suit, standing before a wall of dark books with one hand
resting on the back of a great carved chair as he stared grimly
at the reader with narrow eyes and tight lips. Under the photograph were the words: EDWARD OWEN WHITELAW, 1840–1884.
Turning to the table of contents, I saw a list of titles such as
"The Ebony Box," "Edward Carter," "The Waldstein Sonata,"
"Leonora," "The Octagonal Tower," "Otto von Hennegau,"
"Dr. Eddington's Narrative," "Walter Lasher and William Lee."
There were several black-and-white illustrations on faintly shiny
paper scattered through the volume. One showed a man seated
at a crude wooden table, leaning forward and clutching his skull
with both hands. On the table before him was a small black box.
Under the picture were the words: THE LID WAS OF EBONY, IN-
LAID WITH SILVER, AND CARVED IN ALL MANNER OF STRANGE AND
CURIOUS DEVICES. Another illustration showed a small boy in
knickerbockers. He was standing with a frightened expression
among what seemed to be immensely tall grassblades that towered above him to the top of the picture. Under the picture were
the words: THE KNOWLEDGE DAWNED UPON HIM THAT HE WAS
HOPELESSLY LOST. That evening I plunged into the tales of
Edward Owen Whitelaw. They affected me like dreams of
vague dread from which one awakes with a feeling of oppression
that lasts the entire day. And yet you do not wish not to have
dreamt them, those unpleasant dreams, for they seem to have

been leading you to the verge of an overwhelming secret. A weary traveler, in the year 18—, comes to an inn in the village of D———. An ostler leads away his horse. The inn is deserted except for an old innkeeper who brings the traveler a meal of black soup and red wine. The innkeeper then leads the traveler to a dusky room with a high fourposter bed. There is something dimly familiar about this room. On the wall is an oval portrait of a beautiful sad-eyed lady. The traveler lays his weary head upon the pillow and at once falls asleep. In the middle of the night he is awakened by a faint sound, as of distant weeping. He lights his taper and looks about the chamber. He is alone. He steps into the hall but now perceives that the sound of weeping comes from his room. He returns, disturbed, but after a long search discovers nothing. Exhausted, he falls into a troubled sleep. Waking at dawn, unrefreshed, he remembers the events of the night as if they had been an evil dream. He glances at the portrait, which seems to be imploring him, hurries downstairs, and calls for his horse. The ostler comes promptly, grinning insolently. The traveler rides away, and as the sun begins to shed its golden rays through the green silence of the forest, the traveler feels guilty and oppressed. There the story ends. In another tale a man is invited to the home of a friend whom he has not seen for twenty years. He arrives at midnight before a decaying mansion in a wood. His knock is not answered and he hesitantly enters. By the light of a half-moon he sees that the great parlor is in decay. Obscurely troubled he passes from room to decaying room, dimly reminded of something. In one room he sees a dusty writing-desk with three quill pens; in another room he sees a cracked mirror with a tarnished gilt frame. In his student days he had occupied a chamber with such a desk; in his dead wife's dressing-room had hung such a mirror. He pushes open a creaking door and enters a small room. On a decaying bed lies a headless toy soldier; in one corner a broken rocking horse lies beside a wooden sword. With a feeling of oppression he recognizes the toys of his childhood. A terrible weariness comes over him; he longs "to flee, to stay." "Feverishly, wearily," he comes to the final door. With a feeling of dread he pushes it open and sees a circular stairway. He lights a lucifer and begins to climb. At the top of the stairway he comes to another door, and pushing it open he enters an octagonal tower. All eight walls are lined with books. The room is empty except for a small round table covered with a white tablecloth; on it lie a black mask and a red rose. He is filled with a vague terror; he senses that what is terrible is not the objects themselves but the fact that they are unfamiliar. He gazes at them with dread, oppression, and a "fearful curiosity." There the story ends. The deliberate and as if insolent incompleteness and obscurity of all the stories angered me, exhausted me, and inflamed my curiosity. It was as if the esthetic intention of Edward Owen Whitelaw were to lead you to the verge of an overwhelming revelation and to abandon you there forever, on the verge. When I returned the volumes to Eleanor I expressed my annoyed fascination. "Oh, Artoor," she said, in one of her teasing moods, "do you like happy endings?" "Don't call me Artoor," I said sharply, but I felt anxious and melancholy.

So we talked, Eleanor and I, in the darkening sickroom that she called her tomb, as I sat by the bed that she called her grave; and before long she would grow drowsy and listless. And I looked forward to those dreamy, sleepy moods, when moving down under her quilt she would half-close her eyes. Then a cozy sadness would come over me, and sliding lower in my chair I would gaze at Raggedy sitting on my leg, at the bureau on the other side of her bed, at the dark mirror over the faceted glass vials; and in the quiet, darkening room there would be no sound but the sound of Eleanor's soft breathing and my own. Sometimes our breathing came together, then slowly it would grow apart, only to come together again. And how I longed to stay that way forever, with only the sound of Eleanor's soft breathing and my own. Sometimes her eyes would close, and she would fall into a troubled sleep. From my chair beside the bed I could see the skin between her eyebrows tense as if in thought, and as I watched she would begin to frown deeply and relax, frown deeply and relax; and as I watched I had the sensation that she must feel, like the tip of a grassblade, my sight scratching against her. And as I watched, suddenly her eyes would open, and looking at me with a dreamy, troubled gaze she would rub her forehead with the back of a hand and say: "Oh, you're still here, I thought . . . you don't have to go yet, do you . . . I was in a garden, the flowers came over my head, I was lost . . . say you won't go . . ." And always, always, it was time to go. Then a heaviness would come over me, and I felt that I could not possibly rise from my chair and pull my sluggish body across the room, and pushing lower in the chair and half-closing my eyes I would pretend that I never had to go, never never had to go, but already I could hear the sound of Mrs. Schumann's footsteps on the stairs, as when, on a dark winter morning, through a dream you hear the sound of opening and closing doors. And you recognize the sound of opening and closing doors, but you plunge away from those doors, back into the dream which is already changing, for among the thick trees of a forest distant doors are closing, and you feel, in that forest, the hard pillow-edge pressing up against your cheekbone, then a hiss of turned-on water tugs at your brain and suddenly with a feeling of pain your mind is torn loose from its dream and you bleed into the morning. Thus I tore myself from Eleanor's dark sickroom into the strange world that was not her sickroom, and stepping into my room I would look about in confusion at the worn brown armchair, the standing lamp with its frayed cord, the book lying face downward on the bed, under the pulled-out wall-light.

One dark afternoon when it was time to leave and I had begun to prepare myself for the effort of pushing my heavy body to its feet, Eleanor turned her head slowly toward me, and gazing upon me with her dark, doleful eyes she said: "I wish you didn't have to go." "Oh," I said, "yes, I know what you mean, it's so drowsy here, so peaceful, how can I go, but I have to go, I have to." "Have to," she said, "that's a funny thing to say: have to . . . but wouldn't it be nice if you could stay, and stay . . . forever . . ." "Oh, forever, please don't say that, you make me feel . . .

but Eleanor, I have to go now, your mother . . ." "My mother will not have a nervous breakdown if you stay for two more seconds." Sitting up in bed with her knees raised under the quilt, she embraced her legs and leaned her cheek on her knees; and gazing at me sideways she said: "Don't you want to stay, Artoor?" "Oh," I said, "of course, please don't say that, what do you think, but Eleanor, it's time to go, you know I have to get home, and besides . . ." "Oh," she said, "all right. Good-bye." And throwing off the covers she swung over the far side of the bed. "Eleanor," I said, "what are you," but already, in the dim bedlight, I saw her rounding the corner of the bed on the way to the closet. "Eleanor," I said, rising to my feet and bending suddenly to catch Raggedy as she fell. I placed Raggedy on the chair but she began to slide sideways, and picking her up as the closet door closed I laid her on the quilt and smoothed her dress. "Eleanor," I called, and as I made my way to the closet I felt weary and unhappy, as if I had failed a test. Opening the closet door I quickly pushed my way through the tight row of dresses and came to the wall. I patted about and found the doorknob. At once I opened the door and entered the Childhood Museum. Eleanor had lit the candle again, and again she was sitting before the gabled dollhouse, gazing straight ahead. I came forward and kneeled beside her, on the other side of the candlestick. "Eleanor," I said wearily. Arching her back, and tossing her head, she turned to me with a disdainful look. "Well?" she demanded. Sorrowfully I bent toward her, and as my lips clumsily touched her slightly parted lips I saw, seated there in the darkness behind her, dim dolls all in a row; and wave upon wave of weariness and melancholy rose in me until I drowned.

52

THERE NOW BEGAN a period of lingering, melancholy, troubling kisses, from which I emerged with burning lips and a feeling of weakness, of exhaustion; and sliding lower in the leather chair beside the bed I would half-close my eyes as Eleanor lay upon her pillow with half-closed eyes and slightly parted lips. And how I longed to stay there forever, in the darkening sickroom that she called her tomb, beside the bed that she called her grave; and in the quiet, darkening room there would be no sound but the sound of Eleanor's soft breathing and my own. Sometimes our breathing came together, then slowly it would grow apart, only to come together again. And how I longed to stay that way forever, with only the sound of Eleanor's soft breathing and my own. And always, always, it was time to go. And one day when it was time to go and I sat languorously in my chair, Eleanor turned to me, and gazing at me with her dark, doleful eyes she said softly: "Won't you stay for dinner, Artoor?" "Oh," I murmured, "dinner," I murmured, and far away I heard the sound of footsteps on the stairs. Suddenly there was a rap at the door. "Enter," said Eleanor, and Mrs. Schumann opened the door. "Oh, mother," said Eleanor, "Artoor is staying for dinner. Do you mind?" "Of course not, Eleanor." She paused. "Does Arthur know—" "Oh, he won't mind. What are you frowning at, mother? There's more than enough room." "I suppose so," said Mrs. Schumann doubtfully. "But Arthur, hadn't you better call your mother?" "Oh," I murmured, "my mother," I murmured, and wearily I began to push myself from the chair, and as I rose I heard the faint sound of my pants peeling from the leather. Then I noticed a yellow dishrack, and in my hand was a black telephone. Mother sounded angry, she was worried about my homework, but I assured her that I had "none," and placing down the receiver I returned to Eleanor's soothing sickroom, lit only by the dim bedlight and a small dim lamp on the bookcase of toys; and sitting down in the leather chair I half-closed my eyes. After a while there was a sound of slow footsteps on the stairs, and gentle thumps. I looked at Eleanor, who was leaning back with half-closed eyes. The creaks and thumps turned on the landing, and continued along the hallway, and stopped. Three quiet knocks sounded at the door. "Enter," said Eleanor, and the door opened slowly. Bending forward slightly, leaning on his polished walking stick, slowly he came forward, a gray-haired gentleman in a dark drooping suit. Under his eyes were dark sagging pouches, and against his vest the loop of a watch-chain trembled as he walked. I began to rise, but he made a patting motion with his hand, and sitting down I watched him make his way between the bed and bureau to the head of the bed. Resting his thick-fingered hands on the top of his polished walking stick he said precisely: "And how iss my princess today?" "A little weary, father." And lifting her face she turned a white cheek for him to kiss. "Oh father," she said, "I'd like you to meet Artoor," and vaguely, indolently, she raised a hand in my direction. Slowly straightening up he turned stiffly toward me, and gazing across the bed he said a little too loudly: "How are you feeling today, my boy?" "Oh, fine thank you, Mr. Schumann." "What? What's that? Speak up, my boy." "Fine thank you!" I said. "Good!" he said, without any change in his melancholy face. Then casting upon Eleanor a long sad look, and casting upon me a long sad look, he turned and made his way slowly from the room, stooping slightly and leaning on his polished walking stick. I glanced at Eleanor, who lay with her eyes closed, and sliding lower in my chair I half-closed my eyes; and in the quiet, darkening room there was no sound but the sound of Eleanor's soft breathing and my own. After a while I heard footsteps on the stairs, and then a rap at the door. "Enter," said Eleanor, and Mrs. Schumann entered, bearing a large tray on which sat two plates of steaming food, two tall glasses of juice, two napkins, two sets of silverware, and a glass saltshaker with a silver top. Wearily I began to rise, but "no, no," said Mrs. Schumann, shaking her head. In the dim lamplight she carried the tray over to the desk and placed it down beside the typewriter. She picked up the big doll on the desk-chair and for a few moments looked about vaguely. Then she sat the doll down on the other side of the typewriter, with her head resting against the carriage. She pulled out the desk-chair, and on the slightly rippling wooden seat she carefully set down a plate, a glass of juice, a napkin, the saltshaker, and three pieces of silverware. Gently she pushed the laden chair toward me with her leg, and gazing at me with her dark, doleful eyes she said: "I hope you aren't too cramped for space, Arthur." "Oh, mother, for heaven's sake," said Eleanor, sitting up in bed and holding out her arms with an impatient look. Mrs. Schumann lifted the tray from the desk and handed it to Eleanor, who placed it on her quilt-covered lap. "I'm afraid everything is getting cold," said Mrs. Schumann sadly. "No no," I said. "Oh, mother," said Eleanor, and bending over with a frown she began to cut into a chicken-wing. "Now if you need anything," said Mrs. Schumann, letting her voice trail away; and casting at us both a mournful look she left the room, closing the door softly behind her. In the lamplit darkness of Eleanor's sickroom there was no sound but the sound of a creaking bed, a creaking chair, a gentle rattle of silverware. "Please pass the salt," said Eleanor, and in the days that followed I began to stay for dinner at Eleanor's, much to mother's concern, for she was worried about my homework, but I assured her that I had none, and holding the saltshaker sideways Eleanor tapped the glass with little sharp motions of her forefinger. When we were finished I would gather our dishes and carry them down on the tray, and then I would bring up the milk and dessert. After dessert I would bring the tray back down, and always Mrs. Schumann would say: "What a nice boy you are," and sometimes Mr. Schumann, looking up with a frown, would say: "What? What's that?" and I would look down with a frown. Then I would return to Eleanor's sickroom, and closing the door behind me I would sink into the leather chair beside the bed and half-close my eyes; and sometimes I would lie down on the bed beside her, I on top of the quilt and she beneath. And how I longed to stay there forever, in the peaceful sickroom that she called her tomb, upon the bed that she called her grave; and in the quiet, lamplit dark there would be no sound but the sound of Eleanor's soft breathing and my own. Sometimes our breathing came together, then it would grow apart, only to come together again. And for a long while

I would stay that way, weary, peaceful, and unmoving. Then it would be time to go, and turning to me with her dark, doleful eyes she would say: "Can't you stay a little longer, Artoor ... just a little longer ..."

Mrs. Schumann would drive me home, and when I stepped into my lamplit living room and mother and father turned toward me, I had the sensation that I had fallen asleep far away in Eleanor's sickroom, and was dreaming this room, this father, that frowning mother.

53

ONE EVENING when it was nearly time to leave and I had begun to prepare myself for the effort of rising from the quilt, Eleanor turned her head slowly toward me, and gazing upon me with her dark, doleful eyes she said: "I wish you didn't have to go." "Oh," I said drowsily, "yes, if only, but I can't, it's almost time ..." "But you always say that, Artoor. But why can't you just stay, and stay ... forever ..." "Oh, forever, I wish you wouldn't ... forever ... and no one would ever bother us again ... and if only ... if only ... but you know I can't, it's almost, I have to ... but Eleanor, haven't we had this discussion before?" "Oh," she said abruptly, "if that's the way you feel about it," and throwing off the covers, which fell across me, she swung over the side of the bed. "Eleanor," I murmured, and in the dim bedlight I saw her rounding the corner of the bed on her way to the closet. "Eleanor," I said wearily, lifting my head from the pillow but letting it fall back as the closet door closed. With a tremendous effort I pushed myself up to a sitting position and then swung my legs over the side of the bed, bumping against the leather chair and watching Raggedy slide slowly down until she lay on her back, smiling up at the ceiling. Wearily I sat her up, folding her hands neatly on her lap, and wearily I made my way to the closet, rubbing my eyes. Opening the closet door I pushed my way through the tight row of dresses and came to the wall. I patted about and found the doorknob, and opening the door I entered the Childhood Museum.

The darkness was so black that for a while I clung to the door-knob for fear of losing my balance. "Eleanor," I whispered, but there was no answer. In my mind I began to furnish the blackness with objects. I remembered the large gabled dollhouse in the center of the room, then I remembered the rocking chair with the doll in the far left-hand corner, and the tea-table against the far wall. And as I imagined the Childhood Museum there seemed to emerge from the blackness darker blacknesses, and I saw or seemed to see the black mass of the dollhouse, the black mass of the rocking chair in the corner, the black tea-table against the far wall. Cautiously I began to step forward, holding out my hand and patting the air before me. Suddenly I felt something against my foot and gasped aloud, but when I crouched down I felt the cold wooden cheek of a doll and the hard, sharp eyelashes above a smooth, open eye. "Eleanor," I said more loudly as I squatted there, listening intensely and looking about, fearing that she would reach out and touch me with her long, sharp fingernails, but then I remembered her blunt, flat, bitten-down nails. She gave no answer, and squinting in the blackness, as if all that darkness hurt my eyes, I began to crawl toward the black mass of the dollhouse, which I saw or sensed not too far away. As I crawled slowly forward I lowered my flat palms slowly onto the dusty floor, and as I crawled forward my right palm sank into something soft which cried Waaaa! and I yanked my hand away, listening intensely in the watching dark. Then my fingertips felt the sudden dollhouse, and I began to crawl around it from left to right, knocking over the candlestick with my knee. When I had completed my circle I sat up on my heels and gazed about the room at the little masses of darker darkness, among which I could now discern dim shapes; and here and there I saw or thought I saw the black glimmer of eyes. Aloud I said softly: "You're not here, are you." There was no answer, and for a moment I imagined that Eleanor was fast asleep in the dollhouse, but all at once I remembered the small door in the wall.

Crawling carefully on my hands and knees I came to the far wall, where I could see the black shape of the tea-table and the black shape of the bookcase. Between them I felt the cold wall with my fingertips. Drawing my palm slowly across the smooth surface I came to a sudden metal hinge. The top of the door was at the level of my neck as I kneeled. Halfway down the door I felt a small metal doorknob. Gently I turned and pushed, but nothing happened. Angrily I pushed harder, I felt like shouting or bursting into tears, then I pulled and the door opened smoothly with faint creaking sounds. A coldness touched my skin. Kneeling down and peering inside I could see only blackness, but when I reached out my hand I felt cloth and heard the faint scrape of a hanger.

I lowered my head and began to crawl slowly into the little closet, pressing my head against the thick mass of dresses and pushing them apart. Above the dresses a rod pushed down against my neck, and I had to lie down on my stomach and squirm slowly forward as the dresses pressed down on me and scraped on their rod. Halfway in I reached through the dresses and felt for a wall, but my fingers touched nothing; the air was cold. Then closing my eyes I pushed my head through the dresses and emerged in cold blackness. Still lying on my stomach, with the dresses pressing down on my shoulders, and my legs sticking into the Childhood Museum, I reached out a hand and felt a tickle of cobwebs. Slowly I swung my hand to the left, and came to a wall. On the right was another wall. They were separated by a space the width of the closet. Reaching up, I felt a rough beam at closet-height. It seemed to be a passageway, large enough for me to enter on my hands and knees.

Slowly I pulled my body through the dresses with loud scraping sounds, and as I rose to my knees I felt on my face a tickle of cobwebs. Just above my back the rough and splintery ceiling pressed down. On the floor I felt a rug with my palm.

Moving my hand sideways along the rug, toward the wall, suddenly I felt a little chair. Beside it I felt a little table. On the table I felt two little plates, two little forks, and two little glasses.

Slowly I crawled forward along that black passageway, tapping the rug before me with my fingertips, and as I crawled I kept knocking over little pieces of furniture with my knees. Just above my back the rough and splintery ceiling pressed down, and I thought of giant Alice in the lizard's house, with her monstrous arm sticking through the little window. I seemed to have been crawling for a long, long time, although I was scarcely moving, when all at once I came to another door. It seemed even smaller than the first door. Below the doorknob I felt a tiny metal key. When I turned the key the door opened forward into darkness, and lowering myself to my stomach I began to squeeze my way in. The narrow sides pressed against my shoulders, the top pushed at my back, and for a moment the doorway held me in its grip before suddenly I pulled myself through.

Inside I kneeled in chill blackness and reached out my hand. On both sides I felt empty blackness. Over my head I felt empty blackness. The floor was smooth, cold wood. Slowly I began to rise, keeping my hand over my head; my fingers struck wood. I was not yet standing at my full height but was half bent over. I moved my hand cautiously along the rough wooden horizontal surface, which suddenly turned upward. I moved my hand along the vertical surface and came to another horizontal surface about two palm-widths above. Running my hand along the second piece I felt it turn upward along another vertical piece, which joined a still higher horizontal piece, and all these vertical and horizontal surfaces seemed oddly familiar. Slowly I moved in the direction of the rising slope of the ceiling, and after a few steps I was able to stand at my full height as the invisible ceiling rose out of reach above my upstretched hand. Then moving back a step I steadied myself in blackness against the curious ceiling. As I stood with my hand resting on a rough angle I imagined myself walking upside down along the stair-like ceiling, higher and higher, clinging to the surfaces like a giant insect. Then I felt dizzy, and gripped the stairway above me, which should have been under me. For a moment the whole world seemed upside down, in the blackness I squeezed my eyes shut, suddenly my fingers remembered touching the cellar stairs from below, and opening my eyes I blinked in blackness, but in my mind I saw myself standing in the space under a stairway rising above me. "Eleanor," I whispered, and listened intently. Then I began to advance slowly, holding my hand outstretched before me and tapping the air with my outspread fingers. Carefully I slid each foot forward, bringing the other foot up beside it, suddenly I felt something soft against my foot and gasped, but she didn't say anything, and crouching down I felt a furry animal with one cold eye and one sharp piece of wire sticking out. Then rising carefully I continued to move forward in the cold blackness, sliding my feet along the floor and nudging soft things with my toes, all at once my outstretched fingers struck a splintery piece of wood. It was a narrow vertical beam, projecting from a rough wooden wall. A few hand-widths to the right was another vertical beam. I continued to pat along the wall, and all at once I felt, between two beams, a short crosspiece. Above it was another crosspiece. They rose up like the rungs of a ladder. Slowly I began to climb, gripping the rough sides tightly and stopping on each rung to reach overhead. Once I looked down over my shoulder and could see nothing but blackness. But the motion of my head seemed to tug me backward, I felt myself plunging down, down, then pressing my cheek against the wood I squeezed my eyes shut. And I longed to lie down, and close my weary eyes, but opening my eyes I stepped carefully onto the next rung, and as I reached up I felt the splintery ceiling. For a few moments I patted about, frowning in the dark. Then I pushed upward against the wood, which began to rise slowly and heavily with loud creaking sounds, and as it rose I saw a widening wedge of new darkness, filled with swirling dust.

54

LIFTING THE HEAVY TRAPDOOR with my left arm and shoulder I grasped the floor with my right forearm. I found myself staring at big black trunks and black wooden barrels that rose up before me. Here and there a metal edge gleamed darkly. Over the trunks and barrels a beamed ceiling came plunging down. I climbed out carefully, lowering the trapdoor creakily into place, and then looked about me, in the darkness less dark than the darkness from which I had come. I was standing at one end of a great sloping attic filled with jagged blacknesses. Far away a dim and flickering light cast a fitful glow on a few shadowy beams and touched the general darkness with dark gleams of edges and corners. Not too far from the trapdoor I made out a shadowy handrail and a black stairway plunging down. Between the trapdoor and the stairway a narrow path seemed to stretch away toward the jagged blacknesses, beyond which the dim light cast its fitful glow.

Sucking in my stomach I squeezed between two nearly touching barrels, scraping my hipbones, and stepped onto the path. I began to advance slowly, feeling the cobwebbed rims of black barrels with my right hand and with my left hand the splintery edge of a long wooden table, on which I could feel black cold cans, a black coil of rope, a sagged black beachball, and uncertain objects of cold rubber and metal. At the end of the table black trunks and broken furniture rose up, to the right a black lamp leaned across the way like a fallen tree, far away a dim light flickered, and turning left, toward deeper blackness, I kept my hand on the table-edge as I stepped carefully along the cluttered floor, lifting each foot to the knee and pausing before I slowly lowered it into what seemed a space among black rattling objects. The table-rim ended and I lowered my palm to the dampish padded arm of a chair. There was no cushion, and as I patted about the stiff seat, through which I could feel the bumps of springs, I felt a scattering of play-money coins and a naked wooden doll lying on her stomach with her face turned upward. Past the chair there rose up on the left a squarish black mass that felt like wickerwork, and past the wickerwork object I came to a great black shape that blocked my way. I felt a smooth wooden surface with little wooden protuberances. Turning right, and keeping my left hand on the smooth surface of what seemed to be a bureau, suddenly I bumped against a barrier. On my left was the bureau, on my right rose up another black shape that seemed to be an old refrigerator; the barrier was between them and came up to the level of my waist. I felt a rim of wood, beyond which lay fuzzy firmnesses, a small wooden hand, a fluffy ear; it seemed to be a large open box filled with dolls and animals. There was no way to advance except across the box of dolls. Gripping the rim I kneeled gently into the soft belly of a large black beast, and very softly, far below, I heard a muffled cry which suddenly stopped. Then I put my other knee into the soft and sinking doll-mass, gripping the opposite rim as my sinking knees tried to crawl across heads and paws, but it was no use, and standing up in that quicksand of dolls I lifted first one leg and then the other awkwardly over the opposite rim. I now found myself on another littered path, formed by high rows of piled-up trunks and boxes that came up to my head. As I advanced, carefully lowering each foot, my right foot pressed down on something hard that gave way under me. I yanked my foot away and in the not quite black darkness I saw a black rocking horse wildly and silently rocking. Carefully I made my way between the still-moving horse and the cold trunks, then I came to a high table that blocked my way. Jagged blacknesses rose from the table. I felt a mop in a bucket, an upside-down chair, a piece of sharp metal. A thick, heavy, dampish tablecloth reached to the floor and lay in a black heap. Slowly I lowered myself into a squatting position, bumping something soft with my knee, and lifting the cloth I began to crawl inside, banging my knee against a sharp crosspiece. Inside I dropped the cloth and found myself in total blackness. Carefully I crawled forward inch by inch. Over my head I felt sharp screws pointing down, on the floor I pressed into something sticky with my palm. Then I felt the heavy cloth before me, and pushing clumsily against it, like an actor who cannot find the division in the curtain, I pressed against something on the other side. The barrier rose up all along the cloth. Slowly and clumsily I lifted the heavy curtain, which to the left was pinned under a weight, and I found myself staring at a black flat-looking mass rising directly before me and about two feet high. Lifting the heavy tablecloth over my head and onto my neck, I began to squirm upward and outward, pressing against the firm softness as my knees worked over sharp edges and the top of the table pressed against my neck, and slowly I climbed out and up onto a sagging bed covered with fuzzy animals. Straight ahead black objects rose up, and I began to crawl slowly along the bed to the right, patting among fuzzy limbs, cold eyes, the smooth snout of a bear, suddenly I lay down on my stomach and closed my weary eyes. But at once I opened my eyes, and crawling to the end of the bed I stepped down and began to make my way along a narrow path between piled blacknesses. My foot sank into something hard that gave way with a sprinkle of metal sounds, and yanking my foot away I heard a metallic thud; a little bell rang. Bending down I felt a cold typewriter with a cluster of stuck keys. As I stepped over the typewriter my leg bumped something light that began to sway slightly, knocking softly against my leg as I passed. Then I came to a high bookcase, and turning right I made my way between piles of heavy sharp-edged trunks, some of which rose to my head. Here and there the trunk-tops gleamed darkly. The trunk-path turned left, and I came to a high black squarish mass that blocked my way.

It rose up before me higher than my head. Above it, rising from behind, a square post was darkly visible, faintly touched by fitful light. Gently I felt the black mass with my fingertips; it was smooth wood. My fingertips came to a slightly raised portion, then the smoothness continued. I tapped the surface, which to my surprise sounded hollow, but when I tried to push the mass aside it would not move. Heavy trunks rose up on both sides. Trapped in my maze, wearily I thought of the long way back, along the path of trunks, between piled blacknesses, over the bed of animals, under the dangerous table, but I could not remember what came next, and sitting down wearily on the narrow ledge of a low trunk I bowed my head in the dark. Wearily I raised my head, gazing at the wall of trunks and the high black mass. Then wearily I rose, and turned away, angrily I turned back and went up to the hollow-sounding great box. I ran my palm along the surface to the slightly raised portion, which was about the width of my hand. Then I ran my fingers along the raised surface, tracing the outline of a large rectangle, the bottom of which was about two feet from the floor. I frowned in the dark, tapping about within the rectangle, and suddenly I felt a small protuberance the size of a drawer-knob. I pulled the knob and a door opened, emitting a smell of moth-balls and cloth. Stepping over the rim I entered cold, tickly fur. The coats were tightly packed together, and as I pulled two thick shoulders apart and pushed my face inward I felt tight walls of fur pressing in on me. Standing bent over in that press of fur I pushed through with my head and hand. As my fingers touched cardboard it gave way, and another high door opened.

I found myself gazing at a high dark curtain, over which a dim light cast a fitful glow. At the top of the curtain shadowy rafters came sloping down to the left and right, leaving a triangle of space. I stepped over the rim of the wardrobe, took two steps, and began feeling for a division in the folds of the curtain. The cloth was thick and velvety and gave off a musty odor. At last I kneeled down, placing my face near the floor, and when I lifted a heavy piece of curtain I found myself peering into a little alcove.

It was a flickering alcove lit by a single candle in a holder on the floor. To the left and right the high rafters sloped down to the floor, forming a triangular wall opposite. Against the wall lay a bed entirely concealed by long dark-blue velvet curtains that hung from a high curtain-rod fixed between sloping rafters. In front of the curtained bed, to the left, stood a full-length mirror mounted on swivels. It leaned back slightly, reflecting the dark rafters and, at the bottom, the wavering top of the nearby candleflame. To the right stood a carved wooden chest. Its top was open and a mass of clothes was visible. A wrinkled black sleeve hung over one edge as if it were wearily trying to pull itself out of the chest. On the floor near the chest lay a dead brown flower, a package of spotted letters tied with a faded blue ribbon, and a wrinkled yellowish-white high-heeled shoe. Softly I crawled under the heavy curtain and rose into the little room. Softly I took three steps over to the dark blue curtains. "Eleanor," I whispered, but there was no answer. I raised my hand to a ripple of curtain and pushed it gently aside.

The bed lay directly against the rough wooden wall. In a small round window divided by four strips of wood radiating from a central point, I saw my frowning face and one pale hand holding aside a dark curtain. Dressed in a long yellowish-white gown, Eleanor was lying on the bed below the window with her eyes closed and her arms crossed over her chest. A line of wetness glimmered on her cheek. In the dim yellow light of the trembling candleflame I stood gazing down at her. Under my gaze her closed eyelids trembled. Wearily I lay down in the dark beside her, leaning my cheek against her cold hair.

55

THAT EVENING I arrived home later than usual, and in the days that followed I began to arrive home later than usual, lowering my eyes under mother's deepening frown; and closing the door behind me I would sit down at my desk. Pushing the button of my fluorescent lamp I would watch first one bulb flicker on, and then the next, and opening up a schoolbook I would begin to read. But after a while I would grow tired, and rising from my hard chair I would go over to the bed and push aside the blinds. I would gaze out at the black maple-twigs against the moonlit sky, at the stiff grassblades sticking up through the snowcrust, at the cold swing with its mound of snow; and on my face I would feel the cold flowing from the glass.

One evening after dessert as I sat slackly in the leather chair beside the bed, with the small of my back resting on the edge of the seat, my head leaning languorously against the low back, and my heavy eyelids half-closed, Eleanor, who had been a little moody that day, and now was sitting up with a frown, began to look about the room restlessly. At last, throwing aside the covers, she slipped from the bed, and tying her black robe about her she went rustling toward the footboard, glancing back at me as I gazed dreamily after her. At the vanity table she caught sight of herself in the mirror and stopped. With a quick motion she sat down on the padded bench before the table, and turning on the two dim table-lamps she began combing her hair. Slowly and cracklingly she pulled the comb down through her rich black hair, uttering little hisses whenever she hit a snag, and tossing back her head at the end of each combing. In the dimly lamplit darkness I could see her raised elbow in the dusky mirror. Over her head a mirror-hand with a mirror-comb would appear and disappear. For a while she sat there, combing out her crackling hair, and after a while she said: "Mirror mirror on the wall, who is the fairest of them all?" She stopped combing, as if waiting for an answer. Then she began combing again, with loud crackling sounds, and as she combed she said: "Artoor, do you think I'm fair?" There was another pause, during which her hand stopped combing. Drowsily I murmured: "Eleanor Eleanor by the wall, you are the fairest of them all." Her hand began combing again, and after a few moments she said: "I feel sad tonight, Artoor. Sad and bored." There was another pause. She said: "You're not saying much tonight, Artoor." She put down her comb and leaned forward; through my half-closed eyes I saw her gazing at herself in the mirror. Then she reached for a box behind the mirror-tray. As she lifted the top, revealing a dark red velvet lining, a music-box melody began to play. Removing two earrings she fastened them on her ears, tilting her head first one way, and then the other, and suddenly leaning forward she did something to her face. Turning abruptly she said: "How do you like that?" "Oh," I murmured, "I can't see," and rising from the bench she came rustling toward me and sat at the edge of the bed beside the chair. Turning her head first one way, and then the other, she displayed her earrings, which were small silver flowers; and her eyebrows were blacker and a little longer. In one hand she held a dark red pencil with a very black point. "Well?" she said, frowning at me with her blackened eyebrows, and suddenly she added: "Don't move." Bending forward she pressed the dark red pencil against my right eyebrow. I felt the dull point tracing the curve of first one eyebrow and then the other, and after a while she said: "All right, you can look now." And taking me by the hand she pulled me from my chair and drew me over to the mirror, while I clung to Raggedy, who had almost fallen. Wearily I bent toward the mirror, where I saw that over my drooping eyelids my eyebrows were arched and very black; and as I gazed I saw on my mirror-face a faint smile that I did not feel on my own face. "Yes," I murmured, "that's all right," and suddenly the mirror-face frowned. "Give me that thing," I said. With the red pencil I began to lengthen my eyebrows, but soon they seemed crooked. "But that's all wrong, silly," said Eleanor, "now sit down, no, not that way," and seating me on the bench with my back to the mirror she began to draw the pencil over my eyebrows, stepping back from time to time to examine me with a frown. When she was done I began to turn around, but "Not yet," said Eleanor, "now close your eyes." I heard a metal cap unscrewing. Then I heard the sound of fingertips tapping against tin. The air seemed filled with scented dust. Suddenly I felt powdery fingers on my face. She patted and rubbed my cheeks, my chin, my forehead, my nose, pausing now and then to tap against the tin.

"Keep them closed," she said. A drawer opened. I heard the sound of sliding tin. Then I felt a soft pressure on my eyelids. "Not yet, not yet," she said, and against my lips I felt a firm waxy pressure; and I felt a firm waxy pressure in the center of each cheek. Then I heard another drawer open and a sound of soft things being moved. Suddenly I felt something being pulled over my head, and I opened my eyes. Eleanor was looking at me with a frown, her head tilted to one side and a finger raised along her cheek. "No," she said, "you still lack something," and bending forward she began messing up the sides of my hair. "Hey," I murmured. "Quiet," said Eleanor. "Now let me see, let me see..." and going over to her closet she began pushing clothes around with loud scraping sounds. She returned holding a red dress-jacket with brass buttons. "Now put this on," she said. "Oh, for heaven's sake, it won't kill you." It felt tight under the arms; Eleanor left it unbuttoned. Then stepping back: "Well," she said doubtfully, "that isn't too... I know, take off your shoes." And as I took off my shoes she went back to her closet, pushed around her clothes, and returned with a pair of baggy gray corduroy pants. "Try these on," said Eleanor, adding: "over yours, of course," and as I pulled on the pants, which were tight at the waist but loose at the hips, I felt a strange, drowsy excitement, as if I were enclosing myself in Eleanor.

"All right," she said, "you can look now," and when I turned I saw in the mirror a white-faced clown with a big red smiling mouth, two red spots on his cheeks, turquoise-blue eyelids, and a white woolen cap with a red pompom.

Picking up the lipstick, I made the edges of the mouth droop down sadly.

"Pretty Pierrot," said Eleanor. "Can you dance, Pierrot?"

In the dusty mirror I watched the arms in their red jacket begin to rise slowly and stiffly. As they rose the stiff jacket-shoulders stuck up and the unbuttoned lapels pulled apart. The arms stopped, sloping down like the sides of coathangers. The hands dropped laxly at the wrists, the tired head bent to one side. In the mirror I saw Eleanor sitting on the bed behind me with her legs dangling over the footboard, her knees pressed together and her ankles apart. Under her blackened eyebrows she was watching intently. Slowly, stiffly, I began to turn. And as I turned there rose in me a sad, wild feeling, on the padded bench Raggedy lay face down with her arms thrown out, and suddenly snatching her up I began to waltz slowly, taking one long step and two short ones, turning round and round in the space between the vanity table and the closet. I held Raggedy a little away from me, my right hand on her waist and my left hand grasping her arm, and turning round and round I began to waltz in the narrow aisle between the closet and the leather chair, bumping my thigh on the sharp desk-corner, and as I turned and turned I saw my sad red mouth in the dark glass of the cabinet of dolls; and as I turned I saw Eleanor with her blackened eyebrows and silver earrings, watching from the footboard. Faster and faster I danced with Raggedy, turning and turning in my narrow space, taking one long step and two short ones, and as I danced there was no sound but the soft sound of my socks on the floor and the sound of my breath going faster and faster. And as I danced my hat fell to the floor, my shirt came out of my pants, sweat trickled along my sides. But as if I could not stop I danced faster and faster, my temples throbbed and my breath burned in my throat, and holding out my arms I began to spin around and around, faster and faster, through half-closed eyes in the lamplit dark I saw the glass vials, the silver earrings, the dark gleaming glass of the cabinet of dolls, and round and around and around I went, faster and faster, faster and faster, faster and faster and faster and faster—suddenly I stopped. Gripping the edge of the desk as Raggedy fell I bent forward breathing painfully. But the room turned all about me, round and around and around about me, and sinking clumsily to one knee I grasped the edge of the desk with one hand and the edge of the chair with the other hand, bowing my head as the room turned round and round. Softly the large doll came sliding against me and far away I heard: "Oh, Pierrot, where is your hat, Pierrot?" Wrenching open my eyes I saw the hat lying on the floor beside me. Dizzily I bent over and picked up the hat and pulled it crookedly over my head. "Oh, Pierrot, pretty Pierrot, will you dance, Pierrot?" But gripping the chair-edge I bowed my forehead heavily against my powdered fingers.

56

WE WERE MARRIED one night in the Childhood Museum, she and I, she and I; Eleanor and I. Alone in Eleanor's candlelit sick-room I changed into my wedding clothes. The stiff black jacket, smelling of must, was covered with little wrinkles, and the frayed and shiny cuffs came down over my knuckles. One pocket-flap was bent out of shape and the sagging shoulders rested against my upper arms. My baggy pants, stained on one thigh with a wavering rust-colored line, were spotted here and there with pale patches of mildew. From under the drooping cuffs emerged a pair of black shoe-toes filled with little cracks and wrinkles. In the dim mirror above the vanity table, before the sputtering candle, I adjusted the drooping black bowtie at the top of my cold, wrinkled, yellowish shirt. Far away a tin-kling music-box melody began to play. "All right," called Eleanor softly. Taking a deep breath I opened the closet door, pushed my way through the black dresses, and entered the Childhood Museum.

The room was dimly illuminated by the flickering light of a single candle before the gabled dollhouse. Dressed in the long yellowish-white wedding gown she came softly forward from the opposite wall. The long train trailed behind her and made a soft swishing sound. A stiff crumpled veil covered her face and hung halfway down her back. In her hands she clasped a bouquet of brown stems from which dry brown petals fell as she moved slowly forward. At the dollhouse she kneeled down and gazed before her with a dreamy expression. When the tinkling melody began again I came forward slowly in time to the music. Gently I kneeled down beside her, inhaling a faint odor of must. For a long while we kneeled side by side with the candle between us, listening to the tinkling music-box melody that grew slower and slower as it played over and over again, growing slower and slower and wearier and wearier until each tired tinkling note, sounding after longer and longer pauses, seemed the very last, but then another note would sound, and suddenly two notes sounded in quick succession, followed by a long, weary silence, from which there rose, as if after a tremendous effort, a faint, glassy, barely breathing note, which needed only one more note to complete its phrase. And for a long while I waited for that last, dying note, listening so intensely that I felt a tickling sensation in my inner ear, but the music had ended. When I glanced at Eleanor she was staring before her with a dreamy expression. Then from my pocket I removed a golden ring with a large, many-faceted, rainbow-shimmering diamond on top, held in place by tiny prongs and amber-colored glue. "Eleanor," I whispered. Dreamily she turned toward me and raised one drooping hand, lax at the wrist. Taking her soft, chill hand I slipped the dazzling ring over the fourth finger. Her hand dropped limply to her lap. "Eleanor," I whispered again, and turning toward me she gazed at me with her dark, doleful eyes. Then gently I raised the stiff, wrinkled, scratchy veil, slowly I leaned toward her, but at the last moment she turned her head aside and my lips touched her chill cheek. At once she rose, picking up the candle and throwing her shadow about the room. Slowly she walked toward the far wall, her gown swishing behind her. In the center of the tea-table she set the candle down. Beside the candle I saw a small blue-and-white teapot, and at each place was set a little cup and saucer. The chairs were empty. Pulling out the small chair on the left, slowly and carefully Eleanor sat down, leaning forward with her elbow on her gowned knee and resting the side of her cheek against the back of her hand. Then I rose slowly and walked slowly over to the table. Pulling out the chair on the right I sat down carefully. My cup was one inch high. It had a tiny handle through which I could not insert a finger, and its white and glimmering surface was covered with dark blue pictures showing little windmills, little houses, and little people skating on a pond with their scarves streaming out behind them and one leg bent back at the knee. To the left of my cup was a little napkin on which lay a silver fork two inches long. To the right of my cup lay a silver knife and a silver spoon. With her right thumb and forefinger Eleanor picked up the teapot by the handle. Holding the top with her left forefinger she tipped the spout over the rim of my cup, looking up suddenly with a questioning gaze. I held up my palm, and she tipped the teapot back. Then she tipped the spout over her own cup, straightening the teapot but then tipping it briefly once again, and at last she placed the teapot back beside the candle. Then removing the knobbed top of the little sugarbowl she picked up her spoon, lowered it into the bowl, lifted it gently, and brought it carefully toward the cup, where she tipped the spoon over. She began to stir, making quiet clinking sounds. With her left hand she replaced the top of the sugarbowl and pushed the bowl toward me. Removing the knobbed top of the bowl I picked up my spoon, lowered it into the bowl, lifted it gently, and brought it carefully toward my cup, where I tipped the spoon over. Once again I lowered my spoon into the bowl, lifted it gently, brought it carefully toward my cup, and tipped the spoon over. Then I began to stir, making quiet clinking sounds. Eleanor put down her spoon. Gripping the little handle of the teacup with her thumb and forefinger she raised the cup to her lips, tipped the rim toward her, tipped it back, and lowered the cup onto the saucer with a quiet clinking sound. Gripping the little handle of my teacup with my thumb and forefinger I raised the cup to my lips, tipped the rim toward me, tipped it back, and lowered the cup onto the saucer with a quiet clinking sound. For a long while we drank our tea in a silence broken only by quiet clinking sounds. On the wall behind Eleanor her large dim shadow rose and fell with the rising and falling candleflame and in the corner the doll in the rocking chair stared at me with flaming black eyes. Eleanor placed her teacup down and lifted the napkin to her lips. She patted her lips twice and put the napkin down to the left of the saucer and placed upon it the shiny fork. To the right of the saucer she placed the spoon neatly beside the knife. I lifted my teacup to my lips, leaned my head way back, and then leaned forward. I placed my teacup down and lifted my napkin to my lips. I patted my lips twice and put the napkin down to the left of the saucer and placed upon it the shiny fork. To the right of the saucer I placed the spoon neatly beside the knife. Eleanor pushed back in her chair. Slowly she rose, higher and higher, until her knees were on a level with the table-top and her black hair streamed among the stars. Slowly I rose, higher and higher, and finally stopped. Softly Eleanor pushed in her chair. Softly I pushed in my chair. Arm in arm we walked slowly across the room, leaving the candle on the table behind us. Opening the closet door without a word Eleanor bent down and disappeared through the black clothes. Then I pushed my way through the black clothes into Eleanor's sickroom.

In the dim and flickering light of the candle on the vanity table she was standing at the foot of the bed with her back to me. Silently I stepped beside her. For a while we stood in silence, gazing at our wavering shadows that stretched across the bed and stood up against the headboard and overflowed onto the wall. Then silently she turned to the left and walked along the side of the bed beside the bureau. At the head of the bed she sat down, and leaning back on her elbows she raised her legs slightly and began to make gentle kicking motions. There was the sound of a dropping shoe, the sound of rubbing flesh, the sound of another dropping shoe. Then sitting up at the side of the bed Eleanor drew off one yellowish-white glove, held it up between two fingers, and let it fall to the floor with a soft cloth-sound. She drew off her other glove, held it up between two fingers, and let it fall to the floor with a soft cloth-sound. Then she raised her fingertips to the tops of her shoulders. Slowly she

began to lift, bowing her head and sweeping her hands forward
in an arc until she held both arms stretched out with the palms
upward; and lifting her head slowly, she held up one hand with
the thumb and finger pinched together and the pinky sticking
up. Slowly she opened her thumb and finger, tilting her hand
as she watched the bridal gown fall soundlessly to the floor.
Eleanor rose from the bed and pulled the covers back. Slowly
she crawled under, pulling the quilt up to her chin, placing her
arms above, and closing her eyes. Beside her lay my long and
gently wavering shadow, covering her elbow, her neck, and
part of her hair. Silently I turned to the right and walked along
the side of the bed past the desk and the cabinet of dolls to the
leather chair. I gazed at the cracked and faintly gleaming
leather seat, at the thick quilt with its pattern of faded pink
flowers, at Eleanor's closed eyes. Slowly I reached down to the
top of the covers on my side. As I began to lift, Eleanor's eyes
opened and she turned her head toward me with a frown. At
once I dropped the covers and straightened up, lowering my
eyes as I felt a hot pulsing in my neck. When I raised my eyes
I saw her frowning more deeply at me. And I longed to cry Stop
it! Stop it! Stop it! Stop it! but "Shoes," she murmured, and
gazing down at my feet I saw black shoe-toes filled with little
cracks and wrinkles. Then lifting my right foot I scraped the
loose shoe-back against my left shin and the shoe fell to the
floor. Then raising my left foot I scraped the loose shoe-back
against my right shin and the shoe fell to the floor. Looking
up I saw Eleanor lying back with closed eyes. Slowly I reached
down to the top of the covers on my side. Slowly I began to
pull back the quilt, the blanket, the sheet. And slowly I slid
under the covers on my side, pulling the covers up to my chin
and placing my arms outside. For a long while I lay motionless,
with a beating neck, listening to the soft sounds of breathing
and inhaling a damp, musty odor. Then moving my irises to the
right I saw Eleanor's left arm lying on the quilt. The long
tight wrinkled sleeve covered the entire arm and burst into stiff
lace at the wrist. Beyond the lace I could see the slope of the

back of her hand, with its intricate pattern of tiny lines and a faint shine from the candlelight. One knuckle was sharp and reddish-looking, and two green-blue veins wound around it and disappeared on the other side. Moving my irises to the right until I felt pains in my eyes I saw Eleanor's face turned partway toward me. Her eyes were closed. A single line of black hair lay on her white cheek like a pencil-line. Slowly and steadily she breathed. The candle sputtered. Somewhere a car passed. Then there was no sound but the sound of Eleanor's soft breathing and my own. A weariness came over me, and in the soothing darkness I closed my eyes.

57

As I spent more and more time with Eleanor, I began to notice a subtle change in the universe. It was not so much that a vagueness had come over things as that a partial dissolution had occurred, leaving edges of objects that poked through a medium of mist. Mother had shrunk to a pair of eyebrows frowning over the tops of eyeglasses, father was a plump lamp-lit hand lying on the padded edge of an armchair, and all of high school was a brownish blur from which there would emerge suddenly the hard edge of a desk, William's pained angry face, the short silver lines radiating from a circle of black on a locker, the beads of moisture on the curve of silver that rose from the shadowed white porcelain in its niche—only to dissolve, and gazing dreamily through heavy-lidded eyes I would wander among patches of white and brown, and suddenly the hard white edge of a house would leap out, only to dissolve. It was not, as in some pleasant storybook, that I seemed to inhabit two different worlds, one a sunny and boring dayworld and the other a mysterious realm of night, rather it was as if Eleanor's world were draining away the other world, leaving it pale and insubstantial; so that as I walked along the long brown corridors or pulled my covers up to my chin it seemed to me that I was drifting in a dream of covers and corridors from which I would wake to the weight and hardness and connected precision of the glass vials on the vanity table, the glass-covered cabinet of dolls, the leather chair beside the bed.

As the days passed I began to notice a restlessness in my sick bride. Often when I arrived she would be sitting up in bed, looking at me with a sullen expression, and if I said anything at all she would answer "Yes yes yes" and look away with a frown. Shutting the door softly behind me I would walk softly to the chair beside the bed, and taking up Raggedy on my thigh I would slide down lower and lower and gaze before me with half-closed heavy-lidded eyes. And how I longed to stay there forever, in the darkening sickroom that she called her tomb, beside the bed that she called her grave; and half-alive in the darkening dusk I thought: if only I could stay forever, if only I did not have to break the spell, if only I could fall asleep beside her and never wake up. And half-alive in the darkening dusk I would half-dream of Dornröschen in her tower, and of the prince who had traveled on his long journey. Pushing aside the final branches he stepped into the silent courtyard, where the horses and the hounds lay fast asleep, and on the roof the doves slept with their heads under their wings. Softly, in silent wonder, he made his way across the sleep-enchanted courtyard to the slumbering castle. And when he stepped inside he saw the flies asleep on the wall, he saw the cook in the kitchen holding his hand as if to strike the boy, he saw the maid sleeping before the sleeping black hen. Then he came to a great hall where men and women lay fast asleep, and up above, beside the throne, the king and queen lay sleeping. And there was no sound in that hall but the sound of his own breathing. Then he came to a tower, and climbing the winding stair he came to a little door, and opening the door he saw Dornröschen, lying fast asleep. And she was so beautiful that he could not look away. And the prince knew that when he kissed Dornröschen, her eyes would open. Then the king and queen would awake, and all the court. And the horses in the courtyard would wake and shake themselves, the hounds would spring up and wag their tails, the doves on the roof would lift their heads from under their wings, look about, and fly away. And the flies on the wall would fly again, the fire in the kitchen would rise, the cook would strike the boy, the maid would pluck the hen. Then the wedding of the prince and Dornröschen would be celebrated, and they would live happily ever after. And as the prince stood looking at Dornröschen as she lay fast asleep, a sadness came over him. He thought of the sleeping hounds and the sleeping horses, of the doves with their heads under their wings, of the sleeping king and the sleeping queen, of the sleeping flies and the sleeping fire, and as if he had fallen under the spell of that sleep he went over to where Dornröschen lay, and lying down beside her he closed his eyes forever.

58

IT WAS SHE one afternoon who spoke of death. That day she had seemed more fretful and irritable than usual, and had gazed at me darkly, twirling her hair about a finger and saying how "grateful" she was to me for my visits, while I, sitting drowsily with half-closed eyes, listened to the rush and drip of rain against glass and the suck and gurgle of rainwater in the roof-gutter. After a while Eleanor threw the covers back. She swung her legs over the side of the bed and began to walk up and down restlessly between the bureau and the bed, frowning as she tied her black robe about her. Then she strode around the footboard and began to walk up and down between the bed and the vanity table, pausing now and then to gaze at herself in the dim mirror above the faceted glass vials, while I, half-asleep, sat listening to the soft slap of her slippers and the swish of her robe. After a while she walked over to the desk, leaned forward, and pushed aside a little piece of curtain. A dull gray light entered the room, bringing out a faint gleam on the vanity table, the glass vials, the brass handles of the bureau. "Hey," I murmured. She let the curtain fall back into place, and near-darkness returned. Then she began to pace again, and after a while she said: "You know, Artoor, I've been feeling much better lately"—and suddenly she began to speak of death. She called herself a bride of death; and looking away with dark-flashing eyes she began to speak of famous love-deaths. She spoke of Romeo and Juliet, of Antony and Cleopatra, of Tristan and Isolde; and as she spoke I remembered a picture I had once seen of two lovers lying side by side with their eyes closed, under dark stormclouds, on the brown ground, beside a twisted tree. Then I too began to speak of death—but she was scornful of guns, which reminded her of "cowboy movies for adolescent boys." And she spoke of queens, of goblets, of potions, of poisons, and as she spoke there rose in my mind an image from some forgotten movie: two white hands clasping a gold cup before a crimson curtain.

That evening Eleanor began to plan the drama of our death. I lay drowsily on the soft quilt as Eleanor paced swishingly up and down, discussing possible settings and costumes. "Yes," I murmured now and then, "oh yes, yes, that's fine." "Yes," I murmured, "yes, I'm awake," and the next day when I pushed open the door of her room I saw her standing in the corner by the closet. Her elbow rested in the palm of her hand and her long forefinger lay across her cheek. She was frowning at the bed. The bed was entirely covered by an old-looking black spread with a raised pattern of black wavy lines; a dusty tasseled fringe trailed on the floor. "Well?" said Eleanor, "aren't you going to say anything?" "Oh, it's fine, fine," I murmured. "I don't know," said Eleanor, "I don't know . . . take off your coat and lie down, Artoor," and as I lay down on my back and let my head sink into the black pillow I inhaled a damp, musty odor. Eleanor began walking up and down in front of the footboard, pausing to look at me from various angles. Then she said: "Close your eyes, Artoor," and when I closed my eyes I imagined her coming closer and closer until she was bending over me, gazing at me with her dark, doleful eyes, and suddenly I opened my eyes, but she was standing before the closet door, gazing at me with a frown. "I thought I asked you to close your eyes. Now fold your arms across your chest, no, yes, that's right." Then I heard her footsteps coming around the side of the bed near the bureau. I felt the mattress sink and I heard a spring thud dully as she stretched out beside me, not touching me except for a piece of hair that tickled my cheek. Almost at once she rose, saying "All right," and when I opened my eyes she was standing by the bureau, frowning down at me. I stood up on the chair-side, and when I looked at the bed I saw two head-hollows on the side-by-side pillows and two dim shapes pressed into the black stiff spread. "Yes," I murmured, "that's all right," and looking across the bed at Eleanor I saw her gazing at me with her dark, doleful eyes.

The next day when I pushed open the door of her room I saw her sitting up in bed, frowning down at two knitting needles that she held in the form of uplifted wings. Beside her lay a straw knitting bag with a flower on it, composed of pink beads for the petals and green beads for the stem and two leaves. From the bag emerged a piece of black wool that led to a narrow fringe of black knitting on the long lavender needle. She looked up for a moment and at once looked down, and sitting down languorously in my chair beside the bed I listened for a while to the click of needles as I watched the point of the long green needle deftly gathering up the loops of black wool and transferring to itself the black fringe from the lavender needle. The fringe was about three inches wide and hung down about one inch. After a while I said: "Aren't you going to tell me what it is, Eleanor?" but Eleanor knitted on in silence. By suppertime the fringe had grown to about four inches, and after dessert, when I returned to the room, there was a single row of black stitching on the lavender needle, and on the quilt before the straw bag lay a small black woolen tube about four inches long. "But what is this!" I cried, pulling the black tube over my finger. "Are you making me a glove, Eleanor?" I wiggled my woolen finger; Eleanor knitted on, stopping suddenly and thrusting the needles into her bag. The next afternoon when I entered I saw two tubes on the quilt and a new piece of knitting hanging from the lavender needle. All that day and evening Eleanor knitted on, making two separate pieces about eight inches long and four inches wide, and the next afternoon when I pushed open the door I saw her sitting up in bed beside her straw bag of knitting, gazing at me with a slight frown. She was wearing the long lavender needle in her hair. She held the long green needle so that the point pressed lightly into her shoulder and a forefinger pressed lightly against the silver button on the other end. "No knitting," I said, as she continued to watch me, and only when I reached the leather chair did I see Raggedy smiling up at me in her long black dress and her black wool cap.

The preparations continued. One sunny springlike afternoon when sweating in my heavy wintercoat I pushed open the door of Eleanor's cool sickroom I was surprised to see her sitting in my chair in her black silky robe. Raggedy lay face downward on the bed with her arms spread out and one leg lying up along her back. "Oh there you are," said Eleanor, standing up at once and coming around the bed as I stood by the door holding my heavy schoolbooks. "Well?" she said, gazing down at her feet, lifting her robe slightly, and looking up at me with a frown. "But I can't exactly," I said, coming forward. "Well?" she said, lifting her robe a little higher. "They seem very," I said, gazing at the high tight dusty-looking black boots, "actually they're very, did you find them up there?" "In a trunk," she said, sitting down on the bed with her booted legs dangling over the low footboard. A row of black hooks ran up the front of each boot and around each hook was drawn a black lace. Eleanor leaned back on her hands and tipped her head first one way and then the other way as she lifted first one boot and then the other. "And look," she said, getting up suddenly, "something for you too, Artoor." And going over to the desk-chair she picked up a piece of black crumpled cloth and held it out before me. It looked like a crumpled black dress. "But what is it?" I said. "Take off your coat, Artoor," she said with a frown. "Now turn around." She placed the heavy black cloth on my shoulders; the bottom fell to my calves. Then turning me around she fastened it under my chin, and as I strode up and down before the vanity table, watching myself passing and repassing in the mirror above the faceted glass vials, I saw my black cape rippling out behind me.

As the night of our death drew near, a sadness came over me. One afternoon as I lay on the quilt beside Raggedy, gazing up at the darkening ceiling, I said: "You know, Eleanor, I've been thinking." In the leather chair Eleanor looked up from her book. "Thinking, Artoor?" "Oh," I said, avoiding her eyes, "not thinking, exactly, it's just... don't you feel a little funny about this sometimes?" "Funny, Artoor? Is that what you said? But what is there to feel 'funny' about?" "Oh, I don't know, not funny, but a little strange, as if, as if..." "You're not finishing your sentences, Artoor." "Yes, I know, but you see, it's as if, as if... I don't know... as if... do you really think we ought to go through with it, Eleanor?"

There was a pause.

"Don't be so lugubrious," said Eleanor sharply.

59

OUR DEATH TOOK PLACE in Eleanor's sickroom, one night after dessert. In the flickering candlelight of the Childhood Museum I changed into my last costume. I placed my shoes, my pants, and my shirt in a neat pile beside the gabled dollhouse. Then I pulled on a pair of Eleanor's black knee-socks, a pair of her pressed black slacks, and a bulky black sweater that tickled my bare arms. Around my neck I fastened a black nylon neckerchief. With the aid of a pocket mirror I blackened my upper lip. Over my shoulders I placed the long black cape, slipping my arms through the sleeve-slits and fastening the top at my throat, and over my hands I pulled a pair of long black gloves— so tight, those gloves, that I could scarcely bend my fingers. Last of all I slipped over my face a black mask that covered my nose and eyes. As I waited for Eleanor I paced up and down, clutching the cape with one inner hand and feeling the cloth stream out behind me. The candleflame bent in the breeze of my passing, and pacing and pacing in my black costume I felt hidden and exposed, hidden and exposed, hidden and exposed.

"All right, Artoor," Eleanor called. Adjusting my mask and gathering my cape close about me, I opened the door, pushed through the clothes, fumbled for the knob, and stepped into the candlelit sickroom.

There were four candles: one on the vanity table, one on the high bureau, one on the desk, and one on the bookcase of toys. Eleanor, wearing a longsleeved high-throated gown of black velvet that came down over the tops of her laced black boots, lay on the black bedspread with her head and shoulders propped up against the propped-up black pillows. Her knees were turned to one side, giving her body an undulation. One bare hand lay against the back of her neck, with the black velvet elbow leaning up against the mahogany headboard, and one arm fell along her upturned hip and sideturned thigh. On her white hand a red gem flashed. Her thick black hair was pulled tightly back, held in place by a black velvet band glittering and flashing with bits of faceted green glass, and from the luxurious blackness of her hair there blossomed a violently dark-red rose. Over her eyes she wore a black mask. In the wavering orange-red flamelight her cream-white cheek and hand reflected faintly the candleglow. As I stood by the closet door admiring my Queen of Death she stared at me from behind her mask-slits, and at last she said sharply: "Well? Aren't you going to say anything?" At once I dropped to one knee, and making a flourish with one black-gloved hand I said: "Queen Eleanor is the fairest in all the land." "Arise, my prince," she said, lifting a gemmed and languid hand, and as I rose she said: "Do you really like it, Artoor?" "Yes, my lady," and suddenly she began to laugh lightly, gazing at me with merry black eyes. "What's wrong?" I said sharply. "Nothing," she said, but throwing back her head she continued to laugh, and stepping over to the mirror above the vanity table I gazed at my black mask, my black mustache, my black cape, my long black hands. "Well?" I said, turning fiercely, "I don't see anything wrong." And laughing and laughing and trying to stop she choked out an "Oh, Artoor," laughing and laughing but shaking her head vigorously as if to deny her laughter and making a quick wiping motion with her hand. "It's not," she gasped, "it isn't," and suddenly clenching her fists and controlling herself with a visible shudder she said: "It's just that you look so cute, Artoor." And shocked by that word, for I felt dashing and dangerous, but pleased by that word, for my queen had praised me, I frowned and said: "Well, anyway . . ." As I strode to the leather chair I clutched my cape tightly about me. In the light of the candle on the bookcase of toys I felt suddenly foolish and depressed, and sitting down quickly and placing Raggedy on my leg I pushed back in the chair and wrapped myself tightly in the heavy black cloak. Eleanor had turned toward me, and after a while she said softly: "You're not looking at me, Artoor." Then I raised my eyes, at once looking away from her dark, doleful gaze, and I said: "Let's not prolong this, Eleanor. Now where is the, you said you would—" "It's over there," she said, pointing to the table in the corner behind me, and when I turned I saw a black silken cloth draping a bulky object. Turning back abruptly I said: "Then everything is ready?" "Yes, my lord." "How long will it take?" "The action of the draught should take no more than ten minutes, my lord." "And your mother?" "Will not appear before the stroke of nine, my lord. She is under strict orders." "Very good, my lady. And now—but first, I must bid farewell." And turning

Raggedy around I gazed at the strings of red hair escaping from the black wool cap, at the curved eyebrows, at the three eyelashes painted above her round eyes and the three eyelashes painted below, at the triangular red nose, at the long smiling line of her mouth, at the piece of red-and-white-striped leg visible beneath an upturned piece of black dress, at one hand dangling limply at her side and one hand resting in her black wool lap. "Well, Rags," I began, but suddenly I could not continue, and angrily I turned her around and leaned her against my hip with her legs crossed on my thigh and both hands resting in her lap. When I looked up furtively I saw Eleanor looking down with her chin crushed against her throat and her mask slightly awry as she fussed with something on the shoulder of her gown. "You know what," I said, "I think I'd like to look at that juggler once more. Can I help you with—" "No no, it's just this little piece of—I hope you don't want to wind him up and all that." "Oh no, I just want to look," and bending over I pulled out the satiny green box and placed it on my lap. Sliding the cover slowly toward my stomach I saw the blue tuft of hair and the white top of the head, and as I drew the cover toward me I continued to see only whiteness. His face was blank, his features had disappeared, he was a nightmare man in a spangled shiny-blue costume, suddenly I saw the lever sticking out of his back, and sliding the cover down all the way I turned him gently over. I gazed at the jetblack eyes, at the fringed lashes, at the blue spots in the cheeks, at the stern blue mouth, and troubled by his fierce unblinking gaze I quickly slid the lid over and put him back on the shelf. "There," said Eleanor, holding up her hand and rubbing her forefinger quickly back and forth against her thumb with a little soft insect-like sound. A small white thread came slowly floating down. Adjusting her mask, and looking at me with her dark, doleful eyes, she said softly: "What are you thinking about, Artoor?" Annoyed by her tone I frowned behind my mask and jerked my thumb over my shoulder at the table with its draped object. With a little pout she said: "Methinks my lord seemeth in haste to woo the strumpet Death." "Nay, my lady, mistake me not, it be only—Eleanor, let's not talk this way." "Oh, as you wish," she said, dismissing me with an impatient gesture.

Tucking Raggedy under my arm I rose, stepped to the table, and pressed my hands gently inward on both sides of the cloth until I felt the shape beneath. Lifting it carefully I returned to the chair, where for a few moments I stood looking about uncertainly. Then stepping over to the desk-chair I hooked one black-socked foot around a chairleg and began drawing the chair toward the leather chair as I hopped backward on one foot. The big soft doll came sliding sideways against my knee.

When the desk-chair was between the bed and the leather chair I set my burden gently down, picked up the big doll and sat her on the desk with her back to the typewriter, returned to the leather chair, and sat down.

For a while I gazed at the black-draped object on the chair before me. Then I raised my eyes to Eleanor. She was lying on her side with her cheek leaning against a hand. There was a sulky expression on her mouth, part of which was pulled to one side by the stretched cheek-skin. She was drumming her fingers soundlessly on the black spread. I said: "Do you want to lift it or shall I? Please don't look so bored, Eleanor."

"I'm not bored," said Eleanor with a pout, and leaning over she plucked up the cloth, revealing a pewter goblet.

It was about eight inches high; the rim of the cup was about four inches in diameter. Around the stem wound two slender pewter snakes whose heads, facing in opposite directions, seemed to support the cup above. Their jaws were open and their forked tongues curled out. In a narrow band at the top of the cup was a raised design of small elephants marching. The tail of each elephant was clasped by the trunk of the elephant behind. Below the elephants the sides of the cup were smooth, and shone with a faint sheen in the candlelight.

"But Eleanor," I said suddenly, "it's empty."

Still lying on her side with her cheek on her hand, Eleanor was holding up the black silken cloth between thumb and forefinger, gazing up at it through the slits of her mask. She spread her thumb and finger, and the black cloth fluttered slowly down, falling in undulations upon her hip, rippling to sudden rest.

Turning her face toward me, and sweeping out her arm in a vague, indolent gesture, she said: "It's on the mirror-tray. Extreme left." Her hand hung for a moment in the air. Then it fell suddenly to the bed, where it bounced once and lay still.

Squeezing between the leather chair and the desk-chair I made my way to the flaming vanity table, where on the mirror-tray a diamond-shaped glass vial, three inches high, contained a brownish liquid.

I picked up the glass vial, carried it carefully back to the chair, and sat down. Slowly I lifted the weighty glass stopper, which widened upward; the top half was smooth and transparent, the bottom half was frosted and rough. Lifting the vial to my nostrils I inhaled a sharp, bittersweet odor. My eyes burned faintly.

When I glanced up at Eleanor I saw her winding a strand of black hair lazily around a finger.

"Are you watching?" I said sharply. Eleanor looked up abruptly. With a quick motion I tipped the glass vial over the edge of the pewter goblet. The brown, thickish liquid poured out silently. A small dark pool at the base of the cup rose higher and higher and stopped. I shook out a final drop; the cup was nearly a third full. I placed the empty vial on the chair and replaced the glass stopper. Eleanor had stopped twirling her hair and was now gazing at me solemnly from her mask-slits. In her wide shiny-black pupils I saw tiny orange candleflames. I placed my hand around the stem of the pewter cup, so that the top edge of my hand rested beneath the cold snake-heads, and slowly lifting the cup with its flashing brown liquid I held it out before me and said: "To our death." As I raised the cup to my lips I again inhaled the sharp, bittersweet odor, and pausing a moment I said: "Just out of curiosity, Eleanor: what is it?" "The potion of death," said Eleanor. There was a pause. "No,"

I said, "I meant the exact name." "Oh, for heaven's sake, what difference does it make? Some Romeo." Gently I set the cup down on the chair. "Eleanor," I said quietly, "please tell me what it's called." "Oh, what a fuss he's making!" she cried, and suddenly reaching forward she seized the cup, lifted it to her mouth, threw back her head, and took a deep swallow. Tipping her head forward she looked at me with flashing eyes. "Well?" she demanded, giving her head a toss. And shamed by my queen I at once took the cup and rose from my chair and stepped to one side; and flinging out my cape behind me, and dropping to one knee before her, I raised the cup to my lips and took a deep swallow. I felt a burning in my throat, and when I lowered the cup I saw Eleanor gazing down at me with flashing eyes.

Suddenly looking away and raising the back of a hand to her forehead she said: "Oh, I feel faint, my lord."

"Faint, my lady?"—and as I rose I felt a slight faintness. My temples were throbbing and my heart seemed to be beating too rapidly. Carefully I set the goblet down and pressed one palm against my pounding heart.

"Oh," she said gaily, "let's dance, my lord." And slipping from the bed she stood before me, looking at me with candle-flaming eyes. "Dance," I murmured, "I don't know, dance . . ." "The way you did with Raggedy," said Eleanor. "Ah, the Dance of Death," and taking Eleanor's waist and holding up her hand I began to turn slowly in the narrow aisle, taking one long step and two short ones. And as we turned and turned, Eleanor began to hum The Merry Widow Waltz, saying "DEE dahDEE dahDEE dahDEE dahDEE DEE DEE" while I kept time with "Oom-pah-pah Oom-pah-pah Oom-pah-pah Oom-pah-pah"— sputtering into giggles but stifling them with an Oom-pah-pah Oom-pah-pah as I turned and turned, and suddenly Eleanor burst into giggles, stifling them with a DEE but bursting into giggles again, and throwing back her head she laughed with her mouth open and the bonelike column in her throat outlined against her throat-skin. But turning and turning with my Oom-pah-pah Oom-pah-pah, knocking lightly into the desk and the side of the bed, I danced faster and faster while Eleanor laughed with great gulps and gasps, and lines of wetness streamed along her cheeks. Under my hand I felt the muscles of her back tensing and untensing as she turned, and as I turned faster and faster with my Oom-pah-pah Oom-pah-pah I felt beneath my palm the sudden flare of her hip, the pulse in my neck beat faster and faster, suddenly I slammed my thigh against the desk, the typewriter rattled angrily, the doll fell to the floor, placing a palm against my chest Eleanor gave a push and wrenched herself out of my grasp. Drawing in her breath with a hiss she clasped a hand to her throat and with a painful stifled gasp cried weakly: "Oh God." "Eleanor," I gasped, breathing heavily as I stood bent over slightly with one hand pressed to my pounding chest, "what—" "Death," said Eleanor, while in my mind we turned and turned, passing through the closet into the Childhood Museum, turning and turning, scattering dolls, passing through the little door and down the dark passageway, dancing farther and farther and farther away, growing smaller and smaller, turning and turning, faster and faster, smaller and smaller, forever and ever.

"Death, my lady?" And breathing heavily I raised the back of a hand to my warm, damp forehead.

"Nay, 'twas but a passing fit," said Eleanor, sitting down heavily on the side of the bed. " 'Twill all be over soon, my lord."

"Aye, soon, my lady."

"Aye, soon, my lord . . . swoon, my lord . . . Swoooooooon . . . when I was a child I would turn round and round with my arms out and then throw myself on the bed . . . just to make the room turn all around me . . . then at night I used to close my eyes and make believe I had died, when I opened my eyes it was dark, and for a second I thought . . . What do you really think of me, Artoor?"

"Oh, think of you, think of you, but death, yes, when I was a child . . . but you know, Eleanor, we haven't much time."

"Oh, time enough to die in, my lord."

"Nay, my lady, time waits for no man."

"I am no man, my lord. Ergo time waits for me."

"Ha ha, that was very—nay nay, my lady, not so, not so."

"How so, my lord?"

"Why, thus: if thou'rt no man, then thou'rt no one. If thou'rt no one, then thou'rt dead. If thou'rt dead, time hath not waited for thee."

"Nay, an' if I be dead, what care I for time, or time for me?"

"Ha ha, you're really good at this, Eleanor."

"Good at dying, my lord?"

"And sighing, my lady."

"Out out brief candle! Dying is such sweet sorrow. It droppeth as the gentle rain from heaven. I feel cold, my lord."

"Cold, my lady?"

"Nay, hot, my lord."

"Hot, my lady?"

"Nay, methinks I feel hot and cold, my lord."

"Hot and cold, my lady?"

"Ho hum. Are you going to stand there all day?" And with a fist she rapped soundlessly twice against the black spread.

Pulling my cape close about me I strode around the footboard toward the bookcase of books, and as I strode I felt my cape lifting behind me. At the head of the bed I paused for a moment and felt the cape settle against my calves. At once I lay down on the black spread with my cape wrapped about me. "Now close your eyes," said Eleanor, kneeling on the bed beside me and gazing down at me through her mask. When I closed my eyes I felt her fingers on my gloved left wrist. I felt her lifting my wrist, then I felt the palm of her hand pressing against the palm of my hand, then I felt something passing around my wrist. I felt my hand lowered to the bed and then lifted onto her tense thigh and then lowered to the bed. "Don't just lie there," said Eleanor testily, and opening my eyes and lifting my neck I saw her trying to tie a black ribbon around our wrists. "Put your finger there," said Eleanor, "yes, now hold it, just a, there. There. Good. So." And lifting her wrist she lifted my wrist, gazing at them with her head tilted to one side. Then lowering her wrist she lowered my wrist, and shifting around clumsily on the bed she lay down on her back beside me. We lay with our arms at our sides, our hands palm to palm, and our fingers tightly clasped. Through my thick cape, against my thigh, I felt the hardness of her ring. A candle sputtered. Eleanor pressed the side of her skull lightly against the side of my skull. "Your hair is tickling me," I said. Eleanor began to raise her tied wrist, at once lowered it, and raising her other hand she smoothed away her hair and moved her skull back into place. "Does that suit you, my lord?" "Aye, my lady." Eleanor sighed. " 'Twill soon be over, my lord." "How soon, my lady?" "Oh, can't you feel the coldness rising . . . from your feet . . . to your knees . . . like ice . . . death . . . when I was a child I used to imagine it just that way . . . rising . . . and I could not move . . . I could not breathe . . . then I thought of the sun shining . . . the meadows . . . the willow by the stream . . . and then, when it hit my heart . . . What are you thinking about, Artoor?" "Oh, thinking, but death, yes, when I was a child . . . and then, lying on my stomach before the hedge, looking out at the field, the stream, and then, one day, when Mrs. Schneider went inside . . . and it was so strange, how can I . . . and walking through the snow, the soldiers, the cat with the glass eyes . . . and the black music-box, the white-faced juggler . . . 'How ugly!' you said . . . and then, the afternoons . . . the evenings . . . and you always said 'Stay a little longer . . . just a little longer' . . . and I thought: if only I could stay . . ." "If only you could stay . . ." "Forever . . ." "Forever . . . and you know, Artoor . . ." "Yes, Eleanor . . ." "If only you could stay . . ." "If only I could stay . . ." "Forever . . ." "Forever . . ." "And you know, Artoor . . ." "Yes, Eleanor . . ." "Time's running out, and you know, Artoor . . ." "Yes, Eleanor . . ." "Oh, never mind, and you know, Artoor . . ." "Yes, Eleanor . . ." "Parting is such sweet sorrow, and you know, Artoor . . ." "Yes, Eleanor . . ." "If only you could have stayed . . ." "If only I could have stayed . . ." "Forever . . ." "Forever . . ." "I feel cold, my lord." "Aye, cold, my lady." "Along my legs . . ." "Along my legs . . ." "Now it's at my knees . . ." "It's at my knees..." "When it hits my heart..." "When it hits my heart..." "Death, my lord." "Death, my lady." "And you know, Artoor..." "Yes, Eleanor..." "If only you could stay..." "Only you could stay..." "Forever..." "Forever..." "Now it's at my waist..." "It's at my waist..." "When it hits my heart..." "When it hits my heart..." "Ice, my lord." "Ice, my lady." "Good-bye, Artoor." "Good-bye, Eleanor." "And you know, Artoor..." "You know, Eleanor..." Then her face turned toward me, my face turned toward her, and she gazed at me with her dark, doleful eyes. And as I watched, a small tear formed in the moist pink corner of her upper eye. It swelled, stretched, wet her lashes, and broke free, rolling out of sight beneath her slightly crooked black mask. Then her eyes closed, my eyes closed, lightly our lips pressed together and pulled away, pressed together and pulled away, pressed together and pulled away, and as our lips pressed together and pulled away I felt feverish and weary, desolate and inflamed. "Now it's at my ribs..." "Now it's at my ribs..." "When it hits my heart..." "When it hits my heart..." "Death, my lord." "Death, my lady." "Good-bye, Artoor..." "Good-bye, Eleanor..." "Now it's at my heart..." "It's at my heart..." "I can hardly breathe..." "Hardly breathe..." "Good-bye, Artoor..." "Good-bye, Eleanor..." "Good-bye..." "Good-bye..." "Good-bye..." "Good-bye..." "Oh God!" cried Eleanor, and struggling up to a half-sitting position she began to breathe faster and faster, she grasped her throat, suddenly she could not breathe, I heard a stifled gasping, her face became red, she looked about wildly, with a painful gasp she fell back stiffly on the bed with her head turned away and her black hair streaming against me.

Raising my neck painfully, I gazed at the parted lips of the still-warm corpse. On the white cheek beneath her ear showed delicate dark lines of hair. I raised my tied wrist; her wrist rose limply. I let both wrists fall. "Eleanor," I whispered, "are you dead, Eleanor?" There was no answer. Struggling up to a half-sitting position I slowly reached out a black-gloved hand. With

my outstretched black index finger I pushed gently into the soft
cheek. The cheek went in, pulling slightly the corner of the
parted lips. Slowly I removed my finger, watching the cheek
go out. Reaching across her face I carefully removed the dark-
red rose. The petals were of red velvet and the wire stem was
wrapped in tight-twisted green paper. With my black-gloved
hand I fastened the false rose to the throat of my cape. I gazed
at the waxen white cheek, at the streaming black hair, at the
faint rise of the black velvet breast, at the undulation of the
black velvet hip. I began to breathe faster. My temples were
throbbing, my heart was pounding, suddenly I could not breathe,
I gave a stifled gasp, blood rushed to my head, with a painful
gasp I fell heavily back. My head rolled on one side. Death
clutched my heart.

60

SPRING CAME, that famous season, and in the brightening and
warming air I made my posthumous and ghostly way to the
brightening and warming tomb of my dead bride. Sweating in
my heavy wintercoat I would push open the door and pause for
a moment, gazing about with a faint frown. No longer did I
step into soothing dusk and shadow, for blue sunlight soaked
through the drawn blue curtains, shedding over everything a
deep blue stain. On the pulled-out chair before the dusty desk
sat a large white doll with stringy yellow hair and a faded pink
dress. To the left, the glass door of the cabinet of dolls was
streaked with dust and light. Beside the bed on a small brown
bookcase a black box sat beside a hand-puppet that looked like
a blue rag. In the bed, beneath a pale blue quilt dotted with
little pink flowers, lay my dead bride. From the doorway I
could see quite clearly the waxen blue-whiteness of her skin and
the cold pallor of her bluish lips. A shadow of dark hairs showed

at the corners of her upper lip and a faint shine of oil was visible between her eyebrows and on the sides of her nose. On the floor beside the bed a white sock lay in a clump of dust. Beside the vanity table stood a brown closet door with two panels that showed paintbrush streaks; tacked to the upper panel was a yellowed newspaper cartoon. In the warmth and clearness I would walk to the leather chair, with its nicked brown arms and cracked leather seat, and sitting down with my back to the light I would wait impatiently for evening.

After a while a deepening blueness spread through the room, a coolness came over things, and as I half-listened to the slap of a rope against tar, to the muffled thunder of roller skates on concrete, to the delicate crunch or harsh rustle of bicycle tires on street-sand, swiftly and silently, all about me, on the darkening bureau against the wall, in the shadowy mirror above the faceted glass vials, on the drowsy hand-puppet beside the black music-box, swiftly and silently evening fell.

Only, not too far away, at the far border of the curtain above the littered desk, dust whirled in bright blue light.

As the weather grew warmer a restlessness came over my dead bride. Now when I arrived she was always sitting up in bed, with her dark hair falling about her; and as I settled slowly into my chair and half-closed my eyes, a drowsy ghost, content with eternity, Eleanor would look away darkly. Sometimes she would take up a book and begin to read, turning the pages with loud impatient sounds, and sometimes she would fling the covers back, swing her legs over the side, and begin pacing up and down, up and down, tying her black robe violently about her, as if she were trying to cut herself in half. Sometimes she would stride over to the curtains and push an edge fiercely aside. A sword-slash of sunlight would pierce the room. And for a moment, caught in that light, the slumbering dust would start awake, and look about in wild confusion, trembling with anger or pain. Then the curtain would fall back, the troubled dust would turn over and close its eyes, drowsily recalling its nightmare of the sun, and Eleanor, an unquiet ghost, would resume her restless pacing. Often she would throw me an irritable look, and once, placing her hands on her hips and throwing back her head, she said: "This is an absolutely scintillating discussion." Then she continued pacing.

One day when I pushed open the door I saw her sitting up in bed, reading with a frown in the glow of the bedlight. With her left hand she held the top of the book, which was covered in brown paper, and with her right hand she pressed the base of a dark red fountain pen against her lower lip, so that one side of the lip was pulled partway down. Before her, on the quilt, lay an open notebook. As I entered she raised her eyes but at once lowered them, frowning more deeply, and as I sank into the leather chair she turned the page with a sharp sound and continued reading. As she read she raised her fountain pen and began to twist it slowly in her hair, and looking up suddenly she thrust the book toward me and said: "Let's go over Group I plurals." With a slight frown I took the book. Through tired eyes and with faintly throbbing temples I gazed at two columns of prickly black nouns entitled SINGULAR and PLURAL, beneath which was a list of rules entitled SUMMARY—GROUP I. Eleanor said: "Group I plurals contain: A) Many masculines and neuters ending in -el, -en, -er. B) All neuter diminutives ending in -chen and -lein. And C) Only two feminines: Mutter and Tochter. Correct me if I make a mistake. The four rules of umlaut are: I can never remember these insane rules. A) If a noun already has the umlaut in the singular, the umlaut is retained in the plural. Example: Schüler, Schüler; Mädchen, Mädchen; Fräulein, Fräulein. B) B, B, what is B, I told you I can never, give me the first, no I have it— The vowels e and i never take an umlaut. The vowels e and i never take an umlaut. The vowels e and i never take an umlaut. Example: Lehrer, Lehrer; Fenster, Fenster. C) No, let's go back to A and get it right. A) If a noun already has the umlaut—are you paying attention, Artoor?"

61

As THE AFTERNOONS GREW LONGER, pushing back the night, Eleanor's restlessness increased. She was asking many questions about school. In fact she revealed a relentless appetite for the smallest details of the oppressive schoolday and would grow angry if she felt I was leaving something out. She seemed to remember everyone in homeroom, and in English, and in German, and in homeroom. She wanted to know if Linda Strauss still wore bangs and if Richard Chapko still said "oaf Wiedersehen." She wanted to know what activities were taking place and what announcements were made each morning over the intercom. Once, seeing in one of my schoolbooks a folded mimeographed notice that had been passed out in homeroom, she pulled it out and began reading eagerly. Suddenly dropping it on the bed she stared sadly at the quilt and murmured: "The Spring Dance..." "Oh," I said, "who cares about their boring dances," and looking up with flashing eyes she said: "God, you're prejudiced." Often she would lose her temper with me. If, in answer to a question, I said "Oh, I don't know," or with a weary shrug "Just the same old garbage," her eyes would blaze and she would begin to defend school activities, accusing me of "indifference" and "lack of imagination." I disliked the entire discussion but argued that far from being indifferent to dates, dances, clubs, football games, yearbooks, cheerleaders, school rings, school newspapers, Varsity sweaters, and the rest of that stuff, I actively despised it all, since behind the rosy glow induced by manly imbibings of school spirit, an intoxicating beverage that had no effect on me whatever, I detected a sickening imitation of all that was most dull in so-called adult life. Eleanor, furious, said that only a person of low intelligence was "bored by everything." It was precisely a person of intelligence who was able to enjoy even apparently uninteresting things, which he rendered interesting by means of his intelligence. Moreover if cheerleaders were rather ridiculous there was nothing innately offensive about them, one could think of them as a sort of floral decoration, and some school activities, like the newspaper and the student council, provided valuable experience that could be gotten in no other way. Moreover— "Well," I said, "I don't really want to talk about this stuff," and as she continued to argue, striding up and down, suddenly I imagined myself lying peacefully on my bed, beneath the closed blinds, before an open book.

During the early winter Eleanor had carefully kept up with her assignments, but in the course of time she had let them slide. Now she threw herself passionately into her homework. Not only did she insist on going over her German with me each day, but now I began to visit her five teachers, often with specific questions from Eleanor, and twice I went to the school library in search of books for her history paper. After dinner Eleanor would turn on her bedlight, with its new bright bulb. She would sit up in bed with her knees raised and an open book propped on the slope of her thighs, or she would sit in a crouch over her open notebook, leaning over with a frown as she wrote quickly quickly with her pen. I would sit sulkily beside her, staring at the furious pen, and after a while I would stand up and begin to pace up and down, stopping at the window to push aside the curtain and gaze out at the deepening blue dusk. Eleanor would look up at me with a frown and then lower her head over her notebook. At last I would return to the leather chair, and pushing it against the bookcase of toys I would try to read my history book in the dim light of the small lamp, but after a while my eyes would grow tired, my back would begin to hurt, and again I would get up and begin to pace. One evening Eleanor said: "Why don't you work at the desk, Artoor?" With a frown I gazed at the desk. Then pushing aside the typewriter, removing the large doll from the chair, and turning on the desk-lamp, I sat down and began to read in the yellowish glow. Soon I began to feel uncomfortable, the chair was much too hard, the light glared on my paper and cast shadows from my hands, I seemed unable to concentrate, and turning off the light I returned to the leather chair and sat gazing at the side of the bed.

62

ONE NICE WARM sunny afternoon I made my way to Eleanor's as usual. I still wore my heavy wintercoat, which I no longer buttoned, and as I walked, shifting my heavy books from arm to arm, I felt lines of sweat trickling along my sides. At the front door Mrs. Schumann greeted me with a radiant smile, and as usual I climbed the stairway and walked along the cool, dusty hall, brightened by sunlight from a partly open door on the left. At the end of the hall I shifted my books again, gave a light knock, pushed open Eleanor's door, and suddenly raised my arm as if to ward off a blow.

The room was filled with sunlight. Eleanor, wearing her black robe with the loose sleeves pushed up, was sitting in the middle of the bright bed, bent over her dazzling-white open notebook. Behind the desk the heavy blue curtains had been pulled aside, exposing two windows, through which I saw the black upper windows of two houses across the street, a sparkling red roof and a sparkling black roof, and a slightly tilted television antenna against a hot blue sky. One window was raised slightly, admitting a lazy breeze that ruffled a piece of paper in the typewriter and stirred the yellow strings of hair on the desk-chair doll.

"Oh hi," said Eleanor, looking up with a slight frown as she smoothed from her eyes a strand of hair that fell down again. Without a word I strode around the bed and sat down in the leather chair with my back to the windows.

Eleanor said: "Well, you look hale and hearty today. What's wrong, if I may be so bold?"

After a while I said: "I feel fine, Eleanor, it's just that I'm fairly tired and also I have a slight headache. Actually I'm surprised to see you out of bed in the middle of this fairly cool breeze, which I can feel on my neck. Are you sure it's wise to take chances? You look a little tired to me. Do you mind if I . . . just for a . . ." and standing up abruptly I stepped to the desk, pushed down the window with a bang, and drew the thick curtains tightly together. "Hey," said Eleanor; a dark blueness seeped into the room. "There!" I said, returning swiftly to my seat, "I think that's much, much better. Why don't you get under the covers, Eleanor, it's not good for you to expose yourself like that, no no, don't say anything, and besides, there's really lots of sunlight in here right now, it's really foolish to rush things and take unnecessary chances, just let things happen naturally, don't you think so, Raggedy?"

Quickly three times Raggedy bowed, touching the top of her head to her outstretched legs.

63

So BEGAN ELEANOR's relentless recovery. It was as if her illness were sick, and no longer had strength enough to resist the infection of health. The next day when I entered her sun-crazed room I found her standing with her back to me by the exposed windows, gazing down at the street. She wore faded bluejeans that were rolled up above her pale calves and a white shirt that hung below her back pockets. She stood with her weight on her left leg, so that her left hip was thrown out slightly. The portion of shirt above the left back pocket was raised, and her left hand, facing palm outward, was plunged halfway into the pocket. Her right elbow was pressed against her side, and her right

hand grasped her shoulder from the front, revealing four fingertips. On the left side, her shirt above her hip did not touch her
body, and in the windowlight the cloth was translucent, revealing a shadowline of hip and waist. Over her left shoulder hung
a shirt-dustrag. In the space between the bed and the vanity
table a cylindrical can stood beside a lamb's-wool cloth. A long
wooden mop leaned across the footboard and ended beneath
the padded bench. The floor leading to the cylindrical can was
patched with sticky-looking wet. Her hair was gathered in a
high ponytail, bound by a white ribbon. A few dark wisps of
hair, escaping from the— "Oh," she said, whirling around and
raising a hand to her chest, "you startled me. No, wait! Could
you wait one little second? It's almost dry." A few dark wisps
of hair, escaping from the ribbon, hung down against her white
neck.

Later that afternoon she grew suddenly tired, and lay down
on the bed with her arm over her eyes, but the next afternoon
she continued her spring cleaning, and that evening we ate dinner downstairs in the kitchen.

One sunny, hot, oppressive April morning, when with a slight
headache and faintly burning eyes I stepped into homeroom, I
saw her sitting in the row beside the windows. She was writing
in her notebook with a frown of concentration. She wore a
pleated tan skirt with a wide blue belt, a shortsleeved white
blouse, and an orange sweater buttoned at the throat but hanging loosely over her shoulders like a cape. Her black hair,
combed back on the sides to expose her ears, was held in place
by a shiny red barrette with silver sparkles; she wore bangs
high on her forehead, and her hair was parted in the middle,
showing a white line. During the announcements she looked
over with a smile, and I smiled abruptly and looked down with
a frown, feeling the smile still attached to my mouth. And how
strange it was to see her in English in the morning, and in
German in the afternoon, and in homeroom at the end of the
day ... That afternoon I walked home with her in the dreamlike April sunlight, toward the black iron railway trestle divided

into dark black shade and pale black sun, under the black iron
railway trestle into a sudden coolness and a sharp smell of oil
and damp stone, into sudden hotness, past a smiling cardboard
lady in a white bikini holding up a green cardboard bottle, past
a stern wooden man in a red bathing suit holding up his arms in
an exhausting pose, past a woman in jodhpurs leaning backward
from the waist with her arm before her eyes as a white pith
helmet falls from her long red hair and a yellow lion leaps from
a rock, past a transparent Eleanor through whom was visible a
set of flat silver wrenches growing smaller and smaller, and stepping into the bright but cool living room I felt my heavy coat-
sleeve sliding from my arm, there was a sharp scrape of hangers,
and striding across the room Eleanor sat down on the couch,
kicked off her flat black shoes, tucked her legs under her,
stretched one arm across the sunny couchback, and was still. I
was sitting in the armchair across from the porcelain cat. In the
sunny silence I leaned my neck back against the warm chairback and gazed through half-closed eyes at the pendulum swinging through sunlight above a gleaming silver key that lay on its
side, at a white angel with gold-tipped wings who was holding a
singing-book and looking up to heaven with her mouth shaped
like an O, at a green glass ashtray shaped like a maple-leaf with
a green glass stem and green glass veins, at a flat black shoe lying
on its side before the sunlit brown skirt of a couch. Eleanor
said: "I think I'll go up and change, Arthur. I'll be right back."
"Yes," I murmured, "that's all right," and when I raised my
eyes I saw her coming swiftly down the stairs, holding her hands
on her thighs and wearing her faded bluejeans rolled up above
her calves and her white shirt hanging out. She crossed the room
swiftly and sat down on the couch, tucking her legs up under
her and stretching one arm along the couchback. After a while
she said: "Would you care for a gingerale?" "Oh," I said,
"gingerale, I don't know, no thanks, not really, don't bother."
"But that's silly, it's no 'bother' for heaven's sake," and she
emerged from the kitchen with a tall rattling glass of gingerale
and plump ice-cubes with concave sides. Over the bottom of the

glass and partway up was a covering of orange-and-green wool, as if the glass were wearing a sock. "You're welcome," said Eleanor. "Would you like something to go with it? There are pretzels, I think we have some potato frills..." "Oh," I said, "oh no, no thanks, this is fine, really," and gazing down at the glass I watched it rising slowly toward me and suddenly I felt against my nose a little sharp burst of cold gingerspray. Eleanor said: "That must be mother now," and went to the window. "No," she said, "it's just someone turning around in our drive-way." Eleanor said: "Listen, Arthur, I have something to tell you." I said: "You've murdered your mother and you want me to help you get rid of the corpse." Eleanor laughed. "Yes," she said, "that's it." Eleanor frowned. "But seriously. It's about these visits. This isn't exactly going to be the easiest thing in the world to say." There was a pause. Through moist glass and golden gingerale a porcelain cat rippled. "As you must know, I've enjoyed them very much. I don't think I've ever enjoyed anything so much. When I was sick you were simply wonder-ful, and I'll always be grateful to you. Oh, God, 'grateful,' what a hideous asinine word, I don't mean 'grateful,' I mean that I'll never forget your loyalty and all the things we did together. It all seems like some fantastic dream. But Arthur—and this is the point—now that I'm back in school I'm practically drowned in homework. You can't imagine how bad it is. I still have five back papers, six if you count the one I'm still going insane over, and Mrs. Donahue has given me a whole pile of extra assignments since I missed so much classwork. It's all busywork but it has to be done—not that there's really a danger of my staying back, but you know what some teachers are like, and the fact that I've missed practically four months of school—I'm getting off the subject. The point is, I have a whole lot of back work that has piled up. I don't have any time to waste at all. Oh, not 'waste,' I don't mean 'waste,' God how you must hate me, what I mean is that I don't have as much time to lie around and talk as I had before. Frankly, I don't even have time to breathe. Today for instance I have something like six or seven hours of work staring me in the face, and as for tomorrow, I don't even want to think about tomorrow. Are you listening? What I wanted to propose is this. Why don't you do your homework over here? I know you don't like doing homework together, you've told me that before, but Arthur, there's no other way. You could work in mother's room, or better yet, since mother's room is really not very adequate, are you listening, I could have my room and you could have the Childhood Museum. With a little fixing up that place would make an ideal study. We could bring up the old desk in the basement and put it in front of the windows and you could work in absolute privacy. Then you could stay for dinner and we could see each other then. After dinner we could talk for a while, though not anything prolonged while I have all this homework hanging over me like the sword of Damocles—she said, with a classical allusion. Anyway, she added, looking apprehensively in the direction of the pale youth who sat wrapped in gloomy silence, that's my proposition.

"You're not saying anything, Arthur. Are you angry with me? You don't like my idea, do you. You can't stand 'study-dates.' Well, if you really want to know, I'm not exactly crazy about them either. I'd much rather just stretch out like a great big lazy cat and let things take care of themselves. But alas, things don't take care of themselves. If I don't literally chain myself to my desk, I'm finished. As long as I have all this work to do it's slave slave slave twenty-six hours a day.

"You're not being very helpful, Arthur. I can't think of anything more to say. Listen: think about it. I'm sure we can work something out. If you don't want to work over here—but I hope you do—then it would be better if we didn't see each other for a while—just for a while. Listen: think about it. You decide. If you want to study together, fine. I'd like nothing better. If you don't like that, as I suspect you—that must be mother. Just a minute. I don't see anything... Oh, it's Mrs. Cassetti. I wonder where she's coming from. She never goes anywhere. She wears that same coat all year. Anyway, to get back to— Arthur? Arthur! Arthur, what are you—"

At the landing I turned and took the two remaining steps at a bound. As I strode along the hall I saw in the bright leaning mirror my downhill-plunging feet, my belt, my longsleeved shirt, my pale neck, my suddenly looking-away face. With a rude twist of the knob I pushed open the door of her room. The windows were wide open and in the draft of the suddenly opened door the curtains sucked in their stomachs. The bed was made and the leather chair had disappeared. Slowly the curtains let out their breath. Raggedy, looking pale and tired, lay flat on her back on the quilt with her arms spread out and her pale blue dress turned up to expose her wrinkled bloomers. Beside her the desk-chair doll lay on her stomach with one leg twisted. In the big black typewriter a piece of white paper stirred slightly in the window-breeze. Far away I heard the sound of footsteps on stairs. Striding over to the bed I sat Raggedy up against the pillow with her hands in her lap. I turned the big doll over and rested her head against the pillow. Striding swiftly to the closet I yanked open the door and pushed my way through the heavy dresses, which tried to seize me by my shirt-buttons. On the other side I grasped the inner doorknob, gave a violent twist, pushed open the door, and suddenly stopped.

"Yes," I murmured, "that's all right."

The room was nearly dark. The heavy curtains, trailing on the floor, were still securely drawn. The large gabled dollhouse still loomed in the center of the room, and dark dolls sat all about. At the tea-table against the far wall, two dolls were taking tea. I heard the creak of the landing and a rapid tread along the hall. Stepping across to the thick curtains I patted about and felt the drawcord. The footsteps entered Eleanor's room. A piece of cobweb tickled my face; I brushed it away. Suddenly I heard a sharp scrape of hangers. Slowly I pulled open the heavy curtains, which swished along the dusty floor. Pale dolls raised their arms over their eyes, black shadows sprang into shape, a spider scampered up a glittering thread, and as Eleanor entered, wrinkling her forehead in the hot white shock of the sun,

I swept out my arm and cried: "Welcome to the Childhood Museum!"

That afternoon I returned home for dinner, and as I stepped into the cool dusk of my room, with its drawn blinds, its drowsy armchair, its slumbering lamp with bent neck and bowed head, I felt that I was waking from a troubled dream of sunlight to the reassuring dark.

64

AND WHEN I RAISED MY EYES, in the days that followed, I would see the drawn blinds, the slumbering armchair, the drowsy lamp with bent neck and bowed head. Home from school I would let myself in with my key, and as I stepped into my room I saw the drawn blinds, the slumbering armchair, the drowsy lamp with bent neck and bowed head. On the floor beside the bed an open book lay face downward. On the worn seat of the armchair another book lay closed. And lying down on my stomach on the bed, under the pulled-out wall-light, I would begin to read, and raising my eyes I would see the drawn blinds, the slumbering armchair, the drowsy lamp with bent neck and bowed head. After a while mother would say: "You know you're not allowed to read at the table, Arthur. Now close that book and put it away," and I would look up with a slight frown. And stepping into my room I would see the drawn blinds, the slumbering armchair, the drowsy lamp with bent neck and bowed head. In the morning, as I entered homeroom, I would suddenly lower my eyes, and home from school I would let myself in with my key. And as I stepped into my room I would see the drawn blinds, the slumbering armchair, the drowsy lamp with bent neck and bowed head. And how strange it was to see her in English in the morning, and German in the afternoon, and homeroom at the end of the day, but lowering my eyes I continued reading. That spring I was working fairly hard. In school I ignored everyone, fixing my eyes on my desk, and after school I rode home on the bus and let myself in with my key. And stepping into my room I felt absorbed by the drawn blinds, the slumbering armchair, the drowsy lamp with bent neck and bowed head. Once, as I stepped into the cafeteria, I saw her rising from a table, but jerking my eyes away I gazed at a tall window, where a saltshaker sat on the brown windowsill, and once, rising from my German seat at the end of the period, I heard the slap of her shoe coming closer and closer. Then I stood without moving, frowning down at my desk, and stepping into my room I saw the drawn blinds, the slumbering armchair, the drowsy lamp with bent neck and bowed head. And one afternoon when I stepped into my room I saw her seated at my desk. She was bent over, writing swiftly. An uneven pile of brown-covered books towered on the left. On top sat Raggedy, smiling gaily, with her legs crossed and her hands resting on her aproned lap. Over the back of the chair hung a piece of gray rope. "Eleanor," I said sharply, but she continued writing. Swiftly I strode over and grasped her shoulder, squeezing my fingers in, but she continued writing. Angrily I seized her by the hair and began to pull. The black wig tore off with loud ripping sounds, exposing a bald shiny head with little tufts of hair glued here and there, then my hand touched something hard and cold and I jerked open my eyes, but it was only the wall. In school I ignored everyone, fixing my eyes on my desk, and as I stepped into my room I saw the drawn blinds, the slumbering armchair, the drowsy lamp with bent neck and bowed head.

As the warm days passed a dull contentedness came over me. Neither bored nor burning I was undisturbed, and passed impartially among the obligations of my day. After dinner, in the drowsy dusk, I would sit outside on the long front porch, and raising my eyes from my book I would gaze at the shadowed housefronts, at the sunny bright-green tree-tops above the rising shadowline of night, at the yellow-gleaming telephone wires against the drained and fading sky, and stretching out my arms, and yawning widely, I would lower my eyes and continue reading. Sometimes the screen door would open and I would look up incuriously as father stepped out in shirtsleeves with a folded newspaper tucked under his arm. Rubbing his hands together, and taking deep breaths, he would say: "Mmmm, this is some weather, huh? Reminds me, I've got to get the blades sharpened," while I, finding this interruption neither welcome nor unwelcome, watched him sit down with a great creak on the wicker settee. He would put on his reading glasses, open the newspaper, and begin to fold it in half, slapping out a crease with the back of a hand before completing the fold; and giving the paper a shake he would begin to read with a deep frown, saying: "Don't you go to school with that Cusick kid? Seems they just picked up his older brother and some other kid for robbing DeLancy's down on East Main. Broad daylight, can you believe it?" or "Bases loaded three-two and he walks him— he walks him." After a while, letting the paper slide down, he would begin to talk about how no one ever hit over .400 any more, and how the ball was livelier now, and once he told me about a fishing trip he had taken with his father, in a gloomy lake, among dark pines, in the cold morning before the sun came up. After a while he would say: "It's getting a little chilly out here," and I would say: "Oh, it's a little chilly, I guess. But not too chilly." "Nnnno, no," said father, "I wouldn't say it's too chilly." He paused. "But there's a bit of a chill in the air." After a while the door would open and mother would say: "Well speak of the devil." And sitting down on the padded steel chair she would begin to knit, while I, gazing up at the darkening leaves, imagined the three of us sitting there, on the long front porch, in the cooling dusk: mother, father, son. "It's getting chilly," mother would say—"Arthur, don't you think you ought to put on your jacket?" "Oh, I don't know, I will, in a while," and father would say: "They say this is a bad time of year for colds. It's the sudden change of temperature does it. Hot one minute, cold the next: body can't adjust to it." "Mercy, feel that breeze," mother would say, and father would say: "I'm beginning to feel a bit of a chill." "I hope you're not coming down with a cold, Walter. You don't want to come down with a cold." "Nah," said father, dismissing the idea with a wave of his hand, "I can always tell when a cold is coming. I get that itchy feeling at the top of my nose. Besides, I never catch colds at this time of year. Winter's the time for me." "But what about last spring, Walter? You were sick last spring. You had a temperature of a hundred and one. Don't tell me you've forgotten you were sick last spring with a temperature of a hundred and one." "Son of a gun, you know it slipped my mind completely. A hundred and one. Right you are. Funny how it slipped my mind." "Slipped your mind! I don't see how it could have slipped your mind—in bed for two weeks with a temperature of a hundred and one." "Yes, it's funny, but it completely slipped my mind. And a temperature of a hundred and one. I remember it now, by Joe. It had me laid up for two weeks. Funny the way it slipped my mind." "You've never forgotten you were sick before. I can't understand how you can forget a thing like that, Walter. And with a temperature of a hundred and one. It's not like forgetting a name, or a telephone number. Of course you were always good at telephone numbers. And you never forget a face." "That's true. Just the other day I was telling Jacobson: Bob, I said, I can't remember names to save my life, but I never forget a face. And he knew it. He couldn't deny it." "Of course he couldn't deny it. I've never known anyone like you when it comes to faces. I'm terrible at faces, except of people I know, of course. You remember Rita's sister Lottie. She was terrible at faces. But you should have seen her with telephone numbers. For the life of me I don't know how she did it. I always have to write them down. Then wouldn't you know it I can't remember for love or money where I put the darn fool thing in the first place. I might as well save myself the trouble of writing it down for all the good it does me. Then don't I find it right where I put it just when I don't need it. I keep meaning to call Jean Small. She's still out with that thing in her back. We ought to have them over. I don't see how you could forget you were sick in bed for two weeks with a temperature of a hundred and one." "The funny thing is, it slipped my mind completely. I remembered it the minute you mentioned it. A temperature of a hundred and one. I don't see how you can read in this light." "Don't tell me he's reading in this light. You'll ruin your eyes sure as shootin'. In all my life I've never heard of anyone who reads so much." "I wasn't really reading. Just holding my book open on my lap." "Oh, mercy, what an unusual way to read, holding your book open on your lap and not looking at it. They didn't do it that way in my day. Of course that was a long time ago. In the age of the dinosaurs." "Aw, come on, Mom. I bet you don't go back that far. I bet you don't go back before the woolly mammoth." "The woolly mammoth! Good lord, did you ever? The woolly mammoth!" "Ha ho hum," said father, stretching out his arms, giving a faint shudder, and folding his hands across his stomach. Mother said: "I love this time of day. It's so peaceful now." "Yes," I said, "it's peaceful." "Yes," said father, "this is a fine peaceful time of day. Even if it is a bit on the chilly side."

After a while the three of us would go inside and play canasta on the dining-room table, and then I would go to my room and do my homework.

On the weekends I would join in family excursions: a picnic on a red wooden table beside a babbling brook, a picnic on a gray wooden table beside a placid lake, a picnic on a brown wooden table beside a little waterfall, a visit to a bird sanctuary with winding trails and white arrows painted on tree-trunks and a sudden brown pond with green-headed ducks; and one warm Saturday night father and mother took me to an amusing place where I had never been before. I liked the yellow glow of lights, the bright green strips of cloth framed in red wood, the cries, the shouts, the red-roofed white church three feet high, the lighthouse four feet high, the metal loop-the-loop, the turning mill-wheel, the clown with an open mouth, the soft knock of wood on hard rubber, the little red ball rolling up the bright green ramp, falling into the wide opening at the top, suddenly emerging from a space at the side, rolling swiftly along bright green cloth toward the hole, coming closer and closer and at last veering to one side and bouncing against the red wood frame, the ohs!, the hoorays!, the sound of soda-bottles thudding from a nearby machine, the distant sound of baseballs against backstops—and later, at the baseball-pitching machines, I stood with my bat on my shoulder and waited fearfully as the red metal arm rose slowly, slowly, and suddenly stepping back I swung wildly, feeling in my wrists the thrilling tremor of wood on leather. Afterward I put a dime in the soda machine, enjoying the soft thud of the bottle against the metal door; and grasping the damp cool glass I inserted the bottlecap under the opening and pulled sharply downward, hearing the satisfying hiss and feeling through the glass the bend of the cap. As I rode home in the back of the car, gazing out at the darkness illuminated here and there by a yellow glow above the pumps of a gas station, a red glow above the tall letters of a closed supermarket, a blue glow in the window of a drugstore, a sadness came over me. I thought of a vulgar gesture a boy had made, of father's clumsy stance, of a dark purple stain on the asphalt beside a broken bottle, of a puddle of pink vomit with little lumps in it, of my hideous life, then anguish rose in me and I said quickly: "If I hadn't fouled up in the crummy sand I would have been just three over par, which isn't bad for a beginner." Mother said: "Listen to him, will you? As if you weren't a born player, Arthur." Father said: "He certainly put his old dad to shame." "Well," I said, "I wouldn't say that. What bothers me is the way I kept chopping up that sand and getting nowhere." "Happens to the best of us, Artie," said father, and when I returned to my room I lay down on my bed and began to read, but suddenly I closed the book and began walking up and down, up and down, up and down. Then I lay down and continued reading.

At school I worked diligently, but without much interest, and between classes I would sometimes stroll with a classmate, talking about schoolwork and making occasional jokes. Home from school I would let myself in with my key, and as I stepped into my room I would frown faintly, and lying down on my bed I would begin to turn the pages of various books. One evening I was sitting on the porch beside mother and father, thinking about nothing in particular. A chair creaked, a bird rose in the air; a little piece of fluff floated lazily down. And an uneasiness came over me... Then my mind darkened over, a black telephone pole sticking up against the purple sky filled me with anguish, and wrenching myself up I hurried inside, letting the door slam behind me.

One warm night toward the end of May I was lying in bed with my arm over my eyes, waiting to fall asleep. For the last few days I had been finding it impossible to fall asleep quickly. I would crawl wearily into bed, with tired stinging eyes, and I would lie for hours exhausted but awake, brooding over trivial incidents of the day, erupting into sudden angers, collapsing into odd desolations. I turned onto my left side, and onto my right side, and onto my stomach, and onto my back, where I lay listening to distant traffic, and then I turned onto my left side, and onto my right side, and onto my stomach, and onto my back. Something thumped lightly on the porch. Somewhere a cat cried. Far away soft motors sounded. There was a sudden loud scraping of cat-claws against my screen. I frowned, imagining a dark cat crouched on the outer sill. Wearily I turned onto my left side, and onto my right side, the cat-claws scraped again, angrily I swung my hand against the clattering blinds. Alert, exhausted, enraged, and awake, I sat up in bed and pushed aside the blinds.

Holding a finger before his lips, William was frowning in at me as if in disapproval. He was dressed in a summer jacket and dungarees. Keeping his finger against his lips, with his other hand he pointed in three jabbing motions toward the hedge. Then looking abruptly right, and abruptly left, he turned, took a step, placed his hand on the porchrail, and vaulted over, landing silently on the grass. Without looking back he hurried across the lawn and disappeared through the hedge.

Within moments I had dressed, tiptoed from my room, and closed the porch door softly behind me. Swiftly I strode across the moonlit lawn, and when I pushed through the hedge I saw him sitting on the path of the slope with his arms around his knees.

He turned his head, looking up at me as if in surprise, and at once stood up, slapping at the seat of his dungarees. He looked at me with a frown and then looked away. "But what, is anything," I said, when he did not speak.

William seemed embarrassed. "Oh," he said lightly, "nothing really, I just..." He frowned and kicked at a fern. "Listen, I was lying in bed, I couldn't sleep... you remember that night ... I thought, I don't know, if you felt like doing something or..." He turned to me and said abruptly: "Listen, I'm sorry if I got you up."

"No, I wasn't sleeping, and besides," I added, changing my voice to an orator's voice, and throwing out an arm to the blue night sky, "on this noble occasion, when the great William Mainwaring..."

"Quiet," commanded William, looking about with a frown.

65

MOMENTS LATER we were stalking through the field to the stream. We jumped down into the weeds, hesitated for a moment, and turned right, into the adventurous night. We headed along the grassy edge of the moonlit stream-path, gleaming here and there with bits of glass and patches of mud. Soon the field on both sides disappeared and high back yards at the level of our necks came down to the concrete banks. A dog howled and came bounding toward us; suddenly it stopped, half-choking on its rope. It lurched forward again and again, flattening its ears and baring its teeth and raising one paw with odd delicacy as it gasped and snarled. Moongreen hedges and blue-white picket fences began to appear above the banks, and as we continued the walls grew higher and higher until they rose above our heads. Then the walls turned sharply to the right, and after a while they began to grow lower and lower until they were on a level with our hips. Weedridden back yards gave way to empty fields, and suddenly the stream-path ended in a foot-high cement pipe that went under a road. On the other side of the road the walls disappeared. Tree-grown slopes fell on both sides to a narrow stream-path, half-grown with weeds. The trees shut out the moon, making a dark and rustling place. Something ran across leaves. Suddenly the trees ended and moonlit fields stretched away on both sides. Far away, a black backstop rose from a baseball diamond, and behind it black trees and rooftops showed against the dark blue sky. On both sides of the stream-path high grass rose up to our stomachs. The path became muddier and more indistinct, and finally it disappeared in a moonlit marsh. Dark shallow water gleamed here and there among hard grassy mounds and muddy flats. We stopped, gazing around in confusion. "Too bad," I muttered, kicking a rusty can. With a frown William pointed at the water and said: "Look, there's a current."

In shallow inlets surrounded by reeds, matted whorls of dead grass lay motionless. But here and there, bits of grass floated slowly, attaching themselves to the matted whorls.

Stepping on little islands of solid grassy ground we made our way among shallow pools and inlets. A slow motion of water was visible, dying out in shallow muddy places.

The movement of water toward us became more distinct, and then we came to the hard edge of a sluggish muddy stream. Clumps of grass stuck up through the water.

We kept to the hard edge of the swampy stream, which now and then widened out or suddenly narrowed. After a while the banks stiffened and a shallow stream flowed gently along. Over the shrill scrape of crickets and a murmur of distant traffic came the steady sound of shallow water rushing over stones.

The land began to slope up on both sides and we seemed to descend as we followed the stream-edge. Then we came to a road that formed a high black roof above our heads. As we passed under the road we stepped from moonlight to darkness, but at the far end we saw the rushing moonlit stream.

On the other side of the road a swift shallow stream, about four feet across, flowed between steep tree-covered slopes. Here and there the shadows of the trees shut out the moonlight. "We can sit here," I said, stamping the hard ground, but looking up with a frown at the high trees William said: "No, not here."

The trees began to thin out and the stream flowed between gently rising slopes. There were flat grassy places between the trees, and here and there the wrinkled tops of boulders broke through. "This seems like a good place," said William after a while.

And it was a good place. I sat down against a tree, and in moonshade patched with moonlight I gazed down at the rushing moonlit stream. The shifting white stream-foam against the shiny black water made patterns like sunlight on a dark forest path. Here and there wet stones blackly gleamed. On the other side of the stream the bushy slope rose to the dark blue sky. At the edge of my shade, a little below me and to the left, William stood in the moonlight, frowning down at the water. His face, partially visible from where I sat, looked stern and brooding in the clear light of the moon. He stood with his hands in the back pockets of his dungarees, the fingers inside and the thumbs out. He stood very still, frowning at the water. Across the stream some bush-leaves rustled in a breeze, changing from dark green to silvery green. Then William's jacket sleeve fluttered, a piece of his hair sprang up, against my throat I felt a sudden coolness. William's right hand rose from his pocket, clasping a black object; and tilting his head to the left he began to comb his hair down carefully, curving his left arm over his head and smoothing down the combed hair with his fingers. Then he thrust his comb in his right back pocket and replaced his hands in his pockets, the fingers inside and the thumbs out. He continued to frown down at the water. I said: "This was a good idea, coming here." William did not move, but seemed to frown more deeply. An uneasiness came over me, and I said gently, almost in a whisper: "I'm glad you came over." William continued to frown down in silence, and raising my voice I said with annoyance: "I said, I'm glad you came over."

William looked over his shoulder at me with a frown. Then he turned completely around. In the moonlight his eyes looked black and fierce. Removing his hands from his pockets he stood with his hands on his hips and his legs slightly apart, looking down at me with a frown. His eyes narrowed, as if he were searching for me in my shadow, and I shrank back a little against my tree. And for a while he stood that way, frowning down at me. "Well," I said angrily, "what's the big—" But looking at me with black angry eyes William said fiercely: "Traitor."

66

"I'M NOT A TRAITOR!" I cried, avoiding his gaze; that night I told him about the walk through the snow, the cat with the glass eyes, the white-faced juggler, the Childhood Museum. And the door in the wall, and the bride of death ... At first William sat on the moonlit slope with his arms around his raised knees, but as I continued he leaned back on both elbows with his legs outstretched and his ankles crossed. In the shadow of my tree above the moonlit stream I saw the black box begin to open and a pale ballerina slowly rise. He jerked his left hand to the right, leaving in his right palm the yellow glass ball, which he tossed in the air as he jerked back to receive the falling red glass ball. Under a crimson coverlet a pale yellow-haired lady, covered with dust, lay with her eyes closed. And carefully lifting the delicate, crackling, clinging paper I gazed at a stiff-looking gentleman in a black suit, "Enter," said Eleanor, and bending forward slightly, leaning on his polished walking stick, slowly he came forward, above my back the rough and splintery ceiling pressed down, gripping the little handle of my teacup with thumb and forefinger I raised the cup to my lips as in my mind we turned and turned, faster and faster, smaller and smaller, and catching the falling red glass ball he jerked his left hand to the right, leaving in his right palm the red glass ball, which he tossed in the air as he jerked back to receive the falling blue glass ball, "How ugly!" said Eleanor, slowly I pulled open the heavy curtains, which swished along the dusty floor, and as I stepped into the cool dusk of my room a cool breeze blew against my forehead, in the sudden silence I heard the loud sound of water. On the moonlit slope beside the shadow of my tree William was leaning back on both elbows with his legs outstretched, frowning down at the rushing stream. In the brilliant moonlight his face looked paper-white. A black shadow fell from the eave of his eyebrow over his eye down to his upthrusting cheekbone. He looked like a statue in a garden. After a while he picked up a twig, flung it toward the water, and leaned back on his elbow. The twig dropped in the grass by his foot. Silently William frowned down at the water. Annoyed at the twig, and the silence, and the whiteness, and the blackness, I said sharply: "Well, what's on your mind?" William looked at me over his shoulder with a frown. His eyes in their black caves gleamed; he seemed to be searching for me in my shadow. Then he turned back and looked down at the water. After a while he said: "This is okay here." "Yeah," I said, "it's okay. Sure." William picked up a stone and flung it into the stream. It made a light splash that was instantly overwhelmed by the sound of rushing water. And for a moment he remained fixed in an attitude of throwing: leaning on his left elbow, his head bent slightly to the left, his throwing arm suspended in the air, his hand hanging from the wrist. Then he leaned back on his right elbow. After a while he said: "When I was a kid I read this book about an Indian in a canoe. A carved Indian in a little canoe. He went riding down streams like this. He was a cool little Indian: yeah, he was cool.

Nothing could stop him. Stream like this was a river to him—Ohio, Mississippi, Rio Grande. Finally he comes to the sea. Man, I always liked that Indian—going places. Far. Never come back." In the silence William gazed down at the water. There was no sound but the sound of water rushing over stones. The sound of water was the silence and the silence was the sound of water rushing over stones. I coughed lightly. William remained motionless, gazing down at the water rushing over stones. Then he picked up a stone and threw it into the water. It made a heavier, plopping splash. "Well," I said, "I guess—" "Let's get out of here," he said suddenly, and stood up abruptly, as if angrily. Avoiding my gaze he slapped dirt from his dungarees, straining with a frown to see over his shoulder behind his back; and as I stood up in the chill night air I felt a strange desolation, as if I had been betrayed.

The next day William appeared at my locker after school, standing stiffly with his books on his hip. "Make it home okay?" I asked. He frowned, nodded once, and looked away. At my house we returned to our old games, playing ping-pong in the cellar, and badminton in the back yard, and Monopoly in my room. Never did he mention our moonlit adventure, which soon came to seem remote and strange, and often I wondered what it was that had made him come to me that night, after a winter's absence. He seemed unusually distant and constrained, and sometimes, raising my eyes from the Monopoly board, I would catch him staring off with a slight frown, his head turned slightly to one side and in his eyes a faintly wrong look. Then I would snap my fingers, and he would start slightly, returning to this world with a look of annoyance. In fact he often seemed sullen or annoyed, and one hot afternoon when he dropped the dice on the board as usual and began to move his battleship slowly along, knocking one sharp edge against the board as he counted out the spaces one at a time, suddenly he looked up and said: "I'm sick of this damn game," and lowering his eyes he continued counting out his spaces. "Well," I said, giving a genial shrug, "we can always do something else, chess or something." "No," said William decisively, landing on two of my houses, "there's nothing to do," and with a skilful motion of his fingers he swept up a hundred and placed it in the bank, swiftly removing a fifty, a twenty, two tens, a five, five ones.

As the days grew hotter William began to seem more and more fretful. In the midst of our games, irritable expressions would stray across his face, and he was often impatient and bored. At the same time he began staying later at my house, as if reluctant to depart. Often after dinner, in the warm dusk smelling of street-tar, leaves, and dinners cooking in open kitchen windows, we would sit outside on the long front porch and talk about nothing in particular as the sky faded to shades of gray— and suddenly the streetlights would go on. "Well," he would say, "I'd better get going," and he would not move. Sometimes the front door would open and father would appear, in his slippers and his rumpled khakis and his rolled-up lumberjack shirt. "Evening, men," he would say, hooking his thumbs inside his pants and taking a deep breath. "Mmm, this is some lovely weather we've got around here, huh? Say, Artie, I don't want to break anything up, but Mom thinks you ought to call it a night"—and sitting down with a tremendous creak in the wicker settee he would begin talking to William about whether Mays had a chance at Ruth's record. One evening as father was talking about this and that he happened to touch on the subject of school. Father had a somewhat exalted notion of learning and believed that education was always improving. "You know," he said, "nowadays they teach you guys things in the ninth grade I didn't even hear about till I was oh, way the heck along in high school. You guys don't know how lucky you are." "Yeah," I said, stifling a yawn, "we're lucky, all right. Lucky modern youth, that's us. Light up a Lucky." Lazily I looked off at the street, at the drained and darkening sky, at a shriveled cluster of brown-tinged lilacs leaning over the porchrail, at William seated beside me. To my surprise I saw him frowning down at his knees with tight lips and angry-looking eyes. Suddenly he said:

"I can't take this heat," and standing up abruptly he went inside, letting the screen door slam behind him.

One hot schoolday toward the middle of June, when no air came in through the open window, and the flag hung wearily from the exhausted flagpole, and a sluggish white cloud, inert and fat, lay sprawled on its back in the dead blue sky, I found myself looking forward with sharp impatience to my afternoon with William. The day passed with more than its usual measure of brown boredom, and as I made my way wearily along the dreary brown corridors I kept an eye out for William. That morning I did not pass him on the way to English. I did not pass him on the way to study hall in the afternoon, and as time grew slower, and classes grew longer, and death seemed inevitable, I began to feel oddly abandoned and oppressed. That afternoon after the final bell he did not appear at my locker, and as I rode home on the bus beside a familiar stranger I felt I could never drag my way through the long dull empty day. At my house I let myself in with my key. I passed through the cool brown living room with its odor of furniture polish, through the brighter dining room with a slanting sun-pattern of venetian blinds on the wall, and into the blazing kitchen, where silverware gleamed in the box of the dishrack. Putting down my heavy books I poured myself a tall cold glass of milk, into which I stirred a spoonful of chocolate syrup; when I lifted the spoon the coating of syrup looked wrinkled and cold. As I drank my milk I gazed about at the gleaming silver drawer-handles, at the gleaming silver emblem on the yellowing refrigerator door, at the bright dairymaid on the windowsill—and the brightness, the emptiness, the gleaming silence made me think of a prairie ghost-town I had seen on television, where tumbleweed rolled in the dusty and deserted street, and no one sat in the two wooden chairs on the wooden sidewalk outside the marshal's office, and suddenly, in a gust of wind, one wing of the saloon door swings inward, revealing for a moment the empty tables, the empty chairs, the empty gleaming mirror behind the deserted bar. The door swings out again, and in again, and out, and in, revealing a little less each time, while in the silent street, before the abandoned hitching post, no drowsy horse, bowing its head to the dust, blows wearily through blubber lips and lazily switches its heavy, drowsy tail. Sadly I finished my milk, wearily I rose from the table, and as I lifted my heavy books I felt too listless to move, too restless to remain. Wearily I stepped into the cool brown hall, as if I were going to still another classroom, and when I pushed open the door of my room I stopped abruptly, grasping the doorknob with my hand.

He was sitting sideways with his face turned to me, in the armchair beside my bed. His hands gripped the chairarms and he looked at me fiercely, his chin lifted, his dark eyes blazing. On the floor beside the bed lay his notebook and his pile of schoolbooks. In his lap one of my library books lay face downward. For a while we stared at one another in silence and then he said: "Well? So? You took your time getting here. How was school? Don't worry, no one saw me. I had a sandwich around eleven, I didn't think anyone . . . I've been reading, mostly. What's wrong? Christ. Can't you talk?"

There was a slight pause.

"Why William, you devil you," I said with a smile.

67

ON HOT SUMMER MORNINGS, on stifling summer afternoons, William and I sat sprawled in the warm shade of my closed and blind-drawn room. I would lie on the bed with my cheek propped in my hand, idly reading a library novel or turning through the pages of an old Christmas catalogue, while William sat in my reading chair with one leg hooked over an arm, making little clicking noises as he pushed the tiles of a number-square back-and-forth and up-and-down with his thumb. After a while, with a great effort, we would get up and make our weary way to the shady front porch. There I would lie down on the wicker settee with my head on the hard arm and my knees up, idly reading a library novel or turning through the pages of an old *National Geographic* magazine, while William sat on the wicker rocker, leaning back and making little clicking noises, or leaning forward and making papery sliding sounds as he played clock solitaire on the round steel table. "Goodness," mother would say when she reached the front porch with her clippers, her wooden basket, and her tasseled pillow, "are you boys going to stick around here all day? Can't you find anything to do?" And raising the back of one gloved hand to her moist and reddish face she would wipe from her forehead a few damp strands of hair. "It's too hot," I would answer, frowning and brushing away a fly, and rising wearily I would return to the privacy of my warm room, followed by William. I would lie on the bed with my cheek propped on my hand, idly reading a library novel or turning through the pages of old comic books, while William sat sprawled in my reading chair with one leg hooked over an arm, making little clicking noises, or turning the pages of my abandoned *National Geographic* magazine, or staring at his knee. Sometimes he would turn around in his chair and examine with a frown the books in my brown wooden bookcase. Pulling one out, and staring angrily at the spine, he would twist back in his seat, open it up, and begin to read with a frown. "Feel like doing anything?" I would say after a while. "I don't know," William would answer. After a while I would say: "Think there's anything on television?" "I don't know," William would answer. Sometimes he would rise without a word and leave the room, returning in a while with a glass of milk in one hand and, in the other, a saucer holding a peanut butter and jelly sandwich on rye and above it another saucer on which sat a peeled orange surrounded by half a dozen chocolate-covered graham crackers. Sitting down in the chair and placing one saucer on one arm, the other saucer on the other arm, and the glass of milk on top of two books on the floor, he would return to his book. And after a while I would go out to the kitchen, returning with a glass of pink lemonade, a peeled apple sliced into eighths, and a plate of Oreo cookies.

Sometimes, raising my eyes, I would catch him staring off with a slight frown. Then I would snap my fingers, and he would start slightly, returning to this world with a look of annoyance.

After dinner, in the bright hot air, William and I would stroll out into the sultry summer evening. We seemed to have stepped into a summer afternoon, but the shadows of houses on my side of the street stretched across the tar and halfway up the opposite houses; and over the burning black and red asbestos of the roofs, the sky seemed pale and weary, drained of its richest blue. Dressed in faded dungarees, worn sneakers, and light jackets zippered up an inch, we would stroll side by side through warm house-shadows and the sudden bright-hot spaces between the shadows, past the old two-family houses of my street, across dusty side-streets burning in the low sun, past the fields and vacant lots of distant neighborhoods, onward and onward, heading nowhere. As we walked we looked straight ahead, tight-lipped and frowning, holding our shoulders back. Narrowing my eyes I watched carefully for danger; and in the drowsy, violent air I felt wary and dangerous, tough and dangerous—for there we were, tightlipped and frowning, two tall high-school students towering over children. Now and then I would glance at William, examining with approval his stern frown, his tense arms, his dark hair combed back in a wave. A thick peak of hair at the back of his neck came down over his jacket collar. No longer did he wear his pants on his waist, but low on his hips, where they belonged. Sometimes a breeze would blow, swelling out his jacket behind him and lifting a piece of hair. Then reaching into his back pocket and plucking out his short black comb he would give his hair a few careful hand-smoothed comb-sweeps, and thrusting the comb back into his pocket he would continue without a word, looking straight ahead. Sometimes we would walk to a baseball lot and watch a game in the long shadows of the setting sun. I liked to watch the pitcher leaning forward with a squint, holding his gloved hand bent up behind his back while his other hand, swollen with veins, dangled loosely down. I liked to watch his arms sweeping back and coming forward to his chest, the pause, the glance to first, the lifting leg, the backward stretch, the foul ball banging into the wire backstop, the bat knocking dirt from cleats, the bits of dirt jumping on the tapped plate, the pitcher leaning forward, the pause, the glance to first, the lifting leg, but as I looked my eyes would wander from the game to a nearby face, the darkening sky, a distant rooftop—and suddenly William and I would be off, walking and walking, heading nowhere. And always as we walked I had a tense sense of excitement, as if at any moment, around any corner, something would happen. The sun went down, the west turned red, the east darkened into dusk; on old sidewalks under thick-leaved maples night had begun to fall, while in the street, in the hot dusklight, it was still day. Sometimes we would stop at a corner lot, looking about uncertainly, and then we would strike on, walking and walking; and as we walked in the darkening summer dusk I would look about with growing excitement, as if I were longing for the day to end. And yet there was almost no time at all, for although I wanted the day to end, I did not look forward to the sultry summer night. And as we walked, in the darkening air, I would have the sense of something slipping away, as if what I had desired was only the darkening summer dusk. And I would walk faster and faster, as if in despair, and William would say: "Hey, come on, take it easy." When it grew dark we would continue walking, but already I felt a sense of failure, the yellow windows of dark unknown houses oppressed me strangely, and when we returned to my hot lamplit room I felt restless and listless, exhausted and unappeased. Under the yellow lightbulb we played Monopoly, and through my open screen, with its little sharp-edged hole beneath which a BB pellet lay rusting in the dust of the window-trough, I would hear a screech of brakes, a madness of crickets, the low and high notes of a distant jukebox; and faintly and far away I would hear the sound of heavy trucks rolling on a highway.

And the summer dusk, that summer dusk ... Silence, a sudden shout in the summer dusk . . . And do you know them, the old men of summer ... sitting on porches in the hot shade of a summer dusk ...

Under the hot lightbulb, under the yellow glow, the faint shine of sweat on William's brow ...

Under the hot lightbulb, one sultry summer night, William and I sat sprawled in my stifling room. Outside, in the muggy dark, pallid heat-lightning flickered without thunder. We had broken off a long, inconclusive game of Monopoly, and now there was nothing to do but wait for William to go home. I wanted him to go home, for his presence annoyed me, but I did not want him to go home, for then I felt so uneasy ... He was sitting sprawled in my armchair near the bed. His left leg was stuck out in a straight line to the floor, and his left foot in its wide scuffed-black loafer leaned to the left; between the loafer and the frayed bottom of his dungaree pantsleg a thick white sock was visible. His right leg was bent at the knee and was swung out to the right; near the chairleg his right foot rested with the toe pressed down and the heel lifted, the loafer slipping off the white-socked yellowish heel. His left forearm lay flat on the padded chairarm and the hand hung slackly over the edge. His right forearm was bent sharply at the elbow and cut across the right chairarm. Between the index finger and thumb of his right hand he held a yellow pencil which he rocked swiftly back and forth near his stomach as he stared with a frown of concentration at the blur formed by the pink eraser and the brass. I was sitting on my bed near the window with my back against the wall and my legs stretched out. "Well," I said, "another day shot." I interlocked my fingers and stretched out my interlocked hands, turning the palms outward; a single knuckle cracked faintly. William said nothing, but continued to stare with a frown of concentration at the swiftly rocking pencil. His forehead shone with a faint wash of sweat. A few inches to my left, a light-brown pleated curtain crisscrossed with dark brown and dark green covered the wooden edge of the windowframe. "Christ it's hot in here," I said, recalling at once a stubble-cheeked man with beads of sweat on his eyebrows, seated on a hard chair, under the slowly turning blades of a ceiling fan, in a stifling room, in a Mexican town, in a black-and-white movie on television. "Eee-yep," I then said, "ah thank ah'll jes mosey own day-own to the ol' swimmin' hole. Ah cain't hyardly bureathe in hyar," but William was still frowning at his infuriating pencil, and I said: "Hi, folks, this is Arthur Grumm, speaking to you once again from television land. How're all you fine folks out there today?" but William was still frowning at his pencil, and I said: "Tarbaby, she ain't sayin' nothin', en brer Fox, he lay low," but William was still frowning at his pencil, and I said: "Say the secret word and win a hundred dollars. It's a common word, something you see every day," but William was still frowning at his pencil, and I said: "You know, George, we never asked his name. Who *was* that masked man, anyway? . . . You mean you don't know? Why, that's the Looone Ranger . . ." but William was still frowning at his pencil, and I said: "Death is probably overrated. For all we know, this is it. On the other hand, no one really knows anything about it. Personally I never cared for angels, they were always a little too chubby. Did I ever mention the game Philip School-craft and I used to play? Ho hum, another day, another dollar. Tennis, anyone? Ding dong, Satan calling. Just sign on the dotted line. One to a customer. Sorry, no refunds." William said nothing, but continued to stare at the rocking pencil. Gradually the pencil moved slower and slower and stopped. For a few moments William remained motionless, gazing dully at the pencil. Then leaning his head wearily against the chairback he gazed at me with narrow eyes, and parting his lips slowly, with faint peeling sounds, he said: "Tell me."

68

ON A SUNNY SATURDAY MORNING, a few days later, seven people set out in two cars for a distant lake. William and I, dressed in dungarees, sneakers, and shortsleeved shirts, and wearing our bathing suits under our pants, sat in the back of our car behind father and Marjorie. On the seat between us sat a red-and-silver thermos jug with a small white spout, my loosely folded light-brown towel with dark brown stripes at each end, and William's tightly rolled-up white towel, wrapped round by a green rubber band. Marjorie wore faded dungaree shorts cut from an old pair of dungarees, red sneakers, and a long white shirt through which her bathing-suit straps were visible. She had long bangs and a high-arched ponytail held in place by a red rubber band. From time to time as we bounced along she would reach up and pull at a bathing-suit strap that had slid toward a shoulder. I sat back against the hot seatcover with half-closed eyes, now gazing at the flicker of sun and shadow that passed over the open book on my lap, now gazing out the side window at passing trees. I would focus my gaze on a far tree that moved slowly toward me, drawing my eyes along with it, coming closer and closer and faster and faster until suddenly rushing past it was annihilated by the window-edge, and as if my eyes were fastened to the ends of springs they jerked forward and I would focus my gaze on another tree, which drew my eyes along with it until suddenly it was annihilated by the window-edge, and my eyes jerked forward and would focus on another tree, and another tree, and another tree, and another tree, until at last, letting my weary sight relax, I gazed unseeing at a green blur rushing past and, in the window, a motionless pale reflection of the dark-red front seat and above it father's neck and cheek. William sat leaning back in his corner, frowning out his window, and clasping in one sunny-and-shady hand a closed book that lay on his thigh. Marjorie said: "Oh look, une vache. Bonjour, madame la vache. Comment allez-vous aujourd'hui? How do you say how are you today in German, Arthur?" In a bored monotone I said: "Wie geht es Ihnen heute." "Oh, what an ugly language!" cried Marjorie. "William, don't you think German is an ugly language?" "Not really," said William wearily. In the warm light he half-closed his eyes. After a while Marjorie turned sideways in her seat, and placing a hand on the back of the seat, and resting her chin on her hand, she looked at me and said: "Whatcha readin', Arthur?" "Oh, I don't know. Just a book. It's called *The White Company*." "Who's it by?" "Arthur Conan Doyle," I answered, feeling a secret thrill. To my annoyance Marjorie did not say "Isn't he the author of Sherlock Holmes?" but only nodded slightly and said "Oh," and I added: "You know, Sherlock Holmes and so forth. But this isn't about Sherlock Holmes." "Uh huh," said Marjorie, and turning her chin on her hand she said: "Whatcha readin', William?" William turned from the window with a frown and gazed down at the book he held clasped in his lap, as if he had not noticed it before. Lifting it abruptly, and frowning at the spine, he muttered: "*New Arabian Nights*," and lowering it he turned back to the window. "Who's it by?" said Marjorie. William lifted the book again, and again looked at the spine. "Stevenson," he said. "Is it any good?" pursued Marjorie. "Pretty good, I guess." For a few moments Marjorie remained half-turned in her seat; then she turned around, and raising a hand she pulled up her slippery bathing-suit strap.

We parked beside Uncle Manny's shiny new two-tone Buick in an earthen parking lot at the edge of a wood. Through the concealing trees we could hear far shouts and splashes. Carrying blankets and picnic baskets we walked along a shady winding trail lined by high pines and oaks and beeches. "At least I think it's a beech," I said, "but maybe it's a birch, or a brontosaurus. Basically I only know two trees: maple and telephone pole." "Very funny. How do you say tree in ugly German?" "Ach, du bist ein dummes Mädchen. It's a long word." Marjorie looked at me suspiciously. "Oh," she said suddenly, "la mer." The trail had risen slightly and at the top of the rise we saw before us a thinning out of trees, with brown picnic tables scattered here and there, and beyond the tables a little beach crowded with blankets, and beyond the blankets a small gray-green lake entirely visible and surrounded by trees. A quarter of the way out was the usual row of floating white barrels, joined by white ropes. Toward the right of the beach rose up a white and slightly tilted lifeguard's chair, from which blossomed a dark red beach umbrella; in its shade a languid lifeguard, wearing a white helmet, sat reading a book, like some haughty and turbaned prince in a canopied seat on top of an elephant. On the left side of the beach was a short pier at the end of which four railed stairs rose to a gleaming wet diving board. A girl in a black bathing suit and a white bathing cap stood at the end of the board with her arms held out and her head bowed as if in prayer, and suddenly dived into the water, whereupon a tall broad-shouldered Indian-colored boy with a blond crewcut climbed the stairs and stood for a moment at the top, clinging to the iron railing and watching the still-trembling board; in a moment he let go of the rail, strode with measured steps to the end of the board, and at once jackknifed into the water, while behind him a clowning teenager had already climbed onto the shaking board, and staggering forward, holding his stomach as if he had been shot, at last he threw himself off the end with one leg flung in the air as he held his nose in mock fear.

We found a shady wooden table about ten feet from the shore. It was littered with hamburger-roll crumbs and a few brown pine-needles; there was a dark ketchup stain in one corner, and from between two planks stuck up the small square of a carefully folded waxpaper potato-chip bag. Holding out one arm I recited softly: "Über allen Gipfeln ist Ruh, in allen Wipfeln—" "Oh!" said Marjorie, covering her ears, "how can you stand that language? I don't see why anyone would take *Ger*man." "Aw aw aw," I said. "Parlee voo fraw say? Aw aw aw. Talk about ugly languages." "Just because some people can't pronounce it." "You know what I think?" said Uncle Manny, putting down the grill with a clatter, "I think you're both nuts. Hey, Bill, you taking a language?" "Yessir," said William. There was a pause. "Well? Out with it," said Uncle Manny. "French," said William, looking a little bored.

We carried our towels and blankets past the trees to the brown, hard, and slightly damp sand that formed a grass-bordered semicircle at the edge of the sunny lake. Mother, in her voluminous new skirted suit, sat down beside father on their blanket and spread suntan oil over great pale arms while he lay on his back with a towel over his face. Beside them, on a blanket one inch away, lay Uncle Manny and Auntie Lou. William and I spread our blanket below the adult blankets and carefully off to one side, so that the upper right-hand corner of our blanket began a safe distance from the lower left-hand corner of Auntie Lou's blanket. Marjorie hesitated a moment and then spread her large pink towel directly below the adult blankets and about six feet from our blanket. William and I took off our sneakers and, standing up, quickly slipped off our dungarees and rolled them up to use as pillows. Marjorie kneeled on her towel, frowning down as she unbuttoned her long white shirt. At last she slipped it off, for a moment thrusting out her chubby breasts; then sitting down with her legs out before her she began undoing her sneaker laces as William and I, still standing up, unbuttoned our shirts. William kneeled down on the blanket, where he carefully wrapped his shirt around his book, and still sitting down Marjorie unbuttoned and unzipped her dungaree shorts, slid them off, and quickly lay down on her stomach, turning her head away. Suddenly she reached up behind and tugged down her suit-skirt. Far, far away, Eeyore walked along the bumps of her spine up to her hair. Marjorie laid her hands on both sides of her head. She looked as if she had been banished to a pink island. "Hey, Marge," I said, "you want to go for a swim?"

"Uh uh," she said, not turning her head. Giving a shrug I tossed my shirt onto the blanket, pulled my shoulders back, and strolled with William down to the loud, crowded water.

The lake-bottom was smooth and silky but littered with small round stones; a few feet in, the water was over our heads. William swam straight out to the row of barrels, which now seemed much farther away, while I stood at chest-level watching him lift his face from the water and plunge it in, lift his face and plunge it in. When he reached the barrels he seized one with an arm, wiped the hair from his eyes, and motioned for me to join him. With my slower and more tiring stroke, for I had never learned to put my face in the water, I swam out to him and seized the other end of the barrel. I looked at the noisy diving board, at the shady lifeguard in his tilted chair, at the small and crowded shore where father was sitting up and pointing to us and Marjorie, lying on her back but raising her head, was gazing at us with her hand shading her eyes. Then I turned and looked out at the peaceful gray lake and at the dark green trees beyond. Suddenly a whistle blew, and when I turned I saw the lifeguard motioning angrily to us.

Breathing heavily, dripping in the hot sun, I stood in the sand with my towel across my shoulders while William lay dripping on the blanket. "The outlaws return," said Marjorie, lying on her back and looking up at me with a hand shading her eyes. Suddenly I bent my head over and rubbed my hair, spraying her lightly. "Stop it!" she cried angrily, covering her face with an arm and lifting one plump knee.

I lay down beside William on my blanket, feeling my ribs and hips against the firm sand; and laying my cheek on my rolled-up warm dungarees, I closed my eyes.

Lunch was served at the shady picnic table beside the smoking grill. William, wearing his unbuttoned, damp-bottomed shirt, sat on his towel at the far end of the bench, before a white paper plate on which sat a grilled hamburger in a toasted roll, a long slice of pickle, and potato salad sprinkled with paprika and parsley. Beside the plate lay his book, with a flattened yellow gum-wrapper sticking out. I sat between William and Auntie Lou. A few feet away, Uncle Manny stood perspiring beside the hissing grill. On the other side of the table Marjorie sat across from Auntie Lou, father sat across from me, and mother stood across from William by the table-end, pouring pink lemonade into paper cups. "Come on, come on," cried father, waving a fork at mother, "we're doing fine here, sit down, I'll take care of the rest," and he began to rise, bending forward and grasping the table as he tried to lift a leg trapped between the bench and table. "Sit down," said mother, and father instantly sat down, muttering "Excuse me, sorry," to Marjorie, who had slid a little away. Uncle Manny, wiping his face with an enormous white handkerchief, blew hard at the smoking grill. He jiggled something and suddenly snatched away his finger, shaking it rapidly. "Good lord," said mother, "be careful. Would you care for more potato salad, William?" A fly landed on the lip of the open ketchup bottle. "There's a fly on the ketchup," said Auntie Lou. "You have to say it in French," I said. Marjorie looked up, brushed away the fly, and looked down. The fly circled lazily, landed on the lip of the ketchup bottle, and began rubbing its hands in satisfaction. "Have you heard this one?" said Auntie Lou. "A priest, a rabbi, and a minister were traveling in an airplane, when suddenly they noticed that one wing was on fire. The priest began to say a Hail Mary, the rabbi began to pray in Jewish, the minister—" "Aah no no no," said Uncle Manny, "you left out half the joke. A priest, a rabbi, and a minister are flying from New York to San Francisco, see. An announcement comes over the loudspeaker—" "I think I remember this one," said mother. "Is this the one where the minister says—" "Wait," said father, "I don't think I've heard it." "Zare ees a fly on zee cat soup," I said, and bending toward William I said quietly: "Don't say anything. Leave it to me." William nodded once without looking at me and continued to eat his hamburger.

"How about that!" cried Uncle Manny. "Oh, you shouldn't have," said Auntie Lou, as mother, flushing with pleasure, lowered a great apple pie onto the table.

After the apple pie there was a great cleaning up and putting away, and then came a great gathering of blankets and towels in preparation for a return to the beach. Stretching out my arms, and giving a little yawn, I said: "Ah boy. I think I'll take a little walk with William, if nobody minds. Digest all that food." I slapped myself noisily on the stomach. "Where to?" said mother, standing with her beach-towel over her arm. "Oh, just around. Not far. Down to the car maybe, around there. Don't worry. We'll be back soon. C'mon, c'mon. Well, so long. Bye." "Just a minute," said father, "maybe Margie wants to join you." I frowned slightly. William looked down. Marjorie said instantly: "Oh no, Uncle Walter, I'm sort of tired, really I am. Well, see ya later, alligator. Au revoir, as we say in gay Paree. By the way, coz. How do you say 'Leave it to me' in German?" "Listen," I said quickly, "if she's tired she won't want to go for a long walk." "I thought you said it was a short walk," said mother. "Yes yes, it's short relatively speaking, but not two feet, if you know what I mean, and besides, I no spicca de fraw say. Well, see ya. In a while, crocodile. Don't get any cramps or anything. Auf Wiedersehen, as we say in gloomy Berlin. C'mon." William and I set off along the path toward the car. As I walked I felt a burning sensation on my back, but when I whirled around I saw father and Marjorie walking away. At the top of the rise I glanced back over my shoulder. Through the trees I saw the abandoned picnic table with the thermos jug and picnic basket on top, and beyond the picnic area I saw the beach, the diving board, the leaning lifeguard chair, and father standing in the water up to his knees, his hands folded behind his back as he looked out toward the white barrels. "All clear," I said, and at once we left the path and set off through the trees. Through a tangle of leaves and branches we kept the lake in sight, and soon we came abreast of the pier with the diving board, some twenty feet away. As we advanced through the trees, following the lake, the look of the beach kept changing: now it was a thin bar on which people were crushed together, now it was a widening arc crowded with blankets and running children, now it was cut in half by a protruding piece of bushy embankment, and as we advanced the shape of the lake kept changing, gaining a bump here and a notch there, losing a little cape, gaining a sudden cove, and always turning slowly clockwise around the white line of barrels. Past the barrels we moved closer to the lake-edge, retreating whenever a lone swimmer headed for the barrel-line. We moved easily through the light undergrowth, circling rapidly about the lake, and soon we reached the opposite shore. Crouching down and pushing aside a bush-branch, I gazed out across the lake at the far beach beyond the line of white barrels.

We found a smooth place by the exposed roots of two trees, near the lake-edge but concealed by bushes. I sat down against the deep-ridged bark of a trunk, shifting slightly so that I had a clear view of the lake through bush-twigs and bush-leaves. Crossing my ankles, and placing my hands behind my neck, I said: "This is more like it." "Just a second," said William, stepping out of sight. His crackling footsteps stopped; I heard a loud splashing sound. A few moments later William appeared. He sat down against his tree, leaned forward to adjust a bush-branch, and leaned back. I opened my book, brushed away a gnat, and glanced at William. He sat with his hand clasping the edge of his book, gazing out at the water. Through the leaves I saw the shady brown edge of the lake, where twigs and brown leaves floated, and beyond it the sunny gold-brown water shading into gray-green, then the line of white barrels and far away the splashes of swimmers, the leaning lifeguard stand, the brown semicircle of beach and there, on the blanket, mother sitting up with her head turned toward the dark trees behind her. On the sand beside the blanket father was standing with his back to me and his hands on his hips, gazing at the dark trees, and on the adjoining blanket Auntie Lou was lying on her stomach with her head raised and one leg bent up at the knee while Uncle

Manny stood sideways with his hands on his hips, his head turned toward the picnic tables, and on the pink towel below the double blanket Marjorie was sitting up, shading her eyes and gazing across the lake not quite at our hiding place, and off to one side lay our large empty blanket, with two pairs of rolled-up dungarees, one folded white towel, and one flung brown towel. I glanced at William. He sat with his hand still clasping the edge of his book, gazing out at the water with a slight frown. I said: "Look at that. What are they going to do, send out a posse? They don't leave you alone for a second. Hey," I said, snapping my fingers. William started. I said: "What were you—" "Nothing, nothing," he said irritably, picking up his book, opening it against his raised legs, and frowning down at the page, while his right hand, clutching the yellow chewing-gum wrapper, thrust over and over again at the opening of his shirt-pocket.

69

THE SAME OLD SUMMER CONTINUED. The same old sun shone down out of the same old sky, and the same old William sat sprawled in my reading chair, frowning down at the same old magazine and turning the pages with a sharp, angry, impatient sound, or sprawled beside me on the wicker rocker on the shady front porch, frowning down at the number-square that he clicked with his thumb over and over again, over and over again, while mother's clippers came closer and closer. "You're driving me crazy with that thing," I would say, and there would be a pause, but then the clicking would resume—and sometimes he would stand up abruptly and go inside, letting the screen door slam behind my head. After a while I would go inside, where I would find him sprawled in my reading chair, frowning down at the number-square that he clicked with his thumb over and over again, over and over again, and as the same old summer continued, and the same old sun shone down out of the same old sky, an irritability came over William. He would be sitting sprawled in the wicker rocker on the shady front porch, his head leaning back and his eyes narrowed as he gazed out at the street like a person with a slight headache, and if from my reclining position on the wicker settee I said: "Read any good books lately?" his frown would deepen, as though the sound of my voice had annoyed him. And knowing that I should say nothing more, but annoyed at his annoyance, I would say, "And so, here we are again, two hardworking lads in a land of idleness," and I would watch his lips tighten, and his frown deepen, and I would say: "Cheer up, death is inevitable," and suddenly he would stand up and stride inside, letting the screen door slam behind my head. Between my raised knees I could see the rocking chair going up and down, up and down, as when, in a movie, a frowning man in a gray suit stabs out a cigarette in an ashtray and for a moment the camera stares at the crushed and slightly unfolding cigarette, the thin line of smoke, the dead butts, the ashes, as if it all meant something.

After dinner we would sit on the warm front porch, where there was nothing to do, and sometimes we would walk out into the dying day, where there was nothing to do. When we returned we would sometimes play pinochle with mother and father, and then we would retire to my room, where there was nothing to do. And really we were both waiting for William to leave, so that we would both be left in peace. And I longed for him to go, for his presence oppressed me, but I did not want him to go, for his absence oppressed me. At last he would go, and throwing myself down on the bed I would begin to read, but after a while I would begin to pace up and down, up and down, and throwing myself down on the bed I would begin to read, begin to read, but after a while I would begin to pace up and down, up and down. Sometimes I felt that even though I was doing nothing wrong, even though I was doing nothing at all, I was somehow worsening, as if, in my case, mere existence were a form of decay. And I would be assailed by illicit longings . . . oh, not those longings, but illicit longings, longings for dangerous and unknown realms of freedom at the opposite end of so-called life. In the hot nights I found it difficult to fall asleep, and the next morning William would arrive as usual, and once again we sat sprawled in my room or on the wicker furniture of the shady front porch. Sometimes I had the sense that he was about to say something, something of overwhelming importance, and I would look up suddenly, in order to catch him by surprise; and once I saw him suddenly lower his eyes. And one hot night as we were sitting in my room waiting for William to go away, William began drumming his fingers lightly on the padded arm of the reading chair. For a while I listened with growing impatience to the faint, barely audible drumming which seemed to form a marching tune but kept changing slightly. It stopped, and I returned to my book, but suddenly it started again, and when I looked up angrily I was startled to see him staring at me so intensely that several seconds passed before we jerked our eyes away.

One hot night as we were sitting in my room waiting for William to go away, William began drumming his fingers lightly on the padded arm of the reading chair. For a while I listened with growing impatience to the faint, barely audible drumming which seemed to form a marching tune but kept changing slightly. It stopped, and I returned to my book, but suddenly it started again, and when I looked up angrily I saw him sitting with his head leaning back wearily against the chairback. He said: "It seems like summer will never end."

Irritably I said: "Everybody around here sounds like a movie."

A few moments later I added: "Besides, it'll end," and returned to my book.

One hot evening when William left and I returned to my bright, empty, useless room, an intense restlessness came over me. I lay down on my bed, but at once I sprang up, and began to pace up and down, up and down, and at last I put on my summer jacket and strolled out into the living room, where mother was reading a fat novel. "Hi," I said. "I'm going out for a walk. I'll be back soon. Is that a good book?" "At this hour!" said mother, looking up. "Arthur, I don't want you going out at this hour. You stay in now. It's dark out. I was just getting ready for bed." "Don't yell at me, I can't stand it," I said quietly, slamming the door behind me and taking a deep breath in the liberating dark. Turning left I began to walk swiftly, heading nowhere in particular, gazing at the lamplit windows of dark houses; suddenly a porchlight went out. I began to walk quicker. The dark street was silent and deserted and many houses were already black. In an upper window a light went out. I felt a curious apprehension, as if I had not arrived in time, and glancing over my shoulder, as if I were being pursued, I began to walk still faster, noticing the all-dark houses, the occasional yellow windows. "But this is crazy," I muttered aloud, and a few moments later I said: "Good evening, I was passing by, I wondered... Hello, you probably don't remember me, my name is..." On a dark porch a sudden voice said: "Shhh, someone's coming"; a girl laughed softly as I passed. The sky was black and moonless. Far away, above a rooftop, I saw a murky red glow, from some shopping center or lone diner. After a while I came to a well-lit street where cars passed in both directions; at one corner a closed gas station glowed brilliant yellow. I crossed the street and almost at once found myself in blackness, punctuated by occasional dim streetlamps. In the darkness I watched my shadow growing shorter and longer under the streetlamps. As I approached the dim circle of light I would glance over my shoulder at my shadow stretching far out behind me, growing shorter and shorter as I came closer and closer until, as I passed under the streetlight, I would be shadowless for a moment before the tip of my shadow began to emerge from my toes, growing swiftly from a plump infant to a slender man to a thinner and thinner giant who grew longer and longer and dimmer and dimmer and at last disappeared in the blackness of the road—and looking over my shoulder I would see a long dim shadow stretching out behind me. And sometimes, growing from my shadow at a slight angle, a second, dimmer shadow would appear, caused by some other light, and suddenly it would melt away. The road dipped down and passed under another road, and on the other side I came to a little dark park. Under the pallid glare of a solitary streetlamp a lone bench cast a slatted shadow. I crossed the park and walked along dark sidewalkless roads, and after a while I came to a dark street lined with great overarching trees. Under the leafy black boughs it was very dark. The large old houses were set well back from the road, and here and there I saw a dim glow of yellow lamplight through drawn curtains. "Too late," I muttered, walking faster and faster, glancing at the dark houses on my right. Suddenly I stumbled on a slab of loose sidewalk, but quickly righting myself I hurried on. A cat began to moan, like a wounded child, and in my mind I heard the words: "Do cats eat bats? Do cats eat bats?" and I tried to remember where I had heard that question, but in vain. And as I hurried on I thought: "Do cats eat bats? Do bats eat rats? Do rats eat hats? Do hats eat bats?"—all at once I stopped. Stepping off the sidewalk, I stood beside a high tree that grew between the sidewalk and the street. I peered at the black front walk, at the two high trees black against the black sky, at the two black rows of black-shuttered windows, and high above, in the sloping black roof, three black windows with peaked black roofs. All was slumbering, all was dead—but as I gazed I seemed to see, in the high window on the left, a faintness of light, a tinge of glow, as if the thick darkness were being illuminated by the dying flame of a single match. For a long while I stood there, gazing up at the high dim window: so dim, that window, that at times it seemed completely black. Then taking a deep breath I walked along the cracked front walk. At the dark front door I glanced over my shoulder, and stepping to the right I peered through the thin strip of glass; in the blackness I saw a dim glow of dying coals. I stepped back, and for a while I stood there, frowning at the door. Then I reached up, and grasped the big iron knocker, and let it fall. A great knock sounded through the slumbering night. I waited, breathing heavily; gazing down at my hands I saw that they were clenched. Twice I seemed to hear the sound of approaching footsteps, and each time I stepped back; then I stepped forward and placed my ear against the wood, springing back suddenly, but nothing happened. After a while I turned and walked swiftly away, looking over my shoulder as if I were being pursued.

The houses on my street were dark; the faint yellow light of my two living-room windows fell across the wicker rocker, spilled through the slender porch balusters, touched black leaves with pieces of yellow-green. When I stepped into the dim and shadowy living room, lit only by the low bulb of the reading lamp, I saw mother in her blue summer bathrobe, sitting on the couch with her head to one side and her eyes closed. "I'm home, Mom," I said quietly. Opening her eyes and frowning sleepily she murmured: "Oh there you are, I must have fallen . . . I had the strangest . . . lock the door, Arthur, how many times have I, talking to your mother like that. You were always a well-behaved boy, I don't know where you," and rising wearily and drawing her robe tightly about her she shuffled away, muttering: "He was always so well behaved, I don't know where I, but it's all right, don't worry, what was I . . . in father's garden, why I haven't . . . the little cucumbers . . ."

That night I dreamed that I was climbing a dark stairway. At the top I pushed open a door, and I came to another stairway, and climbing the second stairway I came to another door. Pushing open the door I found myself in a dark hallway with doors on the left and right. Slowly I made my way along the hallway, stepping carefully among white plates that lay here and there, and at the end I pushed open a door on the right and stepped into William's room. The room was lit by candles. He was lying on his back on the bed, smoking a cigarette. Beside the bed stood Eleanor Schumann in her black robe. Her eyebrows were blackened in a frown and her mouth was bright red. She bent over and began to tickle William, who laughed loudly and coarsely. "Quiet!" I said, but Eleanor began to laugh, throwing her head back and squeezing her eyes shut, and when I opened my eyes I found myself lying in my clothes on my still-made bed, in the quiet lamplight, in the empty night.

70

"Oh," sighed mother a few nights later, fanning herself with her cards, "it's been such a lazy summer. I don't know how I'll make the adjustment. It seems as if my vacation started only yesterday. I don't know where the time goes."

"Yes," I said, "that's one remarkable thing about time. It passes. Why don't we play and not talk."

"We can do both, Arthur," said mother, "and I don't think it's necessary for you to be rude to your mother," and looking at me suddenly as if she were studying me she said: "You'll have to get your hair cut."

"I don't 'have' to do anything."

"You can't go to school looking like that."

"Looking like what! Looking like what! What are you trying to do, mock me?"

"Easy, easy," said father, making a little calming motion with his hand.

"Lord! that temper of his. No one can tell him anything. Why, only yesterday—"

William slapped down his cards. "Excuse me, I'm going to the bathroom," he said, striding out of the room.

71

On a hot, too hot, hazy and dusty sort of day in early September, the sort of day when tired dogs raise their heads from their paws and pant hotly into your face with their long pink tongues hanging out, and the not yet dead leaves hang heavily from bowed branches, and the weary and dissatisfied soul, tortured by thirst, lies flat on its back in the merciless dust, no longer able to move, and no longer able to desire to move, on such a day William arrived on his English bike shortly after breakfast. He looked tired and irritable. I greeted him with false cheerfulness. Throwing me a sullen look he sank into my reading chair and gazed off with a frown. All that morning we exchanged not a single word. His tiredness, his air of crankiness, his frown, his sullenness, annoyed and exasperated me, and in the hot, too hot, much too hot, boring and blazing afternoon I suggested a little walk. "It's too hot," said William, not even raising his eyes, and infuriated by the boring and blazing stupidity of it all I strode out alone into the shattering day. The shade of the sidewalk was hot, here and there the sun broke through in white circles, a dog with his long pink tongue hanging out sat panting by the cracked and dust-caked tire of a parked car, in the sunlight the polished hood of the car was intensely green and aglow with tiny shimmering specks of pink and blue, overhead the large motionless maple-leaves looked heavy and rubbery, and when I pushed open the door of my room William looked up abruptly, as if he had been caught by surprise. That afternoon we played a long, listless game of Monopoly, in the evening we sat for a long time waiting for William to go away, and when he left I lay down on my stomach on the bed with one hand trailing on the floor and my chin pressing into the scratchy bedspread.

That night I woke suddenly in the hot darkness. I closed my eyes, but slowly my eyelids opened, my mind was racing, in the darkness I felt exhausted and alert. Wearily I closed my eyes, slowly my eyelids opened, helplessly I gazed up at depthless blackness from which a dim ceiling slowly emerged. In the blackness beyond my toes a slanting pattern of venetian blinds appeared on my dark bureau. It rose slowly, breaking off at the top of the bureau and appearing on the wall behind. It rose along the wall, bent abruptly at the angle of wall and ceiling, and moved slowly along the ceiling until, halfway across, the slats began to disappear one by one, as if they were slipping into a pocket, and as the last slat vanished another pattern of blinds broke off at the top of the bureau, rose along the wall, bent abruptly at the molding, moved slowly across the ceiling and melted away. I waited for the next one, but nothing happened. Through the slightly open window behind my blinds I heard the soft sound of distant passing cars. In the tedious darkness I could make out the band of molding at the top of the wall and the black edge of the ceiling lightshade. Above the windows the blackness faded slightly. Wearily I turned my head to the left, letting my gaze fall to the black base of the standing lamp, the black oblong of the Monopoly box, the black toe of William's loafer, my black sneaker lying on its side. Wearily I closed my eyes, slowly my eyelids opened, in the darkness I sighed aloud. Sitting up wearily with faintly throbbing temples I pushed aside the blinds.

The sky was mostly black, shading to black-blue above the hedge. A few stars glimmered fitfully, like fluttering nerves. Over the hedge a thin crescent moon was tipped back at an exhausting angle, as if it had slipped down a little too far and were straining to pull itself back up. The swing-ropes hung down at slightly uneven lengths; the seat leaned a little forward, and near the edge there rested a large twig that looked as if it should be tumbling madly off.

Irritably I released the blinds, and lay down, and closed my eyes. Slowly my eyes opened, angrily I gazed at the black base of the standing lamp. I gazed at the black toe of William's loafer, at the black base of the standing lamp, at the black toe of William's loafer, at the black oblong of the Monopoly box, at the black toe of William's loafer, at my black sneaker lying on its side, at the black toe of William's loafer, at the dark band of sock, at the black projecting cuff-edge, at the black knee, suddenly I gasped, "Shhh," said William, I sat up with a fiercely beating heart. He was seated stiffly in my reading chair, a breathing black form in the dark. He wore his summer jacket zipped up to his chin. His elbows rested on the back of the chairarms and one dark hand was pressed against his stomach as if he had a pain. In my mind I saw him crawling through the window, tiptoeing along the hall, slowly pushing open the door... "You scared me," I whispered, still breathing heavily; for a moment I had felt like bursting into tears. "You woke up," he whispered, "I thought you knew I was here, I thought you were fooling." "No, no, I didn't see you, how did you..." "The cellar, it's quieter that way, don't worry, I put back the key..." "Oh, the key, it's a good thing you're not a murderer, I never expected..." "Stop faking, you wanted me to come." "Oh, wanted, I want lots of things, and besides, this is probably all a dream, I'll wake up in a few seconds, and then, and then..." "You're lying, don't try to get out of it." "Out of it, out of what, what are you..." Without a whisper William said: "Evenin', Mac, I was..." "Shh!" I hissed, "you'll wake up every..." "Hah!" he whispered, "see." "All right, shhh, what do you..." "He saw you, that night." "He! What are you..." "He looked out the window, he saw you go away. He came down, but you were gone." "You're trying to frighten me, very melodramatic, the darkness, so he saw me, when did you..." "Tonight, after I left you... all this whispering..." "Yes, that's a good word, whissssssssssssssssspering, why did you..." "Oh, to get something." "Get something, then you, did he, was everything the same?" "A little filthier than last time, he looked the same, there wasn't much light. He remembered me right away. Oh, he remembered me." "Remembered you, yes, that time you, I meant to apol, how long did you..." "A half-hour, give or take. We talked about books." "Books! Yes, he always, I suppose he did all the talking, he always..." "No, not all... and besides, I wanted to borrow a book." "Oh, borrow, yes, that's very, and did he..." With a sudden motion William unzipped his jacket. Carefully lifting a dark book in both hands he laid it gently on his lap. "You can't read in the dark," I whispered, pressing back against the blinds. "That's true," he whispered, opening the book and removing a black object. "Don't shoot," I almost sobbed, leaning back and raising my arm to my eyes. "Don't be stupid," said William. There was a spinning sound. It went slower and slower and stopped. Sitting erect he placed the barrel against his temple. "Don't," I whispered. He pulled the trigger. "See!" he cried in a whisper, turning to me in fierce triumph; wearily I bowed my beating head.

72

QUITE SUDDENLY, as if I had not expected it, school began. And how strange it was to see him in Geometry, two rows away and two seats up ... And how strange it was to see him in Biology, two rows away and one seat back ... Biology was the last class before the lunch-shifts began, and one behind the other we slid our brown trays along the curving silver rails that ended at a big black cash register; and stepping into the high brown cafeteria with its rows of loud tables I stood motionless for a few moments with my tray pressing against my stomach and an odor of shepherd's pie streaming into my nostrils as I waited for William and surveyed the alien crowd. Together we walked in search of an empty table in a remote corner, together we put down our trays and sat down face to face, and pushing back in our chairs together we rose together and strolled out onto the pavement at the side of the school. After school he appeared at my locker and together we rode home on my bus. At my house I let us in with my key. Shutting the door of my room behind us I watched William stride over to the windows and close the blinds with short sharp pulls. Then hanging my jacket on the back of the desk-chair I sat down on the bed with my back against the wall as William sat down in my reading chair. Suddenly he stood up. From the closet there came a sound of shuffling and scraping, and flushing faintly from his

bending he emerged holding in both hands a book with a dull
red cover. At the bed he laid it down and opened the cover
and removed the gun. He swung out the cylinder, placed his
finger over one of the two bullets, and spilled the other bullet
onto the bedspread. Then pushing the cylinder back into place
he sat down stiffbacked and tightlipped at the front of the
reading chair. Never did he look at me. He sat motionless for a
while, with the gun resting on his thigh, and his hand resting
on the gun—and abruptly raising the gun he spun the cylinder
fiercely with his left hand. And I felt that cylinder spinning in
my temple, round and round, slower and slower, slower and
slower; in the sudden silence I could hear slight creaking sounds
in my neck. Again he sat motionless, holding the gun awkwardly
and as if painfully erect; his elbow was raised, his biceps half-
flexed, in the silence I could hear the slow sound of his breathing, suddenly he pressed the barrel to his temple. And I felt that
barrel pressing against my temple, his eyes narrowed, my eyes
narrowed, and as he pulled the trigger I felt a sudden tickling
sensation on my cheek, as of a spider running down, and raising
my hand I felt a line of wetness. Then a veiled look came into
his eyes, his hand dropped, his shoulders slumped forward, and
he sat staring at the floor in an attitude of weariness—before
abruptly looking up, staring fiercely before him. He swung out
the cylinder and looked at the position of the bullet, exclaiming
as if in triumph, for it was only one space away; and pushing
back the cylinder he turned to me with a fierce look, holding
out the gun handle-first. Frowning and lowering my eyes I took
the gun and got into position, for I could not endure the
thought of being found dead in a clumsy, ugly posture. At first
I tried sitting at the edge of the bed, but I was afraid of plunging to the floor or of falling back and smashing my head against
the wall, and then I tried sitting sideways on the bed with my
legs straight out and my body tilted back slightly, but I felt
stiff and uncomfortable, and at last I lay down on my back;
and holding the heavy gun above me I spun the cylinder, gazing
up at the black gun as if it were about to fall on me. When the

spinning stopped I lowered the gun carefully into position, one inch from my right temple, laying my flexed arm flat on the bed and touching the wall with my elbow. Then closing my eyes and pressing the barrel to my temple I paused for a moment, imagining William on his chair, gazing at me with fierce, narrow eyes. When it was over I lay drowsily for a while, and at last I sat up wearily, but for some reason I did not want to know where the bullet was, and I gave the cylinder another spin to prevent anyone from knowing. Then I handed the gun to William, who replaced the second bullet, laid the gun in the book, and carried the book back to my closet, and afterward we returned to our old games, avoiding one another's gaze.

We did not play our new little game every day. After the first few times we agreed to perform the deed once a week, as if we feared that chance had already been stretched to the breaking point; and perhaps for this reason the edge of my terror did not lose its sharpness but seemed to cut deeper with repetition. I found myself developing strange sensitivities. When I watched William sitting erect and tightlipped at the edge of the chair, holding up the revolver with its spinning cylinder, I would suddenly lower my eyes, as if I were witnessing something repellent or shameful. Then a rage would come over me, I wanted to spring up and wrest the gun from his grasp and fling it through the window, in my mind I saw the barrel pressing against his temple, my temple began to throb painfully, and I would look up suddenly, but he would still be sitting there, with the gun suspended in the air. And I longed to shout Go on! Go on! What are you waiting for! or Stop! Stop!—and as he lowered the barrel to his temple I wanted to scream or burst into tears; but I remained silent and inert; and as he sat collapsed in his chair I felt my own shoulders slump forward, and I longed to lie down, and close my weary eyes, but already he was holding out the gun with a look of dark exultation. And when I saw his slightly moist forehead, the piece of damp hair sticking to the shine, his fierce narrow eyes, the slightly crooked turn of his lips, there was something about it all that made me look quickly away; and in my blood, in my brain, in the air of the room I felt something beating, beating, as if at any moment it would burst. At the same time I would be enraged by the hint of challenge in his look, and taking the gun I would lie down on the bed, imagining William gazing intensely at me from his chair.

When William left a relief would come over me, and sitting down ardently at my desk I would work until after midnight, but the next day I would see him sitting in Geometry, two rows away and two seats up, and raising my eyes from the lunch table I would see him sitting across from me, bending over his plate with a frown, and after school he would appear at my locker, and together we would ride home on my bus.

One afternoon as we rode home on the bus we happened to have a heated discussion about a problem in geometry. In my room we continued arguing, covering sheets of paper with demonstrations, and suddenly William said, with a significant look: "Let's save this for later." "No," I said, infuriated by his look, "we'll settle it right now," and crumpling up a sheet of paper and hurling it across the room I began scribbling away on another sheet. Suddenly I heard the sound of tires in the driveway. "It's her," I said. "I told you," said William. In silent rage we listened to mother opening the back door and tramping across the kitchen. William and I went out to say hello and then returned to my room. For a while we sat listening to mother's footsteps in various rooms. William sat drumming his fingers against the chairarm. I fiddled with the cord of the venetian blind. When I looked over at William I saw him looking at me; our eyes jerked away. Almost at once I looked over again. He looked over again. William rose, walked over to the door, and turned the lock. "No," I whispered savagely, "she'll know something's wrong." He shrugged and unlocked the door. Then he went to the closet and returned with the book. Listening intently to mother's footsteps in the living room, he took out the gun, removed one bullet, and slid the book and bullet under the bed. He sat down stiffly on the edge of his chair, holding the gun on his thigh and staring fiercely in front of him. Suddenly he raised the gun and spun the cylinder. For a while he stayed that way. Then he took a deep breath, lowered the gun to his temple, and pulled the trigger. A veiled, distant look came into his eyes. There was a sound of footsteps in the hall. "Mmm!" I muttered, pointing frantically at the gun. But as if he were in a trance, William lowered the gun with odd slowness to his thigh and stared dully before him. There were two sharp raps and the door swung open. "I thought you boys might like some cookies," said mother, stepping in with a plate of chocolate-chip cookies. "Thanks," I said, springing up, "but I'd appreciate it very much if you wouldn't come barging in on me all the time." "I don't come 'barging' in," said mother, throwing me a pained look, and gazing about with a frown she said: "How you boys can sit inside with closed blinds on a day like this is beyond me." And turning to William she said: "I'm surprised it doesn't ruin your— Mercy! What's that?" and I thought: kill her, kill her, kill her. "This?" said William, holding up the revolver. "It's an old army revolver of my father's. Completely harmless, of course. I was showing it to Arthur. Care to see how it works?" "Good lord, what next," said mother, frowning at the gun, "no, I don't like guns in any way, shape, manner, or form. You're sure it's not dangerous?" "No doubt about it. It's practically a museum piece. Otherwise he'd never have let me borrow it." "Well," said mother, "be careful. You never know about accidents," but already she was looking about for a place to put the cookies. "I'll take them," I said, and remained standing until she left. When the door closed I walked to the bed and sat down on the edge, bending forward, leaning my forearms on my thighs, and staring at the plate of cookies in my hand. Dully I said: "You'll have to leave before my father gets home, that way we can say you took it home with you," and when I raised my eyes I was startled to see the gun held out before me, handle-first.

One afternoon in early October we entered my room as usual. I placed my books on my desk, hung up my jacket, and sat on the bed with my back against the wall, while William placed his books on the floor, pulled the blind-cords, and sat down in the reading chair. For a while nothing happened, and indeed the last time William had not sprung up almost at once but had hesitated, as if waiting for one of us to speak. He seemed a little tense, and sat drumming his fingers on the chair while I frowned down at my knees. After a while he said: "Did you ever think what would happen if"—and stopped. I said nothing. We continued to sit in silence, avoiding one another's gaze. At last William stood up, and got the gun, and murdered himself as usual, and when it was my turn I lay down as usual, and held the spinning black bomb above me, and watched it stop. Slowly I lowered my arm into position, with the barrel not yet touching my temple. And as always, before that moment, a slight dreaminess or drowsiness came over me, combined with an intense physical awareness. I felt the weight of my shirt lying along my arm, I felt my ribs lifting and falling in my tight undershirt, I felt my too-sharp hipbones pressing into my belt, I felt on my upper lip the faint warm bursts of air from my nostrils, on the white ceiling I noticed a grainy texture as if the plaster were riddled with thousands of tiny holes, and as my elbow began to bend slightly I heard a faint sound of creaking tendons, already I felt against my temple the gentle pressure of steel—"Stop!" cried William. My hand froze. A chair scraped back. My temple was throbbing, and as if I had wakened painfully from a dream I stared in dull confusion as William wrenched from my grasp a gun I seemed to be holding for some reason. Towering over me with an inflamed look, he swung out the cylinder and I half-closed my eyes as the imagined bullet tore through my beating brain. Above me William said "Ah," but it was like a groan; the gun dropped to the bed beside me. In the open cylinder I drowsily saw the bullet two spaces away. "I thought, I was sure..." muttered William, sitting down wearily, but a moment later he was pacing up and down, up and down; that afternoon he proposed the pact.

73

THAT NIGHT I SLEPT FITFULLY; toward dawn I fell into a deep sleep from which I was roused by a hand shaking my shoulder. In school I felt tired and heavy-headed, and as I rode home with William I leaned back against the hot leather seat and closed my eyes in the summery warmth. Warm sunlight lay on the back of my hand, the back of my neck was hot, and when I opened my eyes I saw green, too-green leaves under a blue, too-blue sky, but suddenly the rest of the tree passed into view with its dark red leaves.

Warm sunlight poured through the upward-slanting blinds, filling my room with a thick yellow glow; William strode to the blinds and pulled the cords. Wearily I lay down on my bed, there was a sharp scraping sound, and when I looked up I saw William striding from the room; beside my bed stood the desk-chair. William entered, bearing a dark bottle and a yellow glass. He set the glass and bottle on the desk-chair and sat down in the reading chair, leaning back but at once sitting up. "Are you asleep?" he asked mockingly. "Yes," I murmured, rising wearily and sitting crosslegged before the bottle and glass. I picked up the heavy bottle with two hands and began to tip it toward the rim of the glass; in my fingers I felt the heavy liquid rolling forward. Suddenly it stopped. "What's wrong with you?" said William, seizing the bottle angrily. With his left hand he held it pressed against his chest. His right elbow was raised, his face grew red, I waited for his hand to fly up, but he placed the half-wet cork upside down on the chair and handed me the bottle. Leaning forward he steadied the glass with both hands. Slowly I tipped the bottle forward, suddenly a blood-red stream rushed out. It struck the upper inside of the glass, sheeting down into a rising red pool. Suddenly a dark line rushed across the chair and began dripping from the edge. "What's the matter with you?" scowled William, wiping the seat, the side, the floor; the red-stained crumpled paper creaked as it opened slightly. William handed me a needle and a matchbook. "We don't need matches," I said, flinging them away. They struck a wall, dropped straight down, and were still. I gazed down at my extended fingertip, which looked rosy, as if it contained a great deal of blood. William leaned forward, suddenly I plunged the needle in and gasped with pain. I held my finger over the glass and a thick drop splashed, making a little cloud in the transparent wine. Beside it another cloud appeared, and another. My finger was throbbing, beating out drops of blood; stripes of blood trickled along my finger, fell in the crevices between fingers, ran along the back of my hand. I drew out a wrinkled handkerchief and wrapped it around my finger, shifting to new places as the blood soaked through. "It's all right, don't worry about it," I said, feeling myself smile. William frowned. He wiped the needle-tip on the back of his hand and turned up his finger. Then he lowered the needle into place above his fingertip. "Curge," he muttered. "What?" I said sharply. "What?" exclaimed William, looking up abruptly. In alarm I said: "I just wondered, you said something, I wanted to know..." "Courage, I said." He looked down at his finger. "I forgot to tell you," I whispered—William looked up with a frown—"if you squeeze your finger, like this..." William pressed his thumb against his fingertip, held the needle poised above, and lowered it experimentally, touching the point here and there and pushing it in gently. Under the needle I could see the surface of his skin going down and up, down and up. Then he raised the needle, held it still, and gave a quick jab. A small red blooddrop appeared. "But that's perfect!" I cried. "What are you screaming for," said William. He held his finger over the yellow glass and squeezed out a blooddrop. It fell with a tiny splash. He kept his finger over the glass. "Oh," I said, with a dismissive wave, "that's plenty, we don't need more than that." William squeezed out a second drop. "That's very good!" I said warmly, leaning forward and watching intensely. William forced out a third drop. "There!" he said, raising his eyes; for a moment we stared at one another. William frowned. "What are you looking at?" he muttered, leaning back. Sitting upright he said: "How's your finger?" I stared at my blood-spattered handkerchief. "It's all right," I said. "Well," said William, "that's good." He leaned back, drumming his fingers on the chairarm. "Well?" he said suddenly. I looked up in alarm. Then I began to smile slyly. "Oh," I said, "I know what you're thinking." I looked knowingly at the glass and back to William. He looked away in annoyance. I picked up the glass, held it aloft, and gazed at the cloudy trails. "It looks pretty repulsive," I said, lowering the glass and swirling the wine. Softly I added: "Are you sure you—" "All right," said William, springing to his feet, "forget it, it's obvious you—" "Oh, no," I said, giving a shrug, "I was only thinking of you," and lifting the glass I took a long swallow. When I lowered the glass my eyes burned and I felt a trickle on my chin. William stared darkly. "You're dribbling," he said. He sat down. "Here," I said, handing him the half-drained glass and wiping my chin with a sleeve. William sat erect, holding the glass before him. Suddenly he lifted the glass and threw back his head. His adam's apple went up and down, up and down, and when he tipped his head forward his eyes glistened and his wet lips were slightly twisted. "You look evil," I said, and laughed sharply, and stopped. I closed my burning eyes. Wine beat in my temples. When I opened my eyes I saw William gazing at me as if in expectation. Irritably I said: "There's some blood or something on your lip there. No, there. Over more. Yes, that's it. It's all right now." Closing my eyes I intoned dreamily: "My blood is in your body and your blood is in my body. Now we are blood brothers, William . . . Bill . . ." When I opened my eyes I saw his inflamed cheek-ridges, his burning eyes. "Well," I said, looking away, "that's it I"—suddenly I felt something on my hand. "What are," I said hoarsely, trying to twist my hand away, but he held it in a firm, almost painful grasp.

74

HE RELEASED MY HAND, and as if suddenly a stillness came over things: the dark winebottle, the yellow glass, the silver needle vanished from my room, the wooden chair sat under the desk, lazily stretching its legs, and on the floor across from me sat William, frowning and shaking the dice. His fingers opened, the red dice tumbled on the pale green board, then the dice stopped and the battleship began to move. A stillness had come over things. And how strange it was to see him in Geometry, two rows away and two seats up ... We had agreed on three weeks from the day of our pledge. And how strange it was to see him in Biology, two rows away and one seat back ... After school he appeared at my locker and together we rode home on my bus. At my house we returned to our old games, shaking the dice over the Monopoly board, playing ping-pong in the warm part of the cellar, and shuffling our old cards expertly with our thumbs; William even revived the old record-book, with its columns of little picket fences. Never did he allude to our secret pact. I had looked forward vaguely to the dark comradeship of intimate October afternoons, to cozy deathchats and the blood-warmth of doom, to the flaming out of friendship in the wine-glowing dark; William's stern silence seemed a form of estrangement. At the same time I was relieved by the stillness, for somehow I preferred not to think about all that, and open-ing my fingers I watched the red dice tumble on the pale green board. Sometimes I was troubled by the stillness, I longed to smash it with a shout, but raising my eyes I would see William sitting crosslegged on the floor before me with his neat piles of money tucked under the board, orange October sunlight streamed through the partly open blinds, William's new autumn jacket was draped over the back of the desk-chair, and lowering my eyes I continued playing.

At first the day had come rushing toward me, moving twice as fast as the placidly passing October afternoons, but soon it had stopped moving and had even receded somewhat, remaining fixed in a featureless and immobile future from which particular days would break off and come streaming toward me, passing through me and coming out the other side, in the past.

Softly the days flowed through me, detaching themselves silently one by one, and as the days passed and time stood still I had the sense that something was eluding me. I would be sitting in a classroom, gazing off drowsily with half-closed eyes, and an image would pass across the back of my brain. Then I would half-wake from my half-sleep, and turn my gaze drowsily inward. And there I would see a dusty window, a thick flagpole, a spinning cylinder, an ashen sky. And then in front of me I would see the dusty window, the thick flagpole, the ashen sky. And a weariness came over me... My brain felt thick and sluggish, and desired nothing better than to lie down in a dark corner, and close its weary eyes. At times I felt that this was a dangerous desire, that I must rouse myself before it was too late, but my mind would yawn, and stretch its arms, and close its weary eyes. And it seemed to me that if only I could lie down, and close my weary eyes, then the days would flow through, and then, and then... and again I would have the sense that something was eluding me, some little fact that I had failed to take into account, something dangerous and oppressive that I could not grasp—and flinging open the door of my mind I would try to catch myself by surprise, but as I flung open the door I would see myself sitting motionless on the bed with suddenly lowered eyes, and across from me, in the lamplit armchair, a protruding elbow. And I felt there was something wrong with it all, something I could not quite grasp, and turning my gaze outward I would see William seated beside me on the bus, gazing out the dusty window with a frown. One night as I lay in bed with my arm over my eyes I thought of the bright silver scalpel lying on the black wax of the dissecting pan. Then I thought of the parts of the microscope, the eyepiece, the extension tube, the tube, the nosepiece, the objectives, the stage, the clips, the mirror, the coarse adjustment, the fine adjustment, and suddenly I imagined myself sitting on the bed, with a black gun pointed at my temple. I pulled the trigger, there was a loud explosion, but somehow I was still sitting there. Across from me was a blank space where a chair should have been. Then the door opened, I came striding into the room, again I sat on the bed, again I raised the gun to my temple, there was a loud explosion—and again the door opened, again I came striding into the room . . . Softly the days flowed through me, detaching themselves silently one by one, and one morning as I woke from troubled sleep I imagined that many years had passed and that I was looking back at it all from a great distance, but for some reason this very thought upset me, my temples began to throb, I felt that I was on the verge of an overwhelming discovery, but already it had eluded me, and sitting up in bed I pushed aside the blinds and looked out at the cold blue sky. And a weariness came over me . . . Softly the days flowed through me, detaching themselves silently one by one, and one afternoon as I was sitting on the floor of my room, watching William shake the dice over the pale green board, I was seized by such a rush of friendship that I felt as if I had been struck in the throat. I watched his familiar hand shaking back and forth, back and forth, I heard the clack and click of the clickclacking dice, I saw his fingers open, my temples were throbbing, I could not breathe . . . "Pardon?" said William, looking up suddenly. "Nothing," I muttered, lowering my beating eyes, and the red dice tumbled on the pale green board.

And so I surrendered to the stillness, playing Monopoly, shuffling cards, and taking great pains with my six diagrams of a carefully dissected earthworm. Often William would stay for dinner, and on Saturday father would drive us all out into the country to look at the famous leaves. One sunny, warm, almost hot autumn morning we took a longer drive than usual. The red and yellow leaves were doing their best to resemble calendar illustrations for October and picture postcards of rural Connecticut in the fall. The sky had been filmed in technicolor. Now and then a roadside stand displayed dark green, pale yellow, and speckled gourds, ears of Indian corn with red, yellow, and purple kernels, and flocks of fat orange pumpkins whose thick curved stems pointed in all directions and whose bodies were marked by vertical lines, like the slice-divisions of peeled tangerines. In the hilly distance the rounded tops of little plump trees looked like orange and yellow gumdrops crowded together. Here and there a blue-green spruce or a dark-green pine stood out sternly from the general celebration, like black-clad Pilgrims at a feast of Indians. A billboard showed a copper-colored woman in a white bikini and green sunglasses, leaning up on one elbow on a blanket on the beach as she tipped back her head to drink a sparkling green bottle of soda. From time to time at the side of the road appeared a row of short dark-brown posts joined by twisted strands of gray ropelike metal. Now and then appeared a gray metal stick at the top of which were two disks of orange glass one above the other. In a sudden clearing a derrick with a shiny yellow cabin thrust up its black crisscrossed beam, from which hung a thick black cable that ended in a black hook shaped like an upside-down question mark. Father kept asking mother questions about a map in an open guidebook that she held on her lap, and after a great many red leaves and yellow leaves we came to a dark brown sign shaped like a shield, and at once we turned onto a narrow road that ran into the woods. Father parked on a dirt clearing beside a brown stream with a wooden bridge. We all slammed our doors and marched over the bridge onto a forest path. The trail was thickly covered with spongy layers of old brown leaves upon which lay newly fallen red and yellow leaves, pinecones, a decaying branch, a flattened green Chiclet box with the cellophane window intact. Great oaks and maples and trees unknown to me rose up on both sides, displaying their reds and oranges; thick October sunlight fell through the leaves and lay in warm trembling patches on the shady path. As I walked I dragged my feet in the marshy underleaves, which turned out to be damp and blackish on the bottom. Ahead of me walked mother and William, and far ahead strode father, who stopped and looked back from time to time. Mother was collecting knickknacks for her Autumn Woods Table in school, and she kept stopping to drop into a shoebox held by William a yellow oak-leaf, a red maple-leaf, a twig with two acorns on it, a patch of green moss on a gray stone, a big rubbery sickly-white mushroom with a circle of dark slits on the underside of the hat. William carried the shoebox in his right hand and in his left hand he held open a small book about trees. From time to time he shifted the shoebox under his left arm and turned a page. "Well," William was saying, "it won't hurt to give them an idea of the different kinds of acorns." "Mercy, William, they're only in the first grade. So long as they know it's an acorn." A squirrel scampered up the side of an oak—stopped suddenly, as if to disagree—and continued climbing. The trail turned and began to go uphill. At the side of the path appeared a crumbling dark-brown log mottled with sunlight and pale green lichen. Mother and William were some twenty feet ahead of me, halfway up the hill, and father had already disappeared. Somewhat bored, and somewhat tired, I sat down on the log. My shoulders fell forward, my back curved, my hands dangled between my thighs. Here and there in the warm shade before me, shards of sunlight lay. I gazed at the flat brown broken leaves, at a waxy dark-red oak-leaf part in sun and part in shadow, at a small piece of granite whose flecks of mica flashed in the sun, at a scrap of colorless cellophane with a red stripe running along one edge, at an open matchbook with rain-faded matches chalky pink at the tips, at two dark-blue wildflowers at the edge of the path, at a dark green frond bearing opposite rows of spear-shaped leaves that grew smaller and smaller toward the tip. Warm sunlight struck my wrists and my right cheek. Through my sun-warmed dungarees my thighs felt hot. A pleasant drowsiness came over me, for a moment I half-closed my eyes,

and I saw myself rowing on the warm lake in summer, pulling
back the pines with my oars as William sat across from me in
his open shirt. A warm, sunny tenderness came over me. I
opened my eyes and glanced up the sun-patched path, where
near the top of the hill I saw William and mother moving
through moving patterns of light and shade; leafprints and sun-
circles moved on their backs. Drowsily I let my gaze fall to the
leaves before me. In the summery warmth I felt my heavy
eyelids close. I did not fall asleep, for I was aware of the hard
log under me, of the warm sunlight on my wrists and cheek, of
the dark, dancing redness of my inner eyelids. In the dark,
dancing redness I saw William and mother high above on the
sun-checkered path. William turned to look at me over his
shoulder; then he turned back to mother and continued up the
path. They turned out of view. A moment later William appeared at the top of the path, alone. For a moment he stood
with his hands in his pockets, gazing down at me with a slight
frown. Then he began walking swiftly down toward me, looking back once over his shoulder, and kicking up leaves as he
walked. And as he came down toward me a shadow came over
things, my arms felt cold, I wanted to rise and walk away, but
I could not move. And as he came down toward me the sound
of leaves was louder and louder, I began to breathe quickly,
and as he came down toward me I could see quite clearly his
moist forehead, his twisted mouth, and with a great effort, as
if I were tearing my skin, I opened my eyes. The path was in
shadow, my wrists were in shadow, dead leaves everywhere.
The air was cold. The darkened path was deserted and still.
And it seemed to me that something strange and hideous had
happened, I thought of Rip Van Winkle and his rusty gun, I
thought of the emperor asleep in the mountain, with his beard
growing through the stone table, I felt forlorn, forlorn, under
dark water, at the bottom of the sea, I saw the cold city of
Atlantis, and as I watched, sunlight sprang in patches on the
path before me, the back of my wrists felt warm, sunlight swept
up the hill, and shading my eyes I squinted at the dazzling blue

sky, where half the sun had emerged from the edge of a dark gray cloud. At the bright top of the path William appeared. He looked down at me, shading his eyes. "Hey!" he called, waving me toward him, "come on!" "Coming!" I cried, standing up and hurrying toward him, half-stumbling in the sunny dead leaves.

75

ONE COLD MORNING as I woke from a deep, exhausting sleep I did not open my eyes but lay in a heavy sort of waking. Under my covers I was warm, I was warm, but against my cheek I felt the cold streaming from the cold part of the pillow, and as I lay there thinking of the cold wall, the cold window, the cold yellow sun, I sensed the cold wall and cold window rising on my left, and on my right the open room. Then I felt a slight confusion, a physical unease, and suddenly I realized that I had gone to sleep in the wrong direction, with the cold wall rising on my left, and on my right the open room. And I could not understand how I had lain down that way, with the cold wall rising on my left, and on my right the open room. And although I longed to tear open my eyes, still I continued to lie there with my eyes closed, anxiously enjoying the cold wall rising on my left, and on my right the open room. For I was anxious, I was anxious, I felt that if I opened my eyes something terrible would happen, and squeezing them tight I saw quite clearly the pale green wallpaper just to my left, with its silver and dark-green cross-hatchings, and above it the gray windowsill, and the bell-shaped grip with the fluffy knot sticking out of the bottom. And although I knew I should not move, should not think, should not do anything at all to disturb the strange and fragile backward vision of my room, even so I withdrew my left hand from under the warm covers, feeling the cold enter my loose pajama-sleeve. Holding my fingers spread I began to reach out my left hand, waiting for the sudden hard shock of the wall, but the wall seemed farther away than I had imagined, my heart began to beat faster, and squeezing my eyes tight I reached out, and out, and out, and out, suddenly I felt a plunging sensation in my brain, I was falling, falling, and tearing open my eyes I saw the open room rushing away on my left, and on my right the hard wall and window—and in my mind I felt a small cube swiftly turning. And pierced with disillusion, as if I had wakened from a dream of walking in my bathroom under the sea, I closed my eyes and tried to recapture the backward vision of my room. I felt a sliding motion in my mind, tremulously there rose on my left the pale green wallpaper with silver and dark-green cross-hatchings, and above it the gray windowsill. I felt that if I relaxed for one second the entire structure would dissolve, and this very thought seemed full of danger, as if I had already scattered my attention, and with a renewed effort of imagination I saw so intensely the cold wall rising on my left that all along my left side I sensed the cold closeness of the wall. And because I sensed all along my left side the cold closeness of the wall, I wondered what would happen if for one little second I allowed myself to imagine on my right the pale green wallpaper —and as if I had reached out and struck the wall on my right, all at once the ghost-wall collapsed, and in my mind the real room burst so sharply into view that not until I opened my eyes did I realize that my eyes had been closed. And as I wearily gazed at the now vague and superfluous room there appeared in my mind the precise and detailed image of Philip Schoolcraft's bureau, with its dark green winebottle partially filled with a black-looking liquid, somewhere William threw out his arm and looked at his watch, suddenly I knew that the appointed day had come. Then I closed my eyes and turned onto my side and pulled the warm covers up to my cheek. And I thought how nice it would be to lie that way through all the cold weather, like a bear in a cave, but already my eyes were opening, already I was flinging the covers back.

The morning was cold and clear. A piece of paper tumbled

along a sunny sidewalk, a breeze warm on the outside and cold on the inside entered from the opening bus-door, and when I stepped into homeroom I saw six blazing parallelograms thrown across two rows of desks, and in the bright window-opening above a dark radiator, visible as blown cloth, the thick, heavy, undulating air. And how strange it was to see him in Geometry —but lowering my eyes I stared at the frayed edge of my notebook where gray cardboard showed through the parted blue threads. Toward eleven o'clock the sky darkened over and a cold drizzle fell. Then the rain stopped and a sunless brightness spread. And how strange it was to see him in Biology... Through a translucent dark cloud the furry white sun, shaped like a partially deflated beachball, seemed to be rushing slowly, dreamily along. Now it disappeared behind an opaque layer, now it appeared as a dim white blur. Suddenly a yellow edge slid out, raindrops glittered in the windows, hard black shadows sprang out, wet brown tree-trunks gleamed like polished mahogany, then the tree-trunks darkened, the shadows vanished, the lights went out in the window-drops, evening fell. After lunch William and I walked on the wet asphalt where wet yellow leaves lay flat. No one said anything. William stopped to pull a yellow leaf from the toe of his shoe and as he bent over his face reddened slightly and a small vein showed through the skin of his temple. In the back of my brain a dim gun vanished among wet yellow leaves. I noticed the edge of a yellow leaf sticking out from under my left shoe and as I walked I scraped my sole on the asphalt behind me but when my foot swung into view the yellow leaf was still there. "Just a second," I muttered, and placing the inner edge of my right shoe on the clinging leaf I lifted my left foot, but as I began to walk I noticed the leaf sticking to the sole of my left shoe. Stopping again I raised my left leg over my right knee, clasped my left ankle with a hand, and pulled off the wet yellow leaf, which clung to my fingers. I shook my hand rapidly back and forth but the sticky leaf would not come off. With the thumb and forefinger of my left hand I carefully lifted the leaf by the stem, and opening my fingers I

watched the leaf fall, turning round and round under the spinning stem and falling at last gently against my pantsleg and
clinging wetly there. Angrily I bent over and pulled it off but
the leaf clung to my fingers. Squatting down I pressed the leaf
against the wet asphalt and slowly lifted each finger in turn.
Leaving the leaf on the tar I stood up quickly. "There!" I said.
"That was something! What a leaf!" "What a day," muttered
William, frowning at the dark clouds, between which, however,
blue spaces showed. "Yes," I said, "what a day, this morning,
when I woke up, or rather, I hadn't actually awakened, my eyes
were closed, not that I was asleep, and I had the strangest—"
The bell rang, William turned his head. "Sensation," I said.
"What?" said William, turning with a frown. "Sensation, I said.
The strangest sensation. I had the strangest—" "What sensation?
What are you talking about? Anyway, let's get out of this mess.
What a day. Meet you at the locker, right?" "Yes, right, I guess
I'll, it seems strange, though, not saying anything, if you know
what I, of course I guess you, I don't mean to allude to anything,
ha ha, but then, I don't know." William frowned. "You're
babbling," he said, and added: "You sound like you need a good
night's sleep." "Yes, a good night's sleep, as a matter of fact," but
already he was striding away. Wearily I walked along a dreary
brown corridor, and up the brown stairs, and sitting down at a
desk I leaned my chin on my hand and gazed out the window,
and catching the falling red glass ball he jerked his left hand to
the right, leaving in his right palm the red glass ball, which he
tossed into the air as he jerked back to receive the falling blue
glass ball, while across the watery pale-blue sky stretched row on
row of little fleecy clouds, as if a single vast cloud had begun to
dissolve in a watery solution of sky.

　　That afternoon William appeared at my locker and together
we rode home on the bus. Through the dusty bus-window I
gazed at faint gray shadows barely darker than the gray street.
At the base of a dark telephone pole a watery melting shadow
suddenly darkened and stiffened but at once grew dim and
melted away. Two yellow leaves lay stranded on the shore of a

shrunken brown puddle that was evaporating from the edges, leaving a ragged outline of black wetness. "Actually," I said, turning to William, who looked up with a frown. At my house I let us in with my key, and as I pushed open the door of my room I saw through the open blinds a range of blue ice-mountains. Then the mountains became a large blue cloud with luminous white crests placed one behind the other. William strode over to the bed and closed each blind with a sharp pull of the cord. "You know," I said, "it's incredible, how many clouds, in a single day," and sitting down on the bed with my legs outstretched and my back against the wall I leaned my head against the curtain-covered windowframe and half-closed my eyes. At the other wall William closed the remaining blind and then he sat down on the reading chair. In the dusky silence his fingers tapped a muffled marching tune. I gazed at my wrinkled pants-knees, which stuck up bumpily. "Well!" exclaimed William, slapping both thighs with his hands, "let's get going!" When I raised my eyes I saw him standing before me, holding against his left thigh the folded Monopoly board. "Oh," I murmured, "yes, that's very, that's actually very..." "What's the matter?" he said sharply. "You're not falling asleep, are you?" He looked down at me with mocking eyes. "Oh, as to that," I said, making a dismissive gesture with my hand. William sat down on the floor and began to count out the money swiftly. "You're really getting good at that!" I said, leaning forward and following his agile fingers intently. Wearily I sat down on the floor across from him, leaning my head against the side of the bed. "What's the matter with you?" said William. "You look like you need a good night's sleep." "Yes," I murmured, "a good night's sleep." "Yes," said William, "a good night's sleep," and the red dice tumbled on the pale green board. The red dice tumbled on the pale green board. The red dice tumbled on the pale green board. The red dice tumbled—there was a sharp knock at the door. "Can you boys lend a hand?" called mother. William and I went out to carry in the bags of groceries. "Are you staying for dinner?" mother asked as she loudly flattened an empty bag against her stomach, while I removed a box of cereal, a can of grapefruit juice, a cold box of broccoli.

After dinner we all played pinochle at the dining-room table. Then father and I drove William home. "Good night!" said William, and strode away along the flagstone path. When I returned to the house I went into my room and lay down with my arm pressed over my eyes. There must have been some mistake, and yet it was the correct day, a Wednesday, then he must, it was all . . . and I longed to lie down, and close my weary eyes, but I was already lying down, I had already closed my eyes. Wearily I rose, and went to my desk, and sat down. I opened a big book and leaned my cheek on the heel of my hand, feeling the side of my mouth pulled up by the stretch of my cheek. In the moonlight his eyes looked black and fierce. I gazed at a glossy white page with its thick black print and its fine black print; his eyes narrowed, as if he were searching for me in my shadow, and looking at me with black angry eyes he said fiercely: "Traitor." In one corner a black-and-white drawing showed a slipper-shaped object with a furry fringe, containing little circles of various sizes, and surrounded by pointing lines attached to wormlike words: ectoplasm, endoplasm, macronucleus. After a while I returned to the bed and lay down with my arm pressed over my eyes, and wearily I rose, and went over to my desk, and sat down.

That night I turned onto my left side, and onto my right side, and onto my back. "See!" he said, turning to me in fierce triumph; a frog jumped into the water with the sound of a dropped pebble. "You look like Huckleberry Finn," I said. "Huckleberry Mainwaring," said William. "See!" he said, turning to me in fierce triumph. In the moonlight his eyes looked black and fierce. Removing his hands from his pockets he stood with his hands on his hips and his legs slightly apart, looking down at me with a frown. His eyes narrowed, as if he were searching for me in my shadow, and looking at me with black angry eyes he said fiercely: "Traitor." "Traitor," I murmured, and turned over onto my left side, and onto my right side, and onto my back. "See!" he said, turning to me in fierce triumph. The dark branches moved to one side, and silently, eerily, William Mainwaring squeezed into the moonlit yard. Slowly he crept forward, in moonlit sneakers, and as I moved uncertainly toward a group of laughing boys whom I had not seen since June, I turned to see my double standing on the steps of the bus, holding in one hand a large blue notebook with a rainbow of plastic tabs. "I think I understand you," said William thoughtfully. "You mean you can—but you won't." "See!" he said, turning to me in fierce triumph. The dark branches moved to one side, and silently, eerily, William Mainwaring squeezed into the moonlit yard. Slowly he crept forward, in moonlit sneakers, with the exaggerated tiptoe of a cartoon villain. Halfway across the lawn he stopped, looked sharply to the left and right, and stood frozen for a few moments before continuing. As he approached the back steps the dark branches moved to one side, and silently, eerily, William Mainwaring squeezed into the moonlit yard. "See!" he said, turning to me in fierce triumph. The dark branches moved to one side, and silently, eerily—suddenly I sat up in bed and pushed aside the cold blinds.

Over the clouded bottom of the glass I gazed at the dead black yard, the dead black hedge, the dead black sky.

I released the blinds with a clatter and lay down. I placed my arm over my burning and weary eyes, and catching the falling red glass ball he jerked his left hand to the right, leaving in his right palm the red glass ball, "See!" he said, turning to me in fierce triumph. In the moonlight his eyes looked black and fierce. Looking at me with black angry eyes he said: "Traitor." "Traitor," I murmured, and turned onto my left side, and onto my right side, and onto my back, and suddenly sitting up I pushed aside the blinds and gazed out at the desolate night. Wearily I lay down, the dark branches moved to one side, and stepping quietly from the sink he tiptoed softly across the kitchen into the hall. Slowly he tiptoed to my door, slowly he placed his hand on the dark knob, slowly he began to turn. There was a slight creak. I sat up in bed with a pounding heart.

But it was only the wind, only the wind. "Only the wind," I murmured, and lay down, and I longed to lie down, and close my weary eyes, softly he crept down the dark stairway into the cold garage. He hurried down the driveway, he jumped into the stream, he climbed through the window, he flung open the door of my room. He hurried down the driveway. He jumped into the stream. He climbed through the window. He flung open the door. He hurried down the driveway, jumped into the stream, climbed through the window, flung open the door, and standing with his hands on his hips he said "Traitor traitor traitor traitor" and flinging the covers back I began to dress quickly.

Outside I could see my breath. In the clear black air the brilliant star-points stood out with intense clarity, spreading across the firmament like a vast connect-the-dots picture. Holding my left arm tightly across my stomach I hurried across the crackling back yard. Swiftly I pushed through the scratchy hedge and hurried down the slope and across the dark field, and as I hurried I felt a muffled thump thump thump against my arm and stomach. And as I hurried I felt the slippery book sliding from under my arm, suddenly a bottom edge slipped out, pushing it back up I squeezed more tightly. At the stream I jumped down, landing with one foot on the edge of a tin can and falling to my knees. Scrambling to my feet I pulled myself awkwardly onto the scratchy ledge. Wearily I stumbled up the steep dirt slope to the cinder driveway at the back of the body shop. Swiftly I made my way along the backs of shut-down gas stations and diners and car-wash shops, catching glimpses of red and green traffic lights between buildings, and as I hurried I felt a muffled thump thump thump against my arm and stomach, and always I felt the heavy slippery book sliding down. Swiftly I passed through crunching back yards that seemed to be strewn with cornflakes, pushing through hedges, climbing fences, stumbling over a rake, kicking a sudden football that went tumbling softly away, end over end, end over end, end over end, and coming to a high black hedge that barred my way I turned along the narrow sideyard to the edge of the house. Across the street a row of dark stores reflected a streetlamp and a mailbox. Hugging the book tightly against my stomach I made a dash across the front yard, leaped the pricker hedge, and felt the book slipping; in the glare of two streetlamps I crossed the street half bent over. As I set foot on the opposite sidewalk the book fell out, the cover sprang open, the gun tumbled into the gutter. On the bright deserted sidewalk I squatted down and placed the gun in the book and closed the cover as two headlights sprang into view. Holding the book clumsily in two hands I hurried wearily to the drugstore and stood in the black doorway as the car passed. Then stepping out I turned left onto a quiet street. Behind a thick tree I slipped the book under my jacket. Hugging myself tightly tightly I hurried past small two-story houses behind hedges and black picket fences. At a dark church I turned onto a street with large houses set back from the road. Turning left at the end of the street, and right at the end of the next street, I came at last to William Mainwaring's house, set back from the road with no front walk.

Swiftly and wearily I made my way up the dark driveway. At the dark door I bent over and gripped the cold metal handle. With feverish slowness I began to lift the heavy screeching door, half-inch by half-inch, lifting and pausing, lifting and pausing. When the door was above my knees I held it in place and sat down on the cold driveway. Bending my head back, way back, I began to writhe backward into the black garage. My head banged into something hard and squeezing my eyes shut I held my breath and listened to the dark as a pain began to beat softly at the back of my skull. Through my hair at the back of my beating skull I felt the cold fender against my scalp. Slowly I began to twist my head sideways, suddenly against my cheek I felt the cold crusted metal of the tailpipe. Twisting and squirming I squeezed my cheek below the bumper and lay under the car with my back on the floor and my head slightly raised. The garage door rested on my raised knees and I felt that if I tried to lower my legs they would break under the weight of the heavily falling door. My neck ached from the strain of keeping my head raised and I longed to lie down, and close my weary eyes, slowly I began to lower my knees, suddenly the heavy door scraped down the slope of my shins and fell heavily against both insteps. I began to twist each foot out from under, feeling the hard door pressing through my sneakers, and slowly I squirmed and writhed backward along the scratchy floor with its sharp odor of cement and oil. Against my upper arm I felt the hard rubber of the tire. When the tire was at my hip I writhed and twisted sideways. Soon my head emerged from blackness into darkness, and squirming and wriggling I made my way out from under the side of the car, striking my head lightly against a bag of some hard-packed soft substance. Slowly and unsteadily I rose, hugging my stomach like a wounded criminal. Running my right hand along the cold side of the car I made my way to the cluttered workbench. Clumsily I climbed up and felt along the gritty ledge at the top of the door for the cold metal of the key.

The door opened with a remembered squeak. In the dangerous blackness I could see nothing at all. Slowly I reached out my hand, and as my tingling fingertips moved forward I had the sensation that a hard surface was falling away just beyond my reach. When I had stretched out my arm all the way I began to swing it slowly sideways, but as if I had stepped out of the garage into the black outdoors I felt only a faint wind moving over my moving hand. Then I took a step forward, a wall leaped out and struck my extended fingertips, carefully I ran my hand along cold smoothness. When I came to the banister I began to climb. At the top of the stairs I patted about for the second doorknob, and as I pushed open the second door I tried to recall in sharp detail the hallway with the green bathroom on the left and the telephone at the end. Cautiously I took a step forward, suddenly my foot struck a stair, in my mind the forgotten stairway rose before me. On the left and right darker darknesses emerged from the darkness, only to melt away. As I stepped back from the stair I felt through my sneakers a stiff kind of softness and I remembered William stepping into his living room in brown-and-yellow-striped socks. Hugging my stomach with my left arm I bent over and unlaced my sneakers. I placed them side by side on the strip of plastic at the foot of the stairs. Slowly, on the black rug, I began to climb.

At the black landing I turned right, suddenly I struck a wall, in my mind I made my way along the rippling rug toward the leaning mirror. Shaking my struck fingers I turned left and climbed the two stairs. At the top of the second stair I turned right and stared into the pitchblack hall. Reaching out my right hand I touched the wall on my right. Slowly I moved forward, step by step, now fingering the wall, now holding my hand before me with extended fingertips, and as I advanced I leaned my head back and frowned fiercely, as if in expectation of a blow. I felt the wooden ripple of an unremembered doorframe, and as I advanced I tried to reconstruct the hall in all its detail but I could recall only the green bathroom somewhere on the left, and at the far end the brown table, the black telephone, a mirror of some distinctive shape. And as I advanced I kept seeing in my mind the rippling rug, the leaning mirror, suddenly my fingers touched a smooth round protuberance on the wall. It seemed to be hanging there, and I touched it carefully, fearful that it would come crashing down. It was about two inches in diameter. On the circumference I could feel little raised lines. And I longed to understand that smooth round protuberance on the wall, gently I tried to move it back and forth but it was solidly attached, and as I tried to move it back and forth I found that it could turn like a wheel, slowly I turned it with my fingers and all at once, far away, there was a soft thud, followed by a quiet hum. Then slowly I moved forward, imagining the little table now looming before me, now far away. My hand came to the rippling frame of a second dark door and it seemed to me that this must be the one, but on the other side the wall continued. And now it seemed to me that there were too many doors, that somehow I had entered the wrong hall, the wrong house, the wrong town, suddenly I came to another door, before me I felt the edge of the table, gently I placed my hand on the door-knob and began to turn.

The door opened smoothly, without a sound. Taking one step into the black room I closed the door silently behind me. In the blackness I stood listening intently, but I could hear only my rapid breathing. "Traitor," I whispered, but there was no answer. Taking a deep breath I slowly stretched out my right hand toward the place where the bed should have been. And as I reached out my hand I wondered what would happen if by some hideous mistake I had entered the wrong room, and I paused, listening to the unbreathing dark. "William," I whispered, but there was no answer. Slowly I reached down, imagining the prickly cheek, the soft breasts, the gasp, the cry, suddenly I snatched away my hand but already my fingers had recognized the cool, slightly creased sheet. "William," I whispered, in the suspicious silence. Slowly I lowered my hand to the cool, slightly creased sheet and began to pat softly about. I felt a sudden edge of pajama. "William," I whispered, and poked him with my finger; through the pajama I felt the bed. Rapidly patting about I pressed my palm into the hollowed pillow, I ran my fingers along the line of the thrown-back covers. Wearily I lay down, and laid my cheek on the pillow, and closed my heavy eyes, but at once I sat up. For a while I sat at the edge of the bed, listening to my breathing. Then wearily I rose, and opened the door, and stepped out into the hall, closing the door softly behind me.

Hugging myself with my right arm and brushing the wall with my left, I made my slow way back along the black hall. At the far end the black seemed a little lighter, as if I were making my way through a cave toward the open night. When my fingers came to the smooth round protuberance they turned it slowly backward until there was a click; silence sprang up all around. At the end of the hall I turned left, descended the two steps to the landing, turned right, and descended the stairs. At the dark bottom of the stairway I stumbled on my forgotten sneakers, and sitting down wearily I pulled on a sneaker and began to tighten the lace, starting from the bottom and working my way up. At the top I held up both ends, but the left end stretched way up and the right end barely poked through the hole. Loosening the lace from top to bottom I pulled toward one side and began tightening the lace from bottom to top. At the top I held up both ends, but now the left end barely poked through the hole and the right end stretched way up. Angrily I pulled out the lace from top to bottom, listening to the click of the lace-ends as they pulled through the invisible metal loops. At the bottom I held up both ends until they were precisely even. Then wearily I worked my way up, pulling first one lace-end through a hole and then the other lace-end through a hole. At the top I held up both ends, but the left one was much too short, angrily I loosened the lace from top to bottom and tightened the lace from bottom to top. And when I held up the ends one was still too short, tears burned in my eyes, and it seemed to me that I would have to sit there forever, in the dark, on the bottom stair. And I longed to lie down, and close my weary eyes, far away a dim creak sounded. A door opened on the floor above. Heavy footsteps moved along the hall, suddenly a light went on, looking over my shoulder I saw a dim glow on the landing and the upper steps. The light grew dimmer and dimmer as the steps descended toward me. "Yes," I murmured, "that's all right." Heavy footsteps walked along the hall toward the landing, wearily I leaned back against the balusters and half-closed my eyes. Somewhere a door opened and closed. I sat on my step with my head leaning against the sharp-edged balusters, one sneaker on and one sneaker off, and I longed to lie down, and close my weary eyes, there was a plunging watery sound, a door opened, heavy footsteps walked along the hall. The footsteps stopped, far away a dull thud sounded, followed by a quiet hum. Then the footsteps continued. The light went out, softly a door closed, leaning my head back against the dark balusters I closed my weary eyes, but at once I sat up. I bent over and tied my laces. Pulling on my other sneaker I tied it quickly and made my way down the second stairway to the cold garage.

Outside, the night felt a little colder. In the clear black air the brilliant star-points looked like tiny notes on a vast page of difficult and mournful music. For a while I stood motionless, watching my frosty breath appear and vanish, appear and vanish, appear and vanish. Then hugging myself tightly with my left arm I began to run.

I ran along the driveway to the leafy crunch at the side of the street and turning left I ran past large houses set back from the road. I turned right at the end of the street, and left at the next street, and coming to a dark church I turned onto a street where smaller houses sat behind hedges and picket fences. At the drugstore I waited for the light to change. Then running across the street I leaped the pricker hedge and ran along the sideyard to the back. Softly and swiftly I ran along crunching back yards and the backs of closed diners, and as I ran I felt a muffled thump thump thump against my arm and stomach. I ran across the cinder driveway at the back of the body shop, slid down the dirt slope, jumped into the hard stream. I pulled myself onto the other side and ran across the field and up the little slope. Pushing aside the hedge branches I hurried across the back yard. Carefully I climbed the porch steps, carefully I opened the screen door and the wooden door, carefully I made my way through the kitchen to the hall. At the end of the hall I paused for a moment, breathing heavily and standing bent over slightly. Then softly I opened my door and stepped into the black room.

76

I CLOSED THE DOOR softly behind me and for a few moments I stood leaning back against the door, listening to my heavy breathing and peering into opaque blackness. "William," I whispered, but there was no answer. I raised my hand to the wall beside the door and felt the lightswitch. With a swift click-

click I flicked the overhead light on and off. In the flash of light between blackness William jerked aside his staring face. And for a full second after the return of visible darkness my eyes retained a precise and luminous image of the white curtain-rods, the closed venetian blinds, the gray windowsill, the pale green wallpaper with its silver and dark-green cross-hatchings, the light-brown bedspread crisscrossed with dark brown and dark green, the armchair sitting sideways, William's squeezed-shut eyes, his wrinkled forehead, his partially raised forearm, then the inner light went out, the chair scraped in the dark. In an angry whisper he said: "It's about time you got here." "Oh," I murmured, "yes, it's about time," and making my way through the familiar dark I sat down on the bed with my legs outstretched, my back against the wall, and my eyes half-closed. "Where were you?" he whispered harshly. "Oh, don't sound so angry, William, I was only . . . and you always sound so angry, frowning all the time, disapproving . . . And how do you think it feels, when somebody is always frowning at you, it makes you feel . . . Of course, I haven't been sleeping well. And then, the first time I saw you, it was in the bus, you were sitting in back, I couldn't see you too well, but then, when I was standing on the sidewalk . . . then we became friends, mother always said you were a well-behaved boy, remember the time we, and that summer, the bush-house, we had some good times together, you were always my best, and I'll never, but you were always, you never . . . and you were always so reserved, William, you never . . . of course I'm not expressing myself well, I realize that, but I'm tired now, so tired I could really go to sleep forever, when I was a child my father told me death was like being asleep and never waking up, and I thought, I thought . . ."

"Keep your voice down. What's the matter with you?"

"Oh, the matter with me . . . the matter with you . . . and don't get me wrong, William, you're my best, my only, I've never, but sometimes . . . and then, that spring, when I felt so restless, and I thought, if only I had someone to talk to . . . and all this time, you've never really ... and then, that time, at the stream, you said I was a traitor, that's what you said, a traitor, and I felt, I felt that you, you were the one ..."

"Keep your voice down. So you're backing out, is that it?"

"Backing out, what a thing to, you're really a suspicious person, William, after all we've ... oh, you've always betrayed me ..."

"Betrayed you ..."

"Always concealing everything ... never telling me anything ... and that time you invited me over ... you're so secretive, William, not like a friend, not like a real friend ... at all ..."

"So you're really backing out ..."

"You lie, you lie, and besides ... I forget what I ..."

"And were you any better? What did you ever tell me?"

"Everything! Well, no, not everything ..."

"And talk about frowning, you're the one ... always looking me over ... disapproving ..."

"Now you're angry, William, and just because I tried ... to talk to you ..."

"You call that talk ... telling me I'm not a real ... straight from the heart and all that crap ... so you're really backing out ... after all ..."

"Backing out, you keep saying that ... but I thought that you, that you ... and today, when you didn't say anything ..."

"There was nothing to say ..."

"Oh, nothing to say ... and all this time ... let's talk, William, I feel like talking, you never talk to me ..."

"There's nothing to talk about ..."

"Oh, nothing to talk about ... but what about the time ... and then, what about the time ... and remember the time ..."

"We're wasting time ..."

"Time wastes for no man ... and wouldn't it be fun to talk, and talk, all night long ... and let me say that I've really enjoyed our talk, it's like one of those movies where people talk, and talk, all night long, and then, in the end ... I forget what happens in the end ..."

"Are you through? We have a lot to do."

"Oh, a lot to through . . . a throt to loo . . . what's that?"

"Only the wind."

"Only the wind . . . it's only the wind . . . strange, but when my mother first read me that story, I wasn't frightened by the witch, oh of course I was frightened by the witch, I don't mean, but I was used to witches, I wasn't afraid of being frightened by witches, but what I mean, what I mean, it was Hansel and Gretel themselves . . . those names . . . like the names of devils . . . what's that?" In the darkness I heard the cloth-sound of something being removed from a pocket. There was a papery sound, followed by an abrupt pulling or tearing, then a sharp quick scratchy sound that seemed very familiar. The scratchy sound was repeated, suddenly the room burst into fiery view but at once contracted to the trembling orange-and-blue flame of a match. From his orange-and-black face William stared at me with black glassy eyes; a little matchflame trembled in each pupil. Then he blew out the match. In the blackness a sharp odor of sulfur streamed into my nostrils, making my eyes burn. "You scared me," I whispered. "Quiet," said William. I heard him move in the chair; coins jingled in a pocket. Then I heard a familiar papery sound, as of an envelope opening. The chair moved slightly. I felt the pressure of his hands on the bed. There was a sharp papery flipping sound, followed by a softer, sliding sound. Then again there was a sharp papery flipping sound, followed by a softer, sliding sound. Then again there was a sharp papery flipping sound, followed by a softer, sliding sound. Then again there was a— "Oh!" I exclaimed, bursting into a smile. "Keep your voice down," said William. There was a sharp papery flipping sound, followed by a softer, sliding sound. "Okay," said William, "cut." I reached down, patted about, and felt the cold deck. Placing my thumb on one side and three fingers on the other I carefully lifted a small thickness and placed it on the bed beside the remaining thickness. Then I lifted the first thickness and placed it on top of the second thickness. Carefully I pressed in the edges, squeezing first the long way, then the short way, then the long way. "Okay," I whispered. There was a sharp scrape, a soft explosion; on the bed I saw the dark, glossy, flickering deck. Against a dark green background a big-eared baby elephant stood on a drumlike stand with sloping sides. On his head he wore a sagging yellow cone-shaped hat with a red pompom, over his back hung a red blanket with yellow tassels, and in his trunk he held a staff at the end of which fluttered a yellow pennant bordered in red. "Hurry up," whispered William, and when I looked up I saw his orange-and-black face. "Go on," he muttered, motioning impatiently at the deck. "You mean," I said, making a twisting gesture with my wrist. "That's right, hurry up," said William. I reached down, drew off the top card, and turned it over on the bed beside the deck. In the flickering spotlight of the burning-down match the five of hearts stood out with intense clarity. Three hearts were pointing downward and two hearts were pointing up. The sides of each dark-red heart were slightly concave and ended in a long sharp point, as if the hearts were dripping. In each of the four corners was a red numeral 5 and under each 5 was a little red heart. William slid off a card and turned up a jack of clubs, placing it carefully on top of the five of hearts; the jack slid slightly, revealing part of an upside-down 5 and part of an up-side-down heart. In his rectangular frame the two-eyed jack had a sullen, heavy-lidded expression. The thick strands of his straight yellow hair curled up at the bottom like a scroll. He wore a red crown with black markings. He was dressed in a red-yellow-and-black costume full of stripes and zigzags and he held upright in one fist what looked like a long yellow slide-rule with red and black stripes. Four little white fingers with four little white nails lay horizontally across the yellow sliderule; opposite the four fingernails was a little plump white palm from which a white thumb curved over to rest on the top finger. Beneath the jack was an upside-down jack who grew out of him like the reflection of a mountain in a glossy lake on a puzzle cover. Outside the frame, in each corner, "Hurry up," said William, was a black J under which was a small black cloverleaf.

I slid off a card, "Ssss" said William, the light went out. I froze, holding the unturned card. There was a scraping sound, suddenly the card appeared, my hand continued its motion. On top of the jack lay a jack of hearts. He was in profile and looked superior and disdainful. He wore a red crown with white markings. "Just a second," I said, as William began to turn. Over the downturned line of his mouth the thin line of his black mustache curled up and over into a little spiral. Behind his head was the yellow blade of a battleax and in his fist he held what looked like a yellow flower. He disappeared suddenly under a six of spades. "Did you ever notice," I whispered. "Hurry up," said William. I turned over a three of diamonds. William turned over a ten of hearts. I turned over a two of clubs. William shook out the match. "Hurry up," I whispered, "hurry up." The cards sprang into view. William turned over a king of clubs. He had white hair and a curly white beard and upturned white mustaches. "Hurry up," said William. I turned over a nine of diamonds. William turned over a seven of diamonds. I turned over a— "Look at that!" I gasped, putting my hand on the deck to keep William from turning. He was wearing pointy black shoes, baggy red pants with a yellow stripe running up the side, a puffy jacket with a design of blue and yellow diamonds, and a tall checked hat, red and yellow. His eyes were lowered and his face looked like a white mask. Behind one shoulder peeped out a little white frowning face with a jagged red hat and a jagged blue collar. "Move your hand," whispered William. The light went out. William struck a match. He turned over a two of diamonds. "Oh man," I said, "these diamonds." I turned over an eight of spades. William turned over an ace of hearts. I turned over a five of clubs. William turned over a seven of spades. I turned over a queen of clubs. William shook out the match. He lit another. William turned over a two of spades. I turned over a four of clubs. William turned over a seven of hearts. I turned over a seven of diamonds. William turned over an eight of clubs. I turned over a three of hearts. William blew out the match. He lit another. William turned over a ten of clubs. I turned over an eight of diamonds. William turned over an ace of spades. I turned over a king of diamonds. "What are you doing," whispered William angrily. He picked up the king and put it back on the pile upside down. It was a large gray spade about two inches high, outlined in thick black. Inside the spade was a second spade, outlined in black, and inside the second spade was a black-and-white big-eared baby elephant on a black-and-white stand, wearing a black-and-white hat and a black-and-white blanket and holding in his black-and-white trunk a black-and-white flag. Under the spade were the words: ACE PLAYING CARD CO., ST. LOUIS, U.S.A. Suddenly the card disappeared. In the darkness William let out his breath. Wearily I leaned back against the hard wall. "And you know," I said dreamily, but forgot what I was going to say. I longed to lie down, and close my weary eyes, and I imagined myself lying down, and closing my weary eyes, and waking up, and sleepily remembering the sharp scrape of the match, William's orange-and-black face, the big-eared baby elephant with the yellow hat and red pompom, then a drowsy contentment came over me, in the darkness I closed my eyes, but something was wrong, my heart began to beat faster, opening my eyes I frowned in the dark, which here and there gathered into denser darknesses. And it seemed to me that if only William would go away, then I would be able to lie down, and close my weary eyes. "Give me the book," said William suddenly. And in my mind I heard: "Why don't you get down that book now, and bring it over to me. But be careful. Those old volumes are very fragile." "Yes," I murmured, "that's all right." At once I unbuttoned my autumn jacket and carefully removed the heavy book, placing it on the bed beside me but then pushing it away, far away, far, far away, into the dark. And abruptly withdrawing my hands I felt an intense relief, as if everything would be all right now, and tucking my hands under my armpits I said warmly: "Let's talk, I feel like talking, you never talk to me . . ." "There's nothing to talk about." "Oh, nothing to talk about . . . and besides, we have all night . . . and there was something I wanted to . . . something I meant to . . . it feels strange, don't you think it feels strange ... I wish it was raining ... like one of those movies, at night ... when the movie rain is pouring down ... harder than real rain ... oh, there's nothing like movie rain, like waves dashing against the windows, and all those gurgling gushing sounds, and suddenly the movie thunder comes, and the flames in the candlesticks bend sideways ... and the shutters bang in the wind ... and then, in the end ... don't think you have to ... if you've changed your mind or any ... don't feel you ..." "Changed my, so that's what you ... so you're going to betray me ..." "Oh, betray, how can you ... but then, would it really ... from your point of ... I mean, ha ha, you would never ..." "So you've thought of everything ..." "Oh, every, but then, ha ha, there's a way of making sure, I'm sure you've thought of it ... now and then, now and then ..." "I think I could do it ... if you asked me ..." "Oh, ha ha, thanks anyway, much obliged, very kind of you I'm ... so you'd really ... if I asked you ..." "You'd never ask me ... but you were thinking about it, you were afraid you'd betray me ..." "You keep using that word ..." "Betray, betray, betray, betray ... Swear you'll really do it." "I ... I ..." "No, don't, it's pitiful ... and I should have known, you've always held back ... in the end ..." "Held back, what do you ... held back, how can you ..." "And if *he* had done it, would you ..." "But he would never ... and besides ..." "Keep talking, I'm beginning to enjoy this ..." "Yes, this is fun, William, let's keep on talking, you never ..." A flame burst out, I threw up an arm; William leaned forward, casting over the book a dim orange circle. "Here, hold this," he commanded, reaching out the match. Carefully, delicately, with thumb and forefinger, I took the flaming match, which already had burned down a third of the way. The flame blew away from me as I brought the match toward me, then it sank down. "Hold it closer," said William. The flame blew toward me as I moved the match away. "Closer," said William, painfully I leaned to my left. As if mesmerized I watched the low fitful flame that kept moving forward along the bit of cardboard. In the dim glow I noticed the gaping book, the flaming gun, the frowning orange face, suddenly I sucked in my breath and everything disappeared. Another flame appeared, carefully I took it from William, a moment later the cylinder closed and William sat back in the chair. I gazed at the little flame-animal with its blue belly, at the black hard tip and the shriveling line of charcoal, at the glowing orange spot and the advancing dark line, carefully I moved my thumbtip and fingertip to the very end, then wetting the thumbtip and fingertip of my other hand I gently grasped the burned matchtip, and holding the charred and wrinkled bit of cardboard I watched the little flame move slowly to the very end, suddenly the flame rose and brightened, an orange spot appeared at the tip, then the two orange spots came together, the flame went out. Dreamily I gazed at the place where the orange glow had been, suddenly I sat up with a pounding heart, wearily I leaned back against the wall and drew up my legs and tucked my hand between my knees. "Yes," I murmured, "that's all right. And you know, William, I haven't been sleeping well . . . Of course it's probably all a dream, I'll wake up soon, and then . . . I feel like talking, don't you feel like talking, let's talk, remember the time we . . . but that was a long time ago . . . and you were always my best, I'll never . . . that time with the coasters, The Big Train, remember how you . . . that was fun, that time, rowing on the lake, pulling back the pines, then the island, we ought to . . . next summer . . . and don't think you have to, just because we, of course you were always stubborn, I noticed that from the very . . . and if I've said anything to hurt you, please understand that it was only . . . but let's not talk about that, let's talk about . . . and drawing cards, I hadn't even, you really thought of every . . . of course if I had drawn the ace, and who knows what would have happened, but then, does it really . . . I feel strange, feverish, it's probably all a dream, yes that's it, a dream, I'll wake up soon, and then, and then . . ." Somewhere a shot rang out. In the brief orange-yellow flash that had already vanished I saw for an instant a glossy gun-barrel, a jerking-away head, tense bluish-white knuckles, the bottom curve of a lampshade. In the blackness William moved violently in his chair. A heavy metal object clattered to the floor. Then all was mysteriously still. "William," I whispered, but there was no answer. "William!" I whispered. But there was no answer. I longed to lie down, and close my weary eyes, and it seemed to me that if only I could lie down, and close my weary eyes, then I could lie down, and close my weary eyes, and then, and then, and then, and then . . .

And you, night voyager, my brother, my stranger: you too I sing, O dark romantic . . .

A Note on the Type

The text of this book was set on the Linotype in Janson, a recutting made direct from type cast from matrices long thought to have been made by the Dutchman Anton Janson, who was a practicing type founder in Leipzig during the years 1668–87. However, it has been conclusively demonstrated that these types are actually the work of Nicholas Kis (1650–1702), a Hungarian, who most probably learned his trade from the master Dutch type founder Dirk Voskens. The type is an excellent example of the influential and sturdy Dutch types that prevailed in England up to the time William Caslon developed his own incomparable designs from them.

Composed, printed, and bound by
The Book Press, Brattleboro, Vermont.
Typography and binding design by
Virginia Tan.